THE GOLDEN CAGE

Also available from Headline Liaison

The Paradise Garden by Aurelia Clifford
Private Lessons by Cheryl Mildenhall
The Journal by James Allen
Sleepless Nights by Tom Crewe & Amber Wells
Hearts on Fire by Tom Crewe and Amber Wells
Aphrodisia by Rebecca Ambrose
Dangerous Desires by J J Duke
Love Letters by James Allen
Voluptuous Voyage by Lacey Carlyle

The Golden Cage

Aurelia Clifford

Copyright © 1995 Aurelia Clifford

The right of Aurelia Clifford to be identified as the Author of the Work has been asserted by her in accordance with the Copyright, Designs and Patents Act 1988.

First published in 1995
by HEADLINE BOOK PUBLISHING

A HEADLINE LIAISON paperback

10 9 8 7 6 5 4 3 2 1

All rights reserved. No part of this publication may be reproduced, stored in a retrieval system, or transmitted, in any form or by any means without the prior written permission of the publisher, nor be otherwise circulated in any form of binding or cover other than that in which it is published and without a similar condition being imposed on the subsequent purchaser.

All characters in this publication are fictitious and any resemblance to real persons, living or dead, is purely coincidental.

ISBN 0 7472 5146 0

Typeset by Keyboard Services, Luton, Beds

Printed and bound in Great Britain by
Cox & Wyman Ltd, Reading, Berks

HEADLINE BOOK PUBLISHING
A division of Hodder Headline PLC
338 Euston Road
London NW1 3BH

The Golden Cage

Prologue

The conservatory was filled with a mellow golden light. It filtered almost slyly between the rows of exotic orchids ranged on ornate display stands along the huge picture windows. Their intricately moulded flowers seemed to tremble, lustrous in the afternoon sunlight, each petal fragile and translucent as living flesh.

Placing the book on a wrought-iron table, he walked over to the window and gazed out over the gardens. Before him acres of immaculately groomed lawns rolled away to the distant New England shore, where a grey and discontented sea lashed its tongue against a rocky cape.

He smiled to himself as his fingers stroked the pink-white petals of a rare bloom, savouring the feel of its exquisitely soft vulnerability yielding to his touch. Outside it might be a grey and dismal winter's day, but here in the conservatory, its climate controlled night and day by a sophisticated electronic monitoring system, it was perpetual summer.

Sitting down at the table, he turned his attentions to the book. It was handsomely bound in red morocco leather, the leaves edged with gold. He opened it at the first page: a page filled with the smiling faces of pretty women.

The Agency had excelled itself, he mused to himself as

he turned over page after page of photographs. So many young women, all so beautiful and so eager to leave their old lives behind.

This one, perhaps? His fingers stroked the shiny snapshot. Dark eyes pleaded with him. *Choose me, me, me . . .* No, not her. He turned the page. A laughing blonde with baby-blue eyes pouted her glossy lips, the invitation overt and shameless. *I could give you a good time, you know I could. The best. Try me . . .* Her generous breasts pushed hard against her T-shirt, stretching the cheap cotton fabric, and for a moment he wondered . . . but no. No, she was not the one. Not right at all.

He replenished his wine glass from a rather fine eighteenth-century Venetian decanter and took a sip. The cold, crisp liquid trickled luxuriously over his tongue and sharpened his excitement. There was an ache in his belly, a throb of arousal which drew his fingers to the front of his pants, to stroke gently over the hard flesh beneath the fine woollen gabardine.

That one? His finger paused over the hesitantly curving lips, tracing the generous curve, sensual yet somehow uncertain of their own erotic power. His heart thumped, the blood pounding through his veins. Yes, yes, it had to be her. Dark hair cascaded over bare shoulders in shiny waves, eyes of the deepest jet gazed almost questioningly from beneath arching brows; lips of a warm rose-pink complemented the slight rose tinge of her pale and flawless skin.

She was exactly right. Exotic yet wholesome; knowing yet innocent; strong, even defiant, yet infinitely and deliciously vulnerable. Only she would do. He knew he had to have her.

Closing the book, he got to his feet and walked towards the main body of the house. Stepping into the drawing room he took a small golden key from his pocket and locked the conservatory door.

The latch sprang home with a sharp click and his lips twitched into a smile of pleasurable anticipation.

Chapter 1

Mila Kirovska glanced down at the sleeping figure in the bed and turned back to consider her reflection in the mirror.

She felt the first flutterings of nerves in the pit of her stomach. Was she doing the right thing? At least here in St Petersburg she had a job and friends. What if all her dreams turned out to be castles in the air? That was what Alexander thought and perhaps he was right.

Pulling a brush through her thick, dark hair, she twisted it up into a knot and secured it with pins. Was the look too formal, too unapproachable? She hesitated before rummaging in the old trinket box and taking out her favourite jewellery – long, dangly pewter earrings which made a soft tinkling sound when she moved her head from side to side.

'Mila?'

She turned and saw that Alexander had woken and was looking up at her. He was sprawled across the rumpled bedsheets, leaning on his right elbow, and the bedcovers had fallen back so that his muscular body was naked to the waist. The curve of one bare buttock and thigh drew her eyes momentarily, then she snapped them away. She had other, more important things to occupy her mind.

'Hmm?' she replied wordlessly, one earring clamped between her lips as she attached the other to her ear.

'You're not *still* going, are you?'

Mila took the second earring from between her lips and threaded it through her earlobe.

'I've told you often enough, Alexander. The man from the Agency said I must be there before noon to pay my registration fee. If I don't go soon, I'll be late. I might miss my chance...'

'Forget it, Mila. Stay here with me.' Alexander's voice was half-pleading, half-angry. Mila knew how he felt about the Agency, about bloody rich foreigners coming along and advertising for Russian 'companions'.

'I can't. I said I'd be there.'

'Then unsay it. You're not a thing to be bought and sold, Mila.'

He didn't actually add 'and anyway, you belong to me', but that was the subtext and Mila didn't need to hear it to know that that was what Alexander meant. That was one of Alexander's biggest problems: he was too damned possessive. And Mila had dreams – he'd never really understood that. All he'd wanted, ever since they'd graduated together, was a steady job where he didn't have to work too hard, plenty of vodka and a one-bedroomed apartment in St Petersburg.

That was the limit of Alexander's horizons and for a long time it had seemed to be the limit of Mila's, too. But her job as a translator at the State Bureau of Culture was looking increasingly insecure and unchallenging, this shared apartment was little better than a rat-hole, and several months ago she had realised – to her surprise – that she didn't love Alexander Trubetskoy after all. In fact, she never had. What they'd had had been strictly physical. Now, more than ever, she felt that it was time to move on.

'No one's being bought and sold, Alexander. I'm doing

THE GOLDEN CAGE

this because I want to. I can always change my mind ... and maybe no one will want to meet me anyway.'

Alexander fell silent for a moment, his bottom lip jutting like a sulky child's. It almost made her want to laugh, seeing him like that. She relented and, turning back towards the bed, bent to kiss him on the forehead.

He caught hold of her hand and, pulling it to his lips, began kissing it with a raw, almost savage passion. Half embarrassed, half excited, Mila gave a nervous giggle and tried to pull her hand away.

'Alexander. Alex, no please, don't ...'

He left off kissing her fingers for a moment but did not release her hand.

'You used to want me, Mila.'

'Yes, I know. Oh Alexander, I thought you understood. Things change, people change ...'

'You used to want me and you still want me. You shared my bed last night, you took my cock inside your mouth, Mila. Don't you remember?' He took her index finger into his mouth and wound his tongue around it, making her shiver with reluctant pleasure. 'Of course you remember. Did it taste good, having me come all over your tongue?'

Mila opened her mouth to protest, to tell Alexander that he'd got it all wrong, but what could she say? That she was still sharing his bed because places to live were hard to find in St Petersburg and, besides, she still had the hots for him? Put like that it sounded so, so ... manipulative, whereas all it was was harsh reality. In nineties' Russia, you did what you could to get by. In any case, it wasn't as if Alexander had behaved himself. She'd lost count of the women she'd thrown out of their bed in the two years they'd been together.

'Come here, Mila. I want you.'

'Alexander, don't. You'll crease my suit. You know I spent ages getting ready.'

Alexander's eyes glittered with a playful malice.

'Mmm.' He smacked his lips. 'Good enough to eat.' To Mila's horror he began pulling at her jacket, trying to ease it down over her shoulder, threatening to rip off the buttons.

'You'll tear it!'

'You never used to care about your precious clothes,' spat Alexander, his face momentarily contorted with jealous anger. Then his features relaxed and his fingers unfastened the buttons – one, two, three, all undone. The jacket slid down off her shoulders and he pulled it down over her arms. 'Happy now?'

Underneath she was wearing a prim white blouse in a thin artificial silk, the best she could afford on her modest wage. Alexander didn't bother unfastening it. He just pulled it out of the waistband of her skirt and shoved it upwards, uncovering Mila's bare midriff and the ripe swell of her breasts, encased in underwired white satin.

She let out a little gasp of hot breath as Alexander's bear's-paw of a hand closed around her left breast, the furnace heat of him melting and sizzling into her through the satin of her brassiere.

'Do you like that? You do, don't you?'

A tiny, shuddering sigh escaped from her parted lips and she felt herself yielding to Alexander's rough brand of persuasion.

'This is ridiculous. I have to go...' The words were spoken automatically, empty and meaningless. Already her body had betrayed her and her rational mind was closing down, admitting defeat.

'Don't bullshit me, Mila. I know you only got dressed up

THE GOLDEN CAGE

like that to drive me crazy.' Alexander's voice was no louder than a hoarse murmur, but it seemed to fill the whole room. Underneath it, like the beat of a drum, Mila could hear the pounding of her own heart.

She felt his fingers digging into her flesh as they wriggled their way into her bra cup, prising the flesh out from its shell of cocooning wire and white satin. Her nipple was already firming and, as it slipped between the cradle of his fingers, she felt it grow hard and puckered as a walnut-shell. The whole breast seemed to be tingling and aching, the very crest of the nipple so sensitive that she wondered if she could bear even the lightest touch on its rose-pink head.

Alexander pulled her down until she was half sitting, half lying on the bed beside him. His strong, slightly rough fingers were on either side of her nipple, which was poking out from between them; and he was tightening his grip around the puckered pink flesh, rubbing and rolling it so that Mila thought she would scream out with frustration. The very tip of her nipple he did not touch, and it burned and throbbed as she longed for a warm, wet tongue to flick across it.

Hungry for him now, and almost forgetting her appointment at the Agency, Mila sought out his lips and crushed her mouth against his, showing him that she was no plaything to be toyed with as he chose. She would show him that she could be his equal in passion – and in pleasure.

Her fingers felt for the sheet and drew it back, baring her lover's belly and thighs. She explored him by touch, knowing his body so well that she had no need of sight to picture the tangle of dark-brown curls leading down over Alexander's taut belly to the smooth pink flesh of his manhood.

Even in repose, Alexander's cock was generously formed. Now semi-erect, it fluttered between Mila's fingers like a wounded bird, suddenly regaining its strength from the warm gentleness of her touch. As she cradled and stroked it, she felt it uncoiling, stiffening, thickening in her hand, and a thin trickle of clear moisture made her fingers slide easily over the swelling shaft.

'Mmm,' growled Alexander, his hand clenching and unclenching around the globe of her breast. His nails scratched the soft white flesh and the sensation was almost painful – yet pleasurable too. It was good to feel the strength of the wanting, the power she still had over Alexander's firm young body.

She gasped as the kiss ended and their lips drew apart. Her breasts heaved as she drew in air, dizzy and drunk with excitement. A tingle of exhilaration ran right down to her toes as Alexander gripped her nipple between his strong fingers and began pinching it.

'Alexander . . .'

She twisted and turned, in the grip of a tyrannical need for pleasure which it was hard, so very hard, to fight.

His eyebrow rose a fraction.

'You want me to stop?' His fingers paused in their torture. His voice was heavy with irony.

That wasn't fair, it really wasn't and he knew it, thought Mila as she gazed up into his chocolate-brown eyes. How could she tell him to stop when her breasts were aching for his caresses and the soft pink petals of her womanhood were swelling and blushing with desire?

'Bastard,' she said, trying to fight the impulse to smile.

Alexander pushed her down on to the bed and this time she didn't fight. She scarcely wriggled as he undid first her

THE GOLDEN CAGE

blouse and then her bra – sliding a practised hand underneath her back and releasing the catch with an almost imperceptible flick of his fingers. Alexander was good at undoing brassieres. He'd had plenty of practice.

Mila half expected him to strip her naked but Alexander was in no mood to wait. He pushed up her bra with impatient fingers and contemplated the rosy swell of her breasts.

'You always did have nice tits, Mila Kirovska,' he observed, running the flat of his hand with tantalising lightness over the very tips of her breasts. 'Lovely and big.'

Mila shuddered with pleasure at Alexander's caresses. At the back of her mind was the thought that, if she was late for her appointment, Agency boss Morrison Farley would be less than pleased with her. She might even miss out on the chance she had been dreaming of for so many months – the chance to start a new life somewhere in the West. Maybe even in America...

But the only thing she could focus her thoughts on was the pleasure, and the pleasure was intense, powerful, all-encompassing. There wasn't room for anything else in the whole of her body. Every nerve-ending quivered with anticipation as Alexander knelt astride her hips and stooped over her, his moist pink tongue darting like a snake's towards the firm hillock of her breast.

The first touch of tongue-tip on nipple made her arch her back and let out a low moan of surprise and pleasure. Alexander was not usually so gentle or so inventive. But today, it seemed, he had made up his mind to persuade her not to go, not to walk out of his life and go searching after dreams.

He began lapping at her left breast, his tongue describing circles and spirals of moistness over and over again, never quite touching the epicentre of her erect bud. Her own fingers began to move towards her breast, intent on giving herself the pleasure which Alexander was denying her; but he caught her hand in a vice-like grip and carried it inexorably towards the erect spike of his manhood.

Now fully erect, his shaft felt hot and hard as her fingers closed about it. Hot and throbbing, like living stone; like a volcano of flesh threatening to gush out its burning lava on to her trembling hand.

It was Alexander's turn to moan as her hand began working its way up and down his shaft. Mila knew how to pleasure and torment him, just as well as he knew how to drive her. As adversaries in lust, they were well-matched.

He began moving his pelvis back and forth, gently fucking her fingers as they curled about his swollen prick. And that excited Mila almost more than the feel of his tongue, cooling the sex-hot flesh of her breast with a wet trail of saliva.

There was a curious sense of rhythm in their sex game: the slow, measured tilting of Alexander's hips; the piston-smooth action of his dick sliding between Mila's fingers; the synchronised sounds of their breathing, in time to the pulse and rush of blood through overheated veins.

Suddenly, when Mila was least expecting it, Alexander's mouth moved to the apex of her breast and she felt his lips closing around her nipple, taking the whole of the swollen areola into his mouth.

'Alexander!' The word ended in a shrill shriek as her lover's teeth bit into the flesh of her nipple, sending an electric thrill of pain-mingled pleasure through her whole body. 'Аостатчно!'

'No, my love. Never enough.' Alexander tightened his grip on her flesh.

THE GOLDEN CAGE

Mila writhed and twisted on the bed as Alexander bit and teased her nipple with tongue and teeth, flicking his tongue-tip lightly across the crest as he bit into the puckered flesh.

'Beast!' spat Mila, angry yet laughing with the excitement of the feelings surging through her body. She was more annoyed with herself than with Alexander; indignant that she could be so weak and feeble as to give in to the arrogance of his possessive sexual hunger. 'Beast – get off me, you're hurting!'

It was only partly true – but Mila didn't want Alexander to know just how much she was enjoying it. She pushed him away and rolled sideways, her breast still tingling and aching from her lover's rough caresses.

Alexander's hands caught hold of her and pushed her down on to the bed again, this time belly-down. She heard him laughing, his laughter good-natured, husky and warm with sexual pleasure.

'It's no use pretending,' he chuckled. 'You love it.'

'I do not!' She struggled half-heartedly but Alexander was much stronger than she was and in any case, did she really want to get away? She tried a slightly different tack. 'Look, Alexander, you've had your fun. Stop fooling about and let me get up. I'm not interested in you any more, OK?'

Even to her own ears her protests sounded lame and unconvincing – particularly since there was no denying the telltale warm ooze soaking into the gusset of her white cotton panties.

'No, Mila – let's fool about some more.' Alexander's hands were on her thighs now, pushing up her skirt so that it was up round her waist in a tangled belt of scrunched-up material. He let out a low whistle as his index finger traced the plump curve of her buttock, and the bare inches of thigh exposed between stocking-tops and briefs. 'Well, well, you *did* get dressed up for me today, didn't you?'

'I told you...' began Mila, in exasperation. 'It's not for you, it's...'

Alexander ignored her. He was enjoying himself. OK, so he hadn't always been faithful to Mila, but she was still his woman and he didn't like the idea that any woman of his could just take it into her head to walk out on him. No, he knew what was best for her, what made her feel good; and he'd easily persuade her to change her mind. He knew all the right buttons to press...

Sliding his hand between her thighs, his fingers made contact with the damp gusset of Mila's panties and the touch released a warm, sweet odour of sex which seemed to float like a fragrant cloud in the air around them. He grinned.

'Not interested?' Pushing Mila's thighs just a little further apart, he poked his index finger underneath the side of the gusset and dipped it into the honeypot of her sex. 'You could have fooled me.'

The feel of Alexander's finger slip-sliding into her wet haven made Mila's whole body go rigid with reluctant pleasure. She could have sobbed for frustration and desire.

'Oh! Oh, Alexander, that feels...'

'Good, Mila? I know it feels good. How about *this*?' He pushed a second finger into her and began moving them in and out, in and out, pleasuring her with his fingers, making her juices run and cascade over his hand and wrist.

She had completely given up the fight now. All she wanted was what Alexander wanted to give her. Shameless and hungry, she began thrusting out her buttocks, taking

THE GOLDEN CAGE

his fingers more deeply into her, twisting and turning a little from side to side so that his fingertips and knuckles pressed against the walls of her vagina, stretching the delicate membrane.

Lost in the delicate folds of her womanhood, the rosebud of her clitoris throbbed and pulsed with need. As she moved her hips to receive Alexander's fingers, the plump outer labia brushed lightly against each other and the hood of her clitoris shifted slightly, now covering, now exposing its swollen head.

The caress was too light, too insubstantial to bring her to a climax; but it was certainly enough to drive her into a frenzy of sexual hunger. Her entire body tensed and screamed silently for release as Alexander finger-fucked her.

'You want it, don't you, Mila?'

She let out a long, low moan of surrender as Alexander stopped thrusting into her and began teasing and twisting the inner walls of her womanhood.

'Don't you, Mila?'

'Aah ... yes ...' Her words were little more than a whispering sigh but Alexander knew what she wanted. He took her by the hand and dragged her off the bed.

'What ... Alexander, what are you doing?'

'Remember how we did it that time at Uncle Sadkos's dacha? He and the others were in the next room ... but you were so hot for me, you couldn't wait, not even for a few minutes. You had to do it right there and then. Don't you remember?'

Mila remembered. Remembered how hot and strong their lust for each other had been in those early days, when they were scarcely more than kids. Drunk, too, if she remembered right. Alexander's reprobate uncle distilled a lethal home-made vodka and they'd all had plenty of it that night.

'Well? Do you remember?' Alexander nuzzled into the back of her neck and nibbled the soft white flesh. 'Want to try it again?'

Alexander's fingers were gripping her arm but in all honesty she didn't need much persuasion as he pushed her up against the bedroom wall. The old excitement was flooding into her, making her press her thighs together in delicious anticipation.

The pert, rose-pink bud of her sex blushed crimson as it swelled iron-hard with need, pushing its head out from underneath its fleshy hood, longing for a touch, a caress, a kiss...

Alexander was behind her now, pushing her hard up against the wall, pulling her skirt up higher and higher, tucking it into her belt so that her cotton-clad buttocks were exposed.

'You love it,' he whispered into her ear and felt her tremble at his touch. He lifted up the dark, glossy curtain of her hair and planted hungry kisses at the nape of her neck, nipping the flesh between his teeth as though he longed to devour her. 'You love it, you want it, you want it in you, don't you?'

Famished with hunger for her, he slid down her tight white cotton briefs, baring the creamy globes of her buttocks. They were beautiful, smooth, succulent, good enough to eat.

'You can't get enough of it, can you, Mila? You talk so refined, but underneath you're just a bitch on heat. I'm right, aren't I?'

His words were exciting Mila, he could see that. Hell, they were exciting him too, driving him mad for her.

THE GOLDEN CAGE

Couldn't she see they were made for each other? Like two wild animals, all they had to do to be happy was follow their instincts.

'Is that what you want? Some old, fat American poking his dick into you?' He growled the words, grinding his pelvis into the curve of her backside. 'Is it? Or would you rather have me...?'

He stroked her neck, her shoulder, kissing and nibbling at the bare flesh.

'Screw me,' gasped Mila, surprising herself with the violence of her need. 'Screw me, Alex. I want it now.' Reaching out behind her, she took hold of Alexander's engorged member and stroked its slippery tip up and down the amber furrow of her backside.

Alexander smiled inwardly. He'd known all along that Mila would see sense in the end. And the prospect of scything into that soft, wet pussy made him almost spurt just at the thought of it. Even before he entered her he could feel the seductive heat, the caressing smoothness of her inner labia, closing about his cock in a welcoming kiss. And the smell of her surrounded him, the heavy scent of her sex musky and sweet on his fingers, filling him up with the irresistible need to couple.

His fingers slid into the deep furrow between his lover's arse cheeks, his fingertip just grazing the puckered rose of her anus before moving down towards the deep, deep honeypot. Instinctively Mila shuffled her feet apart, opening herself to him, and he nudged the tip of his cock into the sweet, succulent depths.

'Aaah!' A great, tearing cry shook Mila's body as her lover's sword-thrust pierced her, throwing her hard against the wall. Her head was lying sideways against the wall, her cheek pressed up against the flaking emulsion. Reflected in the curtained window opposite, she saw their two bodies, joined together in seamless, rhythmic passion. It hardly seemed to matter that she'd given up on Alex only half an hour ago; at this precise moment, he was the man of her dreams.

His cock was driving her to paroxysms of pleasure, his fingers sliding between her body and the wall, slipping between her love lips and searching out the hot, hard heart of her pleasure. There was no escape – Alexander knew what he wanted and she wanted it too. That first, electric touch had her crying and laughing and screaming, so out of her head that she didn't even hear the old woman in the next apartment, hammering with her stick on the thin dividing wall.

They moved together, their joining beginning slowly but growing wilder, more desperate. Mila felt almost crushed by Alexander's strong thrusts, and she clawed at the wall, powerless to escape from the pleasure quest in which she had submerged her entire being.

Alexander could feel the excitement rising through his body, making his balls heavy and stiffening his cock until he knew that he could not last out much longer. Mila was so gloriously tight, so luxuriously wet, that each new thrust was like sliding his cock into the welcoming depths of her silky throat.

But it was Mila who surrendered first, her body shaken by spasm after spasm as her sex muscles clenched and wave after wild wave engulfed her, drowning her in breathtaking pleasure. She was so overcome that she scarcely noticed Alexander's hands clutching at her hips, pulling himself into her as he filled her with the first hot, white spurt of his climax.

All was silence in the apartment, save for the regular

THE GOLDEN CAGE

ticking of the carved wooden clock and the distant drip, drip, drip of the rusty tap into the bathtub. Above it all, Mila could hear the rasp of her own breathing, as she fought to overcome the dizzy weakness in the warm afterglow of her orgasm.

Alexander smoothed his hand down the curve of her buttock, squeezing the flesh between greedy fingers.

'Good, huh?' It wasn't so much a question as a statement. Alexander had never been lacking in self-confidence.

Her face still turned away from him, Mila smiled.

'Good,' she conceded. 'Well, not bad anyhow.'

Alexander pulled her round to face him and saw that she was laughing.

'Prick-tease.' He rubbed himself up against her and she felt a frisson of renewed pleasure.

'Animal,' she retorted.

'What d'you say we do it again?' Alexander cupped her bare breast in his hand but she drew away, the cooling trickle of their mingled juices running down the inside of her thigh. She shook her head.

'I told you, I have to go.' She eased her skirt down over her thighs and reached round to fasten her bra over her breasts.

Alexander contemplated her in open-mouthed disbelief.

'You're still going? To the Agency? But I thought...'

'Nothing's changed, Alexander. Just because you screwed me up against the wall, you think that's going to change my mind?'

She stood on tiptoe and kissed Alexander in the middle of his forehead, as if she were kissing a bewildered child.

'Get real, Alex. Get a life. That's what I intend to do. I told you I was going to the Agency and I meant it.'

Chapter 2

Mila walked slowly down Nevsky Prospekt in the heart of St Petersburg. There didn't seem much point in hurrying – she was already over an hour late.

She wondered, not for the first time, if what she was doing was sensible. What young woman in her right mind would sign up with an agency which offered to find Russian brides and 'companions' for wealthy Western men? Come to think of it, what man would take leave of his senses and offer a home, a job, even a life to a woman he had met perhaps only once? On the face of it at least, Alexander was right; it was all very, very chancy.

But then again, life wasn't sensible, and if you wanted your dreams to come true you had to be willing to take chances. It wasn't that Mila disliked St Petersburg – it was a beautiful city and she'd had some good times here. But in the new, free-market Russia, all she had to look forward to was genteel poverty and boredom, and a tiny apartment with Alexander, near the Baltic Station. No, it wasn't enough. This was her big chance to make something of her life and she owed it to herself to take it.

Leaving behind her the golden dome of St Isaac's Cathedral, she walked past the famous Literary Café. The Café Literaturnoye charged an entrance fee just to get past the door – and even if you could afford it, you would have to pay in hard currency. Roubles were practically worthless and Russia had become a paradise for racketeers and spivs.

She glanced in through the window as she passed the café, looking at the laughing faces – foreign faces mostly, English and French and American. She had never been inside the Literary Café. Maybe one day, when she had made a new life for herself in the West, she would return to St Petersburg and pay her entrance fee, watching the doorman's face as she peeled off the dollar bills, one by one.

Dreams. They came expensive in St Petersburg. She walked on, past the Café Druzhba and the closed-down kiosk which, in summer, sold sweet Russian champagne in paper cups. She shivered and pulled her coat more closely around her, wishing she could afford to dress more warmly. Spring came late in this part of the world and all year round there was a keen wind blowing in from the Baltic.

Not far from the elegant stained-glass and plasterwork of Elyseev's food store, she found what she was looking for: a nondescript brown door sandwiched between a rouble café and a tatty department store. Hesitating for just the briefest moment, she put her hand to her hair, patting the stray strands into place, took a deep breath and stepped inside.

In his first-floor office on Nevsky Prospekt, Morrison Farley glanced for the umpteenth time at his Rolex.

Almost a quarter past one. Where the hell was that girl? With each moment that passed, he could see dollar bills melting away before his eyes. And yet, at their initial meeting, the Kirovska woman had seemed keen. Very keen. And the client had been very firm in his requirements.

THE GOLDEN CAGE

He must stop panicking – she would come. A girl like her wasn't stupid and he was about to make her an offer she couldn't afford to refuse.

The American director of the East-West Friendship Agency licked his lips as he thought about Mila Kirovska. As he recollected she was tall but not too tall, with long, long legs and a flair for showing them off to best advantage. She had firm breasts and tight buttocks that rippled under the tight fabric of her skirt as she walked. Waves of dark, glossy hair framing a face that seemed to change subtly with her moods – sometimes pale and fragile as a porcelain doll, sometimes filled with all the fire of a defiant and undauntable spirit. Fragile vulnerability and untamed spirit: the perfect paradox and the perfect combination.

Realising he was getting hard just thinking about her, he rubbed the swelling length of his manhood through his pants. Gently, teasingly – just enough to keep that wonderfully warm feeling of arousal, but not so hard that he risked bringing himself off. Oh, where the hell was that girl?

When she arrived, he'd play it cool with her, not let on that he had a client practically biting his hand off to meet her – and ready to pay the full fee on the strength of just one meeting. He'd string her along a little, make her more dependent on his goodwill. Show her how good that goodwill could be, if only she was prepared to meet him halfway...

A sound made him look up. OK – smile. He sat back in his chair, smoothing the light-brown hair back from his forehead. His heart beat a little faster as the outer door closed and he heard the sound of high-heeled shoes making their way up the bare wooden staircase to his office.

* * *

Mila knocked on the door.

Morrison Farley waited a couple of seconds, just to make her sweat a little, then barked out:

'Enter.'

Nervously she turned the handle and entered. Farley was sitting at his desk behind the high-tech computer on which he stored all his client records.

By American standards the office was not particularly luxurious, but to Mila it represented a different and vastly appealing world. There was deep, soft carpet on the floor and the furniture was modern and Scandinavian. It was nothing like the dark, gloomy office in which Mila worked at the Bureau of Culture.

'You're late,' observed Farley with studied coolness, letting his eyes wander from the front of Mila's blouse to the clock on the wall. 'Very late.'

'Y-yes, I know.' Mila swallowed hard, her prepared excuses drying in her throat. Why had she been so stupid and so weak-willed as to allow herself to be seduced by Alexander? She decided not to volunteer any explanation. 'I know I'm late, I'm sorry.'

Farley swivelled his chair round forty-five degrees, sat back and interlaced his fingers as he scrutinised her. Mmm, even better than he remembered. Even if he'd wanted to, he couldn't have suppressed the enthusiastic stirring of his lust.

'I take it you *are* still serious about this Agency and its work, Miss Kirovska?'

'Yes, of course!' Mila wished Farley would offer her a seat. She felt like a naughty child in the headmaster's office. 'Oh Mr Farley, of course I am!'

'Hmm.' Farley took time out to consult the file on his

THE GOLDEN CAGE

desk. Actually he wasn't reading it, just making sure that Mila felt really uncomfortable. He looked back at her. 'Well, you have a strange way of showing it.'

'It won't happen again.'

'It had better not. Our clients are very busy and important men, Mila.' Farley was putting a lot into his act. He paused. 'Have you brought the balance of the Agency fee?'

Mila reached into her bag and took out a sheaf of crumpled notes. Her life-savings. For a split second she heard Alexander's voice at the back of her mind, telling her she was crazy. Maybe he was right...

'Is it all there?'

'All of it, Mr Farley.'

'In US Dollars?'

Mila paled a little.

'Half of it ... the rest is in roubles.'

Farley shook his head, his face a picture of grave disapproval.

'We agreed dollars, Miss Kirovska.'

'I'm sorry. It's so hard to get foreign currency ... I had to deal on the black market and I was afraid of getting caught...'

Farley gave a tetchy sigh. He didn't let on that the fee Mila paid to the Agency represented not even one fiftieth of what he would get from the client if – or rather when – the deal went through.

'This is very irregular.'

'I've told you, Mr Farley, I'm sorry.' Mila hesitated, then asked. 'Have you ... Has anyone ...?'

Farley placed the bundle of notes in his top desk drawer.

'There has been one enquiry ... er, yes. An American gentleman, very respectable, extremely well-connected.'

'An American!'

Farley rummaged in another drawer and took out a studio photograph of a man in his late thirties, distinguished, good-looking, with pale grey eyes which seemed to see right into Mila's soul. Her hands trembled as she picked up the photo and felt her whole body responding instinctively to the man's warm smile, his clean-cut good looks.

'He's interested in me? Really?'

'Yes. He is looking for an educated companion, someone who could act as a hostess for his business clients. There might be a possibility of a meeting between you. But...'

'There's a problem?' Mila's heart was in her mouth.

'There might be,' lied Farley. 'He has expressed an interest in several of our young ladies, you see. And some of the others on our books have been registered with us for so much longer.'

'I'd do anything. Anything!'

Farley raised an eyebrow, regarding her with a mixture of amusement and pulsating lust.

'Indeed? That's very interesting, Mila. Very interesting indeed.'

'Please, Mr Farley.' Mila had come too far to go back now. She seized his hand, her dark eyes imploring. 'If there's some way, *any* way...'

Morrison Farley allowed himself the luxury of a smile as he listened to exactly the words he had been waiting to hear. He got to his feet and walked round until he was standing behind Mila's chair. She could no longer see him, but she could smell the sweet, slightly sickly spiciness of his aftershave, mixed with the acrid tang of sweat.

THE GOLDEN CAGE

Farley's fingers brushed the side of her bare throat and she quivered at the touch.

'There might be,' he whispered, and he bent to unbutton her blouse.

Farley arranged for the meeting to take place at the Hotel Grand Europe, in the heart of St Petersburg. Mila had never been inside the hotel before, let alone eaten in its fabulous restaurant, with its ornate gilded pillars and painted frescoes.

And she knew nothing about the man, not even his name. All Farley would say was that he was 'wealthy and very interested in meeting you, Mila.'

They met in the restaurant and Mila's whole being sizzled with excitement as she felt the tall American's pale grey eyes wandering over her body, devouring her beauty, as though he were trying to possess her with his eyes...

'Good evening, Miss Kirovska. My name is Hobart. Orin Hobart.'

'It's a pleasure to meet you, Mr Hobart.' The name meant nothing to her, but that voice ... it oozed confidence, authority, potency.

'I understand you are a student of the fine arts.'

'A ... little. I studied painting for a year before training as an English translator.'

'Your English is excellent. You have only the faintest of accents, and it is charming, quite charming.'

'Thank you.'

Mila felt so self-conscious under Hobart's gaze that she could scarcely swallow. His eyes seemed to smoulder, burning into her flesh as they searched out her deepest, darkest secrets. Normally she might have been wary of such a man, but there was something irresistible about Orin

Hobart, something warmly seductive in those pale, clear eyes and that slightly sardonic smile.

Hobart was around six feet two in height, powerfully built with broad shoulders and a muscular torso, tapering to a narrow waist and hips. His glossy black hair was cut short at the back and sides and gelled back from his forehead, slick and smooth. When he raised his glass to drink, Mila saw how his throat pulsed gently, like a snake swallowing its prey.

Yes, there was just the faintest frisson of danger about Orin Hobart: the danger that comes with any man who has power and enjoys wielding it. She knew virtually nothing about this man, save that he was a successful businessman in America, but even if she had known nothing at all she would have sensed the control, the supreme confidence. A confidence which turned her on more than she wanted to admit, even to herself.

'Clearly you are a talented young woman, Mila Kirovska.' Hobart stroked the stem of the single thornless rose which decorated their dinner table. Mila was transfixed by his hands: long, sensitive fingers, an artist's hands, slender and surprisingly delicate.

'I wouldn't say...' Mila caught Hobart's quizzical expression and shut up. 'You're very kind.'

Hobart's face broke into a grin and he laughed out loud. A wave of panic swept through Mila. Had she said the wrong thing? Why was she so gauche? Hobart must think she was some kind of peasant.

Hobart patted her hand.

'Relax,' he purred. 'Please, Mila, be yourself. If we're to get along – and I'm sure we shall – I want to know exactly what you're like; what you think, what you feel. In fact, I want to know everything about you.'

THE GOLDEN CAGE

His touch on the back of her hand, brushing the deep-red petals of the rose across her pale skin, seemed to electrify her whole body. She shifted on her seat, conscious of a stealthy, treacherous warmth creeping from her belly down to the warm haven between her thighs. The silky gusset of her French knickers pressed wickedly against her pubis and, as she wriggled on the chair, her sex opened, drenching the gusset with a flood of fragrant juice.

Mila must have let out a tiny gasp of reluctant pleasure as the wet silk slid between her outer labia and rubbed across the exposed head of her clitoris, for the next thing she knew was Hobart's voice, soft and warm and solicitous.

'Mila . . . are you all right?'

'Yes. Yes, of course, I'm sorry.'

'You seemed miles away.' Hobart's smile returned, lighting up his aristocratic face. 'Aren't I fascinating enough to retain your interest? I really must try harder.'

Mila wanted to tell Hobart that, on the contrary, he was easily the most fascinating man she had ever met – but her throat was suddenly dry as dust and no sound came out. She lifted her glass and took a sip of fizzy water.

'More wine, Mila?'

'No, thank you, really.'

'Just a little?'

Mila put her hand over her wine glass but Hobart nudged it away and poured in more white wine.

'Go ahead. It'll steady your nerves.' He caressed her hand and suddenly her whole body started trembling, not from fear any more but from sheer naked lust. Could he sense the way she was reacting to him – and if he could, would he be shocked? Could he smell the honeysweet ooze trickling out from between her thighs?

She shifted position on her chair, forcing herself to some

Aurelia Clifford

sort of composure. She was painfully aware of her turgid nipples, rubbing and pushing their fat little snouts under the thin blue velour of her cheap evening dress. Any fool could see that she was aroused – and by her calculations, Orin Hobart was anything but a fool.

'Tell me about yourself, Mila.'

'There's not much to tell.' Chills and thrills of pleasure were skating over the bare flesh of her arms and down under the blue dress to the crests of her nipples. 'I guess I'm just not the most interesting of people.'

'I disagree,' replied Hobart smoothly. 'Tell me anyway.'

'I'm a translator. I used to translate foreign classics for the Soviets, make them "politically acceptable", but now there isn't much work and it's a dead-end job.'

'And your love life?' Hobart's gaze was steady and penetrating.

'Practically non-existent,' replied Mila. For all practical purposes she was telling the truth.

'You're bored with your existence? You want something more out of life – something better?'

For the first time Mila felt she could really come alive and say what she felt.

'I'm suffocating in this place. Can you understand that? It's not that I don't like it, I was brought up here and it's all I've ever known. Maybe that's why . . .'

'I think I can understand,' replied Hobart, his even tone unchanged despite Mila's passionate outburst. 'I know what it is to have dreams – to want things you can't have.'

He let go of Mila's hand and she felt suddenly bereft. Her eyes searched his face, almost pleading with him to touch her again.

'There are things you want, aren't there, Mila?'

'Yes.'

THE GOLDEN CAGE

'Things you're almost afraid to talk about, as if admitting to your dreams and desires is enough to make them evaporate. Am I right?'

She found herself smiling as she looked straight into those dark, intense eyes.

'You know you are.'

'Tell me about your dreams.'

'I dream about getting away from the tiny apartment I'm living in and leaving my job and...'

'And?'

She gazed about her, at the Western tourists dining unconcernedly among the splendour, as though all this glitz and glamour was something they were used to having every day. Which, quite possibly, they were.

'And getting away from St Petersburg. Far, far away.'

'To America?'

Mila felt her cheeks burn. She hadn't wanted it to be like this. It was pretty obvious how it must sound: that all she wanted was to meet a rich American who would take her away from her unbearably humdrum existence and open the doors to a brilliant new life. The worst thing about it was, it was true.

Or at least, it had been – until she'd met Orin Hobart face to face. Now that she had felt his touch on her skin, felt his eyes burning into her soul, she knew that it would be oh so easy to get hooked.

'Maybe,' she forced herself to answer. Her mouth was horribly dry again and she took a deep draught of wine. The chilled liquid burned a path of cold fire down her throat. She could feel every last droplet searing its way to her stomach.

'And what else do you want, Mila?'

'Oh... you know. A decent job, a future.' She paused

and looked into Hobart's eyes. 'Someone ... special to share it all with.' It sounded corny, she knew that, but she wasn't about to come right out and admit that she was feeling a powerful sexual attraction for this man whom she'd never met before in her life and knew virtually nothing about.

'Good.' Hobart smiled again and, spearing a morsel of asparagus with his silver fork, he carried it to Mila's glossy, painted mouth. He seemed pleased when her lips parted and she accepted the offering. 'Because that's what I want too, Mira Kirovska; and unless I'm very much mistaken, you're a very special kind of young woman.'

Chapter 3

It was in the early hours of a May morning that she found herself being driven towards Moscow Airport in Morrison Farley's limousine – a sleek white Buick he had had brought over from the States.

As she sank into the soft leather seats she felt a frisson, half of pleasure, half of fear, steal over her body like a cold breeze on a hot summer's day, turning her smooth skin to gooseflesh. This was her first real taste of luxury – this and the clothes Farley had bought her to wear, chic and figure-hugging. Maybe soon, if all went as she dreamed it would, she would be travelling everywhere in a limousine.

She tried not to look at Farley. Offering him her body in return for preferential treatment wasn't something she was proud of – but then again, she'd slept with Alexander Trubetskoy to keep a roof over her head, so what was the difference? And here she was, travelling all the way to America to stay with a man she'd only met once.

What if she arrived to find that Orin Hobart had changed his mind? What if the attraction that had been so strong between them no longer existed? What if the dream turned sour . . . ?

Swiftly she decided to put negative thoughts right out of her mind. No way. She was going to make this work, no matter what. She *had* to, if her dreams of a new life were going to come true. And nothing, absolutely nothing could be worse than living in Russia the way it was now, with its interminable bread queues, racketeers and miserable faces.

Farley slipped his hand into Mila's lap. She tried not to respond but her body was quick to betray her, her heartbeat quickening and a light seasoning of perspiration moistening her palms. His fingers moulded themselves to her thigh and began stroking the flesh gently through the thin woollen serge of her skirt.

'You're good company, Mila Kirovska,' he said softly, tightening his grip just a little and feeling Mila tense with apprehension as his fingers crept a little higher. 'I guess I'm gonna miss you.'

Mila hardly knew what to say. Head turned a little to one side, she let her eyes scan the drifting columns of traffic and the dull rows of identical apartment blocks beyond, avoiding Farley's gaze.

'You've been very good to me. I'm ... extremely grateful to you for all that you have done.'

'Yeah.' Farley smiled to himself as he reflected on just how grateful Mila had been. 'How about showing me ... just once more, let's say for old time's sake?'

She turned to look at him.

'Here ... ? I ... you don't mean it.'

'Sure I do, Mila. Sure I do.'

She swallowed, trying to clear the sudden dryness from her throat.

'We'll miss the plane.'

Farley glanced at the dashboard clock.

'We have plenty of time, I made sure of that. And you can't begin to know how much I want you to suck my cock.'

The abrupt expressiveness of his language reminded

THE GOLDEN CAGE

Mila of Alexander, who had been so very tight-lipped and resentful when she'd gone back to clear out her things and tell him she was going to America – and not intending to come back, either, whatever her three-month visa might say. Like Alexander, Morrison Farley excited her against all her better judgement – filled her with a sort of guilty and secretive pleasure she hated to admit to.

She gave a nervous smile, her heart thumping almost audibly in her chest. Something told her this was an offer she had better not refuse.

'Here?'

Farley laughed, glanced in the rearview mirror and swung the car to the right.

'You Ruski girls sure know how to tempt a guy,' he admitted. 'But getting ourselves arrested by the State Police might not be quite so much fun.'

The car was hardly unobtrusive. Its gleaming white bodywork slid ghostlike through the half-lit streets of the Moscow suburbs as dawn came up over the city, turning the sky to mid-blue streaked with clouds of apricot and dusty pink.

A side street in the featureless outskirts of the city was hardly the place for a romantic rendezvous – but then, there was no romance in what was about to happen, only physical need.

The car slid almost noiselessly to a halt in the dawn light. Farley cut the engine and silence closed in. A few windows in a nearby block glowed orange behind drawn curtains, but there was not another soul to be seen. Farley unfastened his seat belt and Mila heard it slide back with a soft rasping sound and a metallic click.

'If you weren't so set on going to the States...' he murmured. And he pulled her towards him, sliding his hand behind her head and caressing the smooth waves of her hair as he kissed her.

Somewhere at the back of her mind, Mila wondered if it was like this for Erika. Erika was her friend from way back in her college days. Back then, Erika had her sights set on a senior post in the State Bureau of Culture, but her ambitions had changed a little since then. These days, Erika was a high-class hooker, one of the expensive ones who worked the tourist hotels and sold their favours for hard currency. Was that so much different from this . . . ?

Mila wondered if Erika felt this way – excited in spite of herself, a sweetly spicy odour of sex wafting up from her parted thighs, the tiny cotton triangle of her panties moist and irresistibly fragrant. Did she too feel this guilty arousal as a stranger slid up her skirt and used her for his pleasure? Could it be her pleasure, too?

'I want you,' whispered Farley, twisting a lock of Mila's dark hair about his fingertip. *I want you for myself*, he added in the silence of his thoughts. Of course that luxury was out of the question. Even if you owned a candy store, you couldn't keep all the candy for yourself. But Morrison Farley had always found it hard to resist mixing business with pleasure.

Her skin felt so, so seductively soft to his fingertips. And he thrilled to the slight quiver that ran through her as their lips met and he entered her mouth with a smooth, hard thrust of his tongue.

All his lust was in that kiss; all the hard-pulsing energy of his stiffened dick. The miniature shaft of his tongue, muscular and smooth, possessed her as readily as if she were lying beneath him and he was entering her with his penis. Her saliva anointed him with hot, wet kisses, and he imagined how much more exciting it would be to feel it

THE GOLDEN CAGE

dripping and trickling over the glistening dome of his manhood.

Taking hold ▓▓▓▓▓▓▓, he guided it down his belly to his lap. She ▓▓▓▓▓▓▓▓▓ notice how aroused she was, the head of ▓▓▓▓▓▓▓▓▓ hard against the inside of his zip.

'Take out my dick,' he whispered, kissing Mila's throat as he pushed up her skirt and exposed her long, slim, stocking-clad thigh.

Mila did as he asked, almost as though she were in a trance – a trance of sexual anticipation, shackles of lust which would not let her resist the impulse that roared and surged within her.

She slid down the zipper and slid her hand inside. Farley's erect penis was sticking out of his boxer shorts, its shaft insolently and arrogantly hard, a curving sabre of flesh. As her fingers curled around it she heard Farley give a little gasp and groan of contentment. She could feel the desire in him pulsing out through his cock, the fat bluish vein on its underside throb, throb, throbbing in time to the rhythm of his lust. And she began to stroke him slowly, delicately.

'Oh *yes*.' His breath escaped in a soft shudder of ecstasy and his fingers tightened on Mila's thigh, sliding up until they were within a hairsbreadth of her pubis.

He thought of Mila's white lace and cotton panties, so chaste and now so moist; and of the beautiful, silken-haired pussy beneath. He ached to tear off those panties, or simply pull aside the gusset so that he could thrust himself up inside her. *Oh yes, yes, yes*. He pushed his pelvis forward, slowly, trying to control the rhythm as Mila's fingers stroked him to pleasure. Her pussy. Oh, such a pussy. Long, silky curls of dark hair foresting the plump mound of her pubis. Fleshy lips that pursed so modestly until a questing finger – or tongue – made them blossom like some rare orchid.

'Your lips,' he gasped, fearing that he would come almost before they had begun and shoot his load over Mila's fingers. 'I want your lips around my cock.'

His hands moved to her face and he kissed her again, this time with such violence that it took her breath away. Then he was stroking her hair and pushing her head down towards the hard and glistening dome of his manhood.

It wasn't easy, having sex sitting in the front of Farley's Buick, but by now Mila was almost as eager as Farley himself. Her lips parted, and her tongue flicked across them once, twice, leaving them wet and shiny with saliva. She heard Farley's voice. It sounded as if it was coming from very far away.

'Suck me. Suck me now.'

She did not demur. Opening her mouth wide she took him inside, engulfing his hardness with her softness, eagerly swallowing down the salty taste that oozed from him in slippery trickles.

He trembled now; trembled beneath her as she wound her tongue-tip around the head of his prick; probing gently that hypersensitive place on the underside of the tip, where foreskin met glans. He writhed and gasped, holding on to her hair now, pulling and twisting it quite roughly as desire overtook him and he lost what remained of his self-control.

His mind was filled with seductive images: pictures of all the times and all the places he and Mila had coupled since that day in his office, when he'd told her that he could do so much to help her . . . if only she helped him. And how she'd helped him . . .

How deep her throat was; how willing. He caressed her

THE GOLDEN CAGE

hair, twisted it around his fingers, listening to her soft moaning as she felt him grow still harder in her mouth. Those last few priceless seconds before ejaculation seemed to last a blissful eternity, and then...

With a hard shove of his pelvis he forced himself that critical last millimetre into Mila's mouth. She wriggled a little then he felt her relax and yield to the fountaining pleasure filling her up. As the orgasm went on and on, dying away with blissful slowness, he stroked her throat and felt it ripple and undulate as she swallowed down his tribute, every precious, opalescent droplet.

Panting, he sat back and rested against the headrest. The world was spinning, ever so gently and ever so pleasantly.

'You're one talented lady, Mila Kirovska.'

Mila looked up at him, wiping her mouth on her handkerchief. But he pulled the handkerchief away and made her kiss him again, sharing the salty taste of his seed.

'*Real* talented.'

Trying to appear calm and collected, Mila pulled down the sun-visor and looked into the mirror, adjusting a few stray strands of hair and tugging down the hem of her skirt.

'Thank you.'

She didn't quite know what else to say. And she hoped that Farley hadn't noticed the hardness of her nipples, thrusting out from underneath her flimsy bra. There seemed something doubly indecent about not just giving him oral sex but enjoying it too.

Farley opened the glove compartment and took out a buff-coloured envelope which he handed to Mila. She looked at him questioningly.

'What's this?'

'Your false passport and your visitor's visa to the US.'

'But . . . why do I need a false passport?'

Farley sighed.

'I thought I explained. Look, that visa only entitles you to remain in the States for three months, right?'

'Right.'

'At the end of which, Uncle Sam will want to know why you haven't gone back home to good old Mother Russia. You'll be deported as an illegal alien. Unless . . .'

'Unless I enter the country under a false name?'

'Got it in one.'

'Isn't that . . . rather risky?'

Farley shrugged his broad shoulders.

'Of course. I told you, all this is very illegal.'

'And what if . . . ?'

'What if what?'

'What if Mr Hobart and I . . . what if things don't work out, and I have to come back to Russia? Will they let me back in with a false passport?'

Farley's face split into a wide grin.

'Believe me, you won't need to come back. This is going to work out just fine between you two, count on it. There's a great chemistry between you – and besides, you'll be an asset to his organisation. Trust me. You'll be just fine.'

'Morrison . . .'

'What?'

Mila leaned over and kissed him on the cheek.

'Thank you. For helping me.'

'Believe me,' smiled Farley. 'The pleasure's all mine.'

Thirty-five thousand feet above the ground, riding high above a marshmallow blanket of cloud, Mila curled her fingers around the fake passport and dreamed of the new life she was about to begin. She'd long since stopped

THE GOLDEN CAGE

wondering if what she was doing was sensible. What mattered was here, now – and what was to come. The past no longer existed.

After a brief stopover in London meals were served, then most of the passengers either dozed in their seats or watched the endless, mindless output of American videos. But Mila couldn't settle – she felt restless, excited, a little fearful too. Checking her make-up in her handbag mirror, she decided to freshen up.

The washroom seemed miles away, at the far end of the cabin; well, that was Economy class for you. Mila wondered vaguely what it would be like to travel in First – would it be like all those American movies she'd devoured over the years? And would wealthy businessman Orin Hobart have his very own private jet?

She smiled to herself as she made her way down the gangway, between the packed seats. She wasn't thinking like a grown woman, more like a fourteen year-old, fantasising about having sex with that good-looking new teacher. All she could hope was that the reality of Orin Hobart turned out to be as good as the fantasy, that he would desire her as much as she had desired him. And even if their relationship never developed beyond that of employer and employee, wasn't that a thousand times better than the dull existence she was leaving behind?

Mila was so lost in her fantasies that she didn't notice the cabin stewardess coming towards her down the gangway with the food trolley.

'Madam ... Excuse me, madam ...'

The stewardess did her best to get out of the way but Mila wasn't looking where she was going and the next moment they collided.

Stumbling sideways, Mila almost fell into the lap of a

youngish man with sun-streaked blond hair and soft blue eyes. Smiling, he put out his arm to catch her just before she landed on his knee.

'Careful!'

Straightening up, scarlet with embarrassment, Mila clapped her hand to her mouth.

'Oh . . . oh, I'm so sorry.'

The stranger's hand lingered on her arm as he helped steady her.

'Don't mention it. I mean, hey, it's not every day a beautiful young woman throws herself at me.'

His voice was melodious and smooth. An American voice? No, English. Mila had always thought Englishmen rather cold and distant, but that wasn't the impression she got from this one. His friendliness seemed genuine, his smile infectious. He was attractive too, with strong, slightly aquiline features and wavy hair the colour of sun-warmed English honey. A little quiver of mutual appreciation seemed to pass between them as their eyes met and Mila felt her defences weakening.

The stewardess's voice cut in.

'Are you all right, madam?'

Mila nodded.

'Yes, yes, I'm fine. Thank you.'

She could feel her cheeks burning crimson. Only a few hours out of St Petersburg and already she was behaving like a complete idiot, walking into things and falling on top of desirable young men. And he *was* rather desirable, wasn't he? She had to work hard to suppress the laughter that was bubbling up inside her. Was it simply nerves, or the exhilaration of being free at last, off the leash and on the way to a shining future?

'I . . . I'm sorry to have bothered you,' said Mila.

THE GOLDEN CAGE

'I don't suppose you'd consider sharing a drink with me?' The Englishman nodded towards the bottle of single malt whisky on his table. 'They do say it's a bad thing to drink on your own,' he added. 'So the least you can do is save me from myself.'

The stranger seemed captivated by the smile that curved Mila's lips into a sensual scarlet bow, glossy and so kissable.

'It's kind of you, but I don't think so.' Mila got to her feet, brushing imaginary creases out of her skirt, and extended her hand. The Englishman took it, his fingers curling about hers and for a few seconds imprisoning her within the strength of his wanting. 'A pleasure meeting you, Mr . . . ?'

'Delaney, Greg Delaney. But please – call me Greg. Everybody does.'

'Pleased to meet you, Greg.' She turned to go.

'And you?'

'Sorry?'

'You. Your name. You haven't told me.'

'No.' Mila thought of the two passports in her bag. The future spread out before her had nothing to do with this young Englishman, no matter how personable he might be. 'It's not important.'

'I'll be seeing you around, then.'

'Yes. I'll be seeing you.'

When she went back to her seat, Mila curled up against the window and watched the darkening sky, the black expanse of ocean so very far beneath the plane.

Slowly she felt herself dozing, drifting off into dreams in which the young Englishman was quickly forgotten, and she relived the thrill of Orin Hobart's goodnight kiss.

Mila dozed fitfully, she didn't know how long for. The

seconds and minutes and hours seemed to blur. She was jet-lagged, yet curiously alert; the adrenaline rush filling her with a shiver of excitement as the pilot's voice crackled over the intercom:

'In a few minutes' time we shall be coming in to land at Logan Airport, Boston. Please ensure that your seatbelts are fastened and all cigarettes extinguished...'

Mila clutched her passport and visa – the fakes that were so convincing she almost believed that she really was Nadia Muratova, arriving in Boston to spend the summer with her aunt and uncle. The deception worried her a little, but she had no reason to question what Morrison Farley had told her. If this was the only way she could start a new life in the States, then so be it.

They touched down almost dead on time and what seemed like only seconds later Mila was disembarking, smiling to the cabin steward, and stepping out of the aeroplane into another world.

She tried hard to remember everything she had been told, repeating the instructions to herself over and over again. *Collect your luggage from the carousel. Wait by the bookstall for a man called Lars. If anyone asks, you're Nadia Muratova...*

'Passport and visa, ma'am.'

Mila's heart was thumping so loudly as she fumbled in her bag that she was sure the whole world must be able to hear it above the hubbub of the airport. Surely they would notice that the passport was a fake. She'd be caught, arrested, deported! Oh, why had she ever agreed to go along with this?

Her thoughts flashed back to the night when three of her friends had been caught with 'seditious literature' by the Russian secret police, back in the old Soviet days. Glasnost,

THE GOLDEN CAGE

Perestroika, call it what you will – it took more than a few words and fine speeches to erase the deep-seated fear of men in uniforms.

The customs officer glanced at the passport and visa, touched his cap and handed them back.

'Have a real nice vacation, Miss Muratova.'

His friendly smile threw her off balance for a few seconds; then she was being jostled and carried along by the crowd, through the immigration channels and the X-ray security machines to the vast concourse beyond.

Even at eleven-thirty at night, the airport was busy. Mila collected the single suitcase which contained everything she had wanted to salvage from her old life and scanned the concourse. There was a bookstall over to the right, by the pavement-style café where men and women in chic business suits were drinking espresso and cappuccino to the accompaniment of soft, almost formless music.

At the bookstall, she set down her suitcase and checked her watch. What now? She felt exposed here and extraordinarily alone. Everyone else seemed to be going somewhere, meeting relatives and friends, heading out of the terminal towards taxi-cabs and buses and hire-cars. The one-way plane ticket lay crumpled in her pocket, and she was just a small, lone figure in the middle of all this vastness. For the first time, she began to feel really scared.

'Miss Muratova?'

'Yes . . . ?'

At the sound of the false name she spun round, to see a man in an immaculate chauffeur's uniform of dark-blue serge with polished knee-boots and a peaked cap.

'Hi, I'm Lars.' He extended a gloved hand. 'Mr Hobart's chauffeur.' He picked up her suitcase. 'And you must be . . .' he lowered his voice, 'Mila Kirovska.'

Mila nodded. She felt slightly ludicrous, a bit like a very inept spy.

'I've come to drive you to Mr Hobart's summer villa on the coast,' explained Lars. 'He asked me to be sure and tell you how much he's looking forward to seeing you again.'

Chapter 4

The night sky was lightening into the first peachy-pink streaks of dawn as the limousine approached the house on the Massachusetts coast.

Orin Hobart stood at his study window and watched the car glide sleekly up the driveway to the house. A smile of anticipation played about his lips and his fingers toyed with the heavy gold signet ring on his right hand. This moment had been a long time in coming.

Hobart's summer residence overlooked the ocean, the distant waves audible even through the thick double-glazing. Lush emerald lawns stretched down a gently rolling slope, beyond which a tangle of wind-twisted spruce screened the house from the keen breeze which blew in off the ocean even at the height of summer.

It was a secluded place, about a mile from the nearest village and just far enough from the fashionable resort towns to be convenient, yet agreeably private. Orin Wycherley Hobart IV did not invite prying eyes. He preferred to keep his private life strictly private.

As he gazed out of the first-floor window, he saw the car swish to a halt outside the front steps. His fingers tightened on the windowsill as he watched Lars open the passenger door and Mila Kirovska slide out, graceful as a cat and soft as a kitten. He had been thinking about her a great deal lately, ever since their meeting in St Petersburg, but even so he had not quite remembered the fragile beauty of the woman; the delicate features and those great dark eyes, set against the smooth ivory whiteness of her skin.

She delighted him. Aroused him too and he knew, as she raised her face to look up at the house, that he had not been mistaken. She was perfect, absolutely perfect for what he had in mind. Mila might not realise it yet, but Orin Hobart knew exactly what she needed and craved, and he was going to make her so happy that she would fall at his feet and weep.

Weep with ecstasy.

While Lars was getting her suitcase out of the limo, Mila just stood and stared up at the house, gaping like a half-wit at the sheer size of the place.

It wasn't that she'd never seen a big house before – St Petersburg was full of magnificent buildings and she'd done all the touristy places like Tsarskoe Selo and Petrodvoretz and Oranienbaum – but she'd certainly never met anyone who *owned* a place like this, that was for sure. Was this really the house that Hobart had described to her as 'my little summer retreat'?

This was the first time she'd properly confronted the reality of Orin Hobart's extensive wealth, and she realised that she knew hardly anything about him, beyond the face that he was some sort of businessman who dabbled in politics.

The house was a typical New England 'summer cottage' of white-painted pasteboard; in fact it was a rambling Victorian-style mansion with dozens of windows and grounds that seemed to stretch as far as the eye could see. Velvety lawns, summerhouses, gleaming cars parked on

THE GOLDEN CAGE

the driveway ... Hobart's summer residence was just like something out of a movie.

Although it was not yet dawn, a light burned in a first-floor window and she could make out the silhouette of a watching figure, silent and still. Was it Hobart? How long had he been standing there, watching, waiting for her?

'If you'd like to come this way.' Lars indicated to her to lead the way up the front steps and for one mad second she felt like turning tail and running away.

Hesitantly, she climbed the steps, her high heels deafening as they struck the wooden treads. The only other sounds were her own breathing, the distant crash and hiss of the surf and the click, click, whirr of insects in the undergrowth.

The door swung open even before she had reached the top of the steps. A crack of pallid orange grew to a great flood of light and Mila blinked, suddenly exhausted, as she was ushered inside.

The woman was perhaps forty years old, no older, her attractiveness mature yet flawless. Violet eyes shone in an unlined face, framed by bleached hair cut into a short, severe style. She extended a hand and Mila felt the tremendous strength in her clasp.

'I am Cora, Mr Hobart's housekeeper,' she announced, her smile friendly but her eyes peculiarly expressionless. 'I will show you to your room. You must be tired after your long journey.'

Mila nodded, hardly able to speak or move now that the jet-lag had taken hold of her. She scarcely noticed the sumptuous furnishings in the hallway, or the deep, soft carpet on the landing at the top of the stairs.

'This is your room. Everything has been made ready for

you.' Reaching behind the door, Cora clicked on a switch, flooding the room with light. 'Please – make yourself comfortable.'

'Thank you.' Mila stepped inside. It was tastefully and expensively decorated, yet homely. An exquisite antique patchwork quilt was draped over the back of a comfortable sofa, whilst the window was framed by two high-backed Shaker chairs. The bed was a huge brass affair, old-fashioned with a thick, high mattress and a wonderful crimson velvet bedspread.

'I shall leave you now so that you can get some sleep.' Cora patted Mila's hand. 'Mr Hobart will see you later in the morning.' She indicated a tray of sandwiches and a glass beside the bed. 'Do try to eat or drink something before you retire – it will help you to sleep.'

The housekeeper left the room, and the door clicked shut behind her, leaving Mila alone. She scarcely thought she would need any help to get to sleep, but she was thirsty and drank half of the milk before realising that she could hardly keep her eyes open. She was so exhausted that she hardly had the energy to get undressed and slide between the crisp white sheets.

The last things she remembered, as she drifted off into dreams, was the light of dawn, glimmering through the thin curtains, and a cool hand, stroking her brow. Was she imagining it, or did she really feel those cool, gentle fingers sliding under the sheet and caressing her naked breasts? Did she really feel something closing about her wrists and ankles, holding her fast?

Foolish girl, of course she was imagining it. What could it possibly be but a dream? A mad, erotic dream.

'She is waking.'

THE GOLDEN CAGE

'Good. Excellent.'

Somewhere in the haze of her dream, Mila recognised those voices. One was a woman's, the other .. the other, the voice of Orin Hobart. She had been dreaming about him, her body luxuriating in a warm, sweet lake of fantasy, and for a few moments she thought that this was just another stage in that selfsame dream.

But something was touching her, summoning her irresistibly towards wakefulness. She couldn't resist it, though she tried. Somehow she didn't want to wake up.

Her eyes struggled to open, blinking and fluttering in a light which was too intense, too brutal.

There were two shadowy figures beside the bed She couldn't make out their faces yet, because everything was so bright; but she heard their voices and knew that Hobart and his housekeeper must be in the bedroom with her.

Cold ... she felt cold. What had happened to the sheets ... the bedspread? Had she kicked them off in her sleep? She jolted into wakefulness with the sudden realisation that she was naked, her body utterly and completely bare on the bed. She tried to roll sideways, cover her embarrassment, but something stopped her. Something which restrained her wrists and ankles, not so tightly that they caused real discomfort, but with sufficient firmness to prevent her doing anything but sprawl on her back, her arms and legs spread wide like some shameless starfish.

Orin Hobart looked down at his guest with a huge surge of lustful elation. She was everything he had hoped – and might yet prove to be still more.

'Welcome,' he said, his voice quiet and somehow chilling.

'I ... what's happening to me? Why can't I move?' Panic was rising up inside Mila like a cold, black tide.

Strong hands held and caressed her, holding her down, forbidding her struggles.

'Because I don't want you to move, my sweet Mila,' smiled Orin Hobart. 'I want time to ... admire you.'

He bent over Mila and stroked his fingertip down her bare flank. She shuddered and squirmed, but how could she evade his ruthless, relentless exploration of her nakedness?

'No!' she gasped. But she felt Cora's hand on her arm.

'Be silent.' The words were matter-of-fact, almost toneless, but they demanded attention and obedience.

'Please,' she whimpered, afraid and yet aroused by Hobart's touch. 'Why ... ? Please, tell me why you're doing this to me.'

Hobart chuckled as he wound his finger in a narrowing spiral about the pink crest of her nipple.

'It has all been so easy, little one,' he sighed with satisfaction. 'Almost too easy. I chose you, I bought you and you came to me of your own accord.'

'Bought me!' Mila's voice mingled rage and alarm.

'Yes, little one, *bought you*. Or isn't that the way you see it? No, of course not. You wanted some great romance – something out of a fairy tale. You would come to work for me and I would fall hopelessly in love with you ... is that it?

'Well, let me tell you, little one, fairy tales aren't just about sweetness and light. There is darkness in there, too. And darkness can be so bittersweet. I'm going to show you how bittersweet pleasure can be, little one ... '

'Don't touch me!' Mila's voice rose to a screech of anger and she tried to break free of the silken cords which held

THE GOLDEN CAGE

her wrists fast to the bedposts. Cora placed her hand over Mila's mouth but Mila bit savagely into the flesh and she withdrew with a curse. Mila's eyes flashed fire. 'Let me go. Untie me, and let me go. Now!'

'You want to leave me already, Mila? But we have hardly gotten to know one another yet.' Hobart sat down on the edge of the bed and began stroking Mila's bare thighs. 'Now, tell me you don't want me to do this to you.'

Mila was close to tears of anger and frustration – as much directed against herself as against the ridiculous, scary situation she had got herself into.

'I. Don't ... Don't do that.' Nothing more came, her words ending in an agonised gasp as Hobart slipped his hand between her legs and began moving it slowly up her inner thigh towards the fringed pleasure-garden of her naked sex.

'Nothing more to say to me, little one?'

She turned her head to look right into Hobart's eyes and spat at him.

'Bastard,' she hissed.

The white, frothy blob of spittle hit him on the cheek, but Hobart seemed imperturbed. He simply wiped the back of his hand across his face.

'What a little vixen you are,' he commented. 'I can see that I shall have to ask Cora to teach you better manners.'

His hand slipped higher and Mila screwed her eyes shut with shame and guilty pleasure as the side of his palm pressed hard into her groin, parting the fleshy lips of her womanhood. Sweet, spicy fragrance wafted from her open sex, and her juices began to flow as Hobart's hand sawed back and forth between her pussy lips.

'No, no, no,' she moaned again and again, as though the mantra would disengage her from this sweet and subtle torment and transport her far, far away from the humiliating, terrifying reality of this room, this bed, this sensual captivity.

'Yes, yes, yes,' breathed Hobart, silky-smooth satisfaction filling his voice. His eyes gleamed with pleasure at Mila's discomfort. Experienced though he was, even he had not gauged that his latest toy would be quite so responsive. 'Yes, Mila. Don't play games with me. Don't pretend you don't like it, because I know you do. You stink of sex, do you know that? You're a young woman with deep, insatiable desires. That's why I chose you, don't you see?' He chuckled. 'I bet you bring yourself off three or four times a day if there's no man to do it for you. I'm right, aren't I?'

She didn't reply, but her body was already responding for her, her hips slowly bucking against Hobart's hand and her juices trickling out of her on to the plain white sheet beneath.

Hobart smiled and looked across at Cora.

'You may leave us now.'

'Sir?'

'Wait for me downstairs in the training room. I shall have need of your special skills later on. But first, I intend to enjoy my new purchase.'

Purchase! Even through the red mist of her desperate, guilt-ridden desire, that word penetrated Mila's soul. Was that how he saw her – as a toy he had bought for his own pleasure? That much was obvious to her now. She remembered Alexander's words: 'Don't go, Mila. You're not a plaything to be bought and sold...'

Only she was, wasn't she?

She heard the door close as Cora left the room. Now she was alone with her fear, with the man whose hoarse, halting

THE GOLDEN CAGE

breathing seemed to fill her soul as the wall-clock ticked away the seconds to her fate.

'Just you and me, Mila.'

Sounds of breathing; quickening, shuddering, grating. She could hear his arousal in every indrawn breath; knew that inside those sleek designer pants his cock was throbbing and burning for her. The icy waters of terror mingled with the burning tide of arousal within her, too, forcing her to enjoy the sensation of his hand, rhythmically titillating her as though they were both part of some great sexual machine.

'I wanted you as soon as I saw your picture, Mila, did you know that? I knew you were the one. You were so fragile and yet I could see you had spirit. I could see that you would fight me like a wolverine, and it excited me to think of you clawing and spitting and scratching while I pushed my fat dick between your pussy lips.

'It excites you too, doesn't it?'

Mila let out a sobbing moan of distress. She could feel her clitoris distending, hardening, pushing its way out from the pink fleshy hood which had so modestly concealed its arousal. There could be no hiding her pleasure and yet how could she feel pleasure at all? Here she was, at the mercy of some cold-blooded psychopath who probably intended to kill her once he tired of her.

Suddenly she felt pain like she had never experienced before – a sharp, dagger-like stab of pain that began between her thighs but seemed to knife its way through her very soul.

'Stop! Please, no, NO!'

Hobart was pinching her clitoris between his finger and thumb, hard and steadily, not letting up for an instant.

'Feel the pain, Mila. Savour it.'

Sweat was trickling down between her breasts, sprinkling her skin like raindrops, matting her dark hair to her scalp. Her teeth were clenched and her breath could escape only as a low hiss of rage and distress.

'Good, isn't it, little one? So good to feel pain. It makes us feel ... alive. And how much better it feels when we learn how to transform that pain into pleasure. You have to understand, Mila, there is no pleasure in the world half so exquisite as pleasure derived from pain.'

'Please. Please don't.'

'Hush.' Orin kissed his index finger and placed it on Mila's lips. 'Hush, my little one. Be silent in your pleasure.'

Mila's whole body trembled with the effort of not crying out, of withstanding the urge to scream and cry and howl against the ruthless sensations which ought to be repellent to her, but which were slowly, insidiously, whispering to her body of a greater, more exquisite pleasure yet to come.

Slowly, almost imperceptibly, Hobart began to release the pressure on Mila's swollen clitoris. She let out an involuntary shudder of relief as the savage heat of the pain began to subside, ebbing away until it was replaced by the gentler throb of a passion yet unsatisfied. Her muscles began to relax and she lay exhausted on the bed, her eyes wide and watchful.

Hobart surveyed his prize with a proprietorial satisfaction. She really was exceptionally lovely. Not beautiful exactly, or at least not in the classical sense, but striking and distinctive in a way which placed her beauty beyond price. Mila Kirovska was uniquely desirable, uniquely responsive and sensual; and, like any aesthete, Orin Hobart prided himself on his taste for the unique in all things. Especially his sexual playthings.

'Did you enjoy that, Mila?' He looked down into those

THE GOLDEN CAGE

wide, dark eyes and thought of some wild forest creature, fearful and untamed, perhaps even dangerous if pushed too far. He wondered just how far he could push her before she broke like porcelain in his hands. He did not wait for her to answer. 'Of course you did, Mila, you are a sensual woman – untutored, it is true, but with such potential. You will give me a great deal of pleasure.'

His fingers strayed back to Mila's outspread thighs, the flesh just below the dark-fringed sex-lips moist with the sweet juices of her need Hobart let his fingertip stray a little further, toying with Mila's dark pubic curls, glossy with juice and wiry as little black serpents, winding around his finger.

He laughed and his laughter chilled Mila's soul. 'You are a headstrong young woman, Mila, and I shall take great pleasure in taming you.'

'You will never do that,' spat Mila, wriggling furiously to evade Hobart's unforgiving caresses. 'Never!'

'Really?' Hobart regarded her with a mixture of amusement and lust. Her defiance excited him beyond measure. 'I do so love a challenge – especially when my opponent is as beautiful as you.'

'You cannot keep me here.' Mila's words did not even convince herself, but she had to say something, do something to prove to herself that she was not the fool she knew she was.

'Darling fool, I can do absolutely anything I like with you. Anything. Don't you understand? Obviously I shall have to make you understand.'

Mila moaned softly as Hobart bent over her and began licking the inner surface of her thighs. How could he do this to her – one moment cause her agony, the next torment her with pleasure she had not the strength to resist?

His tongue lapped closer and closer to Mila's sex, licking up the sweet, sticky droplets which were welling up out of the heart of her desire. She tensed, afraid of the excitement she was feeling, terrified that Hobart was right and that, no matter how extreme the things he forced upon her, she would find pleasure in them.

Pushing his fingers between the outer lobes of Mila's womanhood, Hobart possessed her with a sudden thrust. One, two, three fingers jabbed into the soft, wet heart, stretching the elastic walls, sending thrills of excitement running all over her body.

'Ah, aaah!' She could no longer keep silent now, Hobart's tortures were too exquisite and too unrelenting. Besides, her whole body felt unbelievably sensitive and aroused, and she was beginning to suspect that the milk she had drunk before going to sleep had contained not only some kind of sleeping draught, but also some subtle aphrodisiac, designed to lower her resistance.

'You are beautifully wet,' observed Hobart in a husky whisper, going down on her with tongue and teeth and lips while he masturbated her, his fingers curled so that the knuckles pushed and twisted against the elastic walls of her vagina. 'Slick and wet and juicy, all for me. I knew you were the one, Mila. I knew that destiny meant you to be mine.'

She wept slow, slow tears as she felt the pleasure growing, expanding, sweeping down on her like a great white-capped ocean breaker, taking over her whole existence. There could be no resistance now, only total surrender. And, as the glittering apex of her pleasure crashed down upon her and she felt Hobart's teeth bite savagely on the hardened stalk of her clitoris, she knew there could be no going back.

THE GOLDEN CAGE

* * *

In a side street in Boston's Combat Zone, Greg Delaney sat alone in the borrowed yellow Chevrolet. It was a hot night, sticky, sultry, suffocating. He loosened the button on his shirt collar but he still felt as if even the air he breathed was trying to throttle the life out of him.

He glanced around him, uneasy and filled with a sort of horrified fascination. This was a side of Boston he hadn't seen before. The Combat Zone lay between the theatre district and Chinatown, but there was nothing artistic about the peep shows and strip joints strung out along Washington Street. On the corner opposite a hooker in a fringed leather miniskirt and hold-up stockings was leaning through the window of a car, her plump arse poking up in the air and the fringes jiggling as she swayed her hips from side to side.

Greg wound up the window. He knew it wasn't safe in this part of the city and he wasn't entirely sure why he had come here, unless it was because they wouldn't think of looking for him here. That, and because he needed time to think about what to do next.

The sound of knocking on the side window made him turn his head. The hooker had walked across from the other side of the street and he could see right down the front of her red PVC top. It was at least two sizes too small and the laces bulged open as they strained to cover her enormous breasts. She wasn't even remotely his cup of tea, but it was hard for any red-blooded male to ignore a figure like that.

She could have been thirty or twenty or a whole lot younger. It was difficult to tell – all hookers tended to have that selfsame expression of world-weary cynicism as they forced their mouths into a smile and set out their wares.

'Lookin' for company, hon?' The alarmingly red lips leered at him, revealing a pink ball of gum between her teeth.

He shook his head and waved her away.

'Come on, big boy, don't be shy.'

He sighed and mouthed 'Not interested' at her through the window. Sticking up her middle finger to let him know exactly what she thought, the hooker stuck her half-chewed gum in the middle of his wing mirror and stalked off across the road. This is no place for a guy like me, thought Greg to himself. But then again, he was rapidly running out of places to be.

He could hardly believe how rapidly things had gone down the toilet since he'd arrived in Boston, just days before. Talk about walking straight into the lions' den. It was all like some horrendous nightmare, only you had to live it to know that it was bloody well real and wasn't going to go away.

What was a mild-mannered English guy doing in downtown Boston with a clapped-out Chevy and two days' growth of beard?

Running away, that's what, thought Greg as he saw the guy across the way slipping the knife out of his pocket. Turning the key in the ignition, he stamped down on the accelerator and wondered where he would end up next.

Chapter 5

'What do you know about me, Mila Kirovska?'

Orin Hobart was standing in the conservatory, gazing out at the ocean. Mila stood, still and silent, before him. In the last few days she had learned not to underestimate Hobart's taste for domination. Hobart did not turn to look at her, but added after a pause:

'You may answer.'

'Nothing. Almost nothing.'

This time he did turn to look at her and she just caught the fleeting shadow of a sardonic smile. It had vanished before his cold grey eyes bored into hers.

'You will call me "Master" at all times. Have I not made myself perfectly clear?'

Mila wanted to spit her anger and her defiance, but her hands were shackled behind her back and Hobart's 'housekeeper' Cora held the end of a leash which led to a heavy silver choke-chain about her neck. If she failed to do as she was bidden, or was too slow in her responses, Cora jerked on the chain, half-strangling Mila.

'I am sorry, *Master*.' It was hard to keep the hatred out of her voice.

Hobart was holding one of his favourite toys, a silver-handled riding-crop which caught the July sunlight and the paler, flickering light reflected off the sea. He extended it and ran the soft leather tip down the side of Mila's face, slowly and tantalisingly, ending eventually at her lips.

'Kiss your mistress, Mila.'

Mila hesitated for just one second and Cora jerked hard on the chain. It was almost as though she was waiting for the slightest transgression which would give her an opportunity to punish the errant Russian girl.

Gasping and coughing, Mila stumbled but Hobart caught her. She was surprised and alarmed by the physical strength she could feel within him. With the greatest ease imaginable, he pushed her to her knees on the marble tiled floor.

Again he put the riding-crop to her lips.

'I gave you a command, Mila. Do you dare disobey me?'

This time Mila obeyed, kissing the tip of the riding-crop with unwilling lips. The leather smelt of sweat and blood and other scents, more subtle and shameful. The scents of sex. How many other young women had submitted to this cruel and knowing mistress?

Mila's body and brain ached with the transformation that had come over her since her arrival in America. How cruelly the dream had turned to dust, how suddenly she had been forced to realise that she had been a little fool.

Catching sight of her reflection in the huge windows of the conservatory, Mila hardly recognised the creature she had become. Painted lips, a black rubber sheath-dress and scarlet shoes with four-inch stiletto heels had transformed her into the very image of a cheap slut.

Hobart caught her looking at her reflection and gave her a sharp flick of the riding-crop across her bare shoulders. She winced, but did not cry out. By now, she knew better than to make a stupid mistake like that.

'Do you like the new you, Mila?' demanded Hobart tauntingly. 'Do you recognise the slut you have always

THE GOLDEN CAGE

been?' She opened her mouth to reply, but Hobart silenced her with a flash of his grey eyes. 'Yes, Mila, this is the true you – not the demure Russian girl with her smart suit and her brushed hair. Your body is made for sex and I intend to show you how to use it to pleasure me.'

He slid the riding-crop down over Mila's bare shoulders, then over the firm mounds of her breasts. She was profoundly ashamed of her hard, erect nipples, pushing so shamelessly against the inner surface of the skin-tight rubber. Perhaps Hobart was right after all. Alone here, his prisoner and his plaything, she was fast losing touch with reality.

'So, you know nothing about me.' Hobart stroked the fragile white petals of one of his prized orchids. 'And still you came to me, my little one. Such innocence and such blind faith.

'These orchids – they are beautiful, are they not? Ah, but not as beautiful as you, Mila. They are my creation, my treasure; and you shall be my creation too. I have the power to turn you into anything I want you to be, and you are going to learn to be whatever I want of you. Today, Mila, I wish you to be the perfect slut.'

He met her angry, fearful gaze and smiled.

'You may hate me now but it will not always be so. You will learn to love everything I do to you, the pleasure *and* the pain.'

'Never,' whispered Mila and instantly she felt the chain jerk and tighten about her throat.

'Already you have begun to love me.' Hobart's voice was a quietly menacing whisper.

He brought the riding-crop down on her skin with ferocious skill, the whiplash tip making a sharp cracking sound as it bit into the flesh of shoulders and bosom. Mila let out an involuntary gasp, half discomfort, half exhilaration, for the pain was not so severe that it obliterated the warm, sensual glow of excitement.

The blows rained down on her with a sort of manic precision; their rhythm apparently random, yet their aim so exact that each new blow made her shiver with an unexpected frisson. The blows were precise but light, reddening the skin without breaking it. She swayed under the sensual assault and would have fallen, but Cora was behind her, gripping her shoulders, her painted nails digging into the bare flesh.

Hobart paused, his breath hoarse and shallow. Mila's skin glowed as though there were a dull red fire just below it, the coals smouldering with a passionate intensity.

'Strip her.'

'Certainly, sir.' Cora's voice was filled with a dark and sultry pleasure and Mila realised, not for the first time, that Cora was not simply an obedient servant – she was Hobart's willing accomplice. Mila could smell the heat of her body and she knew that Cora was as sexually aroused as her master.

Cora's sharp fingernails dug into the clinging black rubber of Mila's dress and tore it away in great shreds, leaving it hanging in tatters from her bare breasts.

Hobart admired Cora's handiwork with a connoisseur's eye.

'Such a pretty canvas you have given me to work with.'

'Thank you, sir.'

The tiny black tattooed letter H stood out against the snowy white of Mila's left breast. She tried not to look down at it, but even with her eyes closed she saw it with horrible clarity – the symbol of her degradation.

'Free her wrists.'

THE GOLDEN CAGE

'Yes, sir.'

While Cora was unlocking the manacles, Hobart carried on talking in a soft, even voice loaded with eroticism.

'You make me hard, Mila, do you know that?' He ran his finger down over the bulging crotch of his pants. 'I want you to feel how hard.'

Mila's hand trembled as he took it and guided it to the front of his trousers, to the obscene bulge beneath the smooth grey worsted flannel. Such delicious, seductive obscenity was concealed beneath the respectable exterior. As Mila touched him through the fabric she thought how that was a metaphor for Orin Hobart's whole life. A perverse, unforgiving hunger behind the flawless façade of ultra-respectable New England society. A society which fawned at the heels of its favourite billionaire Republican.

Orin Hobart hadn't just duped Mila Kirovska. He'd taken in the whole damn world.

'Do you want to touch it? Do you want it in your hand?'

She did not answer immediately, her heart thump-thumping in her chest and her brain sick with dizziness. A red mist swam in front of her eyes, a mist of guilty, impure desire. She shook her head mechanically but it would not go away. It was taking her over, making her do things she didn't even want to think about doing.

'Answer!' Mila felt the slap of Cora's ringed hand across her cheek. It stung, bringing a film of tears to her dark eyes. Refusing to abandon this last bastion of defiance, she blinked them away. She would not weep, not for Orin Hobart. She heard Cora hiss: 'Insolent child. Leave her to me, sir, I will soon tame her. As I tamed the others.'

Cora's words chilled Mila's blood. The others – what others? How many had there been? And what had happened to them? Had Hobart let them go when he had tired of them? Not even Mila was naïve enough to believe that.

'I do not doubt it.' Hobart's voice was creamy-smooth, velvety and soft. 'You are a good and loyal servant, Cora.'

'Thank you, sir.'

'Perhaps later on I shall let you have the girl to play with. But for now...' His words tailed off into a husky sigh of satisfaction that was at once soft and menacing. 'For now, I shall take personal direction of her sensual education.'

Taking hold of Mila's hand, he tightened his grip on it, so suddenly and so devastatingly that he almost crushed her fingers in his, and she let out a tiny gasp of pain.

'I asked you a question, Mila. Do you want to touch my penis?'

Mila's tear-misted eyes moved slowly upwards, her eyelids flicking up until she was looking into her master's eyes, her hatred and her fear not masking the lust she felt, in spite of everything that had happened to her at the hands of her captor.

'Yes.' She paused for a fleeting instant, instinctively weighing her defiance against her fear, her knowledge, her lust. 'Yes, Master,' she corrected herself, catching sight of Cora's hand, lifted to strike her once again.

'You may take it out and touch it.'

For some reason, Hobart's words filled Mila with a great wave of excitement. Rationally, she knew that this was crazy: why should she be grateful to this arrogant, perverted bastard for letting her do the very thing he most wanted her to do? It made no sense at all, not one iota. But to her body, her poor, overheated, frustrated body, it made all the sense in the world.

Every nerve-ending in her back and breasts tingled from the strokes he had given her with the riding-crop, and a

THE GOLDEN CAGE

deep, fiery warmth that began in her belly was spreading out to thighs and breasts and anus and sex, pinking and plumping her pussy lips, making her womanhood trickle with the sweet stickiness of desire.

Her fingers shook slightly as she fumbled with the ivory buttons on Hobart's fly. Her wrists still ached from the handcuffs, two red burn-marks on the white flesh from the ropes which had secured her wrists to an iron ring in Hobart's bedroom wall during that last, long night. Slowly, clumsy in her hunger, she succeeded in unbuttoning Hobart's cock from its prison.

His cock-scent reached her even before her fingers made contact with the rose-pink flesh of his manhood. Tangy and strong, the aroma of his aroused penis made her clitoris throb with unsatisfied hunger. She knew he had kept the scent of fucking on his dick deliberately, to drive her crazy. Hobart was an expert in the arts and sciences of sex. He had forced Mila to watch him screwing Cora on the huge waterbed in his room, knowing instinctively how it would make her squirm with need, watching his dick pumping in, out, in, out, and Cora's white thighs wrapped tight about his waist...

The scent of Hobart's dick brought back that last night's torment. She had hung there all night, the ropes biting into her wrists as she was suspended by her arms from the iron ring. She had wanted to turn away, to stop looking, but somehow she hadn't been able to, her eyes locked on the sight before her as though by some horrible fascination. The sight of Hobart's white sperm, silently spurting from his cock-tip on to Cora's ecstatic, upturned face; the agony of watching as she took him once again between her thighs, her breasts, her lips...

The warmth of Hobart's cock flooded into her fingertips

and she drew in breath, her entire soul captivated once again by the scent of him. The scent of naked, rutting lust.

'Take it between your fingers. Feels good, huh? Feels *big*.'

Hobart's penis was not abnormally large, but it was beautifully hard and thick, its purplish-pink head ripe and juicy as a plum, glistening with its own juice.

'Masturbate me.' Hobart began to move his hips, slowly at first, pushing his shaft back and forth between Mila's fingers so that the lubricating juice trickled over her fingertips. 'Do it, Mila. Do it to me.' His teeth were clenched now, his face fixed in an expression of strange intensity, as though one moment's abstraction would cost him the unique power of his pleasure.

As the juices dripped down her fingers, so very close to her face, Mila felt a desperate need to taste them, to lick them off and savour their sensual potency. Unbidden, she parted her lips and put out her tongue, its pointed tip stretching out towards the mingled scents of Hobart's ejaculate and Cora's honeydew. So close, so very close. Just one taste, just one . . .

'No!'

The choke-chain tightened with devastating suddenness about Mila's throat and suddenly she was clawing at it, fighting for breath, her world turned to a spinning mist of broken images.

'Insolent bitch!'

As suddenly as she had begun, Cora let the chain slacken, and Mila slumped to her hands and knees on the floor, the chill sweat of terror trickling down her bare back to the base of her spine.

'Well, well.' Hobart's creamy-smooth voice was filled with a deeper satisfaction now – the satisfaction which

THE GOLDEN CAGE

comes from the contemplation of another's suffering. 'You have disobeyed me, Mila. And you know I will not tolerate disobedience from anyone – least of all you. Now I shall have to punish you. Have you any idea how much that *saddens* me, Mila?'

She dared to look up at him and his eyes were as cold and glittery as shards of glass. He glanced towards Cora.

'Bind her.'

Cora's thin lips split into a smile of pleasure.

'Sir.'

She tightened the choke-chain and, forcing Mila to her feet, led her towards one of the ornate ironwork pillars which supported the glass roof of the conservatory. Mila closed her eyes, but the pictures would not go away. She knew what would happen next, it had happened before. She would be chained to the pillars by her wrists and ankles and subjected to whatever punishments Hobart deemed necessary for her 'correction'. How could she have been so stupid as to disobey him?

And yet ... And yet the prospect of his punishment stiffened her nipples, made her sex ooze anew with honeysweet juice.

The leather thongs were pulled tight about wrists and ankles, and she half stood, half hung between the pillars, completely at the mercy of her master; almost naked and entirely helpless in her scarlet boots and the tatters of her black rubber dress.

She waited for the chastisement to begin, her eyes straying involuntarily to Hobart's smooth, hard cock, still thrusting out of his pants. If anything it seemed even harder and more menacing in its hunger.

Hobart turned back to Cora.

'Unlock the cupboard and bring the box to me.'

Cora walked across the conservatory to a small cabinet of inlaid walnut and maple, unlocking the door with a tiny golden key. Inside lay a black lacquer box.

Hobart's cruel mouth curved into a contemptuous yet lustful smile.

'You know nothing about me, Mila Kirovska.' He laughed, and his laughter seemed to come straight from Hell, shaking the iron pillars and making the windowpanes sing with tension. 'Which is as it should be, for you are nothing.' He took the box from Cora and opened it. Inside lay two passports. His eyes did not leave Mila's face as he took them out. 'Nothing'

Panic rose inside Mila. She had almost forgotten about the two passports – the real and the false; the two identities. Instinctively afraid, she began to struggle in her bonds, but Cora seized her by the hair.

'Be still, bitch.'

'Please – you're hurting me . . .'

Cora's left hand ran over Mila's right breast and her scarlet talons gave the nipple a swift and savage tweak.

'I said, be still.'

Mila slumped between the pillars, temporarily defeated by the hopelessness of her situation.

'Those are mine,' she said flatly.

'Indeed?' Hobart contemplated the two passports with a sort of humorous detachment. 'But, my dear girl, how can they be? You are nothing. Nobody.'

Hobart snapped his fingers and Cora stepped forward again, this time with a silver dish. Reaching into his pocket, Hobart took out a gold-plated cigarette lighter.

Mila realised what he was about to do.

'No, please, you mustn't!'

Hobart did not even bother to reply, merely arching an

THE GOLDEN CAGE

eyebrow at Mila's defiance as he flicked on the lighter and a two-inch orange flame licked at the edge of the first passport.

This time, Mila could not suppress her tears. They were tears not of defeat or pain or surrender, but of anger. An anger that would never, ever be stilled until it had been avenged.

She watched in bitter silence as Hobart dropped the burning passports into the silver dish; watched as they shrivelled and charred, turning within moments into unrecognisable greyish-black flakes of burnt paper.

'You see, child? Gone. Gone forever.' Wiping his hands on his handkerchief, he stroked her tear-stained cheek and – despite her anger and her bitterness – she felt a shiver of desire rippling through her body. 'Nothing, that's what you are. You belong to me now and that is the only identity you will ever need.'

'No! No, no, no!' Mila's rage exploded from her in great choking screams, her stiff-nippled breasts quivering as she strained to free herself from the bonds which held her fast. 'I am not nothing. I am Mila Kirovska. Mila Kirovska!'

Hobart laughed as he kissed her, pushing himself hard against her resisting body.

'Nothing,' he whispered. 'Nothing but my possession. Mine for ever.'

'No...' Her whisper was almost inaudible.

'But you gave yourself to me. You came to me... you are mine now, mine to do with as I wish.'

She felt Hobart's hands on her thighs but all her strength seemed to have drained away, and the only force left within her was the treacherous force of her sexual desire, welcoming his cock as it forced its way between her legs and into the haven of her secret pleasure.

With a single hard thrust of his pelvis he entered her, his cock possessing her as completely as the leather thongs about her wrists and ankles, as unforgivingly as the black rubber caressing her hips and thighs. She arched her back, letting out a shuddering cry of anguish as his thick manhood stretched her soft vaginal walls, awakening a dark and secret pleasure.

'Mine.'

He took her with a rhythmic brutality, paying no heed to her desires yet knowing that with each thrust he was transporting her, body and soul, to a world of sensual bondage; a golden cage of pleasure from which she would never escape.

'Mila. I am Mila Kirovska...'

He laughed at her whispered sigh of defiance.

'Not any more,' he told her, biting the soft flesh of her neck as he possessed her. 'Now you have a new name.

'And that name is Slave.'

Chapter 6

Had it been two weeks, or three? In the haze of her captivity, Mila had lost all track of time. Days melted into nights; ice-cold, fire-hot nights where pain might suddenly blossom into pleasure, or pleasure end in a cry of anguish...

The training room had been converted from the extensive cellars running under the length of Orin Hobart's summer retreat. It was reached through a perfectly respectable-looking wine-cellar and no one would ever have suspected what lay behind that innocuous, cobwebby door.

The door was in fact made from four-inch-thick steel plate; just one of the many sophistications Hobart had had built into his pleasure-ground to ensure that no one and nothing should risk disturbing his sexual recreation.

Mila had come to know the training room very well over the last couple of weeks. It was a place of demons, icy-cold and damp even at the heat of noon; a place where a slave might quickly learn the value of silence. For, no matter how loudly you might scream, the sound was instantly absorbed by the thick stone walls, lost in the blanketing silence.

Sometimes, in the half-light of the smoking candles and guttering oil-lamps, Mila thought she made out leering faces in the gloom, eyes watching her from the rough-hewn walls. And she saw their mouths opening and closing, telling silent stories of other girls, other slaves who had known the pleasure and pain of this room.

The ceiling was quite low, a barrel-shaped vault hung with oil lamps. On either side rough stone walls stretched into the tunnel-like darkness and there were no windows to let in any natural light. Grotesque shadows danced in the smoky lamp-light, hobgoblins formed from Mila's own fear.

At one side a wrought-iron spiral staircase led up to the steel door – seemingly the only way in and out of the training room. Dotted around were the instruments of sensual torture: a metal discipline frame, made from two thick lengths of steel piping, welded together to form a wide X; a punishment table, covered with a sheet of black rubber and with leather cuffs for neck, wrists and ankles; a saw-horse; and a vast array of whips, masks and set toys.

Mila shivered as Cora unlocked her manacles and pushed her forward into the light. Hobart stood half in shadow, half in light, his features almost satanic in the gothic chiaroscuro. He was clad all in black leather: a tight-fitting suit criss-crossed with studded straps and buckles, and heavy boots such as a motorcyclist might wear.

The soft, supple leather gleamed like wet oil against his well-muscled skin. A zipper ran between his legs, the metal teeth bulging over the generous swell of his manhood. His testes seemed huge and heavy beneath the tight-stretched leather, his semi-erect cock pointing upwards across his lower belly in a fat diagonal swelling.

Heavy black leather gauntlets covered his hands, shiny metal studs on each knuckle. As Mila watched, he rubbed his hand over his crotch, smoothing his fingers over the swollen beauty of his manhood, making it grow longer, harder, fatter...

THE GOLDEN CAGE

His eyes roamed all over Mila's nakedness, drinking in the fullness of breast and hip, the tautness of belly and waist, the sleek smoothness of calf and thigh. She was a real beauty, this Russian girl. A fine slave, curiously sensual beneath that apparently virginal exterior.

'Hair,' snapped Hobart, his eyes never leaving Mila as he continued to rub his cock through the leather trousers.

'At once, sir.'

Cora took the pins from Mila's hair and it came tumbling down over her shoulders in wild, glossy waves. Tendrils crept down over her right breast, coyly caressing the plump white flesh like timorous fingers. The nipple, already stone-hard, peeped through the dark veil like the point of a lewd pink tongue.

'Good. I much prefer you like that, slave. Reduced to the primitive creature you truly are.' He leered and Mila could not take her eyes from the swelling hardness of her captor's manhood, so clearly delineated beneath the black leather. 'A creature of pure sex, made for sex and for nothing else.' He caressed Mila's long, dark hair with his gauntleted hand. 'That *is* what you are, isn't it, slave?'

She defied him with the lightning flash of her eyes, but punishment was swift in following. Hobart twisted a long tendril of hair about his fingers, twisted, twisted, so very tight...

Mila tried to put up her hand to stop him, but he simply twisted it harder, until her face was contorted into an agonised grimace and she was moaning in anguish.

'Isn't it, slave?'

'Yes,' whispered Mila.

'Yes, what?' He gave another twist, harder this time.

'Yes. Master.'

Releasing her hair, he let her go, and she stood gasping

and resentful before him, wanting to scratch and spit and weep and run away, all at once.

And fuck...

'Your tits please me, slave.'

Mila knew the script by heart.

'Thank you, Master.'

'They are nicely formed. Heavy but firm. I like my slaves to have good bodies. The very best.'

Hobart turned, picked up a small glass bottle from the table and threw it to her, the cobalt-blue glass sparkling in the candlelight as it flew through the air. Luckily she caught it, her fingers closing over it just in time. To have dropped it would have been unthinkable. Her brain whirled, her body strangely exhilarated by this small success though her entire soul rebelled against Hobart and his despicable taste for domination.

'Pour the oil over your breasts and massage them.'

She did not defy him. To do so would only have meant some worse punishment, some more dreadful humiliation. Out of the corner of her eye she saw Cora watching. The older woman was wearing a white shift dress and no bra, and her dark-brown nipples showed clearly through the thin, silky fabric. Were they hard because of the cold, or because it turned her on to watch this helpless Russian girl caressing her own naked body for their Master's pleasure?

Taking the top off the bottle, Mila breathed in the heavy, almost sickly smell of the oil. It was obviously a blend of herb and flower scents, mixed with something musky, intensely erotic. The smell alone was potent enough to fill Mila with the dull ache of need.

Tipping the bottle, she poured a few drops into the palm of her hand. Her skin tingled as the oil met her skin.

'All of it, slave.'

THE GOLDEN CAGE

'Master?'

'The whole bottle.'

Hobart was thoroughly enjoying himself. No other slave had excited him as profoundly as Mila Kirovska. Even in the most abject depths of humiliation, there was a flash of danger in those dark eyes, a spark of Slavonic defiance, wild and unpredictable. This girl was a true primitive, naïve and vulnerable yet with a store of instinctive cunning which made her entertaining and arousing prey.

The oil was slightly warm and flowed freely as Mila tipped up the little blue bottle, the liquid flooding her palm and trickling between her fingers.

'You must not spill it, slave, or I shall be very angry with you. *Very* angry.' Hobart's fingers were lightly stroking the front of his pants. 'So angry that I may not let you have my dick in your mouth.'

Mila dared not look him in the face, afraid that her hunger would betray itself in her eyes. She hated this man; loathed and despised him to the point of obsession. Yet she also desired what he was offering her, felt the guilty excitement of the lust deep within her, and because of that she hated herself even more.

'Rub the oil all over your tits.'

She obeyed him, lifting her dripping hands to her breasts and cupping them, so that the warm liquid dripped and smoothed over her firm white globes.

The sensations produced by the oil were unexpectedly strong. She let out a gasp as it began to soak into the skin. First a dull, distant warmth, and then other sensations, magnified tenfold as she started to massage her breasts. A tingling, amplified gradually to a low, insistent burning, spread right through her, centring on her nipples but throbbing and searing through her whole body. As the burning subsided to a hot glow, Mila began to realise that her skin had become much more sensitive to stimuli. She could scarcely bear to touch her nipples, the slightest contact sending electric shocks of sensation through her body.

Was this pleasure – or pain? Mila was beginning to understand what Hobart had said about the interchangeability of the two worlds, the blurred line where the two met and mingled, inextricably intertwined. Pain and pleasure, black and white; in this world of shadows, there could be no absolutes any more. Not even the absolute hatred of Orin Hobart...

'Good, good. Oh yes...' Hobart was murmuring to himself as he watched, almost as though he could feel every sensation that passed through his captive's body. As she smoothed the oil over her bosom, his eyes followed every movement, his cock hard as an iron bar beneath the fine black leather pants. 'Now massage your belly... that's right, down over your belly, yes, good.'

The oil smoothed and trickled over Mila's belly, warming and then kindling it into a deep, hot flame of desire. This was such wickedness, such torture. Hobart knew exactly what he was doing to her.

'Now lower. Your thighs.'

'Please,' she gasped. 'No more. I can't take any more.'

She felt the blow across her back and shoulders as though it were the bite of a thousand scorpions. As she stumbled and cried out, she saw Cora's thin-lipped smile of satisfaction, her arm raised and the bundle of supple twigs in her hand.

'You had better learn to mind your manners, bitch,' snapped Cora. 'Or you will feel far worse than the kiss of the switch on your back.'

THE GOLDEN CAGE

Mila's head was reeling, her whole body screaming with the realisation of what Hobart was doing to her. Panting from the discomfort, she turned to him, her naked breasts and belly glistening with a fine sheen of fragrant oil.

'What have you done to me?' she demanded, quite forgetting that she was the humble slave. 'What have you done?'

Cora grabbed her round the waist and dragged her back but Mila shook her off and lunged at Hobart, who caught her wrists and held her fast.

She twisted and turned, screaming her rage:

'Оставьте меня впокое! Leave me alone, let me go! What have you done?'

Throwing back his head, he laughed at her fury.

'Done to you, slave? I have done nothing – all that you are feeling, you have done to yourself.'

Mila tried to pull free, but Hobart was strong, much too strong for her. He held her fast, forcing her to look deep into his wild eyes, insane with a dark and ferocious lust. Oddly enough, she realised that she felt no fear.

'What was in that oil?' she demanded, wriggling and writhing, trying to rake Hobart's flesh with her nails. Perhaps it was the oil that had done this to her too, making her brave and reckless and stupid beyond belief.

'Ah, the oil.' Hobart smiled, completely undisturbed by Mila's outburst. 'A little blend of my own devising. It contains flower-oils and spices ... a little ginger and musk...'

'And?'

'That would be telling, my sweet. Rare and beautiful essences to give you pleasure; to make you feel a thousand times more than other people feel. Is that not a great joy and privilege – to feel a thousand times more pleasure?'

'And a thousand times more pain?'

'Precisely, my dear slut. You understand me so well.'

Hobart's gauntleted fingers let go of Mila's left wrist and closed about her nipple. She let out a piercing shriek of anguish as he pinched and twisted the engorged flesh, cursing him in every language she knew, screaming and writhing and kicking and biting.

Bored with this game, Hobart pushed her away and she fell to the floor on hands and knees. Crouching there, she glared up at him, her dark hair in disarray and a scarlet smear of lipstick like a bloody gash across her smooth white cheek.

'Bastard,' she hissed.

Hobart gave an ironic bow.

'You flatter me.' Then the smile disappeared from his face. 'I told you to rub the oil into your belly, Mila. I don't believe I told you to stop.'

'Go to hell.'

She pushed her tousled hair back from her face, smearing a little of the scented oil over her skin. It gleamed in the dancing candlelight.

Hobart stepped forward out of the shadows, unhurried, seemingly dispassionate. Only the throbbing baton of flesh at his crotch betrayed his excitement. He could not have wished for a more arousing scene – his slave crouching at his feet, her naked body dripping with oil and her dark hair falling in tendrils about her perfect shoulders. How it excited him to look at the reddish stripes across her smooth, white back.

'If I do, little one, I shall be sure to take you with me.'

Stooping over her, he took a handful of her hair and used it to pull her to her feet, snarling and writhing in his grasp.

'The saw-horse, sir?'

THE GOLDEN CAGE

'Indeed. An excellent idea, Cora. Prepare the manacles.'

Mila found herself being dragged across the smooth stone floor of the training room, completely unable to free herself from Hobart's clutches. She felt as helpless as an errant child in his grasp, his strength overwhelming her, his fingers bruising her as he pushed her against the wooden saw-horse.

'No. No, let me go, let me go!'

She wondered why she had chosen this particular moment to show a spark of rebellion. Perhaps she had just woken up after so many long days and nights at Hobart's mercy. It made no sense to resist him – she knew perfectly well that it would only make things ten times more difficult for her – and yet she could not take any more. If she did not do something, anything, to show that she was not his plaything, she feared that very soon she would have forgotten who she once was.

Mila Kirovska. She was Mila Kirovska and nobody's slave. One day, very soon, she would find a way to show Orin Hobart that she was not simply his plaything. She had been stupid, dangerously stupid, but she was learning fast – and the day must surely come when she would be able to turn the tables on her captor.

'Tie her down. Securely – she fights like a she-cat.'

'Sir.'

Cora's voice was filled with a syrupy satisfaction which sickened Mila. She knew now how much sexual pleasure Cora gained from watching her degradation, and a dark corner of her own soul longed to see Cora humiliated as she had been, used and abused and defiled. It disturbed her that she found the thought arousing...

Resisting with all her strength, she was pushed forward over the old wooden saw-horse, so that her back and backside were exposed and her head hanging down. Rusty iron cuffs snapped shut around her wrists and ankles, and at last Hobart let go of her. She did not struggle – what was the point? She was completely at his mercy now, unable even to see as the tangled curtain of her hair obscured her face.

Hobart ran his gloved hand over Mila's backside.

'Such a pity I have to punish you again,' he said softly. But Mila knew it wasn't a pity – it was a pleasure for him. Hobart liked nothing so much as an opportunity to punish his slave. 'But you see, my sweet, I really must teach you a lesson. I am hosting an important party in a few days' time, and I have already decided that you are to be the star attraction. You shall be my sweet little *hostess*. Wasn't that what we agreed when we first met in St Petersburg?'

Mila's body tensed. A party? She had assumed that Hobart was going to hide her away forever, keeping her away from questions and prying eyes. Was this some sort of trick?

'And so, my sweet, you see that I must tame you, no matter how much pain it causes me.' He ran his tongue down Mila's back and the cooling trail of saliva raised goosebumps of pleasure on her skin. 'Why will you not obey me, little one? Submit to me and I shall teach you ways to such pleasure as you have never even dreamed about.'

All was very quiet in the training room, the silence broken only by the sound of breathing and the pounding of Mila's terrified heart.

The first touch of Hobart's gloved fingers on her backside was unexpectedly pleasurable, the cold leather and metal studs agreeably smooth, almost soothing on her sweat-sprinkled flesh.

THE GOLDEN CAGE

'Such a fine ass you have,' commented Hobart, his voice husky with sex. 'I wonder how many men have enjoyed its pleasures...'

Pulling apart Mila's bottom cheeks, he poured a little oil into the deep amber-coloured valley, watching it ooze and trickle down from the base of her spine to the puckered rose of her arsehole. Mila twitched and wriggled at the contact, as the stimulants in the oil began working, absorbed through her skin to drive her crazy with need; amplifying the slightest sensation, overwhelming her with guilty desire.

'I am going to fuck you in the ass, Mila,' announced Hobart, his voice quiet and matter-of-fact.

'No.' Mila's voice was scarcely more than a strangled whisper, her resistance a futile token. 'No, I won't let you...'

But I want you to, whispered a voice in her head, a wicked voice that knew her deepest, darkest secrets. *I want you to possess me utterly. I want you to ram into me, pump and thrust and fill me with your come. I hate and despise and fear you, and yet I want your cock inside me now, now, now!*

His index finger, smeared with oil, teased the tight membrane of her sphincter, the rough seams of the leather gauntlet tormenting her with thrills of intensely pleasurable discomfort. The very tip flicked across her anus, making it alternately dilate and contract, as though it were unsure whether it should welcome or resist the intruder.

She shuddered half in fear, half in excitement, as she waited for his assault.

'Remember, little one, I am doing this as a punishment; but I am also doing it because I care deeply about you. No one understands you like I do, my sweet slave. No one knows what you desire like I do.'

'You understand nothing about me,' hissed Mila.

'Oh but I do. I understand how you came to me for a new life, a new beginning. A life of luxury...'

'Luxury!' If Mila had not been so angry she might have laughed. 'You have caged me and made me your slave.'

He smiled to himself as he contemplated the beauties of his slave, laid out before him, a plaything who was both his discovery and his creation.

'If I cage you, my sweet, it is a cage of purest gold. Obey me, satisfy my desires, and you shall have every luxury you have ever dreamed of. And pleasures so exquisite that they are beyond your imagining.'

As his cock nudged between her buttocks, she screamed her fear and her anger. Hobart's cock was an instrument of exquisite torture, an engine of dark and unwilling pleasure. Her hypersensitive body awoke to its torments with a torrent of sensation, a tidal wave that threatened to overwhelm both body and soul.

As he took her, possessing her with a casual arrogance, Mila fought the tide of exultation that rose within her. No, no, no. She must be strong. She must resist, close her mind to the treachery of her pleasure. Or had Hobart been right when he told her that it was pointless trying to resist, since her own pleasure would always betray her?

Opening her mind and body at last to the waterfall of sensations, she surrendered to the pleasure, the dark, bleak, terrifying pleasure. But at the back of her mind she was already thinking of ways to escape from Orin Hobart's golden cage.

Chapter 7

The next few days passed in a haze. Hobart's 'housekeeper', Cora, knew every trick and treat to bring an errant slave into line, and the aphrodisiacs he had obtained on his travels in the Far East had a unique power to subdue the reason and release the deepest, wickedest levels of desire. Robbed of her inhibitions and her power of resistance, Mila felt she could do little but surrender to Hobart's plans.

But if Orin Hobart possessed her body, he had not yet gained the power to see inside her mind. And in her mind Mila was plotting her escape; collecting information; waiting for the one chance of freedom that might present itself. If and when it did, she would not let it pass. Mila Kirovska was not created to be a slave.

'I have brought your clothes.'

Cora laid a small suitcase on the bed in Mila's room. Being more obedient to her master's wishes had earned Mila a number of concessions – one of them permission to return to her own room.

Mila watched as Cora unlocked the case and threw open the lid.

'You have bathed as Mr Hobart instructed you?'

'Yes.'

'Very well. Then you may dress.'

Mila peered into the suitcase. Something scarlet and shiny met her gaze. She frowned.

'These . . . these aren't my clothes.'

Cora gave a dry laugh.

'They are the clothes chosen for you by your Master. You are a very fortunate slave.'

'Fortunate?'

'Your Master has given you permission to attend his party tonight. In fact . . .' Her mouth twitched faintly at the corners, as though she were suppressing some secret mirth. 'You are to act as hostess to his guests. Don't you remember?'

Turning on her heel, Cora left the room, closing the door behind her with a soft click – swiftly followed by the dull clunk of the key turning home in the lock. Orin Hobart might have relaxed his vigilance a little over the past few days but he was still taking no chances.

Walking across to the window, Mila pushed aside the curtain and peered out through the elegant ironwork which formed such a pretty cage. In the distance, beyond the lush, manicured lawns and fertile orchards, the ocean crashed against the rocks, a fine sea-spray misting the summer air like the spittle of some angry Titan. Beyond the coastline, the ocean stretched away in shades of fading greenish-blue and grey, towards the far-distant horizon: a charcoal smudge between sea and sky, the very edge of the world.

Mila's thoughts were drawn back to immediate reality by the sound of a car engine. Looking out to the right, she saw the sleek, dark shape of a stretch limousine gliding up the long driveway to the house, its tinted windows glinting in the evening sunlight.

As she watched, the car drew up in front of the house, its tyres scrunching on the gravel as the driver braked and

THE GOLDEN CAGE

swung the car to a halt. The chauffeur got out first, resplendently kitsch in a uniform of grey tunic and breeches, peaked cap, leather gloves and polished riding boots.

He opened the passenger door and a man stepped out. Mila was sure she had seen him before. There was something vaguely familiar about the square jawline, the distinguished greying hair swept back from a high forehead. But she could not quite place him – and anyway, this was obviously one of Orin Hobart's rich American friends. How could she possibly have seen him anywhere before?

He turned back to the car and stooped, picking something up. Something long and thin which tightened, then slackened as a dark shape moved towards him from the interior of the car.

It was a woman, her long legs stretching out before her as she slid out of the limousine. Long, slender legs clad in stiletto-heeled shoes and black stockings. There was a brief glimpse of thigh, then slim fingers in black lace gloves smoothed down the short black skirt and the woman emerged into the sunlit evening.

An electric shock seemed to pass right through Mila, and her hands clutched at the window-sill as though it were the only solid and dependable thing left in the whole world. The woman was elegantly and sexily dressed, in a black Versace skirt and silver velvet bustier, with black lace elbow-length gloves. Whether or not her make-up and hair were equally sexy, Mila had no way of knowing. For the woman's face was completely obscured by a leather mask.

The mask covered her entire head, with a small hole for the nose and zippers covering her eyes and mouth. About her neck was a studded leather collar, from which led a long leather leash.

Mila watched in a state of shock as the woman got out of

the car, smoothing down her skirt, and walking passively behind the man as he led her by the leash towards the front door of Hobart's house. Up to now, Mila had been living from day to day, trying to survive by simply not thinking about what might happen next. But the sight of these two guests had forced her to accept that this evening's social event was not going to be any ordinary dinner party.

Her palms sweated and she felt a lump in her throat, half choking her with fear. What exactly had Cora meant when she talked about Mila being Hobart's 'hostess'? It was obvious that Hobart's friends shared his sexual appetites and preferences. Perhaps he was intending to present his latest acquisition to them for their approval...

'Slave!'

Cora's voice penetrated Mila's consciousness and she felt a cold shiver pass down her spine.

'Yes...' Her imagination was already running riot.

'Are you dressed yet?'

'I ... almost. I am almost ready.'

'Ten more minutes, slave, then I shall come in and inspect you. You had better not disappoint me – and you had better not keep our guests waiting.'

'I won't.' Mila's heart was pounding like a steam-hammer in her chest. She stood stock-still with icy-cold apprehension, listening to Cora's footsteps retreating down the corridor towards the top of the stairs.

Despair flooded over her in a black wave. Why had she deluded herself that she could get away? There was no escape. There had never been any chance of escape, right from the moment when she had walked through the doors of the Agency.

Come on, she told herself. *Pull yourself together. You got yourself into this mess and now you're going to get yourself*

THE GOLDEN CAGE

out of it. Somehow. The trouble was, she still hadn't the faintest idea how. For now, all she could do was go along with whatever Hobart demanded of her, no matter how se, no matter how dark and terrible.

walked across to the suitcase and looked down at the olded clothes. Shiny red PVC glared up at her and she lifted the garment out of the case. It was a mini-skirt, the right size but very, very short – so short that once it was on, it would scarcely skim her backside. She put it to one side and examined the other clothes. There were black PVC thigh-boots with four-inch spiky heels, spiked leather straps to wear round her wrists and a slave-collar of polished silver. Nothing else. No top, no stockings, no bra or briefs.

Nothing. Orin Hobart was certainly playing this one for maximum kicks.

She began by zipping herself into the red mini-skirt. Funnily enough, she felt more exposed wearing it than she had done naked. It was as though the skirt had been expressly designed to reveal far more than it veiled, to hint at scarcely hidden obscenities – like a frame around a pornographic picture.

It was hellishly difficult to get into the boots, which were skin-tight and so pointed that she could scarcely crush her toes into them. The four-inch heels made her feel curiously good: tall, slinky, sexually potent. But the spiked cuffs and slave collar brought her straight back down to earth. She was a slave, nothing more. Orin Hobart's slave, who must do whatever she was told to do, obey every command.

'You are ready, slave?'

'Yes.'

The key turned once again in the lock and the bedroom door swung open. Cora had changed into a black cocktail frock which showed off her small, firm breasts and tight derriere. Her hard, muscular body looked superb in the skin-tight lycra.

'Turn round, I want to see what you look like from the back.'

Mila turned.

'Bend over that chair.'

Surprised, Mila obeyed; and felt the mini-skirt riding up, baring her buttocks. Seconds later, she felt Cora's hand smoothing over the naked flesh, pinching and slapping.

'Excellent.' Cora's voice was heavy with sensual satisfaction. 'Your master will enjoy reddening those pretty ass-cheeks. You may stand up now.'

As Mila straightened up, she felt something on her face and, as she swung round, the blindfold closed over her eyes, blotting out the light. She tried to clutch at it, scrabbling with her fingers, but Cora had already tied it tightly, and was now pulling her arms behind her back, joining the two spiked cuffs with rope.

'That's better.' Cora's voice was smooth and syrupy now, like Hobart's when he was really hard and hungry for her. A voice filled with sex, hot and dirty. 'Much better. Now, I think, you are ready to meet your master's guests.'

Hobart's manhood throbbed and yearned for release. He had allowed Cora to give him head half an hour before, to take the edge off his sexual need and ensure that tonight's pleasure did not disappoint him. But the aphrodisiac cocktails served as an aperitif to this sensual feast had reawakened his lust and, in any case, his appetite for Mila Kirovska was constant and insatiable.

He glanced around the dining-room at his guests. They were twelve in all, six wealthy and influential men and their

THE GOLDEN CAGE

slaves; like-minded men who had good cause to know the value of discretion and whose generosity was boundless. For what could be more generous than to share your slave with your friends?

The guests sat around the table, their slaves waiting patiently and obediently at their masters' feet, living only for the moment when they would be commanded to perform some sexual service. Such devotion warmed Hobart's heart. He had high hopes that in time, Mila too would develop into the perfect slave. And when finally became bored with her, she would fetch a good price in Africa or the Middle East where feminine obedience was especially prized.

But it would be a long time before that. Mila aroused him to the point of frenzy. She was like a half-broken filly, sometimes docile, sometimes a spitting, bucking fury; and he could remember no other woman who had provoked such a violence of passion in him.

'That was an excellent dinner, Hobart,' commented the man to his right, lifting his wine glass in a toast.

'Naturally, Curtis,' cut in a youngish man with wavy brown hair. 'Hobart is true gourmet.' He winked. 'And we're not just talking food.'

He turned to the slave kneeling beside his chair, naked save for an elaborate harness of shiny, electric-blue straps and chains. Taking a morsel of fruit from his plate, he held it above her head as though she were a dog begging for a titbit.

'You have been a good girl, you may eat.'

The girl opened her scarlet-painted lips and he dropped the fruit in to her mouth.

'Good girl.' He took her by the hair and pressed her face close to his crotch. 'Now suck my dick.'

Aurelia Clifford

Hobart watched through hooded eyes, sitting back in his chair as he savoured the spectacle of his guests enjoying themselves. There were some famous faces here – two Republican congressmen, a film producer, an actor and two prominent businessmen. Gourmets every one, with impeccable sexual taste.

To his left, film producer Carey Ronstein was fondling the breasts of his slave – a tall, elegant woman in a black skirt and silver velvet bustier, completely masked so that she seemed like some profoundly sexy android, a creature half-woman, half-machine. Ronstein had pulled her breasts out of the bustier and they were lying on the top of it like juicy apples on a platter. It would be so good to taste them, to bite them and lap up their juice. Hobart was almost tempted to break his self-imposed fast . . .

'Sir?'

Hobart turned to see Cora standing in the doorway, chic and a little haughty in her black cocktail dress.

'Yes.'

'Your . . . hostess is ready to join you and your guests.'

A slow smile spread over Hobart's face.

'Bring her in.'

His body was tense with expectation, all other temptations forgotten as he anticipated the joy of seeing Mila again, the sheer, unalloyed sexual thrill of watching her terror and her arousal. There was an air of expectation in the dining room, every thought focused on what was to come.

The door opened again and this time there were two figures standing in the doorway: the tall housekeeper and before her, blindfolded and half-naked, the full-breasted, delicious slave who had once been Mila Kirovska.

'Go and meet your Master's guests,' hissed Cora, her

THE GOLDEN CAGE

voice taunting as she pushed Mila into the room. 'And be sure you do not disappoint them.'

With her hands still tied behind her back, she was unable to save herself as she stumbled, and she fell against Carey Ronstein, crying out as the film director's hands explored her body, squeezing her bare breasts.

'No, no, don't touch me, let me go! Покалуйста, please...'

She wriggled, trying to escape from her unseen captor, but she was helpless to defend herself, and Ronstein forced his lips against hers, pushing his tongue into her mouth as his fingers worked their way underneath the hem of her micro-skirt. His kiss half-suffocated her, possessing her, filling her mouth with the taste of brandy and the darker, subtler taste of some exotic spice. Something that had awakened a demon of lust in this already lustful man.

When he pulled away from the kiss, she was gasping for air, filling her lungs with hoarse, sobbing breaths. Ronstein laughed.

'You sexy bitch,' he hissed appreciatively. 'See how she wriggles. I thought you had her trained, Hobart.'

Hobart smiled.

'Her training has scarcely begun. I thought it might entertain you to continue her education yourselves. Do anything you want to her. For tonight, she is yours.'

A strange feeling tore at his heart as he spoke those words. What was happening to him? Was he becoming possessive in his old age? He'd never felt like that about a slave before. When all was said and done, they were half-trained animals, domestic pets who existed only to be disciplined and to provide for their master's sexual needs. The last thing on his mind was getting addicted to just one woman... wasn't it?

Ronstein's slave was pawing at his leg, her scarlet-tipped fingers clawing and clutching at him as she moaned her jealousy.

'Please, Master. Please. Give me your dick, I want it...'

He thrust her away, pushing her to the floor, where she lay whimpering like a kicked spaniel.

'What you want is irrelevant, slave. All that matters is what I want. Remember that. You will be punished for that later. Now be silent.'

Lost in the darkness beyond the blindfold, Mila found that the loss of sight had heightened her other senses. Tastes and scents surrounded her: brandy and semen, candlewax and fresh cream ... She must be in the main dining-room, but whose were these hands on her, roaming over her bare flesh, exploring and possessing? And how many other strangers were surrounding her, getting off on the spectacle of her nakedness?

Whispering voices seemed to be everywhere; she tried to follow them, but the conversation moved too quickly, and still the hands were probing and possessing, demanding and taking.

'Is she a good fuck?'

'Wild.'

'You've butt-fucked her?'

'There's nothing she likes better.'

'Mmm. Tight like a virgin.'

A finger jabbed with brutal suddenness between Mila's bare buttocks, but there was no refuge from the relentless invader, and her unwilling excitement betrayed itself in the wetness between her thighs.

'The hot little bitch has wet all over my pants.' The feigned disgust concealed lustful satisfaction. 'Is *this* what you want, bitch? Is it?'

THE GOLDEN CAGE

Strong hands lifted her up as though she weighed no more than a feather. Something hot and hard nudged between her thighs and suddenly she was forced downwards, on to a fleshy, curving spike.

'Aaah!' she cried, her breath escaping in a great roar as she arched her back and strained against her captor's arms.

Ronstein's finger pushed deeper into her arse, and she felt it through the thin wall of her vagina; it was like being entered by two men at once, possessed by two lovers who cared for nothing but the satisfaction of their own hunger.

'Hot and sweet. Just how I like them. You make me want to spurt, d'you know that, bitch?'

Ronstein danced her on his lap, one hand pushing her up and down on his manhood, the other toying with the tight sphincter of her arse. Her body had no power to resist him, her juices flowing clear and sweet, the flower of her womanhood blossoming about the stalk of his penis.

She fought the feelings of rising pleasure, but they were too powerful. It was much too late to close her mind to the flood of sensations, the burning swell that filled her belly, stiffened her nipples and turned her clitoris into a burning seed of ecstasy.

Hobart watched with breathless excitement. Outwardly he was in control, the absolute master, but inside he burned in a hell of jealous desire, yearning to take his slave back from Ronstein and have her all to himself again. It both excited and angered him to see her in the arms of another man, her red PVC micro-skirt up round her waist and the heavy globes of her breasts thrust out as she arched her back in unwilling surrender. He wondered if she had the faintest idea what she was doing to him.

Aurelia Clifford

It made him crazy with excitement, but he hated it: hated to see another man's cock between his slave's thighs, another man's finger playing with her beautiful firm ass.

The other guests were watching too, mesmerised. One of the congressmen had dragged his slave on to his lap and was mimicking the movements of Carey Ronstein as he dreamed he was the one possessing Mila. The actor was moaning softly, eyes half-closed, as a girl with an angel tattoo milked his semen into the deep furrow between her enormous breasts.

Sex, sex, sex. The need was like boiling lava within him. Hobart unzipped his pants and took out his penis. It seemed unutterably beautiful to him, a wonderful thing of smooth, blood-warm stone, marbled with bluish veins; an instrument of pain and pleasure. Slowly he began to stroke it, all the time gazing at Mila's face. He wished he could see her eyes, feast on the terror and the hatred and the desire and the ecstasy. Her lips were opening and closing in soundless agony, her body tensing and relaxing; tensing, tensing, tensing...

He sensed her orgasm in the split second before she cried out, her cry a long, sobbing outrush of breath. The sight of her climaxing made his manhood burn with jealous desire. And when Ronstein pumped into her for the last time, pulling her down hard against his groin so that his seed spurted deep inside her, Hobart thought he would go mad with need. He seized his neighbour's slave and prised her lips open with his fingers.

'Suck me.'

She was not Mila, but as her lips closed about his cock-tip he imagined that she was. Sweet Mila, little vixen, grazing his cock with her sharp little teeth...

THE GOLDEN CAGE

'You're right, Hobart, she's a hot vixen. But does she know how to take her punishment?' Ronstein got to his feet and Caswell, the oil company boss, took her from him.

'Wanna keep her to yourself, huh? Time you shared her...'

He grabbed hold of her and Mila shivered as he slid his hand between her thighs, scooping and smearing the mingled juices of her coupling all over her thighs and belly and backside.

'Dirty-minded little slut,' he hissed, and Mila trembled at the darkness in his voice. His fingers pushed into her mouth, and she almost choked on the taste of sex-juice and semen. 'Like that, don't you? Like the taste of your own sinful lust? Ronstein's right, you need to be taught a few lessons.'

'Cut her loose. Let her fight, it's more fun when they wriggle a little.'

The next thing she knew, something was cutting through the rope binding her wrists together. Then, before she could do anything to free herself, she was being picked up and spreadeagled on her back on the dinner table. China and glass clattered and rolled out of the way, and she felt the wetness of spilt wine on her bare skin, the stickiness of food crushed beneath her back and backside.

'A little initiation, I think, my sweet little slave.'

This time it was Hobart's voice and instinctively she focused on it, everything else fading into the background. She heard his footsteps coming towards her, the soles of his handmade shoes tap-tapping slowly across the polished parquet floor. Somewhere in the distance a clock chimed the half-hour.

'Haven't you anything to say to me, slave? No words of welcome?'

'M-master?'

Mila froze, afraid to struggle any more, suddenly convinced that something terrible was about to happen. A fingertip touched her lips, then travelled slowly and luxuriously down over throat and breasts and belly, pausing only when it reached the margin of her dark pubic curls.

'That's right, my little one. I am your master, and I shall continue to be your master for ever, for all time. Already I have marked you, but perhaps you need something else... another token of my possession? Don't you agree?'

She remained silent, not knowing what to say, afraid that Hobart would trick her again.

'Answer me, slave.'

'I . . . yes, Master.'

'Excellent. You see, already she is learning the virtues of obedience.'

Hobart was filled with the most tremendous sense of well-being – and he had not even climaxed yet, not even masturbated over his slave's body and watched his seed spurt in creamy-white gobbets over her matchless skin.

He turned to Ronstein.

'Bring it here.'

he uncovered the silver tray with a flourish, his cock stiffening as he picked up the golden ring and the needle which would pierce his slave's plump labia. The mark of his passion and his possession.

And after he had marked her, they would have her – all of them, joining their bodies to hers in a sweet celebration of her submission and their power.

It was long after midnight. Mila was alone in the dining room, listening to the sounds of laughter and passion.

THE GOLDEN CAGE

She had been alone in here for several hours, locked in by Hobart when the party moved to the conservatory. Sated with her, satisfied with what they had done, they had left her here, roped to one of the chairs.

At first, she had hated the golden ring, hated it for what it symbolised, piercing her outer labia like the teeth of some wild animal. But slowly, gradually, it had seemed to become part of her, causing her sensations which were almost pleasurable. Hobart had not defeated her only taught her a new way to experience pleasure.

It had taken a long, long time, but gradually she had managed to work the ropes loose, easing her wrists from the loops until at last she was free.

She tried the door – it was locked, naturally. Hobart didn't like to take chances with his property. Or did he? Putting her eye to the keyhole, she saw that the key was still in the lock on the other side. If only she had something to slide under the door...

A stiff damask napkin would serve the purpose, if she was very, very careful. With painful slowness, she eased the edge under the door, praying that no one would come along and catch her. The handle of a teaspoon fitted neatly into the lock. She wriggled it, easing out the key; and for a split second it seemed to hover in mid-air, hesitant, teasing.

It fell with a soft thud on to the napkin, and Mila drew it back under the door, holding her breath, convinced that the gap would not be large enough and the key would be pushed further away from her. But it slid towards her and seconds later it was in her hands, a tiny miracle, the key to her freedom.

The key turned with a click and a grate, and the door slid open on squeaky hinges. She peeped outside. There was no one in the corridor, but she could hear laughter and music filtering out from the conservatory. Screams too. Screams of pleasure.

Mila had had plenty of time to think, but thinking didn't always make things work out the way you wanted them to. Hadn't she thought long and hard about the Agency?

Wait. Wait a moment. She couldn't just leave like this – she had nothing, no money, no passport, absolutely nothing. The least Orin Hobart owed her was the means to survive. She turned and scanned the room. Like the rest of the house, it was full of rare and beautiful things – silver, crystal, even gold. But you couldn't live on silver spoons and Limoges porcelain.

Carey Ronstein's dinner jacket hung over the back of his chair. She slipped her hand into the inside pocket. *Yes!* A wallet, stuffed with plastic and a few notes. She took the paper money and discarded the wallet. Stolen credit cards were no use to her, and in any case she wasn't a thief – just a lone woman in a foreign country, trying desperately to survive.

As an afterthought, she took the jacket, and slipped it on over her bare breasts. Just as she was leaving the room, she caught sight of the little glass cabinet where Hobart kept curios, little objets d'art he had collected from his travels all over the world. There was nothing really valuable there, surely nothing he would miss. And there was something about the jade tiger which had captured Mila's imagination the first time she'd seen it. On an impulse, she slipped it into the jacket pocket. It was heavier than it looked. If Hobart came after her, she could always hit him with it.

With agonising slowness, terrified that she would be caught, Mila tiptoed across the hallway, opened the front door and stepped into the night.

The air was cold for a summer night and filled with the

THE GOLDEN CAGE

tang of sea-spray. How many weeks was it since she had breathed the fresh air of freedom? But there was no time to stand and think. She had to get away from here.

Cars were parked in a semicircle around the front of the house. The first one she chose was locked, but the second – a black Mercedes – yielded smoothly and silently, the boot springing open at her touch.

She stole one last glance behind her at the house – the cage which had held her prisoner for so long – and she felt a curious ache of loss, as though Hobart's words had not been entirely untrue. Perhaps he really had tapped some hidden vein of darkness within her, sensed some secret need?

But no. She was deceiving herself, the way he had deceived her. And Mila Kirovska was never going to be anybody's fool, ever again. Swiftly and silently she climbed into the boot of the car, curled herself up and pulled the lid down, holding it so that it was almost but not quite closed.

Praying that no one would find her there, she lay in wakeful silence until she heard the sounds of laughter and farewells – and the sounds of approaching footsteps. People clambered into the car and at last the engine roared into life. Then she felt the car begin to move slowly down the driveway, away from the house and away from Orin Hobart.

For ever.

Chapter 8

Where was she?

In the chilly light of morning, Mila was beginning to regret ever leaving the boot of the Mercedes. When the car had stopped she had taken the opportunity to slip out and scurry into the trees at the side of the road, stretching her chilled, stiffened muscles.

She needn't have bothered hiding, because the occupants of the Merc were much too far gone to notice her. In fact, they were so drunk that it was amazing they had made it this far without an accident.

They got out of the car, laughing and kissing, and climbed into the back seat. Mila could hardly believe it. They were making out right there, in the back seat of the Mercedes. Mila could see the guy moving up an down on top of the girl, heard her squeals and groans as he pumped into her.

Mila didn't stick around to see what happened next. She headed into the woods and started walking across hilly, forested country, hoping to hit another road. Maybe if she stuck to the country tracks, she'd be OK and no one would notice her. She glanced down at herself – half naked beneath Carey Ronstein's jacket – and couldn't suppress a smile. Who the hell was she kidding?

Without a watch, she had lost all track of time; but it

was a long time past dawn and the chill, golden light cast grey, filmy shadows on the soft, sandy earth between the trees. She wanted to stop and rest, but she was hungry and afraid. She needed food and proper clothes, and she needed to put a lot more miles between her and Orin Hobart. By now he was probably out looking for her...

She hit the road in the late morning. It was more of a track really, running between fields and orchards. There was pretty country all around, with some spectacular mountains in the distance, but Mila was past caring about pretty. A strawberry field yielded a few juicy berries but by now she was starving. The high-heeled boots were making her back ache, and it was pretty obvious what she looked like from the cat-calls of the few drivers who passed.

'Wanna ride?'

'Get in, sweetcakes.'

'You sure are the prettiest little whore I seen in a long, long time. Great little ass...'

'Your momma know you're out, hon?'

She heard a car pull up alongside her, and for one horrible moment she thought Hobart had caught up with her already. A hand caught her wrist.

'Where you headin', sweet thing?'

Fearful, she turned, trying to pull free. The driver leered up at her from the cab of his pickup truck. It wasn't difficult to guess what was on his mind.

'Let go of me.'

'You ain't from these parts, huh? Foreign chicks – I love 'em. Real exotic.' He just kept on grinning, his fingers tight about her wrist. 'Love the way you dress. Why don't you take off that jacket and let me get a good look at your tits?'

THE GOLDEN CAGE

'I said...'

'Yeah, hon, I heard what you said. Only I don't listen good, see. 'Cept when I'm listenin' with my dick.'

His hand was on his groin, rubbing it, hardening the flesh underneath. There was no one else in sight, and nowhere to run to even if she got away. He unlocked the door and opened it, at the precise moment that Mila heard another car approaching with a squeal of brakes.

'Come on, hon. Just be nice to me an' I'll be nice to you, okay? I'll pay you good, you see if I don't.'

'Let her go.'

Mila turned to see a woman standing beside a small blue car. She was tall and slender with short brown hair, and well-dressed in white jeans and polo shirt.

The man laughed in her face.

'What you say, little lady?'

'I said let her go.'

'Oh yeah, and what if I don't? You gonna make me?'

The woman smiled.

'I have the number of your licence plate and I see you work for the county forestry service. One phone call to the sheriff's office...'

'Okay, okay. Just get off my back.' He stepped on the accelerator. 'Didn't want the fuckin' bitch anyway...'

Mila watched the car disappear into the distance in a cloud of exhaust fumes, and ran weary fingers through her sweat-dampened hair.

'Thanks.'

The woman shrugged, laying a hand on Mila's shoulder. Instinctively, Mila shrank away.

'You okay?' The woman sounded genuinely concerned, but Mila had got out of the habit of trusting people. Anyone.

'I . . . yes, I'm fine.'

'You look . . . I don't know, it's none of my business, but you look like you've been in some kind of trouble. Can I help?'

'It's all right, really. I'm fine.'

'Can't I give you a lift? Say to the nearest town?' Her touch felt soft, beguilingly gentle. 'My name's Jaime, by the way. And you are . . . ?

Mila didn't answer, but turned to look the woman in the face for the first time. She looked okay, but . . .

'Where am I?'

'Where?' The woman looked puzzled.

'I don't know where I am. I . . . was brought here. In the night.'

'Oh. I see.' Jaime didn't look as if she did, but she kept on smiling anyway. Mila was starting to like her, in spite of her mistrust. 'You're in New Hampshire.'

'Oh.'

'Look . . . I don't want to pressurise you or anything, God knows that dickbrain already did enough of that, but I just want to help. You understand? No questions asked.'

Mila looked into Jaime's face. It seemed an open, honest face. There was a warmth in the eyes, a soft sensuality about the mouth. Even without make-up, she was striking, handsome even; and Mila could feel herself warming to her.

'Well . . . maybe you could drive me to the next town,' began Mila, still doubtful.

'Sure I could. And you look like you could use a bath and a good meal. What d'you say we stop at a motel someplace? I've been driving all night and I could use some sleep.'

THE GOLDEN CAGE

Jaime's hand rested lightly on her shoulder. It didn't feel threatening, just reassuring and warm. Maybe this was a chance she could afford to take. Surely she'd be safe with another woman? And if not? She could hardly be worse off than she was now, half naked and hungry on a New Hampshire backroad.

'Thank you,' she said, following Jaime back to the car. 'Thank you, you're very kind.'

Orin Hobart IV tore the fragile bloom from its stem and crushed it between his strong fingers, scattering the torn and bruised petals over the conservatory floor.

'Bitch,' he hissed between clenched teeth, the muscles of his handsome face tensed and his eyes narrow and glittering with rage. 'Cunning little bitch.'

'Sir, I . . .' cut in Cora.

'Will you be silent!' He raised his fist as though to strike her and her expression softened, almost welcoming his violence, opening herself to the cruelty of his love.

'Forgive me.' Her voice was almost a contented purr.

Hobart's fist halted in mid-air, hesitated for a moment, then unclenched and returned to his side.

'I do not intend to give you the satisfaction of pain,' he said coolly. 'I know your tastes too well to punish you with pleasure.' He drummed his fingers on the table. Next to his hand lay the leather-bound album in which he had seen Mila Kirovska's picture. He did not open it. He did not need to see her photograph to remind himself of how she looked.

His mind was indelibly imprinted with her image. Those waves of dark hair that twisted into a thick, glossy rope just made for holding her fast as she sucked his penis. Those plump, slightly pouting lips, naturally red and so beautiful when they were glossy with his semen. Those breasts, heavy yet firm, with nipples as long and hard as blush-pink almonds.

Cora watched him in silence. To be beaten by her master would, as he surmised, have been a pleasure to her. An honour. Her real punishment was to love him and to know that she would forever take second place to women like Mila Kirovska – worthless slaves, pieces of meat she was forced to prepare for her master's table. She despised them all.

'I want her back,' said Hobart. 'I *will* have her back. And I must have what she has taken from me, I must have it at all costs. You have taken steps as I instructed?'

Cora nodded.

'The investigators are waiting in the lobby, sir.'

'They are specialists in this type of work?'

'They come on the very highest recommendation.'

'Very well. You may bring them in.'

He ran his fingers over the cover of the album, felt its electricity tingling into him. *Her* electricity. The bitch; deceitful, disobedient, thieving little bitch. As soon as he had her back he would punish her and how he would enjoy that punishment.

He had a hunch that she would enjoy it, too. Eventually.

Cora ushered the two detectives into the conservatory: a man and a woman, both in their late twenties or early thirties. The woman was only moderately stunning, with her red-blonde hair, pale complexion and grey-green eyes; but her extravagantly curving mouth indicated a sensual nature which Orin Hobart found both interesting and attractive. In other circumstances he might have taken time out to explore the playground of her sexuality, but that time was not now.

THE GOLDEN CAGE

The guy was a good foot taller than the girl, lean and spare but with a hidden strength under the well-cut sports jacket and chinos. A fringe of fine, dark-brown hair slipped down over a tanned forehead, piercing blue eyes dominating a hawkish, slightly gaunt face. Hobart found him intriguingly attractive, too. But then Orin Hobart IV had never believed in setting boundaries to his sexual experiments.

Cora announced them.

'Mr Caleb Steadman and Ms Darsey O'Brien, sir.'

'You may leave us now.'

Cora left the room, pulling the door quietly shut behind her. She hated being excluded and longed for Hobart to recognise her true loyalty and invest his trust in her.

But Hobart was not thinking about Cora. His thoughts were entirely taken up with Mila Kirovska and what she had done to him.

'I sincerely hope you are not going to let me down,' commented Hobart, opening the photograph album and turning it to face the two detectives.

'We have never failed to complete an assignment to the client's *complete* satisfaction,' replied Darsey O'Brien, her green-tinged eyes bright with self-assurance.

'And we have no intention of beginning now,' added Steadman, running long, slender fingers through his hair and pushing it back off his face. 'Pretty,' he observed, glancing down at the photograph of Mila Kirovska.

'So sweet. So vulnerable.' The girl detective's fingertips skimmed across the picture, as though by stroking its surface she could absorb the essence of its subject. 'It's hard to imagine her being so defiant. 'You'd think she would make the perfect slave – obedient, compliant...'

'The picture doesn't do the bitch justice,' snapped Hobart. 'But the likeness should be sufficient for you to track her down.'

'You want her brought back?' It was more of a statement than a question.

'Of course.'

'Alive?' enquired O'Brien, her face a picture of innocent curiosity. Hobart found himself respecting her. She had such potential for cold, sensual cruelty.

'Certainly. She is of little use to me dead and I have invested a great deal of time and money in acquiring her for my pleasure. Besides, I have scarcely begun her education.'

'Alive is more difficult, of course,' Steadman pointed out.

Hobart anticipated Steadman's train of thought and waved it aside with a dismissive gesture.

'Money is no object. Just bring my slave back to me – and another thing.'

'Yes?'

'I want what she stole from me. With or without her, I *must* have it back, you understand?'

Steadman shrugged.

'Sure. But why . . . ?'

He shut up at the sight of Hobart's expression.

'Yeah, yeah, OK. No questions. Right.' As Steadman prised the photograph from the album and slipped it into his pocket, Hobart felt a curious jealousy – as if this fellow was stealing away from him the only part of Mila he still possessed.

Of course, that was crap. He still possessed her, every beautiful atom of her, locked away inside his head. It didn't matter how hard or how far she tried to run away from him. Once Steadman and O'Brien had brought her back to him, he would make her accept the glorious truth: that he possessed her for ever, body and soul.

Chapter 9

The Sweet Dreams Motel consisted of a collection of prefabricated chalets, set in parkland half a mile or so off the freeway. It reminded Mila vaguely of the holiday village on the Black Sea coast where she had spent one childhood summer, courtesy of local branch of the Communist Party. In those days, she'd often dreamed about the capitalist West, the wonderland that must be America.

But she'd never dreamed it would be quite like this.

It was evening when Mila awoke, sprawled on top of the bedsheets. For a few moments she didn't know where she was, then for a second she panicked, thinking she was back at Hobart's house in Massachusetts. Finally reality clicked back into place in her brain. The man in the pickup truck ... the drive across New Hampshire ... the motel.

Blinking, she lifted her head from the pillow. A figure stood silhouetted in the doorway, unrecognisable in the half-light filtering through the drawn blinds. Scared out of her wits, Mila let out a cry of panic.

'It's OK, sweetheart, it's only me.'

A switch clicked and a wall light came on, filling the room with a dull orange glow.

Mila let out a shuddering sigh of relief. Jaime.

'You ... startled me.'

'I'm sorry, I didn't want to disturb you. You looked like you could use some sleep.'

Mila felt the warmth of Jaime's eyes, her inquisitive gaze travelling over her body. It was suffocatingly hot in the chalet and she was naked, the bedsheets damp with her sweat. Her first instinct was to cover herself up, but then she thought how foolish that would be. What did she have to hide from another woman? What could she possibly have to fear?

'That's an unusual piercing you have there. I've been thinking of having it done myself – they say it's a very centring experience.'

Mila reddened with shame as she followed Jaime's eyes to the golden ring, glittering on her pierced and shaven labia, the mark of her submission.

'And the tattoo. "H". Who's that? Someone who means a lot to you?'

Mila shivered, bringing up her hands instinctively to cover her breast.

'Someone ... someone I hate. You'll never know how much. A man ...'

'Ah.'

Jaime set two brown paper bags down on the table by the window.

'It's OK, you don't have to tell me. Look, I brought some more food.' She produced a glossy plastic carrier bag. 'And I got you something to wear. I hope they're the right size ... I had to guess.'

Mila rolled over on to her belly, propping herself up on her elbows.

'I don't understand.'

'Understand what?'

'Why you're being so ... so good to me.'

THE GOLDEN CAGE

'Why shouldn't I be?' Jaime sat down on the bed beside Mila and stroked her hair back from her face. 'You're a woman alone and it's not safe out there, especially for a foreigner. I can see you've been through hell ... I just want to help. And besides, I like you.'

'I like you too,' Mila found herself saying.

'Then let's let it drop, huh? No more guilt, OK?' She planted a kiss on Mila's forehead. It felt warm and soft and sensual, a mother's kiss, or a sister's.

Mila smiled, accepting the reassurance of Jaime's arm about her shoulders.

'OK.'

Jaime got up and busied herself taking the clothes out of the carrier bag.

'You speak great English,' she observed.

'Thank you.'

'Where is it you come from – somewhere in eastern Europe, maybe?'

'I ... er ...'

'Don't wanna talk about it? OK, that's cool. Look, why don't you try on these clothes? Let's see how they fit.'

'I think I should shower first, I'm so hot and sticky.'

'I'll go run the water for you.'

Mila found it hard to adjust – just one day earlier, she'd been Orin Hobart's slave, whipped and pierced and abused. Now she was being looked after, cosseted even, by a woman who didn't even know the first thing about her. She felt chastened, and followed Jaime into the shower-room.

'Mila,' she said.

'Hmm?' Jaime looked back over her shoulder.

'That's my name. Mila.'

Jaime smiled.

'Thank you, Mila. Thank you for trusting me. You can, you know. I'd never dream of hurting you. I only want to make you feel really, really good.'

To Mila that seemed a strange thing to say, but everything was strange about her life right now. The water roared out of the shower-head, a light frosting of steam filling the cubicle.

'Hot or cold, or just warm?'

'Just warm would be great. 'Спасибо . . . thank you, you are very kind.'

Jaime tested the water. Just right. Cool enough to be soothing in this airless heat, warm enough not to chill.

'All ready for you, hon.'

Mila stepped into the cubicle. Normally she would have drawn the shower curtain but somehow it seemed so normal not to. What did she have to hide from Jaime?

She picked up the tube of shower gel and squeezed a little into her hand. It smelt fresh, like a piney forest glade; and as she began massaging it into the skin of her arms and shoulders she felt it start to tingle, invigorating her as it bubbled into a white, creamy lather.

Her hands slid down from her shoulders and throat to her breast, lingering just a little on the nipples, savouring how good it felt to enjoy this simplest and most innocent of pleasures. Closing her eyes, she leant back and allowed the water-jet to play on her breasts, sending creamy runnels of lather trickling and dripping down her belly, her pubis, her thighs, to disappear in marbled swirls around her feet.

She stayed like that for a long time, savouring the soft, sweet caress of the tepid water, stroking her body like a lover's fingers. Her mind drifted. Carried by the fresh,

THE GOLDEN CAGE

verdant smell of the shower gel, she thought back to her youth, to holidays in the forest, to those fumbling moments of adolescent passion beneath the trees with Alexander Trubetskoy.

Reaching out for the shower gel, she felt another hand on hers.

'Let me. I'll soap your back.'

It was Jaime's voice, gentle as a summer breeze. Why resist? Why refuse when she really rather liked the idea of a woman's kind, soft hands smoothing over her tired, abused body?

The gel felt cold on the skin of her back, but Jaime's fingers were warm and subtle, knowing just how to relax and soothe, and perhaps also how to excite...

'Poor, poor, Mila.' Jaime's voice was quiet and serene and sympathetic, almost one with the sound of the rushing water hissing out of the shower-head. 'Your back is so bruised. And these red weals look sore.' Mila winced briefly as the gel seeped into a tiny cut in her skin. 'Someone has been cruel to you and I hate them for it. I hate *him* for it. It was a man, wasn't it, Mila?'

'A man... mmm, yes, a man,' Mila murmured dreamily, hypnotised by Jaime's soft voice and the gentle sensuality of her caresses. When she felt Jaime's lips pressing against her skin, leaving a trail of kisses down her spine from nape to base, she shivered with irresistible enjoyment.

'But everything's all right now, my dear, sweet Mila. Everything's going to be just fine from now on. I'm going to look after you. Don't be afraid, just trust me...'

The next minute, Jaime was in the shower cubicle with her, her clothes dripping wetness as the shower-head covered both of them with its warm cascade. They kissed, and the warm water mingled with the taste of their saliva as Jaime's tongue explored her mouth.

'Come to me, baby. Come to me and let me make you feel real good.'

Mila was so astonished by the pleasure she felt that she scarcely thought of resisting. It had never occurred to her before that she might enjoy having another woman make love to her. But how good it felt, having Jaime's kisses on her breasts, her caresses sliding down her belly towards the burning-hot heart of her sex.

What was happening to her? She was waking up to a whole new realm of pleasure, that's what. And Jaime was clearly no newcomer to girl-on-girl sex. There was subtlety and skill in those fingers and, when you thought about it, it made perfect sense that only a woman should know the secret ways of making another woman feel great.

But there was something not quite right, something that nagged at the back of Mila's mind. The pleasure was there, yes, but so was the old inhibition. Buried, but still there.

'Jaime,' she breathed, half-heartedly pulling away from the other woman's embrace.

'Hush, hush, honey.' Jaime's kisses devoured Mila's throat and breasts as her fingers crept down her body, searching out the hot, wet secret of the Russian girl's desire. 'Everything's all right, just you wait and see. Everything's going to be just fine.'

'Jaime . . . I can't. I'm not . . .' It was so hard for Mila to explain, not because she didn't have the words to express herself, but because she hardly believed her own protests.

'You're not . . . ?' Jaime's face was tanned and handsome as she looked questioningly into Mila's eyes. Her

THE GOLDEN CAGE

short, dark hair was glossy-wet, waterlogged tendrils dripping warm tears down from her brow to kiss cheeks and lips.

'Really, Jaime. You don't understand.' Mila's eyes closed in unwilling ecstasy as Jaime's fingers moved surreptitiously closer to the apex of her need, her silk-smooth fingertips caressing open Mila's thighs in an instinctive gesture of welcome.

'Oh sweet, sweet child. Sugarplum.' Jaime's expression softened into laughter and she kissed Mila's right breast, her teeth toying very gently with the rose-pink crest of her nipple. 'What don't I understand? That you're not a dyke? Honey, every woman's straight until she finds out who she really is. It was a long time before I could be honest with myself about the way I felt for women.'

She paused for a moment.

'The way I feel for you.'

The two women stood stock-still, gazing into each other's eyes; Mila on the defensive, Jaime full of a sensual, yearning intensity. The only sounds were the rhythmic counterpoint of their breathing, and the soft rush and hiss of the shower. It was like standing under some remote tropical waterfall, somewhere primeval, the only two women on Earth ... Jaime's eyelashes glittered with water droplets, and in a mad impulse Mila wanted to kiss them away.

Jaime kissed her index finger and placed it on Mila's lips.

'Don't fight me. Let me show you how good it can be.'

Mila let out a tiny whimper as Jaime's fingers began to play with her pussy, stroking apart her thighs so that the pleasure of her caresses make Mila's feet slide a little further apart. Half-swooning with pleasure, she leant back against the wall of the cubicle, the tiles cold against her overheated flesh.

The gold ring shifted slightly as Jaime's fingers toyed with her now-shaven pubis, provoking another wave of unbearable sensation.

'Beautiful,' whispered Jaime. 'Have you any idea how you make me feel?'

Mila had no chance to answer, for in the next moment Jaime was throwing off her shirt and jeans, tearing at the buttons and throwing the sodden clothes out on to the bathroom floor. Underneath she was wearing a thin cotton crop-top in place of a bra, and white briefs cut in a masculine style. Mila could not help feeling intense stirrings of lust at the sight of Jaime's arousal, her hard nipples like pink rosebuds underneath the wet, stretchy cotton.

'Won't you undress me, Mila?' coaxed Jaime, taking Mila's hands and placing them so that they cupped her small, pert breasts. At the feeling of another woman's breasts in her hands, a sudden gush of warm sex-juice trickled out of Mila's parted labia. 'Please, Mila, I want to feel you stripping me. I want to feel your fingers on my breasts.'

Automatically, almost mechanically, Mila obeyed the impulse of her lust so eloquently expressed in Jaime's soft whisperings. Her fingers slipped smoothly under the elasticated bottom edge of the crop-top, feeling the taut smoothness of Jaime's skin. An electric thrill tingled into her as her fingertips made contact with the underside of the American girl's breasts, experiencing for the very first time the feel of another woman's aroused body.

'Pull it up. Please Mila, I can't bear it. Pull it up. I so want you to suck my tits.'

THE GOLDEN CAGE

It was almost as if the situation had been suddenly reversed. One moment, Jaime was in complete control, the experienced lesbian lover seducing the novice into guilty, mysterious pleasure; the next, Jaime was the supplicant, begging her new lover to take control and take pity on her need.

For a few seconds, Mila had the oddest sensation of objectivity Even in the red mist of her desire, she knew that if she wanted she could walk away from this situation, say no to Jaime and Jaime would be powerless to force her. But if she wanted, she could choose to stay. She could choose to explore what Jaime had promised to show her.

In a wild, crazy act of lust, she chose pleasure.

Her hands slid right up underneath Jaime's top and took hold of her breasts. The nipples felt hot and hard and seemed to pulse with the urgent need that Mila now shared.

Hungry now, she squeezed the apple-firm globes, her body aching with desire as she felt Jaime at her touch.

'Oh. Oh yes, Mila. Do that some more. Strip me and rub me and kiss me.'

Although this was an entirely new experience for Mila, she now scarcely needed Jaime's words to guide her. Her hands seemed to know what Jaime wanted her to do. While her left hand caressed Jaime's breast, her right pushed up the cotton-top, sliding the tight, wet fabric up so that both breasts were fully exposed. Jaime lifted her arms and Mila slid the top off over her head, letting it fall into the swirling whirlpool at her feet.

'Kiss me . . .'

Jaime's voice tailed off as Mila's lips tentatively sought out hers, and they kissed again. This time, Mila's tongue penetrated Jaime's mouth, eagerly exploring the warm, welcoming wetness. At last her lips left Jaime's and began the long, slow descent from lips to cheek to chin and throat and down, down, down, with agonising slowness, to the pert crests of her nipples.

Her whole body vibrating to the rhythm of her desire, Jaime slid her right leg forward, pushing it gently between Mila's thighs. Taken by surprise, Mila welcomed this new caress, opened herself to it, parting her thighs still more so that Jaime's thigh pushed right up against the hidden heart of her womanhood. She gasped and moaned, her lips tightening about Jaime's nipple as the burning-hot sensations of lust rippled through her, from clitoris to belly and breasts, until her whole body seemed aflame with the need to climax.

'Sweetheart. Sugar-honey,' murmured Jaime, her leg moving rhythmically between Mila's thighs, sliding slowly back and forth, never letting the sensations fade even for a second. 'I could bring you off like this, sweetheart. Would you like that? And then I could bring you off again.'

Mila was past knowing what she wanted; only what she needed. And what she needed was the great, crashing climax which was building up in her sex. The slippery-wet juices of her need were dripping from her now, their clear wet trickles smearing across Jaime's thigh whilst runnels of warm water spiralled and trickled down her own thighs. She began moving her hips to the rhythm of Jaime's lovemaking, masturbating herself, bringing herself closer to the summit of pleasure. And all the time she was licking and biting, sucking hard on Jaime's nipple.

Jaime took hold of Mila's hand, this time guiding it down until it was on her pubis.

'I want you,' she groaned. 'And I want you to taste how much I want you.'

THE GOLDEN CAGE

As Mila felt the plumpness of Jaime's pubis through the thin veil of her wet panties, it began. That familiar, unstoppable sensation which began as a deep, sensuous warmth and spread, magnifying and multiplying until the whole body held its breath, waiting for the moment.

'Oh! Oh, oh, aaah!'

Mila's climax made her whole body jerk, forcing her vulva down hard against Jaime's thigh, so that the intensity of the pleasure was both prolonged and augmented, taken to that hairsbreadth line between extreme joy and agony.

Jaime held her close, one hand stroking her long, wet hair, the other pulling her tightly against her bare breasts, savouring the delicious discomfort as pleasure tensed Mila's body, making her bite harder into the rubbery flesh of her nipple.

'Will you?' Jaime's voice floated into Mila's dizzy consciousness, an unreal whisper. 'Will you taste my pussy? Will you lick me out?'

The ache of ebbing ecstasy seemed to go on for ever, leaving Mila on a high. It was like living a dream, being in a place where you could do anything. Anything at all. Nothing felt wrong, not even licking out another woman's sex.

She slid down Jaime's body until her face was on a level with her panties. They clung like a second skin, the wet cotton so transparent that it hid nothing – neither the dark cushion of her pubic hair, nor the strong, musky scent of her arousal. She felt Jaime's hand on her hair, caressing, soothing, urging.

'Please, Mila. I want you so much. Won't you do this for me? I'd do it for you.'

It seemed right. It even felt right. For the first time

since she had left St Petersburg, Mila actually felt as if the pleasure she was experiencing was innocent, guileless. She hooked her fingers under the waistband of Jaime's pants and slid them down, peeling them slowly and sensually over slim hips, tanned thighs, revealing a plump and tender sex.

She hesitated. Should she? Could she? She had never even dreamed of having sex with another woman, not until today. Was it possible that she'd been hiding these feelings for years, or was what she was feeling just gratitude? Perhaps she would never know.

Uncertain at first, she put out her tongue, flicking it lightly over the sodden maidenhair. It tasted good, a mixture of the saltiness of this shower gel and the sweetness of Jaime's own juices.

'Go on. It's all right. Taste me, I want you. I need you.'

Jaime opened her thighs, opening herself to Mila. Stroking her hair, she pushed her lover's face gently against the dark triangle of her pubis.

'I'm so wet for you, Mila. Wetter than I've been in a long, long time.'

The scent of her lover's blossoming sex made Mila thirsty for Jaime's sweet elixir. It trickled freely from between the plump, coral-pink petals of her vulva, glistening and slippery, scented with the sweet spiciness of musk.

Holding Jaime's thighs, Mila pressed her face into the soft wetness of her vulva, letting her tongue probe the tropical paradise, scooping up the honeydew with a strange new eagerness.

It tasted good, incredibly good. So sweet, with an aftertaste of bitterness that made her thirsty for more and

THE GOLDEN CAGE

yet more. She had left all reason behind, and all she could think about now was the desire burning her up, the throbbing between her thighs.

As she explored Jaime's sex, Mila's tongue-tip glanced across the head of her clitoris and her lover let out a sharp cry of anguish.

'Ah! Gently now, I'm so hot for you it hurts. Do it again. Gently now, gently, oh yes...'

Tutored by Jaime, Mila began licking her again, this time avoiding the exposed head of her clitoris and instead licking around it, making little circular motions which forced the fleshy hood back and forth over the pink stalk, now baring it, now covering it. Mila knew that it must feel good, because Jaime was moaning a wordless song of joy, and all the time honeysweet liquid was trickling out of her on to Mila's upturned face.

On impulse, she slid her index finger between Jaime's thighs and stroked it along the deep, wet furrow of her sex. Jaime groaned and thrust her pelvis forward, silently begging for more, more, more. Mila's fingernail teased the entrance to her tiny, tight vagina, stroking and gently scratching, smoothing the wet secretions round and round as she kept on lapping at Mila's love-bud.

In a single, smooth movement she slipped her finger inside Jaime's vagina. To her astonishment, it would not swallow the full length, and her fingertip came up against something tough, unyielding.

'The first, Mila,' she heard Jaime murmur. 'You're the first. The only one.'

With a shock Mila realised that she was pushing against Jaime's hymen, that Jaime was a virgin. That she had never, ever had a man inside her.

A moment later, she felt Jaime come, her orgasm

tightening the vaginal walls so hard that it was almost painful for Mila, the flesh tightly clenching, holding her finger inside.

She could scarcely breathe, for Jaime was holding her face pressed hard against her pussy lips, her head thrown back and moaning her pleasure in words that only she could understand. Cascades of sweet juice covered her face, and she drank it down greedily, each droplet inflaming her own desire.

At last it was over, and Jaime took her by the shoulders, drawing her up until they were face to face. Jaime kissed the taste of her own juices from Mila's face. Mila was trembling, she didn't know why, as Jaime took her by the hand and led her towards the bedroom.

'I'm gonna take you back with me to Texas. Oh, honey, it's gonna be so great, just you and me. I'll take good care of you, no one's ever gonna hurt you again.'

'I . . . no.'

'You're mine now, Mila. Mine to take care of – and I will, I promise I will.'

Keeping her eyes on the road, Jaime slipped her hand on to Mila's thigh, squeezing it through the white cotton drill of her jeans. Mila flinched, afraid of the sensations she felt: the uncomfortable mixture of excitement and repulsion.

'Jaime, I don't think . . .'

Jaime shook her head dismissively.

'Don't you worry, he won't find you. And if he did, I'd kill him. I know how to handle a gun. Relax. Everything's going to be fine from now on.'

As the car sped westwards into the gathering dusk, Mila felt a ache tighten around her heart, a sickness in the pit of

THE GOLDEN CAGE

her stomach. What had she done? What had she got herself into this time? Jaime had been so, so kind to her. And yet ... was it really kindness, or was it just lust, the need to possess? She had the horrible feeling that with Jaime, she would be as much a slave as she had been with Orin Hobart. No matter how you looked at it, a cage was still a cage.

'You've been really good to me, Jaime,' began Mila, her mouth dry with the realisation of what she had to say. She'd been working up to it ever since they left the Sweet Dreams motel that morning, but if anything, that just made it harder.

'That's OK, hon. You know how I feel about you.'

'Y-yes. That's why I have to leave you.'

Jaime did not react for a few long moments, but just kept on driving, the only sign that she had heard a slight tremble in her hands.

'Don't talk nonsense, sugar.'

'It's not nonsense.' Mila felt her eyes blurring with the beginnings of tears and wiped them ruthlessly away. The last thing she needed, right now, was to fall apart at the seams. But it seemed so cruel, besides which Jaime was offering her the chance to get a good long way from Orin Hobart, make a new life ... 'I have to go. You've been wonderful to me, but ... but I just don't feel the same way you do.'

Jaime's voice sounded curiously flat, as though she was trying to keep her emotions in check.

'You can't leave me. Not now. Back at the motel ...'

'I was lonely and afraid. You were good to me.'

'You *wanted* me. Don't try to tell me you didn't.'

'I'm not.' Oh, why was this so difficult? But she had to do it, and now. 'That was beautiful, but it wasn't me. You understand? I'm straight, Jaime. If I stayed with you I couldn't make you happy.'

'But Mila . . . you're mine. I found you and you're mine. You have to stay with me.'

Jaime's voice was very quiet, and for a moment Mila was afraid. Then she saw the tear trickling down Jaime's cheek. She stroked it away, leaned over and kissed her lightly.

'Someone else thought that,' she said. 'But he was wrong, too.'

Jaime tried a different tack.

'You can't leave me, it's dangerous for you, you told me so. Stay with me just a while longer, maybe you'll change your mind.'

Cars flashed past on the freeway, a long straight ribbon leading from yesterday to tomorrow. She shook her head.

'Let me go, Jaime.'

Jaime did not answer for a while. Then she took a deep breath.

'I'll take you to the next town, right?'

'No, please. Tonight.'

'Here? In the middle of nowhere?'

'There's a . . . what do you call it? . . . a truckstop just ahead.' She nodded to an illuminated sign in the shape of a giant hamburger. 'Drop me there!'

'It's not safe.'

'I'll manage.'

Jaime swung the car into the forecourt.

'You're sure?' Jaime took hold of Mila's hand as she turned to open the car door.

'I'm sure.' Mila clasped Jaime's hand briefly, then gently pulled away. 'Thank you, Jaime. Thank you for everything.'

THE GOLDEN CAGE

Then she walked away towards the truckstop diner, hardly daring to look back in case she changed her mind.

'Well, hi there, sweet thing.'
'Wanna spend a little time with me?'
'You all alone, little lady?'

The inside of the Onestop Diner was something of a culture shock. Raucous catcalls and whistles greeted Mila as she walked in and crossed to the counter. Pinball machines and a CD jukebox added to the general cacophony, and for a few seconds Mila just wanted to cover her ears and make it all go away. With a jolt she realised she was the only woman in the place. Jaime had been right. It wasn't safe.

But it was too late to change her mind now. She'd get a meal, take some time out to think about what she was going to do next. Sliding on to one of the seats by the counter she picked up the menu.

The man behind the bar was in his forties; the typical greasy-aproned short-order cook. He leered appreciatively at Mila as she sat down.

'What can I getcha then?'
'I ... er ... a cup of coffee and a hamburger, please.'
'Kingsize or regular?'
'I don't know.' She felt incredibly stupid and ignorant. A two-month university exchange trip to Liverpool had hardly prepared her for life in the USA.

'Kingsize, huh? I reckon you're a lady who likes things *big*, am I right?'

It was impossible to miss the innuendo, particularly as he was rubbing his cock through his pants as he spoke. But Mila decided to play it dumb.

'Regular will be fine.'

'Where you from?'

'Poland,' she lied, she wasn't quite sure why.

'That so? My cousin shacked up with a girl from Krakow once. Great tits.' He pushed the coffee and burger across the counter, followed by the check. 'Bit like yours.' He grinned. 'Enjoy your meal.'

'Yeah. Thanks.' Creep, she muttered in Russian under her breath, as she felt in her pocket for the money.

The money!

She could picture it now, sitting in the pocket of Carey Ronstein's dinner jacket – on the back seat of Jaime's car. As she put her hand into the pocket of the denim jacket Jaime had bought her, her fingers came into contact with only two things: a scrunched-up tissue and Orin Hobart's stupid model of a jade tiger. She almost threw it across the diner in frustration.

'You gotta problem with that?' demanded the cook.

Mila's mind whirled in the darkness of confusion.

'I've lost my purse,' she lied.

'Oh yeah?' The cook's tongue flicked over his lips, as though he were savouring the prospect of an appetising meal. He caught her by the wrist and she almost panicked. 'Well, there's other ways of payin' your way, if ya get my meanin'.'

A thousand unpleasant pictures reeled through Mila's mind. Pictures of the training room at Orin Hobart's mansion. Pictures of herself cast in the role of victim, yet again. No! She tried to get up, but he had her wrist fast. She glanced around, hoping one of the truckers would help her, but they were studiedly looking in the opposite direction.

'Look, I'm sorry,' she said.

THE GOLDEN CAGE

'No need to be sorry. Just do me a few favours and you can have all the hamburger you can eat, know what I mean?' With his free hand, he unzipped his pants.

A new voice, a very different voice, broke through the deadlock.

'Excuse me, but is this man bothering you?'

Mila swung round, and her jaw dropped. They had only met once, briefly, but she recognised him instantly. He smiled, his mind and body aching with the pleasurable reminiscence of their last, tantalising encounter

'I ... I'm fine. I just lost my purse, that's all. I haven't any money...' She flushed crimson with embarrassment.

'No problem.' Greg Delaney flashed a dark look across the counter, and with the utmost reluctance, the cook let go of Mila's wrist and slid up his zipper. 'Right. How much does the lady owe?'

Chapter 10

After settling the bill, Greg Delaney joined Mila outside the Onestop Diner. The night had turned chilly, and she looked frail and vulnerable in that little denim jacket, those dark eyes huge and lustrous in that pale, oval face. Lost, too. Just what was she doing out here, on her own, in the middle of the night?

She turned to look at him. Half smiled. His cock reared in his pants. Down boy, he commanded it, but then it had always had a wayward streak.

'Thank you,' she said, in that husky, slightly exotic voice. 'For what you did in there.'

He shrugged. The narcissistic part of him rather fancied being the object of this beautiful young woman's undying gratitude, but when all was said and done he hadn't exactly done much, had he? Just paid her bill and got her out of that place in one piece.

'At your service,' he said, grinning.

In fact he couldn't stop grinning. He'd been having wet dreams about this girl ever since he'd seen her on the flight from St Petersburg, and now, incredibly, he had met up with her again. Common sense told him that getting even slightly involved with her would only complicate his already-complicated life – not to mention hers. But he'd never been very good at taking his own advice.

Perhaps he was just being led by his dick, but somehow he felt there was more to it than that. He'd met her once and couldn't get her out of his mind. What would it feel like if he let her go a second time?

'Where's your car?' he enquired. She looked so cold and forlorn in that thin jacket, completely different from the way she'd looked on the plane – all sharp suit and immaculate make-up. All he wanted to do was put his arms around her and squeeze that beautiful body. Maybe kiss her all over . . .

'Car?' Her face registered confusion, then realisation. 'I haven't got a car.'

'Then how did you get here?' He surveyed the neon-tinged darkness, the occasional car or lorry rumbling past and into the distance.

He watched her face, could almost see her brain working as it formulated the lie.

'I hitched.'

'Really?' He tried not to sound too disbelieving. He supposed it could be true, though a hunch told him it wasn't.

'Really.' This time she was more confident. She'd thought it through. 'I'm here on a . . . what do you call it? . . . Рюкзак? – a backpacking holiday. Someone gave me a lift, but he turned out . . . well, it didn't work out so I made him let me out of the car.'

'And he took your money and all your things?'

'Yes.'

She didn't look like someone on a backpacking holiday. Greg wondered why she needed to lie to him. But then again, he would almost certainly have to lie to her if she asked him any awkward questions. The last thing he wanted to do was drag her into the bottomless swamp of his

THE GOLDEN CAGE

troubles. She certainly didn't deserve to become a part of all that. Maybe he'd better resist temptation and not offer her a lift after all . . .

'Fancy a lift?' he asked, as casually as he could with a mouth as dry as a bag of Hoover fluff. So much for self-control.

It was strange how her facial expressions changed. Pleasure, then the shadow of something darker, something that looked like suspicion, or something darker still. Pure, naked fear.

'No. It's kind of you to offer, but no.'

'But how will you get away from here?' he pointed out.

'I . . . don't know. I'll think of something.'

'You know it's not safe here? All those gorillas back there in the café . . .'

She smiled, a little bleakly.

'And I'd be safer with you, would I?'

Greg could have kicked himself. It was obvious she'd had a bad experience, even before that bonehead had made a grab for her in the restaurant. The last thing she needed was some creepy guy trying to lure her into his car.

'You're right of course,' he sighed. 'For all you know I'm some sort of pervert or an axe-murderer or something.' He reached into his pocket and took out two fifty-dollar bills. 'Look, if you won't let me give you a lift, at least take these. You look like you need all the help you can get.'

He stuffed them into her hand, curled the fingers over the palm and set off across the parking lot to the embarrassingly battered Chevrolet. Mila watched him, open-mouthed with astonishment, aching for the golden-haired Englishman and wondering if she dared be stupid enough to trust him, even for a moment.

For his part, Greg wished he was driving something a little more impressive. The old heap did nothing to bolster his image as a solid citizen. It might once have been a gleaming seducer of a car, but now it looked like a casualty from some crap seventies' cop series. Still, unimpressive meant unobtrusive, and right now Greg couldn't afford to draw too much attention to himself.

He stuck the key in the lock; as usual it jammed. So much for Mr Smooth. He aimed a kick at the nearside hub-cap and it fell off with a clatter. Somewhere behind, he heard laughter. Great, so now she was pissing herself laughing at him. He bent down, retrieved the hub-cap and turned to face Mila. Her face was a picture. Maybe it was pent-up tension, maybe it was relief, but she just kept on laughing until the tears came.

'You're offering me a lift in *that*?' she gasped through the giggles.

'It's the only way to travel,' retorted Greg. 'Believe me, you have to experience it to appreciate it.' Life was so bloody peculiar at the moment that all you could do was laugh. 'I suppose this means no?' he added ruefully.

'Well . . .' Mila could hardly believe she was even contemplating this.

'Look, it's OK.' Greg succeeded in unlocking the driver's door, leaned in and threw the hub-cap on to the back seat. 'Good luck. I hope it works out for you.' He got in, closed the door, started the engine. He didn't want to look at her, she was too hellishly beautiful. He wanted her too much for his own good – or hers.

As the car slid into gear and began to move off, he saw Mila walking towards him, and wound down the window, slowing to walking pace.

'Does this mean you've changed your mind?'

THE GOLDEN CAGE

'I don't know . . . maybe.'

'Drive you to the next town and take it as it comes?' Their eyes met and he felt the incredible heat pass between them. The heat of lust. 'What do you say?'

She hesitated only for a moment, then nodded.

'OK.' She opened the passenger door and slid in beside him, her thigh briefly brushing his as she wriggled on to the seat and leant over to fasten her seatbelt. Her sensuality seemed to crackle in the air between them, like static electricity. Oh how he wanted her . . .

'Did you know you speak English with a Liverpool accent? It's been bothering me ever since I first spoke to you on the plane. How does a lady from St Petersburg get a Scouse accent?'

She laughed.

'And how does an Englishman like you come to be driving a car like this?' she countered. Her lips glistened, moist and so kissable. Greg forced himself to keep his eyes on the road.

'I don't even know your name,' he said, as casually as he could manage. 'You wouldn't tell me, remember?'

'I remember,' replied Mila softly.

She didn't know why, but she desperately wanted to trust this Englishman. And more than that, she wanted to go to bed with him. Was that totally insane? Maybe he was out to destroy her, but then again, maybe the whole world was out to do that. Sometimes you just had to take a chance.

'My name's Mila,' she told him, and this time when her thigh brushed against his, the touch was not accidental. 'Mila Kirovska.'

It was a great party. Not so much a party as an orgy, but

then Darsey O'Brien and her colleague Caleb Steadman were accustomed to depravity. It was their job. They feasted upon it.

The poolside area at Jac Tyrone's villa formed the focus of the evening's entertainment. Tyrone, a fabulously wealthy maker of underground sex-films, had bought the house in the Hollywood hills as a hideaway: somewhere he could go to entertain in his own personal style, make a few of his more outrageous movies, live life the way he liked to live it, free from outside interference.

For Tyrone, that meant a place where he could keep and train his slaves. Tonight, noted Darsey O'Brien, several of them were in evidence: pretty boys and girls dressed in leather and chains. Finest leather and silver chains, of course: Jac Tyrone would have nothing but the best.

In the pool, illuminated by underwater lamps in pink and green, a black man and a Navajo girl were swimming naked, their bodies eerily unreal in the ripples of coloured light. Darsey felt a flicker of interest as she watched them coupling, the man's huge penis like black marble as it slid between the girl's willing thighs and she rode him, head thrown back and jewelled breasts sparkling in the artificial light.

'So what do you think of my entertainment?' enquired Tyrone. He was lying on his back on a sunbed, enjoying the ministrations of two Chinese girls who were licking cream from his naked body.

'Very fine,' replied Steadman. 'But then again, Mr Tyrone, your parties are always a success. I know people who would kill for an invitation . . .'

Tyrone laughed. The idea appealed to him, excited him even. Anyone who had seen his films knew how closely he liked to associate pleasure, pain, even death. Some said

THE GOLDEN CAGE

they were 'brilliant masterpieces of macabre sensuality.' Others simply called them sick.

'And so to what do I owe the honour of this visit?' His plummy voice, somehow curiously appropriate for a magnificent pervert like Jac Tyrone, rose with ease above the cacophony of shrieks and laughter as the party hotted up.

'We've been engaged to look for someone.' Darsey O'Brien sat down next to Tyrone and shooed away the two Chinese slaves. She knew just how to deal with Tyrone to get what she wanted. 'We thought you might be able to help us, give us some ... guidance.' She bent over Tyrone and, very delicately, licked a thick gobbet of cream from the stiff shaft of his penis. He gave a murmur of appreciation.

'Is that so? Well, as you know I'm always pleased to see you both, especially you, Darsey. It's such a pity you're dedicated to investigation work, my dear, I have always thought you would make the perfect slave. After a little training, of course.'

Darsey bent over him a second time, this time digging her sharp fingernails into his scrotum as she licked cream from the dome of his glans.

'Sweet slut,' he gasped. 'Oh, you hot, delicious bitch.' He slid his hand under Darsey's skirt and right up the length of her stocking-clad thigh. No panties, just the way he liked her. 'OK, what d'you want to know?'

'We're looking for this girl.' Steadman took Hobart's photograph of Mila from his jacket pocket and handed it to Tyrone.

'Mmm, pretty little bitch isn't she? What's her name?'

'Mila. Ludmila Kirovska. She's Russian.'

'And why are you looking for her?'

'She's an escaped slave,' replied Steadman. 'She had entered into a binding business arrangement with our client. She reneged and we've been retained to bring her back.'

'Ah, I see.' Tyrone licked his lips. 'I wouldn't mind a slave like her myself. She looks ideal: a little spirit makes discipline all the more pleasurable, don't you think? I'd like to put her in one of my movies, see those pretty lips around Big Carlo's dick.' He nodded towards a tall, naked Hispanic who was drinking iced beers with a group of businessmen beside the barbecue. It wasn't difficult to see where he got his nickname from.

'But have you seen her?' demanded Steadman.

Tyrone shook his head.

'Regrettably, no. And if I had, I might well have kept her for myself. By the way.' He took a sip from a lurid cocktail. 'Who *is* your client?'

Steadman paused. He didn't normally give out confidential information.

'Orin Hobart,' cut in O'Brien, flashing Steadman a look that said 'I know what I'm doing.'

'Really.' Tyrone chuckled to himself. It was no secret that he and Hobart were deadly rivals. 'Well, well. I would have thought Mr Hobart would have been a little more careful with valuable possessions like this one.'

'Can you help us?'

'I might he able to.'

'Where do you think the girl could be heading?'

'It's hard to tell. She has no passport, of course, no papers to identify her?'

'Of course not. Mr Hobart took care of that.'

'Then she has to be still in the country. A vulnerable girl like that, alone . . . well, there are plenty of men who would pay to possess her. I will make enquiries. And in the meantime . . .' He laughed. 'You may be interested to

THE GOLDEN CAGE

know a few things I've heard about Mr Orin Hobart and his business activities.'

'Greg?'

Greg turned to his companion. Her elbow was resting on the open car window and her dark hair fluttering prettily in the slip stream. It was all he could do to keep his mind on his driving.

'Hmm?'

'Where are we?'

Greg shrugged.

'I'm not sure. Somewhere in New York State. I think we passed through Syracuse, but that was ages ago. You reckon we should have stuck to the main roads?'

Mila gave a dry laugh.

'You were supposed to be dropping me off, remember? "Just a lift to the next town", that's what you said.'

'Yeah. Sorry.' He flashed her an ingenuous grin. 'Guess I forgot.'

'Guess we both did.'

Mila's voice was low and sexy and Greg wondered – no, hoped – that it meant what he thought it meant. Did she feel the same way about him as he did about her?

'I'll drop you off at the next place we come to, if that's what you want,' he hazarded. 'Scout's honour.'

Mila turned to look at him, her eyes dark and lustrous in her pale face. She was smiling, the most relaxed he had seen her since they'd met.

'Maybe.'

'Mind you, I'd rather spend some more time with you,' he found himself confessing. 'I ... I've enjoyed it. How about you?'

She smiled.

'So far, so good – that's what you say in English, isn't it?' Their eyes locked for just a split second and she wondered if she could bear the intensity. Surely there was no mistaking the lightning-flash of need that had passed between them. Her fingers slipped from the dashboard and lingered, for just a moment, on his forearm. It was muscular, hard, beneath the golden tanned skin sprinkled with dark-blonde hairs.

'You'll need to get some more clothes and things,' went on Greg, talking garbage to keep his mind off sex. 'And I expect you'll want to contact the Russian Embassy, or something? I mean, if you've lost your passport...'

He could not fail to notice the look of alarm on Mila's face.

'I don't think so. Not yet, anyway.'

'Is there something wrong? Something you haven't told me about?'

Mila forced a smile

'No, of course not. Why should there be?'

'No reason.'

They drove on a little further. Greg had been feeling like a nervous teenager for hours now, overheated and awkward. It was late afternoon but it was getting warm, too warm for comfort. He rolled up the sleeves of his crumpled cotton shirt.

'Anyhow.' remarked Mila, raking her fingers through her hair and shaking it free of her forehead. 'You're a bit of a mystery yourself. You haven't really told me what you're doing in the States.'

'I'm on holiday, I told you. I decided to drive across America, coast to coast. The pretty way.'

'In *this* car?'

'It's very ... authentic. I borrowed it from a friend.'

THE GOLDEN CAGE

Which was true. The bit about the car and the friend, anyway. The bit about being on holiday, well . . . what else could he tell her? Though he did feel he owed her some sort of explanation. But time was short, and he couldn't be sure when or how his troubles would catch up with him. Right now, he just wanted to enjoy what he had – while it lasted.

Mila smiled.

'I thought a man like you would drive something a little more luxurious.' Her long, slender fingers caressed the dashboard. Greg's vivid imagination pictured them caressing his prick and suddenly his 5Ols felt much, much too tight.

'Like what?'

'I don't know . . . a businessman's car. When I saw you on the plane, you looked like a wealthy businessman. Not like a man who drives across America in – in a car like this.' She laughed, stroking the sun-warmed vinyl. 'You're crazy.'

'Cheek!' Greg patted the wheel. 'It's a great car this, a real Yankee classic. We could put the soft top down if you like, pretend we're Thelma and Louise.'

'Thelma and . . . ?'

'Sorry, my favourite road movie. Didn't much care for the ending though. Look, you would tell me if there was anything wrong, wouldn't you?'

'I told you, there's nothing wrong. I just got into a little trouble, met a bad person, OK?'

'OK.'

Thelma and Louise, thought Greg to himself. Yeah, or Bonnie and Clyde. He had the distinct feeling that he wasn't the only one around here with a secret to keep.

Mila felt her eyes closing. The sun was setting and it had been a long, long day. After all she'd been through, was it any wonder she was tired out? Funny how, despite everything and all the lessons she had learned, she was beginning to feel safe with Greg Delaney. She didn't entirely believe his story about the holiday, but then again did he believe hers? Something about this blue-eyed, thirty-something Englishman made it difficult not to trust him.

Greg glanced across.

'We'll stop at a motel if you like? Assuming I ever manage to get us back on the right road.'

Mila closed her eyes, drowsy and warm.

'No need. I can sleep in the car.'

As she drifted off to sleep, she slipped a little sideways and Greg felt her heaviness resting against his shoulder, the long, dark curtain of her hair almost obscuring her face.

He knew he shouldn't, but he couldn't resist it. It wasn't as if he had much left to lose – except perhaps Mila, of course. Listening to the soft, whispering rhythm of her breathing, he pushed aside a lock of hair and brushed his lips, very tenderly, against her cheek.

'Forty-thousand bloody damns!'

Mila jolted awake as Greg thumped the dashboard and the car stuttered to a halt. Her heart was pounding, her thoughts hopelessly confused. In her dream, she had been transported suddenly to Orin Hobart's villa, locked in an airless room with bars on the darkened windows.

'Нет, нет . . . Я не могу. I cannot, please . . . !'

She was shaking and thrashing about, only half awake. Startled and alarmed, Greg turned to her, taking her by the shoulders and holding her still, wondering what in God's name had made her eyes so wild, what had made these cold beads of sweat stand out on her white skin.

'Mila, it's me. What's wrong with you? It's me, Greg,

THE GOLDEN CAGE

don't you understand? It's OK, it's my stupid fault. We've just run out of petrol that's all'

Mila's wide-eyed stare relaxed a little, her body slumping in Greg's arms. Instinctively he stroked her and she burrowed against him like a frightened little animal.

'What was it, Mila?' he whispered.

I can't tell you, I want to but I can't.'

'OK, OK, I won't ask again, I promise. You don't have to tell me anything if you don't want to. But it was bad, wasn't it, what happened to you?'

She nodded and he drew her towards him again, kissing her now.

'It was bad and I'm afraid it will come back.'

'Not if I have anything to do with it.'

What was he promising her now? He could hardly believe he'd said that. What could he offer her but even more insecurity and danger? But something in her – her fragility, her hidden strength he did not know quite what – made him ache for her. He'd promised himself he wouldn't take advantage of her, the way others obviously had; but now he could feel himself losing control, giving in to the powerful urge that condemned him to a delicious servitude.

His lips were dry and burning as he darted kisses over her upturned, shivering face, her trembling neck and throat and the bare skin of her shoulder where the open-necked shirt had slipped down.

'I'm sorry,' he said. 'I'm sorry for what happened to you, but I won't let it happen to you again. Not if there's breath left in my body.'

As Greg's hands crept down her back, stroking her, soothing her, Mila knew that even if he was lying to her, she would listen to his lies. His kisses inflamed her, his touch was enough to make her body sing with delight.

He cradled her in his arms, holding her to him, gently easing open the buttons of her shirt.

'What . . . ?' she murmured as she felt his hand on her bare skin.

'I'm making love to you,' he replied.

'Oh. Greg, I don't know . . .'

'Tell me to stop if this isn't what you want and I will. I give you my word I will.'

His lips brushed her closed eyelids and she let out a little sigh. He felt her growing less tense in his arms, and then she reached up and pulled his face down to hers, joining their mouths in a long, long kiss that seemed to draw his soul out of his body.

She was lying across the front passenger seat, reclined back so that it was almost horizontal. Greg hadn't made out in a car since he was seventeen, but it was a skill he hadn't forgotten. Besides, he would have gone through hell for just five seconds of Mila Kirovska's breathtaking nakedness.

Mila, eyes half-closed and hands roaming over his body, lay beneath him, her body moving sinuously on the old moquette seat. She was speaking to him, but her words meant nothing to him – soft, wild, almost primitive murmurings, Slavonic and darkly sensual. Still, he had no need of words to understand what she was telling him.

He unfastened the last button of her shirt and it fell open, revealing plump breasts encased in a simple underwired brassiere of white broderie anglaise, almost virginal yet profoundly alluring, the tiny holes in the embroidered panels displaying the beauty of the flesh beneath – pink, white, dusky and sweet.

'You're a dream,' he murmured. 'A dream some true. I can't believe this is happening to me . . . it's not real . . .'

THE GOLDEN CAGE

It wasn't the first time over the last few days that Greg had had a sense of unreality, of living in something dreamed up by Dali or Kafka. But it was the first time that that dream had changed for the better and become something beautiful, desirable, wonderful.

Mila Kirovska wasn't the first beautiful woman he had made love to – not by a long, long way. But she was the first to captivate him with just a look, a touch, a breath. She was a drug and he was hooked.

She looked up at him with those dark, dark eyes and he was lost.

'I want you,' she breathed. 'I want you to make love to me, you crazy Englishman.'

I want to lose myself, she thought to herself. *Even if only for one night, I want to lose myself in this dream, find out how good it can be again to have a man's kisses on my breasts and his cock inside me.*

It was a velvet-dark night, with a thousand stars glinting in the cocooning blackness. Few cars came along this remote highway and fewer still noticed the old Chevy parked half-on, half-off the roadway. In the darkness, Mila and Greg discovered each other by the dull orange glow of the car's interior light. But they needed no light, for their other senses showed them the way – touch guided their fingers to the most sensitive places; taste and smell sought out the fragrant, spicy juices of desire.

Easing off his lover's shirt, Greg reached behind Mila's back and released the catch on her bra. It yielded silently, the elasticated straps springing forward and the cups slackening their grasp on her breasts.

He gasped as she reached up and pulled off her brassiere.

H. The tiny black letter was crudely but efficiently tattooed into the flesh of Mila's left breast. He traced it wonderingly with the tip of his index finger and, for the first time, felt her flinch.

'No questions,' she breathed. 'Please, you promised.'

'No questions.' He bent over her and licked the hardening flesh of her nipple, loving its taste and texture on his tongue.

Mila unfastened the belt of his jeans. They were tight and the metal buttons were stretched practically to bursting by the painful swell of his cock. He had been erect for her practically continuously since he'd picked her up at the Onestop Diner and the sheer anticipation of her yearned-for touch brought him close to climax.

One, two, three; he felt the buttons pop open as her questing fingers slipped down his fly. Four, and he was free, his manhood a curving sabre springing forward, pushing against the thin black silk of his boxer shorts, now dampened by his arousal.

Mila was breathing quickly, hoarsely, her hunger overtaking any lingering doubts. Whatever terrors there might be, waiting for her around the next corner, for this one, precious night she was free. Free to explore the limits of her desire.

With fingers that shook with need, she slid down Greg's boxer shorts, easing them over the hard spike of his cock, marvelling at the simple beauty of his swollen dick, his tense and heavy balls. He let out a faraway cry of anguish as her fingertips softly grazed his hardness, stroking down the length of his shaft until they met the curly fuzz of his pubic hair. Wiry, golden hairs curled about the juicy globes of his testes, inviting kisses and caresses. When her fingers brushed against them, the skin of his scrotum tensed in delicious expectation.

'Please,' she begged. 'Please . . . on your back.'

THE GOLDEN CAGE

...h he yearned simply to unzip her jeans and slide
... did as she asked, rolling on to his back with
...icking off first his shoes, then his jeans and
... lay in a crumpled tangle over the brake
...nowhere. But he was going somewhere: on a
... the centre of Mila Kirovska's desire.

...felt curiously vulnerable, not just out of control but
...der the control of his lover. Now she was taking charge of
his desire, kneeling over him, loving him with her lips and
tongue and fingers.

'You have such beautiful skin,' she whispered. 'Such
beautiful golden hair. ангел. Like an angel.'

Her voice was another caress, her fingers simply carrying
out what her voice ordained, their touch on his skin its
corporeal form. They skated over his belly, teasing the
hairs. A shiver of pleasure ran through him like a rippling
breeze across a cornfield.

His body jerked upwards, jackknifing with sudden
delight as Mila's mouth closed over the upraised spike of
his penis. The inside of her mouth felt like hot velvet, its
tropical wetness trickling over his swollen flesh, at once
soothing and arousing.

'Oh! How do you do that . . . where did you learn to suck
like that? You're a witch . . .'

Greg was scarcely coherent any more. Desire had
numbed what reason remained in his brain and he no
longer thought in any logical way any more. His cock had
become the centre of his entire universe . . . that, and the
desire to climax inside Mila's beautiful body.

She sucked him with a gentle, subtle skill he had never
encountered before, not even among the high-class geishas
who had occasionally been provided for him by his contacts
on business trips to the Far East. There was something

different about Mila: something delicate, naïve, almost innocent; something instinctive and yet deeply, almost obscenely sensual. She was like the innocent embodiment of sensual, a woman with a virgin's touch. And that touch was carrying him far far away, on the fast track to paradise.

At last, when he was on the brink of coming, and thought he couldn't hold back, not even for one second longer, she abandoned him. She slid his cock out of her mouth and sat back on her haunches, naked to the waist, her beautiful tattooed breast stiff-tipped and quivering.

He writhed between her straddling thighs.

'Mila, you're not leaving me like this . . . are you?'

Was that it? he wondered. Was that the secret he'd been looking for when he searched the deep, dark pools of her eyes? Was she some kind of sadist, who got her kicks from taking her lovers to the edge and leaving them there?

'You want me, crazy Englishman?'

He laughed, his voice cracking with emotion and frustrated lust.

'Are you kidding, Mila? You *know* I want you. If you don't make it with me, I really will go crazy.'

'Me too,' she whispered. 'You see I'm crazy too, Greg. I'm so crazy for you I think I'll die if I don't have you.'

She bent down to kiss him and he felt for the button of her jeans, fumbled it open and felt the zipper give way, baring her belly down to the swell of her pubis, sadly veiled by her white cotton panties.

Mila knelt up and peeled her jeans down over her thighs, briefly rolling off him in order to wriggle out of her clothes. The unveiling of her nakedness was like a banquet to a starving man. He clawed at her bare thighs, transfixed by the sight of the gold ring glittering in the plump flesh of her pussy lips.

THE GOLDEN CAGE

He asked no questions. He had promised not to. And in any case, there was no time to say anything because those bare, silken thighs were sliding on either side of his hips, her taut backside moving slowly down towards the hard spike of his penis.

She took hold of his manhood, her sweat-moistened fingers slipping a little as they gripped the moist shaft. Positioning him between her thighs, she made a single smooth, downward thrust and Greg felt his brain and body explode with the pleasure of it.

He was inside her. She was astride him, one hand on the car seat and the other stroking his face as they coupled. They were moving together, and America suddenly seemed the best, the greatest, the most exhilarating place that there ever could be.

Bar none.

Chapter 11

'How was I to know there was a gas station just a mile up this road?'

Mila pouted her mock disapproval.

'It was just a trick, wasn't it? A trick to have your wicked way with me!'

'If it had been,' replied Greg, pouring the last of the petrol into the tank and shutting the bonnet, 'it would have been well worth it.'

Mila was leaning against a tree. Behind her spread dense woodland, which extended as far as the eye could see on both sides of the road. The early morning sunlight filtered between the trees, casting dappled patterns on her legs, quite bare beneath the oversized shirt.

You're a terrible temptation dressed like that,' observed Greg. 'Or should I say undressed.'

'It's summer. It's too hot for jeans.' She ran her fingers up her thigh, ruching the shirt up a little further. Too hot for panties too, thought Greg with a thrill of approval.

Mila giggled to herself. She felt peculiarly elated, like being drunk on vintage champagne. Surely even Orin Hobart wouldn't think of looking for her here in the middle of a forest? For a fleeting instant the dark shadow of her fear passed over her mind, reminding her that she was alone had no passport, no money and her former master was not a man to give up easily ... but the sunlight was warm and so were Greg's kisses. The memory of last night would stay with her for a long, long time, even if the badness caught up with her again.

'I've worked out where we are,' announced Greg.

'Where?'

'The middle of nowhere!'

'Idiot!' She threw herself at him and they wrestled, struggling half-naked on the grass verge; a struggle which ended in kisses.

'No, seriously, I do know where we are. In a couple of hours' time, if we wanted, we could be at Niagara Falls. Fancy going there?'

'Mmm, yes.' Mila drew him to her and slid her hands down his bare back, just at the moment when a battered VW camper-van came rattling past, its occupants bug-eyed with appreciative astonishment at the roadside entertainment. Whoops and catcalls erupted in the still air, but Mila and Greg didn't care.

'We can't go just yet, though,' she said.

'Why not?'

'Because there's something I want to do first.'

She took Greg by the hand and led him away from the road and into the forest. It was dark and fragrant, a dappled twilight where sudden shafts of honey-coloured sunlight dazzled in the darkness.

Twigs snapped underfoot and birds fluttered into the air, startled by the sudden intrusion. A groundhog scuttled away into the undergrowth and then there was no sound save the silence.

'Still hungry?' enquired Greg, leaning against the trunk of a tree and surveying the delicious figure of the woman who had given herself to him last night and who now, by some minor miracle, wanted more.

Mila pushed herself against him and gently nipped the crook of his neck with eager little teeth.

'Ravenous.'

'This time though,' smiled Greg, 'I think it's my turn to choose the menu.'

She was as light as swansdown, feather-light in his arms as he slid his hands under her buttocks and hoisted her up in his arms. Wrapping her legs around his waist, she put her arms about his neck and he buried his face in the beautiful valley between her breasts, still fragrant from the long night's passion. In his mind's eye he could still see the opalescent trickle of his semen, the long pearly trail running between her breasts.

He could smell the scent of his desire on those breasts and now it was awakening all over again, a new hunger to be shared and satisfied.

Holding her with one hand, he worked at her buttons with the other and quickly bared her breasts. They seemed even more beautiful in the pale green light filtering through the trees. He wondered about the tattoo, but knew he must not ask too many questions or she would run from him, as she had run from whoever it was that had done it to her.

His tongue ran down the deep valley of her cleavage. It tasted salty-strong, a pungent, piquant blend of sweat and semen. Licking at her nipples erected them into cones as delicious as cherries, biteable and juicy.

But Mila was already rubbing herself against him, her legs and backside bare, and her thighs wrapped tightly around him as she excited herself.

'So that's what you want, is it?' Greg slipped his finger

between Mila's parted bum cheeks and began to tease and stroke her.

'Oh! Oh Greg! Oh please, I can't bear it!'

Mila squealed, wriggling and laughing with pleasure as his fingertip crept along the secret furrow that ran from anus to pubis. Her juices were abundant and, as his finger reached the warm, soft heartland of her sex, he could not resist exploring her wet and willing depths, darting his fingertip into her vagina.

She was tight and so slippery-wet that she felt as though she were melting; a perfect, luxurious confection melting like sugar-candy, just for him.

'Like it, Mila?'

'Oh Greg, please!' She was breathless with laughter and excitement now.

'Don't you like it when I play with you? I could have sworn you were enjoying it!'

He slid his finger out of her and held it up to her face.

'See?' He opened his mouth and slid his finger into it, licking off the juices with intense pleasure. 'Oh Mila, you taste so good. So good, I could do this to you for ever.'

Mila's response was to tighten her thighs, grinding her pubis harder against him, desperately trying to find some relief from the burning, throbbing torment of her swollen clitoris.

'Then do it, Greg. Do it to me and don't stop.'

'Well?'

Orin Hobart's voice was clipped and impatient, with a menacing timbre which Caleb Steadman knew only too well. He tucked the receiver under his chin and beckoned to O'Brien for another quarter.

THE GOLDEN CAGE

'We haven't found the slave yet, sir, but we will. We won't let you down.'

'You already did.'

'Look, Mr Hobart, you know our methods. Stealth and subtlety – lull the subject into a false sense of security.'

'Always assuming you know where the subject is,' observed Hobart with acid sarcasm.

'Before long we shall, Mr Hobart, you have my word on that.'

'And make sure you bring me back that jade tiger as well, Mr Steadman. The bitch stole it from me.'

'We'll do what we can, but what if she's got rid of it . . . ? It's only some jade gewgaw . . .'

'You will bring it to me, intact. It is of the utmost importance to me, is that understood?'

'Understood, Mr Hobart.' Steadman mentally jabbed his middle finger into the air, making faces at Darsey O'Brien and mouthing silent obscenities.

'I hope you're not thinking of crossing me, Mr Steadman. You know what happens to people who cross me.'

'I told you, we won't let you down.'

'God, you're useless, Steadman,' cut in Darsey. 'Here, give it to me.'

O'Brien snatched the telephone receiver from her colleague.

'Listen, Hobart, and listen good. I think it's about time we made it clear just who needs who. We're your best hope – correction, we're your only hope of getting that girl back and you know it. Just think about that, next time you're thinking of shooting your mouth off.'

She replaced the receiver on its hook with a satisfying click.

'Asshole,' she observed; and Steadman wondered just

who she meant as she pulled his face down to hers and kissed him, her pierced tongue forcing a brutal entrance into his mouth. 'Now that's done, let's go find the bitch and bring her home to Daddy.'

'You really shouldn't talk like that to Hobart,' hazarded Steadman, taking her by the shoulders and pulling away, focusing on the hard blue diamonds of her eyes. 'It could be dangerous.'

'He's just another guy . . . a crook too if you can believe Jac Tyrone.'

'He's one hell of a rich guy, that's for sure. A guy with a big temper and a whole lot of dangerous friends – and enemies.'

'Just another shit-headed macho man with a dick for a brain. All men are led by their dicks.'

'Aw c'mon, Darsey . . .'

'Yes, even you. Isn't that so, Steadman?'

She clawed him like a cat, her fingers raking down his back and her hard, pointed breasts pushing against his open-necked shirt. She was pure, naked sexuality, wrapped up in a veneer of aggression so erotic that Steadman purred with pleasure.

'If this is what you mean then yeah, sure, I'm led by my dick. Wanna feel?'

He answered the force of her embrace, rubbing against her so that his swelling member, tightly imprisoned inside his pants, nuzzled against the flat firmness of her belly.

'You want her don't you, Steadman?'

'Who?'

'The slave. You want to fuck her. Don't bother saying you don't I saw the look on your face when Hobart showed you those pictures he took of her in his training room.'

'And if I do? What's it to you?'

THE GOLDEN CAGE

'I want to fuck her, too.'

'You!' He drew slightly away, momentarily taken aback. He had seen Darsey O'Brien involved in some heavy sex-scenes – had even joined her in one or two – but this was news to him.

'That's right, Steadman. I swing both ways. Why limit yourself to only fifty per cent of the population when you can have all of them? If I see a chick I want, I go for it. Girls and boys together too, doesn't that turn you on? Wouldn't you like to share a bed with me and one of my dyke lovers?'

Steadman would. He really, really would. He could picture it now, clear as day: him and Darsey O'Brien and some girl with a shaven head and tiny, hard boobs.

'Could be.'

It was hard to play it cool with O'Brien's taut belly rubbing slowly and rhythmically across the burning stalk of his penis. He wasn't wearing any underwear, and the bare tip was being abraded by the inner surface of his zipper – just gently enough to be pleasurable, just hard enough to be on the delicious margin of pain.

'So let's do it.'

Steadman put his head on one side and looked into Darsey O'Brien's eyes. You couldn't take anything she said at its face value. She was a cruel bitch, a beautifully cruel bitch.

'*Do it?*'

'She's beautiful, Steadman, you saw the pictures. All that dark hair, twisted into a rope to tie her up with. Those dark eyes, all moist and pleading. That scarlet mouth, those magnificent ass cheeks.'

'Magnificent.' Mmm, thought Steadman, more than magnificent.

And he remembered the five by seven colour photo of

Mila kneeling on the scrubbed stone floor, her arms shackled behind her back by a chain which led to a hook in the ceiling. Those full, juicy breasts, hanging like ripe fruit. That curtain of blue-black hair falling forward as she hung her head, obscuring her face so that she was reduced to a featureless symbol of perfect, selfish enjoyment.

That sweet, firm ass-curve, the smooth globes divided by a dark and tantalising fissure...

'Don't you remember how she looked, Steadman?'

When Steadman replied, his voice was dreamy and distant.

'She had a trickle of spunk running down between her thighs. I wanted to put my cock in there...'

'And I wanted to put my whole fist in there, Steadman; my whole fist uncurling inside her like a flower opening. I wanted her to scream loud as I possessed her.'

'Yes. Oh yes.' Steadman wrapped a wavy swathe of Darsey's red-blonde hair around his fist and twisted it tight, until she growled with satisfaction.

'So let's do it. Let's screw the little bitch. When we find her, let's have her, you and I, and teach her a few new tricks before we deliver her back to Hobart.'

'Could we?' Steadman thought of Hobart. Hobart would be angry if he knew, but then he wouldn't, would he? He threw back his head and laughed out loud. 'Yeah, we could, couldn't we?'

He felt Darsey's fingers working away between them, and when he looked down he saw that she had hitched up her black mini-skirt. It was a hot day and, underneath, she was wearing nothing but the tiniest of g-strings. In a second she had stepped out of it and, wiping its fragrance across Steadman's eager face, she dropped it on the roadway at her feet.

THE GOLDEN CAGE

Steadman whistled.

'You sure are one upfront bitch. Don't care who sees you, do you?'

O'Brien smiled. That special smile, like a dagger between the shoulder-blades and a kiss between the thighs, all rolled up in one.

'Oh but honey, I do. I *love* it when people see me, don't you? Don't you love it when people watch?'

She glanced behind her. It was a pity the phone booth was on a backroad and not downtown or by the side of the Interstate. But one or two cars had slowed down to get a better look as she stepped out of her panties, the drivers treated to the sight of long, slim legs and firm tanned buttocks decorated with a tiny tattooed salamander.

'Ever done it in a phone booth?' she demanded.

Steadman slipped his hand under her ruched-up skirt and slid his finger between O'Brien's thighs. It was like sliding into warm, melted butter. The well of her sex was overflowing with juice. Why not? he thought. Why the hell not.

'If that's an offer...'

She shook her head.

'It's an order. I'm the senior investigator on this case, remember.'

He took her by the waist and lifted her up so that she was sitting on the shelf which had once held a phone book. It was at exactly the right height, perfect for caressing and fucking her.

'You really don't give a damn, do you?' He ran his fingers up the insides of her thighs, already dampened with sex juice.

'Nope.'

Thighs spread wide, she looked wonderfully blatant, the

antithesis of virginal modesty. He pushed one finger inside her, then a second and a third, and her tight tunnel widened in a kiss of welcome.

'Mmm, maybe I was wrong about you, Steadman. Maybe you do know how to show a girl a good time.'

'You better believe it.' Four fingers, five ... whole fist, curled inside her and sliding upwards to the neck of her womb. O'Brien's body tensed and her fingers clutched at his shoulders.

'Yes.' Her claws bit into his flesh but he didn't care. 'Yes, yes, yes.' Her cries were staccato gasps of pleasure.

'Is this how you want it? Is this what you wanted to do to Hobart's little slave-girl?'

Steadman began uncurling his fingers, splaying them out like the petals of a flower, the spokes of a wheel, moving them round and round and in and out of her womanhood. Darsey rewarded him with growls and sighs of appreciation, and a flood of clear, slippery juice which trickled warmly from fingertips to wrist.

'Do it to me. Then do it to me some more.'

He slid his fingers in and out of her in a twisting, almost spiral motion, his knuckles pushing against the walls of her vagina and teasing that most elusive of pleasure zones, the g-spot on the front wall, quite close to the opening of her vulva. By now O'Brien was gasping and fighting to master the waves of excitement which were flooding her sex-hardened body and brain.

'Like it?' he enquired, surprisingly cool and detached though inside he was burning for her, his cock incandescent with need. Reaching down he released it from its imprisonment and it leapt free, a joyous weapon of hardened and glistening flesh.

'I want it.'

THE GOLDEN CAGE

'OK. Say please.' He felt exultant, for the first time ever truly in command of Darsey O'Brien, the cold-hearted slut who had so often used sex as a tool for manipulation. The fingers of his left hand slid lightly up and down his shaft, teasing himself into ever-greater hardness.

For once, she did not argue.

'Please.' Her lips framed the word so prettily that he almost spurted over her.

Although they were making out in a glass-walled phone booth, his back was to the passing traffic and he was half shielding her from view, his body masking the full beauty of her glistening sex. He fantasised about filming their fucking and broadcasting it on a giant video wall, fifty feet high, right above the Interstate. He wanted to think of all those drivers, their hands on their cocks as they watched Steadman and O'Brien doing just what they damn well pleased.

And as the dream drove him closer to the edge, he slid his fingers out of O'Brien's pussy and replaced them with the hot, ruthless shaft of his aching prick.

Niagara. Mila had read about it in books, seen it in old Hollywood films even, but nothing had prepared her for the reality.

The approach to the Falls had been, to say the least, disappointing, a seemingly endless procession of burger bars and fast-food joints, horrible motels and cheapjack wedding chapels. And Niagara Falls 'city' wasn't like any city she'd ever encountered – it was a sort of smelly, shabby industrial eyesore.

'It's not quite what I'd expected,' commented Mila, peering out of the window at a huge sign advertising 'Gutermann's Pure Beef Burgers'.

'It gets better,' said Greg. 'I promise you, it gets better.'
'How did it get like this?'
Greg shrugged.
'That's good old rampant capitalism for you. Take over something nature's provided free of charge and sell it to people ... don't you ever wish you were back in the good old days of the USSR?'
Mila laughed.
'It was safer then ... more secure. You knew you would have a job and food and a tiny apartment. But it was boring. I wanted something more.'
'Which is why you decided to come on holiday to the States?'
'Holiday? Oh yes – on holiday.' Her eyes met Greg's. 'Just like you.'
Greg looked away, unable to bear the intensity of that questioning gaze, or the dark thoughts it conjured up inside him. He wondered how much longer they could go on playing these games with each other.
'Anyhow, you can't come to the States without seeing the Falls. It's compulsory.'
'You've been here before then?'
'Just the once. Most of my trips to the USA have been business trips. I've never had much time just to have fun. That's why I decided on this holiday. It's good to have you with me, Mila.'
'It's good to have you too, Greg.' Mila stroked the back of Greg's hand. She was wondering, too. Wondering how long it would be before this small slice of happiness would be consumed and gone for ever. Even if Orin Hobart didn't catch up with her, this road trip would soon come to an end and what then? She decided not to think about it. 'You still haven't told me what you do for a living.'

THE GOLDEN CAGE

'Like I said, I'm a businessman. I'm a director of an electronics company. See, I told you I wasn't very interesting.'

Mila leaned over and ran her tongue down the side of his face, from temple to throat.

'Oh, but you are,' she said. 'At any rate, you interest me.' She listened for a moment, suddenly aware of a new sound above the cacophony of car engines and canned music. 'What's that noise? That roaring sound?'

'That's the Falls. You wouldn't believe how much noisier it's going to get. See!' Greg's gaze snapped forward and Mila followed suit her eyes suddenly transfixed.

There before them, like a glittering mist, hung a huge cloud of spray thrown up by the waters. And across the sky, from horizon to horizon, stretched the shimmering crescent of a perfect rainbow.

The *Maid of the Mist* bobbed about on the turbulent waters like a cork dancing on an ocean swell as it headed towards the base of the Horseshoe Falls.

Huddled beneath the boat's canopy, Mila clutched at Greg's arm, squealing with delight as the boat continued its rollercoaster progress towards the foot of the thundering waters.

Snatches of the guide's commentary floated across; against the deafening counterpoint of water crashing 180 feet into a boiling maelstrom of white foam and blinding spume.

'On the American side you can see the Bridal Veil and the American Falls, on the Canadian the famous, dramatically curving sweep of the Horseshoe Falls...'

Mila and Greg were alone at the rear of the boat, braving the deck whilst the rest of the passengers stayed near the front, protected by the thick perspex of the viewing window.

Neither spoke, but they knew they were sharing the exhilaration of the moment, the naked joy of being so very, dangerously close to nature. His hair plastered in streaks to his dripping face, Greg pulled Mila towards him and kissed her. Even on this hot summer day the water was ice-cold and she drank it from his lips, joining her pleasure to his. She was shivering but dazzlingly, wonderfully alive, and as she ran her hand down the front of Greg's pants she discovered that he too was aroused.

'... and during the nineteenth century, the tightrope-walker Blondin carried a man across the Falls on his back. Many who tried to cross in barrels were swept and crushed to their doom in the mighty waters...'

Somehow, the melodrama of the commentary seemed to add to their excitement. It was crazy of course, getting it on here and now, in a tiny boat packed with sightseers.

But then again, life was crazy.

Greg sat down on the bench which ran along the stern of the boat and Mila lowered herself slowly on to his lap. She felt his hand release the buttons on his jeans and the sudden warmth as his bare prick slid between her thighs.

His wet cold lips pressed against her shivering skin but she felt his kisses as fire, an irresistible burning, a silver blade so sharp that it penetrated her skin effortlessly, reaching into the very depths of her soul.

Her wide, floaty skirt fell in folds about her, hiding the secret of her shameless pleasure, as Greg parted her buttocks with his fingers and slipped his manhood into her welcoming haven.

Silent, she must try to keep silent. She must not show the

THE GOLDEN CAGE

pleasure which was spreading through her. She scarcely dared move, for fear that she would draw attention to their coupling. But it was so difficult not to respond to the blissful hardness within her silk-soft sex.

At first they moved slowly, imperceptibly, each tiny movement of the hips sending shivers of excitement through them. But it was not enough. Each touch multiplied the excitement, the desire for more, more, more. A touch became a kiss; a tiny movement, a long, slow thrust of the hips.

Harder, faster, more intense ... They were lost in the crashing of the waters on their upturned faces, the thundering of their hearts as they moved together as one.

Mila slipped her hand under the hem of her skirt and, as she rose; curled it underneath her, cupping Greg's balls. His cock jerked and stiffened in excitement as she thrust down again, so that the tip of his sex nudged hard against her cervix.

The beating of her heart drowned out the sound of the Falls. The blood was pounding in her veins, her breath coming in harsh, rasping gulps of air as her body readied itself for the ultimate pleasure. She couldn't hold back much longer. She was coming, coming, coming ...

At the moment of crisis, ecstasy opened her eyes. A cloud of spray surrounded them like a mist of shattered crystal, but through it she glimpsed the figure of a man, standing some yards away on the deck. She could not see his face, had no idea who he might be, but she could see that he was facing towards them, stock-still.

Watching.

Darkness seemed to descend on Mila's soul like a tropical night, sudden and impenetrable. The hand of fear clutched its cold fingers about her heart as she thought of

Orin Hobart. Hobart, who had sworn that he would never let her go.

How could she have doubted, even for one second, that he would come and find her? He would pursue her to the ends of the earth, if that was what it took to get her back.

Chapter 12

Two days later, they drove along the side of Lake Michigan and into Chicago. It was the sort of city that gave you plenty of warning of its existence, surging up out of the surrounding landscape a long time before you actually reached it. Its skyscrapers dominated the vast, monotonous flatness of the prairies, gradually growing larger and more impressive as the old Chevy chewed up the miles between Cleveland and Chicago.

And suddenly they were there, gliding past the gleaming glass towers of The Loop, past Union Station and the Sears Tower and towards the Magnificent Mile, famous for its high-class department stores and shopping malls.

'Where are we going?' asked Mila.

'To the best hotel in Chicago.'

'But...'

'It's OK, I can afford it.' Which wasn't a lie, because Greg had an attaché case full of money in the trunk – all he had been able to salvage when things went sour; a parting shot at those who had succeeded in destroying him. Hell, he couldn't have much time left before they caught up with him. He might as well enjoy spending it.

Later that evening, Mila came out of the shower to see Greg sitting on the edge of the bed, throwing the little jade tiger into the air and catching it one-handed. A tiny frisson of unease made the hairs stand up on the back of her neck.

'Don't do that. Please.'

'Don't worry, I won't break it. Anyhow, it's only a lump of stone. Pretty though. Where did you get it?'

'I . . . I sort of found it.' She could hardly own up and tell him she'd stolen it from Orin Hobart, along with the money from Carey Ronstein's wallet . . .

'Handsome little beggar, isn't he?' Greg let himself fall back on to the bed, turning the little tiger over and over in his hands. 'Look at the way the sun catches it if I hold it up to the light, makes it look like green fire. Pity about the crack.' A long, hairline crack ran from the corner of the tiger's gaping maw, along its flank to the root of its tail. 'Still, you'd hardly notice it unless you knew it was there. Tell you what, he can be our mascot.'

'Mas-cot?' Mila's moist, scarlet lips pouted as they framed the unfamiliar word.

'You know – a sort of good luck charm.' *I hope it works*, he thought to himself. *Not for me – God knows, I've not got much left to lose – but for you, Mila.*

Whatever it was that hurt her must have been really bad; because it was obviously still going on hurting her, eating away at her from inside. He didn't want to be the cause of yet more trouble for her – but on the other hand, he was far too besotted with her to say goodbye and walk away from her for ever.

Mila sat down on the edge of the bed, the irony of the 'good luck charm' silently echoing inside her head. Her skin was moist and warm from the shower, her wet hair fragrant and shiny. She shook it off her face and a spray of droplets flew free, falling on to Greg's bare skin. She wanted to kiss each one away.

THE GOLDEN CAGE

Greg put down the jade tiger and grabbed hold of her wrist, pressing her still-moist palm against his lips and letting his tongue-tip tickle that most sensitive of places. She giggled and tried to pull away, her fingers instinctively curling over her palm, but Greg shook his head.

'You're not getting away with it that easily,' he smirked. And with his free hand he pulled the towel away from her body.

He couldn't get over how delicious she was. Hers was not, perhaps, a classically proportioned or perfectly beautiful body, but it was all the the more alluring for that. The proportions were certainly perfect as far as he was concerned, the embodiment of his every wet dream – and more.

Her breasts were the dominating feature of her body, full and firm, natural globes of nacreous flesh; their skin so pale and fragile that a network of bluish veins marbled their surface. The areolae were a dusky pink, large and flattish in repose but puckering eagerly to the faintest touch of fingertips or lips. The nipples themselves were long and pert, pointing almost defiantly upwards like the stamens of exotic flowers. At the touch of cool air from the ceiling fan they grew longer, harder; inviting bolder kisses.

Below the generous overhand of her breasts, Mila's body was slender without being lean. Her waist seemed tinier than it was by virtue of the womanly swell of her hips, which flared into the most adorable pair of blush-pink buttocks he had ever seen. Her legs were long, impossibly long and silky smooth, and her thighs framed the nascent down of her dark pubic hair.

He ran his finger over her pubis, rubbing the tiny hairs up the wrong way, making Mila squirm and laugh.

'Stop – it feels...'

'What?'

'I don't know, funny.'

'You know, you probably won't believe this, but I've never slept with a woman with a shaven pussy before.'

'Well, I don't ... not usually ...'

Greg gave her a sidelong look.

'Aw ... don't spoil my fantasy!'

'You like your women shaven?'

Pushing her gently down on to the bed so that she lay across the satin coverlet with her toes still touching the floor, Greg bent and placed the first of a dozen kisses on her plump mound of Venus.

'I'd never really thought about it before. You've converted me. I like *you* shaven.' His tongue toyed with the golden ring that pierced her sex lips.

'Oh.' Mila was excited by Greg's words, but also a little confused. After all, it was Hobart who had decreed that she must be shaven, Hobart who had marked her with the tattoo and the gold ring.

'It's all right, Mila,' Greg reassured her, seeing her expression. 'You don't have to do anything for me. Let it grow back. I'll be just as hot for you then as I am now.'

'Greg ...' She kissed him, rolling on to her side so that they were facing each other.

'Hmm?'

'I want you to do something for me.'

'Anything.' He returned her kiss. 'As long as it involves making mad, passionate love to you.'

'I want you to shave me.'

His cock stiffened into an iron bar at the sound of her soft, husky plea.

'You're sure?'

'I'm sure.'

THE GOLDEN CAGE

'When – later? After dinner?'

'We can eat late. I want you to do it right now.'

Greg's mind exploded into a thousand different colours. His body ached for her. Taking her hand, he guided it to his penis.

'Feel what you do to me?'

Her fingers were cool and moist, butterfly-soft as they cradled his iron-hard shaft. He felt so aroused that he wondered if he could possibly stand to leave her even for a second – all his instincts screamed at him simply to slide into her, relieve the incredible need in his burning, aching balls.

With a supreme effort of will he slid off the bed.

'Don't move. Promise me you won't move.'

Mila rolled on to her belly, propping herself up on her elbows.

'Hurry. I want you.'

Greg went into the bathroom. Switching on the light, he caught sight of himself in the mirror. A little above average height, he was broad-shouldered and quite muscular. All in all, thirty-five years hadn't been too unkind to Greg Peterson. On the other hand he was no Greek god, just a reasonably good-looking English guy, pretty ordinary really. So why did these extraordinary things keep happening to him? He didn't know whether to be bitter or ecstatic.

Collecting his razor and a can of shaving foam, he clicked off the light and walked back into the bedroom. Evening sunlight had flooded the room. They hadn't bothered closing the blinds – there hardly seemed much point when you were thirty floors up. Mila's skin had taken on the golden glow of clarified honey and her wet hair shone like glass.

He knelt on the bed.

'I'm not even sure I know how to do this,' he confessed. 'I've never had the chance to practise on a woman.'

'Practise on me.'

'I don't want to hurt you.'

'You won't.' Her eyes met his and she heard herself say: 'I trust you not to.'

She lay back on the bed, stretching out on the pink satin bedspread, her thighs parted and one knee flexed.

Greg shook the can of shaving foam and squirted a little into his hand, then smeared it at the base of Mila's belly. She murmured her pleasure as the cool, scented foam caressed her still-damp skin.

The razor glinted as he picked it up. Whispered softly as he pressed it against her flesh and – holding the skin taut – cut a first swath through the creamy-white foam.

Wiping the razor, he drew it across the skin again and again. Mila lay very still, her eyes closed, but he could hear her breathing quickening and knew that she was every bit as excited as he was.

'Draw up your legs, Mila.' He eased her thighs apart and applied more shaving foam, this time spraying it directly on to the coral-pink, glistening heart of her sex.

He felt her tense at the cold caress of the foam, and heard her breath escape in the quietest of sighs.

'You excite me,' she whispered.

Greg's hand trembled slightly as he began the infinitely delicate task of shaving the hair from Mila's pussy lips, gliding the razor lightly and deftly across the swollen flesh.

'Oh. Oh, Greg. Be careful . . .'

'Did I hurt you?'

'No, no, it doesn't hurt. It just feels so strange.'

Shaving away the last tiny hairs, Greg wiped away the last traces of foam.

THE GOLDEN CAGE

'Do you like it, Greg? Do you like the way I look?'

'Oh Mila. You're more beautiful than ever.'

His wondering fingers traced the satin-smooth contours of Mila's shaven sex; the generous swell of her pubic mound, the smiling lips of her womanhood, the deep-pink, glistening heart, running with the juices of her desire.

'Kiss me, Greg.'

She was holding out her arms to him, but he did not kiss her on the lips. Kneeling between her thighs, he bent to pay tribute to the intimate beauties of her sex. He felt her tremble as his fingers eased apart the plump pussy-lips, as his own lips found the secret garden of delight and began to kiss her to the summit of pleasure.

The restaurant at the Hotel Michigan was the grandest thing that Mila had ever seen. Even in the old days, when she had occasionally acted as an interpreter at grand Soviet receptions for visiting foreign dignitaries, she had never experienced such casual, effortless luxury.

She glanced down at her dress – the evening dress which Greg had insisted on buying her. No matter how much he had protested, she had known he wouldn't take no for an answer. The funny thing was, all of this – the dress, the hotel room, the restaurant with the penguin-suited maître d' – was what she'd dreamed of when she first went to the Agency.

'You look incredible,' whispered Greg, squeezing her hand.

'Not as incredible as she looks.' Mila nodded towards a woman sitting at the next table.

'Hmm, freaky. Morticia Adams, isn't it?'

'Don't! She might hear you.' But Mila kept on looking at her, as if unable to tear her gaze away.

Aurelia Clifford

Greg could see why Mila might be fascinated by the woman. He found her curiously compelling too, in a repellent sort of way. She was very thin – almost unnaturally so, with a sort of gaunt, cadaverous beauty which was both horrible and powerfully erotic.

Her jet-black hair was drawn up into a tight chignon secured with two silver chopsticks, giving her a faintly oriental look. She was heavily made-up, pale-faced with black kohl around deep-violet eyes, and lipstick that glistened like fresh blood. Her evening gown was a pencil-slim sheath of clinging crêpe-de-chine in a shade of deep mourning violet, and her throat glittered with a collar of diamonds and amethysts. She was ageless and seemed very aware of her unusual magnetism; like some dark spirit drawing its energy from those around her.

Sitting opposite the woman was a man in his early forties, ordinary by comparison but exceptionally well-dressed. Even in his tuxedo you could see he was the kind of man who bought Brooks Brothers suits by the dozen just for slumming about in and probably jetted across the Atlantic to have his finest clothes hand-sewn in Savile Row. Slicked-back hair glossy with pomade, hawkish features and a gold-banded, tortoiseshell cigarette holder gave him a slightly anachronistic air, like something out of a Noel Coward revue.

'Dessert, madame, monsieur?' The waiter appeared from nowhere, hovered at the table and handed out the menus. His *faux* French accent verged on the comical, but Greg managed to keep a straight face.

'Mila?'

'Nothing for me, thank you.'

'Oh go on. I'm having the *feuilleté* of strawberries.'

'Well, maybe just a little fresh fruit.'

THE GOLDEN CAGE

'A basket of *fruits de la saison*, madame? Certainly.'

The waiter whisked away toward the kitchen and Mila's gaze drifted back to the bizarre couple at the next table. They were totally wrapped up in each other, nothing existing beyond their own tiny, hermetic world. As she watched, the man took a silver spoonful of cream from his plate and offered it, slowly and seductively, to his companion.

Her crimson lips parted and she put out her long red tongue. The muscular tip stretching to reach the bowl of the spoon, she lapped up the cream in long, slow movements. Mila watched the woman's long, white throat ripple as she swallowed the cream, then took a sip of wine.

'*Prosit*,' she whispered; her voice softly, huskily Germanic. And then she turned her eyes, quite suddenly on Mila, raised her glass, and smiled.

At that moment the waiter returned with dessert and when she turned back, Mila saw that the couple had gone.

'Shall I do that?' Greg's voice broke into her trance.

'Hmm?' Mila turned back, suddenly ashamed to have neglected Greg. 'I'm sorry, what did you say?'

'What they were doing – shall we play that game?' He scooped up a little cream from his plate, lifted the spoon to his mouth and let the cream run into his mouth. 'Mmm, it's so cold. Wouldn't you like to taste?'

Mila leaned a little way over the table, the boned bodice of her turquoise moiré dress displaying the ample charms of her bosom. Greg took another spoonful of the cream – runny double cream that was just made for pouring. He had a sudden, mad urge to take the whole silver cream jug and pour its contents over Mila's exposed breasts. What would it look like, feel like? In his mind's eye he could imagine how it would be to watch the cream trickle thickly down

Mila's flesh, dripping into the deep gorge between her breasts, filling it until it became a miniature river, brimful of cream...

Another spoonful. The bowl of the spoon so over-full that only surface tension kept the cream from spilling over.

'Open wide, darling,' he whispered.

And Mila's lips parted in a sensuous smile, the dark-pink interior of her mouth welcoming the cold silver and the chill white cream.

'Oh Mila, darling, I want you to drink my cream. All of it, drink it down...'

She swallowed, and he smoothed his fingers down her pretty white throat, lusting after her with a power and an intensity which almost alarmed him.

'Now you,' she smiled. She picked up a nectarine, a beautiful globe of red and gold, firm, juicy, sweet. Polishing its smooth skin on a damask napkin, she raised it to her lips, biting into it with sharp, pearl-white teeth.

Juice sprang from the pierced flesh like golden blood, trickling over lips and tongue; the stickiness escaping down her chin in a single clear, honeyed runnel. She licked her lips, juicy-wet, and wiped the juice from her chin, licking it from each finger in turn with obvious pleasure.

'Now you,' she said, holding out the fruit. 'Your turn, Greg. Won't you taste my juice? It's so sweet.'

Sweet and juicy, tender and suggestive... Greg's whole body cried out for Mila as he bit into the ripe flesh, sucking and biting, swallowing the sweet pulp and drinking down the juice.

Mila leant across the table, joining her lips to his, kissing away the trickles of sticky juice. Suddenly aware that all eyes in the restaurant were upon them, they stopped in mid-kiss and drew apart, laughing like naughty children.

THE GOLDEN CAGE

Not taking his eyes off Mila for a second, Greg snapped his fingers and the waiter glided across to the table.

'Sir?'

Greg indicated the plastic 'smart' card which served as a room key.

'Room 1502. Put it on the check.'

'As you wish, sir. But you have not finished your dessert. Was there something wrong?'

Greg got to his feet and slipped the key into his pocket.

'It's OK,' he said. 'We've made other plans for dessert.'

Total silence.

That was one of the funny things about the Hotel Michigan. Although it was huge and accommodated hundreds of guests, you scarcely ever saw anyone walking about, or even heard any noises coming from beyond the thick hardwood doors. Each of the identical corridors stretched away into the distance, deserted, strangely muffled.

Mila and Greg stepped out of the elevator on the thirtieth floor and Greg slipped the attendant a five-dollar bill.

'Why thank you, sir, madam. Have a nice day.'

'Don't worry, we intend to.'

They walked down the corridor towards their room, Greg's arm around Mila's waist, his hand occasionally slipping down over the delicious curve of her backside.

'Dessert?'

'Dessert. We could maybe call up some cream from room service . Or ice-cream, even ...'

They kissed, Mila with her back against the expensive flock wallpaper, the wall light casting patterns of light and shadow on her face. So engrossed were they in each other that the sudden explosion of light and noise came as a complete shock.

'What the hell is that . . . ?' Greg wheeled round.

A door at the far end of the corridor was standing open. Multicoloured lights flashed and heavy rock music thundered out. A woman was standing in the doorway and, even from the other end of the corridor, both Mila and Greg recognised her instantly.

'It's her . . . the woman from the restaurant,' hissed Mila.

And she was walking up the corridor towards them, her sheath-dress floating open along a thigh-high split as she walked, revealing a leg clad in a black fishnet stocking with a violet satin garter.

'*Guten Abend*,' she greeted them huskily. She was no beauty, yet her angular features and spare frame held a grace and eroticism which were impossible to ignore. 'Allow me to introduce myself. My name is Grethe.'

'Good evening,' replied Greg, fascinated by her. Mila tugged at his arm but it was his turn to be enraptured by this most unusual of women.

'I trust our little celebration does not disturb you too much? The music is perhaps not quite to your taste . . . ?'

'No, no, really, it's fine.' Greg knew he was babbling like an idiot, but his brain seemed to have lost control of his mouth.

Mila felt the woman's violet eyes exploring her, body and soul.

'You are very pretty,' she observed, quite coolly.

'I . . . er . . . thank you.'

'And quite exotic.' Grethe turned to Greg. 'And you . . . ah, the perfect Englishman. Such an underrated race, the English. Find your way beyond the cold exterior and you will find searing, volcanic passions.' She licked her lips and

THE GOLDEN CAGE

Mila found herself thinking of a lizard, or a snake – just before it strikes. 'Won't you join us?'

'I'm sorry?' Greg shook his head, trying to clear his alcohol-fuddled thoughts.

'Join us. At the party in my suite. Anton and I would be more than delighted to welcome you.'

'Well, I don't think...' began Mila, but Greg had already taken his first step towards the open door.

'I'm sure you and your companion would find it an interesting, not to say stimulating, experience.'

'Yes,' he said. 'We'd love to. Why not?'

The slave knelt, blindfold, at the centre of the room, ropes attached to her wrists securing her to the foot of the bed. A leather slave-harness criss-crossed her naked body with shiny black straps; straps which pulled apart the soft mounds of her breasts and the tanned globes of her arse cheeks, leaving her utterly exposed, mocking her most precious secrets.

She had been there a long time, hours probably, but she had lost all track of time. She was a slave. It was not her place to question or complain, only to serve as she commanded.

Her servitude was her joy and her desire.

The party quests almost filled the room. Some were completely naked, others dressed in fetish wear: micro-dresses and spanking pants in black and scarlet rubber, shiny PVC and patent leather boots, chains that pleasured as they mortified the flesh.

They had only one thing in common: they were masked. Some were faceless and inhuman in full-face leather masks adorned with zippers; others wore simple eye-masks. The slaves – around a dozen of them – were blindfolded with silk scarves and leather straps. They wore shiny black harnesses and studded dog-collars, and some were chained like dogs to the furniture. Not that there was any particular need to restrain them, for they crouched obediently at their masters' and mistresses' feet, living only for the next command, the next delicious humiliation.

'Hot bitch,' hissed an old man, naked save for a hangman's mask and leather apron. He ran a bullwhip through his fingers, savouring the suppleness of fine leather woven into a vicious serpent as he surveyed the beauties of the slave-girl tied to the bed.

'Give her a taste of the lash,' suggested a woman standing next to him, a glass of champagne and her own slave's leash in the other. 'She loves to feel the pain.'

The old man raised his arm and brought down the tip of the lash at the very base of the girl's spine, making her twist and turn in a dance of delicious agony. He laughed.

'Bitch, bitch, bitch!' With each syllable he whipped her again, and as the girl's shrill cries rang out, it became obvious why the music was playing so loudly...

It wasn't until they had crossed the outer room that Greg and Mila realised just what they had walked into.

Smiling, Grethe ushered them through the doorway into the bedroom.

'Anton – give our guests a drink. One of the *special* drinks.' She smiled at Greg. 'I have an ancient recipe, passed down through generations. It is guaranteed to intensify both pleasure and pain.' She laughed. 'But then again, I have never recognised any distinction between the two.'

Greg took the proferred glass but did not drink. He was totally mesmerised, his brain scrambled and his hormones at the screaming point of confusion. He wanted to think

THE GOLDEN CAGE

that this was all disgusting, depraved, intolerable – which of course it was. But his body wanted to know more, to immerse itself, to share the intense, electric atmosphere of total stimulation.

It was all laid out before him – a beautiful hell of pleasure and pain. An S/M party. He'd read about them, of course, even known one or two colleagues who'd been into domination, fetishwear, C/P, the whole scene. He'd laughed at them then, but that was before he'd found himself in the middle of this underworld of forbidden pleasure.

The music thumped and crashed around him, the sound bouncing off the walls, imperfectly masking the screams of the girl who was being whipped in time to the bass line. *Thump, thump, thump*. With each beat a new stroke, a new crimson welt across the snowy back, a new cry of fearful ecstasy.

He took a step forward.

'Welcome.' A tall woman extended a gloved hand, the scarlet gauntlet tipped with long claws of silvery metal. Her masked eyes showed no expression, but her full lips curved into a carnivorous smile.

'He's beautiful . . . is it his first time?'

'Help him undress – then give him the whip and let him have some real fun.'

'He shall have my slave, then Cassandra shall cleanse his prick with her tongue.'

'But who is *this*?'

Suddenly Mila, transfixed with terror, felt the eyes of the whole room turning on her. Her mouth opened, but she could not say anything, not a sound, not a word. Pictures were flashing through her brain, strobing with the real scene around her, until she lost track of where she really was and what she was doing.

A slave-girl, clad only in a harness, her body secured by wrist-ropes to the end of a bed...

Suddenly she was back in the training room with Orin Hobart, his voice a low hiss of cruel satisfaction as he possessed her. Faces crowded around her, the faces of Hobart's friends, urging him on...

'She's pretty.'

'Real cute. *Real* cute.'

'She'd be cuter still on her back...'

Mila froze for a split second, lost in the limbo between memory and reality. Greg was talking, laughing, obviously unworried by what he'd got himself into. But then, he didn't know, did he? Didn't know what she'd left behind and what she was afraid might catch up with her at any moment?

A hand touched her, stroked her arm. And then another, easing down the side zipper of her dress, baring her breasts, caressing her nipples and making them stiff with unwilling desire.

'Want some, my pretty?'

The voice awoke her from her trance.

'No. No, get your filthy hands off me! Leave me alone. No, no, no!'

Turning on her heel, she ran, pushing people aside in her desperation to get away. She didn't stop until she was back in her room, with the door locked from the inside.

'Mila.'

Greg rattled the door handle but the door wouldn't budge. He checked the number: 3002, then tried the door again. Silence.

'Mila, what's going on? Let me in.'

After what seemed an age, the door opened an inch or

THE GOLDEN CAGE

two. Mila's face peered out at him, her eyes huge and dark in a white face.

'Leave me alone.'

'What's the matter, Mila? It was only a party, OK it was a bit weird, but don't you think you over-reacted a bit? I mean, you ran out of there like a startled rabbit.'

'I can't tell you.'

He peered into the room over her shoulder.

'You're sitting in the dark. Why are you sitting in the dark?'

'Maybe I like it that way.'

'For pity's sake, Mila. Let me in. Won't you?'

'Please...'

'It's me.' He slipped his hand through the chink in the door and stroked Mila's hand. 'Greg. I thought you trusted me.'

Slowly the chain slid back and he heard it jingle against the door as it slipped down. The door opened and he stepped inside, shutting it behind him. The lights of the city filtered into the room through the open drapes, casting patterns of light and shadow across Mila's face.

She shrank back but he seized her hands and forced her to stand her ground.

'Look at me, Mila. I said, look at me.'

Her dark eyes met his.

'Now, please, I think you have something to tell me, yes?'

She was shaking convulsively as he drew her to him. At first she resisted, then seemed to collapse in on herself, her body limp and shivering in his arms. He stroked her hair, speaking softly to her as though she were a frightened animal.

'If I tell you,' she began, 'you will hate me.'

'I doubt it.' He wondered what she would think of him if he dared open up to her. What she would think when, as was pretty much inevitable, she found out what had happened to him.

'That girl ... at the party.'

'The one tied up?'

'Y-yes. The slave.'

'What about her, sweetheart? She was just a girl, anyhow I think she liked it. They're like that, these domination freaks.'

'Do you think I'm like that, a – a domination freak?'

'Of course not. Why?'

Her eyes moved slowly upward until they were looking straight into his. He would never know how much courage it cost her to meet his gaze while she confessed her shame.

'Because that's what I am, Greg.' Taking her shielding hands from her breasts, she bared the tiny tattooed 'H'. 'Do you know what that tattoo is, Greg? That's my master's mark.'

His eyes widened a fraction, but he did not speak, afraid that if he did she would clam up and refuse to tell him any more. Beyond Mila's shoulder the Chicago skyline glittered in the darkness, almost as unreal as the words he was hearing.

'That's right, Greg. I'm a slave. An escaped slave. And when my master finds out where I am, he'll stop at nothing to get me back.

'I'm afraid, Greg. I'm afraid that he'd kill me rather than let another man have me. And maybe he'd kill you, too.'

The woman in the violet dress pulled the silver chopsticks from her hair and it tumbled down to her waist, uncoiling into jet-black waves.

THE GOLDEN CAGE

She drummed her varnished black talons on the top of the nightstand as she dialled the number and waited.

'O'Brien.'

Her thin face assumed the faintest shadow of a smile.

'Darsey, *darling*. I had one of my little parties tonight.'

'Really.' O'Brien's silky voice sharpened with interest. 'You're still seeking information?'

'Of course.'

'So many interesting people attended tonight. Old friends, of course – and one or two unexpected guests, too. Such a pity they didn't stay long enough to enjoy the celebrations.'

'You're not telling me anything, Grethe,' snapped O'Brien. 'Look, our client is offering a considerable reward for information. If you want that reward, you'd better quit talking in riddles.'

'You always were such a delicious bitch, darling,' purred Grethe. 'Very well, your client may be interested to know that one of my guests tonight was a girl with dark hair, a Russian accent . . . and the prettiest little tattoo on her left breast.'

Chapter 13

It was dark in the hotel bedroom, but Mila watched Greg's silhouette pacing in front of the wide picture-window.

'That was some story,' he commented after a long silence.

'Do you want me to go?' she asked flatly.

He stopped, turned on his heel, stared at her. Starlight cast her features into a ghostly pattern of light and shade.

'Go?'

'I knew you'd hate me if I told you. That's why I didn't tell you before, but I was wrong. I should have.'

Greg's fear exploded into anger.

'For God's sake Mila, stop torturing yourself, will you? I don't hate you, I never have. If I start hating you I'll let you know OK?'

'Sorry. So if you don't want me to go, what do we do now?'

'I have to think.'

'Look, Greg, it's been wonderful. But I don't want there to be any danger for you.'

He crossed the room and, quite unexpectedly, took hold of her face and bent to kiss her eyes.

I know you don't. But it's a bit late for that.' He paused. 'OK, it's honesty time.'

'But I've already told you everything, Greg. Everything.'

'I know. But there are a few things I haven't told you.'

'I don't need to know.' In her heart, she wondered if she even *wanted* to know.

It's already long overdue. When you hear what I have to say, maybe you won't want to stick around anymore. I couldn't blame you if that's the way you feel. God, I've been so bloody selfish I can hardly believe it.'

Mila did not reply. Things were moving too fast for her. One moment she was afraid that Greg would reject her; the next, he was forcing her to share his own secrets. Almost as if he wanted to drive her away.

'Go on,' she said quietly.

Greg turned away and looked out into the starlit depths of the Chicago night. Beyond the skyscrapers and the Art Deco apartment blocks glittered the distant silver ribbon of the Chicago River. Murky-green with pollution by day, it took on an undeniably romantic aspect in the moonlight. Thirty floors down, the traffic of the night glided silently by, little more than a blur of red, white and green light in the hazy darkness.

'I know I look like an ordinary guy,' he began. 'And believe me, my life was ordinary enough until a month ago. I think I told you, I am – was – international finance director of a company which produces electronic components. I joined the company eight years ago, before things really took off. Anyhow, one thing led to another and the company turned into a major corporation, with subsidiaries all over the world. One of those subsidiaries is in Boston.

'A few weeks ago, I got a call from the company Vice-President in Boston. It seemed the auditors had found

THE GOLDEN CAGE

some discrepancies in the accounts. Would I please come over and sort out the problem? I didn't realise then, but I was already under investigation by a special agent from the FBI.'

'The FBI!' It sounded incredible to Mila. The FBI was something that existed only in films. Yet something inside her recoiled instinctively from the thought, remembering the old days when her schoolfriend's father had fallen foul of the KGB.

'I know. Totally unbelievable, isn't it? Anyhow, the moment I arrived in Boston I realised something was seriously wrong – I think the police escort and the arrest warrant had something to do with it. I couldn't understand it until they showed me the hard evidence they'd turned up on the computer accounting system.

'Hidden files – they knew what to look for because somebody in the company had tipped them off. It seems the US Government were already getting suspicious about the company's activities and this guy wanted to save his skin.'

'Greg, I don't understand.'

'No. Neither did I. I still don't, not really. Apparently the company has been involved in illegal arms deals in the Middle East. And those files . . . well, they implicate me up to the neck and then some.'

'You've been . . . you're an *arms dealer*?'

To Mila's surprise, Greg laughed, great sobs of laughter shaking his whole body.

'Of course I'm bloody well not.'

'But the evidence . . . you just said . . . Where did that come from? It was false evidence, yes?'

'I don't know how, Mila, but somebody in the organisation has stitched me up good and proper. I guess they sensed the FBI were getting a little too close and decided I

191

was going to be sacrificed. Take the rap for whoever it is that's been a naughty boy.'

'You can fight though. Get a lawyer. Prove that this evidence was made up.'

He shook his head.

'I went through it a dozen times with my attorney. They've got all they need on me and they're going to damn me to hell. Anyhow, I got a chance and I decided not to stick around and wait for it to happen.'

'You escaped?'

'I dodged bail. It's hopeless of course. Once they catch up with me they'll lock me up and throw away the key. But I decided to borrow the old Chevy, take what money I had and head across America. Does that sound crazy? It's something I'd always wanted to do but I'd never had the time. Maybe this will be my last chance for a long time.'

Mila listened, stunned. It sounded far too fantastic to be true, yet the funny thing was that she believed him. Why? Perhaps because Greg Delaney was such a hopeless liar.

'But why? Why run away?'

Greg shrugged.

'A last act of defiance. I know it's pointless, but I just wanted to do something for myself for once, before it was too late. Then I met you . . .'

'So we've both been hiding secrets from each other.'

'It's daft, I know. I just couldn't face telling you, any more than you could face telling me. And now I have . . . well, maybe it's best if we go our separate ways.'

'I thought you said you didn't want me to go.'

'I don't. But it's dangerous for you. For all I know the FBI know exactly where I am and they're just biding their

THE GOLDEN CAGE

time, waiting to see what I do next. That guy on the boat at Niagara, the one you said was staring at you. Maybe he was staring at *me*.'

Mila's knuckles tensed and untensed as she clenched and unclenched her hands.

'What will you do – when you get across America?'

'*If* I get across. When I get to San Francisco I'll turn myself in. There's no point in me trying to get out of the country – they've got my passport.'

'I'm coming with you,' said Mila.

'Think about what you're saying.'

'I already did, crazy Englishman. I'm coming with you to San Francisco. If you're not afraid to be with me, why should I be afraid to be with you?'

It took them another two days to hit the Kansas border, passing through the unappealing outskirts of Kansas City on Interstate 70, through the wooded, scrubby country around Topeka and Abilene and on to the Great Plains.

On every side, cornfields extended as far as the horizon and beyond, the land flat and acre upon acre of rippling golden cornstalks interrupted only by the odd farmhouse or barn. The silence was punctuated by the lazy drone of the occasional tractor.

It was a jewel-bright July day, the sun beating down out of a sky of blazing blue and – unusual for wild and windy Kansas – hardly the faintest breath of a breeze. With the soft top down, the Chevy created its own cooling currents of air, caressing Mila's bare arms and blowing her hair back from her face.

'If we make it to San Francisco . . .' began Greg.

Mila's fingers stroked his thigh, stopping a few, tantalising millimetres from the swell of his balls.

'*When* we make it,' she corrected him. Since they had opened up to each other, she felt as though a black cloud had lifted from her shoulders. The darkness and the fear were still there, the threat of Orin Hobart's vengeance an ever-present menace, but voicing the fear seemed to have lessened it. Even demons lost some of their menace on a baking-hot, sizzling July day.

'OK, *when* we make it to San Francisco, I'll take you to the Russian Consulate.'

'I can't go there. I left Russia illegally. Morrison Farley made me use a false passport and then Hobart burned all my documents.'

'You have to, Mila. I don't see what alternative you have.'

'But what would they do to me? Besides, I don't want to go back to Russia, not ever.'

Greg sighed.

'You're pigheaded, Mila Kirovska. And you're very irresistible.'

He gave a growl of pleasure as Mila's fingers stroked the plump swell of his balls, making them tingle with anticipation. No matter how often he felt her touch, no matter how often they made love, Greg couldn't get enough of Mila's brand of loving.

Greg wasn't a violent man but he would have liked to kill Orin Hobart for daring to do what he'd done to Mila. As he submitted to the total pleasure of her caress, his mind fantasised on what he might do if they ever met.

Hobart. He'd heard of the guy, somehow, some way. As a businessman, probably, and as a Republican – an aspiring senator, or so he vaguely recalled. What would the good people of Massachusetts say if they knew the truth about their favourite son?

THE GOLDEN CAGE

'Mila, you're a witch, you must be. It can't be more than half an hour since you sucked my dick.'

She laughed.

'I'm ... what's the word? ... a nymphomaniac, didn't I tell you? Don't you want me? I want you.'

Her fingers moved fractionally higher and Greg's hands twitched on the steering wheel, sending the car into a sharp swerve. Gasping for breath he swung the bonnet back into line, just as a huge animal-feed transporter appeared from nowhere and thundered past in a cloud of dust.

'Do that again, and we'll be off the road in that field,' he gasped, his pulse racing.

Sweat was trickling down from his scalp, and his lips tasted salty as he ran his tongue over them. His shirt was sticking to him and he dreamed of jumping with Mila, fully clothed, into a stream. How good it would be to feel the shock of the cold water on his skin, to touch the hard buttons of Mila's nipples through the sodden fabric of her T-shirt.

'I made love in a cornfield once,' observed Mila, lazy as a lizard in the sunshine.

'Tell me more.' Greg could feel his cock uncoiling, stretching like a waking serpent.

'It was when I was sixteen, in Ukraine. I went to spend the summer near Lvov, on the collective farm where my aunt and uncle lived. I was a bit of a rebel then and I hated my mother going on and on about what a 'nice' girl I was. I was just a kid. I wanted to show them that I could be different, whatever I wanted to be.'

'As soon as I got to the farm I knew I wanted this guy. He was much, much older than I was, maybe thirty-five or even older; tall, stocky, with great powerful arms and rough hands. He was a labourer on the farm, a peasant with dark curly hair and tanned skin, like a gypsy. I knew my mother would despise him, and I suppose that's why I wanted him. I knew I had to have him.

'His name was Georgei. He talked to me like I was some kind of slut, and that just got me so excited. No one had ever talked to me like that before. I wanted more.

'He must have known I was still a virgin and maybe that excited him, too. I used to help him feed the animals and sometimes he would touch me – like it was an accident, only I knew it wasn't. His great, hard fingers would brush across my backside, or stroke my breasts as he squeezed past. And as he did, I felt this great thick, hard thing pressing against my belly. I was so naïve, I'd never even seen a man naked. But I knew enough to feel his hunger, the heat of him burning into me as he rubbed himself up against me.

'"You want it, don't you? You want it inside you?" he whispered to me one day when we were in the barn. "Toffee-nosed little bitch, you're just a whore inside."

'He made me touch the front of his pants, and there was this huge, hard thing there. That was the first time I started to be a little bit scared. I didn't know what I was doing, Mother had told me to stay away from men and my girlfriends were no wiser than I was. Now I'd got myself mixed up with this guy, and I could see what was going to happen, and I started to wonder if, maybe, he would do something bad to me.

'The next time I saw him was in the woods, where I'd been sent to find one of the lambs which had run away from the flock. It was dark and lonely there – some people said they had heard wolves howling at night Then I heard footsteps behind me . . .

THE GOLDEN CAGE

'The next thing I knew, Georgei had me pinned against a tree, so hard that the bark scraped my cheek. And he was whispering to me – things that disgusted me but drove me wild with excitement.

'"Don't try to hide it, I know you're a hot bitch. I know you want it. Never had it inside you, huh? I'll bet you're wet for me, aren't you? I can smell your pussy, you're like a mare on heat."

'I think I must have been moaning and crying, but I don't remember what I said. I'm sure I didn't make any sense at all. I felt these clumsy, rough fingers pushing up my skirt, pulling down my knickers. Then the cold air on my bare buttocks. He slapped them a couple of times, not very hard but it came as a shock to me – my parents had never lifted a finger to me. I would never have admitted to myself, let alone to him, that I liked it, but I got the funniest thrill through my whole body, and I wanted to rub my belly up against the tree bark as though I was trying to scratch an itch that I didn't want to go away.

'He put his penis between my buttocks – he didn't try to penetrate me, just pulled apart my bottom cheeks and sort of laid it between them. It felt huge, impossibly long and thick. Then I felt him thrusting. He was grunting and then I felt something wet trickling down the small of my back.

'This went on for a couple of weeks. I didn't know whether to be afraid of him or to seek him out. No matter how often I told myself that this wasn't the sort of guy I ought to be with, I kept finding him "by accident". He fascinated me. I lusted after him without even understanding what I was doing.

'He took my virginity in the cornfield on a hot summer's day – a day just like this one. No, he didn't take it, not really. I gave it to him. I wanted rid of it and I wanted to show my mother that I could defy her.

'Georgei kissed me for the first time and I tasted his breath, it smelt of beer and garlic. It excited me, do you know that? Excited me to know that I was doing something totally forbidden. If they'd known about it, my aunt and uncle would have killed me.

'He didn't bother undressing me, just threw me down amid the cornstalks and pulled up my skirt. He just ripped off my panties and threw them away.

'"Wet", he grunted, and I saw a smile of satisfaction passing across his face. "Dripping wet for me. I always knew you were a little whore at heart."

'At that moment, Georgei was the most attractive guy in the universe to me. I was so hot for him, I'd have done anything he asked of me. Anything. But when he unbuttoned his fly and took out his cock, I nearly screamed with fear.

'It was larger even than I'd dreamed: a full nine inches long and so thick that his fingers scarcely went round it. Its clubbed head was a smooth, purple dome, divided by a deep cleft which oozed and dripped a clear fluid. Beneath it hung his balls – huge, juicy fruits I longed to lick and suck.

'When he entered me I tried to cry out but not a single sound emerged. He was not rough with me but the size of his manhood stretched and tore at my tight sex. Wetness dripped and ran from me, but nothing was enough to ease that first thrust. The thrust that made me a woman.'

Greg drove on, desperately aroused by what he had heard. It was incredibly difficult to concentrate on the road ahead, especially as Mila's fingers were teasing him so beautifully through the crotch of his pants. His mouth was dry and he had to clear his throat before he spoke.

THE GOLDEN CAGE

'Did he make you come?'

'Not with his cock. With his tongue. Then he showed me how to make myself come with my fingers.'

'And was it good?' Greg pictured the rough farmhand, his face pressed against Mila's tender quim, licking his juices from the deep well of her sex.

'It was the first time. It was ... unforgettable.'

'What about me, Mila? Am I unforgettable? Will you remember me when ... when we're not together any more?'

'Don't ... Greg, please don't.'

'You know it has to happen. The Federal Department of Correction has my future mapped out for me for the next – what? – ten years, twenty even. And you'll be going back to St Petersburg...'

Mila's eyes blazed a warning.

'I will *not!*'

'You bloody well will, if I've got anything to do with it. I'm not leaving you to fend for yourself with that maniac after you.'

'I could stay here ... wait for you.'

'What? Are you completely crazy? Either Hobart will get his claws into you, or the cops will catch up with you and you'll be deported as an illegal alien.'

'I don't want to talk about it. I chose to leave that place, and I'm not going back. You can't make me and neither can ... neither can *he*.' She glared at him. Oh, but she was irresistible when she was mad at him, her dark eyes flashing like polished jet, her pale complexion flushed rosy with passion, her parted lips glossy and crimson.

'For God's sake, Mila, will you see sense, just for once?'

'If I'd had any sense, as you call it, I'd never have met you,' Mila pointed out. Her voice grew a little softer and she turned her head away as she spoke. 'And now I've found you I don't see why I should be forced to let you go. Do you?'

Greg stretched out his right hand and it met Mila's, the fingers intertwining.

'No. I know. Don't think I don't know, but...'

Suddenly hopelessly tongue-tied, he didn't know what else to say, not really. Declarations of undying love made him break out in a cold sweat and, besides, it hardly seemed like the time. Undying lust was easier to confess to but then he sensed that she knew that already.

'Greg.'

'What?'

'Let's not think about it, not out here. It's a beautiful day and we're together. Free...'

Her fingers slid between his legs and Greg felt his body relax into a different, altogether more pleasurable sort of tension. She was right of course. It *was* a beautiful day, a flawless blue sky-dome arching over the shimmering roadway which stretched into the far distance, to a horizon which seemed to go on for ever and ever. On either side of the car, the ripening cornfields rippled in the lightest of breezes, like the thick, soft pelt of some slumbering beast.

'Did you like it?' he asked cryptically.

'Like it?'

'Doing it in a cornfield. Fucking out of doors...'

'Oh yes.'

'Fancy doing it again?'

She caught his glance in the rearview mirror and burst out laughing.

'I thought I was the sex maniac around here.'

Greg smirked.

'You've corrupted me.'

THE GOLDEN CAGE

'So it's my fault is it?'

'Absolutely. That body of yours is more temptation than a red-blooded Englishman can bear.'

Mila stretched back in the seat, her hair floating out behind her, her desire-hardened nipples clearly visible beneath the thin silk sleeveless top. He wanted her more than he'd ever thought possible.

She opened her eyes and looked at him questioningly as he eased off the gas and the car slowed down.

'Time for a little recreation,' he smiled, steering the car to a halt just inside the opening to a farm track. Acre after acre of smoothly rippling maize extended into the distance – a golden ocean he longed to dive into.

Getting out of the Chevy, he opened the passenger door and took Mila's hand.

'Come on, we're going for a little nature-study walk.'

'What are we going to study?'

'How much pleasure the human body can stand.'

They waded in among the corn, the dried stalks and leaf-blades scratching the skin like a lover's fingernails.

'Won't the farmer mind?'

Greg kissed her doubts into silence.

'He won't know.'

She relaxed into his kiss, giving herself to him totally as the warmth of the sunshine entered her bones. It was impossible to have doubts or fears on a day like this, in a place like this: a place that was so deserted, silent and uninterrupted that it felt almost as if the two lovers had been transported to some far-distant planet where only their pleasure held any meaning.

'How did he take you?'

'Georgei?'

'Mmm, that's right. Georgei. I want you to tell me again,

but very slowly this time. I want to do it all to you. I want to see if I can do it to you better than he did.'

'He laid me down in the corn. Just sort of picked me up and laid me down. He was so strong...'

Still kissing Mila, Greg lowered her on to her back among the corn. She drew him down so that he was kneeling astride her, the curving spike of his erect penis distorting the crotch of his chinos.

'And what did he do before he fucked you? Did he take off all your clothes?'

'He didn't bother undressing me.'

'Not even your shirt? Didn't he pull up your shirt like this...' Greg slipped his hand underneath the hem of the silk top and eased it up over her breasts. 'And then put his hand inside your bra?' It was a lightweight cotton bra and slipped easily upwards, baring the plump, ripe melons of her breasts and their engorged nubs.

Mila giggled.

'No, he didn't.'

'Then he should have done.' Greg bent down and took Mila's left nipple into his mouth, biting it hard enough to make her squirm and cry out, cupping his head in her hands and pulling him down still further, making him do it to her...

'Harder, Greg. It feels so good. Do it harder.'

As he bit her left nipple, his fingers teased and pinched the right, drawing it out until it was a long, hard spike, surrounded by a puckered, rubbery areola.

When he drew away, his lips were moist with saliva, and Mila's nipple glistened in the blazing sunshine.

'That felt so good.'

'Didn't he do that to you? Didn't he suck your tits?'

'He pulled off my panties and then he took me.'

THE GOLDEN CAGE

Greg eased Mila's skirt up over her thighs until her panties were just visible, The pink lacy nylon was fragrant and moist.

'And were you all wet for him? As wet as you are for me now?'

Mila's voice was no louder than a husky whisper.

'I've never been wet for anyone the way I'm wet for you.'

Her voice was like a caressing hand on Greg's yearning prick.

'Please,' he murmured. 'Please take out my cock. I want to feel you touching it'

She reached up and eased down the zipper. Underneath, his white silk boxers were clinging to the head of his manhood, the wet ooze of his desire making the fabric translucent as clouded glass.

'You're wet for me too,' she smiled.

'Always. And if you're not careful, you'll make me wetter. Much, much wetter. I shall spurt all over your face ... and your breasts ...'

The thought excited Mila and as she reached through the front vent of Greg's pants she imagined the sudden warmth, the cooling heaviness of the droplets, the salty taste of semen staining her lips.

'You could come between my breasts,' she breathed, running her hands lightly over his shaft. 'Why don't you put your prick between my tits?'

The firm, white swell of Mila's plump and perfect globes called to him, whispering their welcome.

'But first ... let me do something else. Come closer to me, that's right, lower yourself over my face.'

She smiled as she stroked the tense purse of his scrotum. He groaned. Her touch was so light and yet so skilful, her fingers cool even on this scorching July day. He hardly dared hope that she was about to do what he desperately wanted her to do.

She was.

Opening her mouth, she put out her tongue and started to lick his scrotum, at first lightly teasing the golden frizz of his pubic hair. Each wiry hair seemed connected to an electrical circuit which sent shivers of pleasure through his entire body as she worked her magic on him.

'Oh Mila, Mila,' was all he could manage to gasp, his brain robbed of the power to frame anything more coherent.

She did not answer in words, responding far more eloquently with caresses. His balls ached with joy as her lips opened in a wide and shameless O of desire. He saw her long, pink tongue glistening with saliva, then her lips closed about his right testicle.

The feeling was exquisite, indescribable, as the warm cavern of her mouth tightened around the throbbing egg, firm and heavy within its puckered purse of rose-brown skin. Her saliva was hot and slippery, making his testes roll around inside the scrotum, captured for brief moment within the prison of her kiss, then escaping again, producing new and wonderful sensations.

Greg's eyes were shut, but the sun glowed red through his closed eyelids, crimson like Mila's lips, crimson like the passion surging and bubbling through his veins. Think of the paradise of sensation if only she could take both testes into her mouth at once . . .

That thought alone was almost enough to make him spurt; and when Mila turned her attentions to his left testicle, he wondered just how much longer he could hold out without climaxing.

She seemed to sense that the point of no return was near,

THE GOLDEN CAGE

for just when surrender seemed inevitable, she opened her mouth again and released him, his saliva-moistened testes feeling strangely cool in the hot sunshine.

'Won't you make love to me?' she pleaded. Her sexy Russian voice drove Greg mad with the need for her.

'Ah, but *how* shall I make love to you, you insatiable little witch?'

'Fuck my tits. I want you to fuck my tits ... and then begin all over again.'

He could feel the excitement within her, a delicious tension inside her as he slid his shaft between the firm white globes of Mila's breasts. She was holding her tits, and as he slid between them she squeezed them together, very firmly, holding him as tightly as the virgin-tight sheath of her womanhood.

It was approaching noon, the hottest part of a scorching hot day. Sweat trickled over their bodies, moistening and lubricating Greg's penis as he pushed back and forth in the deep valley between Mila's breasts. It was too good to last very long, that was obvious to him. He was doing his damnedest to hold back, but pleasure was creeping up on him, determined to betray his resolve.

Her breasts were silky soft, the skin smooth and slippery against his prick. He looked down, mesmerised by the way the flesh rippled and flowed, fluid as a milky ocean; watching the way it parted at each stroke, allowing the glossy purple tip to emerge – a spitting cobra unhooded and ready to strike.

'Mila ... Mila, it's coming...'

'Don't hold back. Let it come.'

There was no choice; control wasn't an option any more. The bright, many-faceted colours of ecstasy were already filling his consciousness, and the last few strokes seemed to carry Greg along with them, like flotsam on a wild and tumbling sea.

'Now, Mila, it's now.'

He withdrew as the seed bubbled and boiled in his balls, shooting up the shaft of his prick in sudden, burning spurts. Ejaculation had seldom felt so good. There, among the swaying cornstalks, he ejaculated over Mila's breasts, the creamy droplets falling in a pearly rain on her smooth, bare skin.

'Lick me clean,' she breathed; and taking his head in her hands, she pulled him down to her breasts.

He put out his tongue, hungry for the taste of their coupling. He had tasted his own semen before – what curious adolescent hadn't? – but it had never turned him on before. This was something new, something that tasted both wicked and blissfully right. There was a creaminess in its taste, mixed with salt and a slightly bitter aftertaste which excited him much more than he had expected it to.

'Drink it all down, darling,' whispered Mila, her dark hair glinting copper fire in the sunlight. 'Then drink my juices. Lick me between my legs.'

Feverishly he lapped at the few remaining droplets of semen, filling his whole being with the taste of his seed and her sweat, his prick already rearing its head in anticipation of this new and honeysweet feast . . .

'Well, ain't that just the cutest thing you ever did see?'

The voice behind him, loaded with sarcasm, made Greg freeze, his blood suddenly thick with cold. Moving very, very slowly, he raised himself on his arms and saw Mila's face. She was looking over his shoulder, her eyes wide with terror. Could it be Hobart's men, come to take Mila from him? Or Federal agents who'd finally decided to put an end to the first real adventure of his life?

THE GOLDEN CAGE

Was the dream ending already, before it had really begun?

'You done now, mister? Only we got a few questions need askin'.'

With a deep breath for courage, Greg rolled over and turned round, clumsily zipping himself up.

His eyes travelled upwards, over shiny black boots and jodphurs, leather jacket and mirror shades, white helmets and a gun holster, slung at the hip. Motorcycle cops.

'Highway Patrol,' announced the taller of the two men, flashing his ID then thrusting it back into the inside pocket of his leather jacket. 'Me and my partner, we got a few questions fer you an' your...' His voice tailed off into a slightly lascivious smile. 'Your little lady.'

'Not so little though, if ya know what I mean.' The second cop spat into the corn, taking off his mirror shades to get a better look. With a look of purest venom, Mila wriggled her bra and silk top down over her exposed breasts.

Fear of the consequences seemed almost irrelevant to Greg, knowing that the eventual consequence was bound to be the State Penitentiary. If he went down, he wasn't going without a struggle – or without protecting Mila from these two gorillas. He allowed his anger to bubble to the surface.

'You have no right to talk to her like that.'

It was a huge relief, after so many years of being what everyone expected him to be – the perfect, politely spoken Englishman. He fantasised about what it would feel like to take a swing at that smug, leering face. He'd never broken a man's nose before. It might even be fun.

'That's where you're wrong.' The first cop seemed to pay little heed to Greg's righteous outburst. 'We got any damn right we choose – ain't that so, Clyde?'

Clyde took off his leather gauntlets and thrust them through the belt of his jodphurs. Taking a note book from his jacket pocket he flicked it open.

'What d'ya say, Officer Mulgrew – offending public decency? Corrupting morals?'

'Sure. If they don't co-operate.'

Greg felt Mila's hand on his arm, heard her whisper in his ear: 'Don't try to be a hero. Just do what they want.' She was trembling, quivering and icy cold.

'OK, OK, we'll answer your questions.'

'That's better. Now if you'd just come with us.'

They had little option. One cop walked in front of them, the other right behind, so close that Mila felt his hand on her backside. Mulgrew led the way towards the yellow Chevy.

'This your vehicle, sir?'

'Yes – no. That is, sort of.'

'You lyin' to me, sir?'

'No, of course not. I borrowed it.'

'You got the documents?'

Greg felt his pulse race. The questions were getting uncomfortably near to home. What if the police had already worked out who they were, and were just playing with them? What if they hadn't, but his clumsy responses pointed them towards the truth?

Mila cut in.

'They were stolen,' she said. 'Along with our passports and most of our money.'

'Is that a fact? You reported the felony, of course?'

'Of course.' Greg prayed the cops wouldn't ask any more questions, but it seemed incredible that they could possibly fall for a transparent – and pretty desperate – lie. To his relief, they changed tack.

THE GOLDEN CAGE

'Where you headed?'
'Nowhere special. We're just on holiday.'
He felt Mila's arm slip round his waist.

'We're on honeymoon, officer,' she said, doing her best to smile whilst working out the best way to escape, should things turn unpleasant.

Officer Mulgrew's face split into a smile which was anything but pleasant to behold. Mila recalled the feel of his hand on her backside shivered. The cops had guns, they had nothing to defend themselves with but their wits.

'Couldn't wait to get to yer honeymoon hotel, huh?'
'Kind of,' agreed Greg.
'Can't say I blame ya, she's a tasty piece of ass. Wouldn't mind a taste of it myself.'

Mila quaked inwardly but stood her ground. She longed to vent all her fury on this contemptible man, who got turned on by other people's fear – exactly the same way that Orin Hobart got his kicks.

'A CBs breaker radioed in that your car was abandoned on the highway,' cut in Clyde. 'You need a tow to a garage?'

'Er no, no, the car's fine.' Greg watched the policemen looking it over, praying they didn't find something which incriminated one or both of them, hoping with all his soul that they didn't recognise his face from the syndicated police mugshots.

'Front nearside tyre's worn. You want to get that fixed, 'fore you get yourself into trouble.' The cop's eyes seemed to glitter behind his shades, 'Accidents can happen.'

'I'll get it fixed,' replied Greg hastily. 'Next town we get to.'

'OK then. That seems to be in order.' To Greg and Mila's astonishment, the two cops got back on their motorbikes and the engines kicked in.

'You don't need to ask us any more questions?' Mila couldn't believe this was happening.

'Not unless you want us to take you in for . . . interrogation,' replied Clyde, and revved the throttle on his Harley-Davidson.

'Mind how you go,' was Mulgrew's parting shot. 'And be sure you have a *real* nice day, y'all.'

The tiny town of Endurance, Kansas, was so small that it barely made it on to maps. The sheriff's office stood about halfway along the main street, flanked by a general store and a doctor's consulting rooms. It wasn't much to write home about – but then again, the citizens of this small settlement were unusually law-abiding.

Inside, Officer Mulgrew and his colleague Clyde Honey sat drinking black coffee and watching confiscated blue movies on the sheriff's own personal VCR.

'You ever see *Deadly Weapons*, Clyde?'

'Nope. I seen *Deep Throat* a time or two, though.'

'You wanna watch *Deadly Weapons*. It's a real classy movie. Jeez, that Chesty Morgan sure is somethin'. She has these great fifty-two-inch tits that she kills her lovers with. It's one horny movie. I got me a boner just thinkin' 'bout it.'

The outer door opened, then slammed shut. Clyde and Mulgrew turned to see the inner door burst open.

'Well, hi there, Mr Steadman, Mizz O'Brien.'

Darsey O'Brien stalked into the sheriff's office ahead of her colleague.

'It was them?'

THE GOLDEN CAGE

'Sure was.' Mulgrew drained his bottle of Bud.

'You're *absolutely* sure?'

'Lady, I *absolutely* don't make mistakes. Not 'bout girls with great tits...'

'And you did as we instructed you?'

'Sure did.' Clyde got up, walked over to the desk and slid open the top drawer. Inside sat a small black box, a little like a TV remote control. He flicked a switch and it began to emit a regular bleeping noise. 'They never suspected a thing – just couldn't wait to get away. They'll never guess we bugged their car.'

Blip. Blip. Blip.

'Excellent.' O'Brien took the control set with a smile of satisfaction. Now they had Mila Kirovska within their grasp. Any time they wanted, they could pounce. And in the meantime, they could track her and the idiot Englishman, find out what they were up to and where they were headed. 'You'll be rewarded.'

'We want a girl. A blonde, big ones...'

'You'll have her. Just as soon as I can arrange it.'

'Make it soon. My dick's burstin'. Don't suppose *you'd* be interested in relieving a man's nat'ral frustrations?'

'Take your filthy hands off me.' Darsey lifted Mulgrew's hands from her buttocks with an air of cool disdain.

'What about the other matter?' interjected Steadman. 'The jade tiger?'

'I dunno – I ain't seen no tiger thing. You seen it, Clyde?'

'Nope.'

'Did you search the car?'

'Kind of.'

'Kind of isn't good enough, *officer*,' hissed O'Brien.

'Maybe they got rid of it?' suggested Clyde.

Steadman shook his head.

'Why would they bother? No, they've still got it. One of them is probably carrying it on them.'

'We'll have it soon,' purred O'Brien, pacified by the rhythmic bleeping of the control set. 'And when we do, we'll use it to barter with Orin Hobart for what we want.'

Chapter 14

Mila opened the glove compartment and took out the little jade tiger.

'You know, I think you're right,' she said. 'He is lucky. Lucky for us, anyway.' She stroked the tiger's head. 'Maybe I sensed that. Maybe that's why I stole him.'

Greg looked at her sharply.

'You stole him? I thought you said you found him.'

'I did – in a cabinet at Orin Hobart's house. I figured he owed it me.'

'And the rest.'

Greg's hands tightened momentarily on the steering wheel as the familiar anger returned. If he had anything to do with it, Hobart would pay for his treatment of Mila with more than a poxy jade model of a tiger.

Mila yawned.

'I'm tired. It'll be evening soon. Shall we stop somewhere?'

Greg surveyed the countryside around them. They were in stunningly beautiful, wild America now – the remote and unearthly canyonlands of Arizona, where mesas and buttes rose up like jagged teeth from the desert floor. To the right, saguaro cactus covered sun-drenched, hillsides of rich red volcanic stone. Further away to the left, were a series of deep gorges filled with giant cottonwood trees.

This wasn't just off the beaten track – it was a wilderness like nothing you could find anywhere else in the world. And it wasn't a place you'd want to get lost in, either. Wander off and you might never be found. Unless the rattlesnakes or the scorpions happened to find you...

'I'm getting a bit tired myself,' confessed Greg. 'But there haven't been any motels for miles, not since we came off the Interstate. Maybe should have stuck to the main roads – or stayed another night at that bed and breakfast in Grand Junction.'

'Oh, not there. The landlady was falling in love with you!'

'That's what I like about the Americans – they have such good taste.'

'You really think so, do you? Well I ... oh look, what's that?' Mila pointed to a sign coming up at the roadside. Greg focused on it as they drove past.

'San Hernandos Indian Reservation,' he read. 'Looks like we've just moved into native American country.'

'Is it safe?'

Greg chuckled.

'You've been watching too many westerns. Of course it's safe I wonder if they get many tourists round here. It's not exactly Piccadilly Circus.'

They drove on a few miles and the road took a sharp bend through a rocky valley. They emerged into a collection of wooden huts, two prefabricated portakabins, one or two tepees, a corral full of piebald ponies and a parking lot dotted with large American cars. Geronimo meets Ronald McDonald, thought Greg as they drove past a youth with long hair and fringed buckskin trousers, carrying a ghetto blaster in one hand and a can of Coke in the other.

THE GOLDEN CAGE

'Look – there's a general store.' Mila pointed to a wooden cabin to the left of the parking lot. 'Maybe they could tell us where to find somewhere to stay?'

'Could be closed – it's well after six.'

Mila checked the sign.

'"Eight till late". What does "late" mean?'

'When the last customer leaves, I imagine, and there's no more money to be made.'

They parked the Chevy alongside a brand-new Datsun jeep, watched by a small gathering of black-haired children wearing jeans and trainers. There was not a pair of moccasins in sight. Six pairs of watchful eyes followed them all the way to the front steps of the store, up on to the front porch and through the door.

Although the store was unlocked it seemed deserted and they had time to take a good look around. It appeared to sell everything from animal traps to beer, souvenirs, bread, clothes, and even a fearsome array of shotguns inside a locked glass cabinet marked 'Sporting Goods'. The low-beamed ceiling was hung with unidentifiable joints of meat and bunches of leaves, slowly drying in the hot, bone-dry air and giving off warm, savoury-sweet, smoky smells.

'Do you suppose it's shut?'

'It can't be – the door was open.'

'Won't the owner mind us being in here?'

'How should I know. I expect he'll be back in a minute.'

Mila wandered across to one of the hooks, looked up and prodded a wrinkled, blackish-brown thing dangling from the ceiling.

'What's that?'

Greg peered at it, screwing up his eyes.

'Looks like . . . I'm not sure, some kind of dried lizard or something.'

Mila pulled a face and wiped her hand on her skirt. She turned to the glass-topped counter.

'Oh, look at these, Greg – they're so pretty. Coloured beads, and necklaces. That's real turquoise, I'm sure it is . . .'

The sound of a door opening and closing, somewhere at the back of the building, announced the shopkeeper's arrival. A bead curtain swished and she emerged into the half-light of the store.

'Hi. You folks need help?'

She was a woman of perhaps forty-five, still quite handsome; in her youth, Greg estimated, she must have been positively stunning. Her face was quite broad but high-cheekboned, giving her an exotic and faintly aristocratic air. She wore her still-dark tresses in a single braid, decorated with thin strands of coloured leather plaited and woven into the hair. Her clothing was western in style – jeans and cowboy boots, and a fringed shirt left open at the neck to reveal supple, tanned skin.

'Oh, hello. We were wondering . . . is the store still open?'

The woman smiled.

'We never close. You looking for anything particular?' Her accent was hard to define – a slightly clipped blend of southern American and something else, something older and more romantic.

'Well, we could do with a little food and something to drink.' Greg rummaged in his back pocket and took out his wallet. 'It's thirsty work driving across the desert.'

'Sure is. Can be a dangerous place, too, if you don't understand it and respect it.' The woman disappeared

THE GOLDEN CAGE

through the curtain and reappeared moments later, carrying a crate of bottles and cans. 'I got Coke or Dr Pepper or root beer.'

'Coke's fine.'

'You want me to fix you something to eat? Coupla club sandwiches maybe?'

'That would be great. It's a long way to the next town – longer than we'd reckoned.'

The woman's expression did not change, but her voice registered curiosity.

'So you're planning on driving through the night?'

'We haven't much choice,' Mila explained. 'We're miles from anywhere. We were hoping to find a motel, but . . .'

'You want a place to stay?'

'You know somewhere?'

'Sure.' The impassive face broke into its first smile. 'You can stay here.'

'That would be great!' enthused Greg, relieved at the thought of not having to drive through the desert at night. It struck him as the sort of place that might be beautiful by day but was just plain scary by night. 'You rent rooms here for visitors?'

'We do, but we don't get too many visitors here. Most of the tourists drive straight past on the freeway, go to see the bigger reservations with their gift stores and visitor centres.'

She extended her hand in greeting.

'My name is Sudden Lightning. You are very welcome here.'

'Mila Kirovska – and this is Greg Delaney.'

'You are lovers, yes?'

'Well . . . yes.' Mila could feel her cheeks burning, but Sudden Lightning seemed perfectly unconcerned.

'It is not difficult to divine. There is a great deal of sexual energy around you.' She laid her hands lightly on Greg and Mila's foreheads, closed her eyes and thought for a moment. 'But I see fear also.'

Mila stiffened, a cold shiver running over her like the caress of an icy hand.

'Not fear of each other, no. Fear of something else ... something that you cannot yet see or touch. A great darkness which pursues you. Am I right?' Her eyes sprang open, questioning them, challenging them to protest that she was mistaken.

'Kind of,' admitted Greg after a long silence.

'There is no reason to be afraid of me or of anyone here. It is not our business to ask questions. But perhaps the old ways could help you to find your own answers?'

'Answers?'

'Our people believe in the importance of freeing both the body and the mind. Fear is one of the shackles that bind us to the darkness instead of to the light of the great spirit. Perhaps we can help you ... but I see that you are tired. Come with me, please. I shall take you to my brother's house.'

Greg and Mila followed Sudden Lightning down the steps and out of the store. Behind them, faded wooden signs proclaimed 'Jewelry, Gifts, Moccasins, Saddle Tack, Purses.'

Mila noticed that the Indian village was bigger than it had seemed from the road. In sharp contrast to the Hollywood image of tepees and feathered headdresses, this was a settlement mainly of sturdy, functional huts – some of wood, others daubed with a reddish, clayey mud which had baked hard in the fierce sunshine. Towards one side stood a

THE GOLDEN CAGE

small school and community centre, a jumble of prefabricated huts brought from the nearest big city. Like the Coke cans and the sneakers, they looked out of place against the red rocks and the tall cacti, out of place and out of time.

'Black River.' Sudden Lightning knocked at the door of one of the wooden huts. 'Black River, get out here.'

'Please, if we're causing you any trouble...' began Mila, but Sudden Lightning snorted dismissively.

'He is a lazy dog. Black River!'

'All right woman, all right.'

A latch scraped and clicked, and the door swung inwards, to reveal an Indian perhaps in his early forties, not tall but well-made and ruggedly good-looking. He was naked except for a pair of stonewashed jeans and a bright beaded headband, two long, jet-black braids of glossy hair swung over his deeply tanned shoulders.

'What's the hurry... oh.' His eyes took in Mila's body in a couple of seconds, drinking in her beauty. Approving of what he saw, he extended his hand. 'Hi there.'

'Pleased to meet you.' Mila tried to avoid his eyes, but they seemed to draw her, coaxing her to look deep into them. They were a deep hazel in colour, velvet-soft yet wild as a coyote's.

'I brought you some guests,' announced Sudden Lightning.

'So I see, sister.'

'They will stay the night with you. You take good care of them, yes?'

'The best.'

Greg wasn't sure he liked the way Black River was eyeing up Mila but when all was said and done hospitality was hospitality. If he wasn't careful he could see himself turning paranoid.

219

Black River led them inside his home. Mila was surprised to find that, despite its rough exterior, the inside of the cabin was extremely comfortable and stylish. The furniture was simple, but there was a TV and VCR in the living room, with a portable PC on the table. The decor was a pleasant mixture of the ethnic and the modern – plain wooden walls decorated with beads, woven blankets and carved animals' heads; a polished floor scattered with colourful rugs in geometric designs. Traditional music played softly on the CD deck.

'You folks don't mind sharing a bed?' Black River looked back over his shoulder as he led them through into the smaller of the two bedrooms. 'Don't answer that, I can see you don't.'

The bedroom was small but cosy, a simple wooden bedstead covered with blankets and a patchwork quilt.

'This is really kind of you,' began Mila, but Black River put up his hands to silence her thanks.

'It is our way to welcome guests.' He laughed. 'And we have few enough guests here, as I expect my sister has told you. I don't think we are quite *commercial* enough to make money from the tourists.'

'How do you live?' enquired Greg

'Most of us have jobs in the towns. One or two work as tour guides, some work in Flagstaff or Phoenix, a friend of mine breeds and schools riding ponies. I'm the teacher at the school here. I try to keep my students interested in the old ways as well as the new. It's not always easy.' He leaned a little closer to Greg and Mila. 'How about you?'

'I'm ... an accountant,' said Greg and instantly wished that he was. A nice, safe, boring accountant in a cosy office somewhere like Croydon or Runcorn, thanking his lucky stars for his daily dose of monotony.

THE GOLDEN CAGE

'I translate books,' said Mila. 'Or I used to.'

'From what language?'

'Russian.'

'Your English is superb. I would not have guessed that you were Russian.'

'Thank you.'

'But I do understand how hard it is to express oneself in a foreign language. American English is entirely foreign to me, just as it is to you.'

Black River's eyes seemed to look deep, so very deep into Mila's soul, reaching inside her and finding out all the truths she was afraid and ashamed to confess. She hardly knew if she was attracted to, or repelled by, this strange man.

'You look tired,' he observed.

'We're bushed,' agreed Greg.

'Hungry? Folks say I fix some real fine tamales.'

'Sounds wonderful.'

'But first . . .' Black River's eyes twinkled with a distant, secret brightness. 'It seems to me that you need to relax, both of you.'

His fingers pushed Mila's hair back over her shoulders and wound it up into a loose knot, while the fingers of his other hand slid over the bare skin of her neck, now tanned a light golden colour.

'Hmm, so very tense.' He exerted a little pressure and Mila gave a yelp of pain. 'Hurts, huh?'

'Like a knife in my shoulder.'

'It is as I thought. That is a trigger point, the sign of very bad tension.' He let the hair fall and it spiralled down as the knot loosened, falling in a slightly twisted coil down her back. 'You too are tense and in pain, Greg?'

'Well – I suppose so, a little. It's been a long day's driving.'

'And you have worries too? No, Greg, don't look at me like that! He laughed. 'Whatever it is that's freaking the two of you out, I don't want to know about it. I really don't want to know who you are, or what you've done. But I've gotten enough of a sixth sense over the years to know when someone's afraid, *really* afraid.

'Let me give you one piece of advice, both of you. You don't have to take it. Get rid of the fear, else it's going to eat away at your insides till there's nothing left but this empty shell. And once you get like that, there's not a damn thing you can do to save yourself. You lose the strength of will, see?'

Greg felt Black River's hands on his shoulders, gently massaging and kneading away the tension. It felt slightly odd to have another man massaging him, but boy did it feel good.

'Mmm, feels great. Where did you learn to do that?'

'I didn't have to learn. All my family have the gift. We're healers as well as teachers. Look, my friends, before we eat why don't I show you the best way in the world to leave your tensions far, far behind?'

Why not? thought Greg as he and Mila followed Black River out through the back door of his cabin and across the dusty tracks which criss-crossed the village. It was moving towards late evening now, the shadows lengthening and the fierce heat of day moderating to a bone-deep warmth which shimmered above the dark-red, dusty earth. The still air was filled with the buzz and click of insect-song, the chirrup of unseen crickets.

Some way distant from the rest of the village, in the lee of tall, rust-coloured, age-weathered rocks, stood a small

THE GOLDEN CAGE

rectangular cabin. On the face of it there was nothing remarkable about it – but this wasn't quite like any of the other buildings in the village.

The cabin was built from split logs, smeared over with hard-baked mud which filled the cracks in between. It was roofed with moss and branches, again bound together with mud.

The oddest thing about it was that there were no windows – only a tiny door-opening, large enough for a man to crawl through on all fours. Wisps of white smoke or steam were escaping through the few cracks which had not been blocked up.

Seeing Greg and Mila's puzzled expressions, Black River explained:

'This is what we call a steam lodge. It is a little like a sauna, but our people do not use it just for cleansing their bodies, or for simple relaxation. It is a place where we go to get in touch with our spiritual selves. Will you enter it with me?'

His eyes met Mila's and again she felt that selfsame, cold thrill. Part of her wanted to say no, to turn away and walk out of this man's spooky, unreal world. But a greater part of her was consumed by curiosity: curiosity and perhaps just a little excitement.

'Yes,' she whispered.

'We must undress first,' Black River instructed them, unbuckling the belt of his jeans.

'Hang on a minute, I don't know about this...' began Greg, but he too could feel the first stirrings of excitement. He looked across at Mila, and saw that she was mesmerised, her nipples standing proud beneath the crumpled silk top and her lips parted and glistening, as though wet with sheer anticipation.

Black River's olive skin glistened with a seasoning of sweat in the evening sunlight. Slowly he unzipped his jeans. Mila couldn't take her eyes off his fingers, sliding down, down, down, baring the secrets beneath.

He wore no underwear, and Mila felt a profound thrill as he exposed millimetre after millimetre of bare flesh. First the taut, tanned belly and the little trail of dark hairs leading down from navel to balls. Then the bliss of glimpsing his long, fat cock as it emerged from its imprisoning cocoon.

It wasn't erect, but even in its flaccid state it was beautiful: long, thick and tanned the same olive-gold as the rest of his body. As Black River slid down his jeans and stepped out of them, it swung free, standing slightly proud above his heavy balls. It was a full five inches long, a golden serpent, sinuous and full of life, its circumcised glans moist and glistening in the evening sunlight.

The Indian stood very still, not saying a word; waiting. Slowly, Mila began to undress and – his mind a maelstrom of mixed feelings – Greg at last followed suit. It felt bizarre in the extreme to be taking off all his clothes in front of this complete stranger, not two hundred yards from the centre of an Indian village. More bizarre still to find himself increasingly attracted to the man who stood before him, the man with the large and menacing penis.

This was the first time Greg Delaney had ever felt any sort of attraction towards another man. Normally he would have been freaked to hell by it, disgusted even; but here, in the middle of the desert, it was like being in another world where the old rules simply didn't apply. Besides, it wasn't as if he was actually going to do anything about it, was it . . . ?

THE GOLDEN CAGE

'You are ready now?' Black River crouched on his knees before the doorway to the steam lodge.

They nodded. Mila was first to get down on all fours, her incomparably beautiful arse driving Greg to an insanity of desire as he watched her crawl towards the open doorway, her body wreathed in tendrils of hot steam.

Men and women. Black River and Mila Kirovska. Sexual desire was so confusing. How could it be possible to desire her to the point of explosion and yet to want him too?

No more questions. It was time to follow Mila into the lodge, just a caress behind her. Black River led the way, lowering his head to crawl into the enfolding steam; then Mila, her gorgeous frame gradually disappearing from view as she entered the lodge.

It was Greg's turn. The savage, wet heat of the steam hit him quite suddenly, filling his lungs and making him cough. He couldn't see a thing, not one damn thing: the steam stung his eyes, and moved in thick, swirling clouds about him.

He heard the door close behind him and felt a momentary surge of panic. He was locked in! Trapped! Memories of childhood claustrophobia were creeping up on him. How on earth did he get himself into these situations?

Black River's voice reached him through the swirling, muffling steam. It sounded calm, patient, serene.

'Relax, Greg. Try to breathe regularly and you will soon become accustomed to it.'

Breathing was easier said than done. The steam seemed to contain all sorts of aromatic scents – herbs, spices, other things so potent that they made his head start to swim.

'I can't! I feel as if I'm suffocating.'

'Breathe deeply. Let yourself go.'

He managed to control his twitching diaphragm and hawked in a lungful of steam. This time, the reaction was quite different. A weird, wonderful, otherworldly sense of elation swept over him, like a great wave of liquid sunshine and he heard himself laughing. It sounded very far away, as if someone else was laughing for him.

'That's better, Greg. Much better. Enjoy...'

Mila's eyes were becoming accustomed to the faint light inside the steam lodge. It was illuminated by a series of coloured candles, mounted around the wall. Their feeble light danced amid the steam, making phantasmagorical patterns. She could just make out the shape of Greg, kneeling on the ground, his whole body shaking with uncontrollable laughter. It didn't seem like an odd thing to be doing, because she felt like that herself. A sensation of incredible lightness had taken her over, wiping out her every worry and inhibition at one sweep of its angelic hand.

Her hands found the edge of a stone bench and she pulled herself up on to it. It felt cold against her overheated flesh, the trickles of mingled sweat and steam running down her face, her breasts, her belly, her thighs. She was bathed in wetness, the secret moisture between her pussy lips almost lost in the slippery joy of being.

Black River threw a handful of powder on the charcoal fire and it flared up, green and red and blue and white. Water made it hiss and spit, and sent yet more clouds of steam billowing around the interior of the cabin. As he turned round Mila saw that he was now erect. Beautifully, magnificently erect. The five inches of pliable golden flesh had turned into almost ten of hard, golden stone.

The Indian's penis danced as he came towards her, the curving sabre pointing its tip at her. Behind him, Greg was

THE GOLDEN CAGE

still on his knees, his body shaking with a silent and joyful laughter. Through the swirling steam, Mila saw that he was watching, tense with excited anticipation.

Black River did not speak but stood in front of Mila, his eyes forming an inextricable bond with hers, their message very clear.

Slowly her lips parted and he took a step forward. Mila's fingers touched him, like touching someone in a beautiful dream. Something so perfect could not be real, yet it felt real. It tasted real. It couldn't be wrong, could it? Because this was just a dream . . .

Her tongue-tip skated across the tip of Black River's manhood, at first barely touching it. Then she grew bolder and took the glans between her lips, kissing and licking it.

Greg saw them together, watched them through the moving white curtain of steam. The misty veil parted and he saw Black River's huge, iron-hard dick sliding up to the hilt into Mila's mouth, pushing right down her throat, the Indian's back slightly arched backward as his hands fretted convulsively with Mila's hair.

Greg wanted her too, but he didn't feel jealous . . . he wanted them both. Wanted sex more than he wanted breath, or life, or anything else. At this moment there was only one drive within him and it was unrelentingly sexual.

'Relax, Mila,' soothed Black River's voice. 'Suck, my darling. Suck like a little babe. Let the taste fill your whole being. Let the feelings flow within you. Free yourself . . . discover the truth of your own desire.'

His hands moved down over Mila's cheeks and throat, down, down, down to the soft pillows of her breasts, and Mila began to tremble as he started stroking her nipples. Her throat relaxed instinctively as he began thrusting into her; not brutally as Orin Hobart had done, but with the utmost gentleness. She found that she was the one who wanted to force the pace, sucking and devouring his sex with a savage eagerness.

Greg crept forward, still on all-fours. He was excited, desperately so. He wanted to laugh, to cry, but most of all to fuck. Jealousy seemed a complete irrelevance. He no longer cared if he had to share Mila with Black River – in fact, the idea turned him on so much that he almost came. His cock was a painfully erect spike, aching to impale soft flesh.

He was kneeling behind Black River now, and it seemed the most natural thing in the world to reach out and touch him. To run his fingers over the dripping-wet flesh of his buttocks. Rivulets of water ran down from the small of his back, collecting in the little hollow at the base of his spine then spilling over to form runnels that dripped down the firm, muscular curve of his buttocks.

Hands stroking the wet flesh, brushing the short, dark hairs, Greg felt the rhythm of Black River's pelvic thrusts, felt as though he were almost a part of his coupling with Mila. On a wild, joyful impulse, he pressed his lips to the flesh of Black River's backside and began to kiss it.

He had never kissed another man before, never tasted another man's flesh. It tasted good and with each breath of steam he took, it tasted even better. His fingers grasped the flesh, kneaded it, stroked and probed, discovering as a child discovers – wonderingly and without prejudice.

'Ah. Ah yes. Yes, Greg, that's so good. Lick me, bite me...'

Black River was thrusting harder now, his cock pushing against the back of Mila's throat, then, as he withdrew, pushing his buttocks hard against Greg's face. Greg's tongue explored the flesh, pushed into the deep furrow

THE GOLDEN CAGE

between the buttocks, tasted and teased, experiencing the thrill of forbidden mysteries...

With a cry of pleasure, Black River climaxed in Mila's mouth, his hands tightening around his Russian lover's sex-swollen breasts. Greg felt that he shared in the climax, feeling the quivering, shuddering pleasure travelling from the Indian's body into his own, magnifying his excitement.

But now he wanted more. Much more.

Black River turned round. Greg couldn't take his eyes off the Indian's manhood, glistening with semen and saliva and still so very erect.

'There is much for you to discover about yourself, Greg,' he said softly, raising Greg's head with gentle hands until it was on a level with his dick. 'Kiss me, Greg. You know you want to, you know you'll enjoy doing it. Understand. Nothing is forbidden, all things are possible. Only pleasure matters.'

Greg did not hesitate. The piquant scent of Black River's cock was driving him crazy. He pressed his lips against its base, feeling the wiry curls against his lips and chin; then ran his lips and tongue slowly upward, along the length of the swollen shaft.

'Don't be afraid, Greg. Taste me. And taste your lover's pleasure on me.'

The tip of Black River's prick slipped smoothly between Greg's lips, filling him with the glorious, strong taste of sex. Seed and saliva mingled into a cocktail of pleasure. He sucked and licked, driven by a desire which swelled with each breath he took.

'Please, Greg. Suck me now.' It was Mila's voice, softly pleading. 'I'm so wet, I can't bear it. Won't you lick me out?'

'You must give your lover what she needs,' urged Black

River, withdrawing from Greg's mouth. 'And I shall give you what you need, my English friend.'

Not yet quite understanding Black River's words, Greg looked towards his lover. Mila was still sitting on the stone bench, her thighs spread wide and the wet pink mouth of her sex smiling at him.

'Lick me out,' she repeated.

He knelt before her, dazzled by the discovery of this new and sparkling sexuality, the realisation that nothing in the world was unnatural or wrong, and that he could find pleasure in anything he chose to do.

She was more beautiful even than he remembered, her pink lotus-blossom opening to him at the very first touch. He spread its petals with the fingers of his left hand, and the hard stalk emerged, stamen-like and glossy-bright, from its fleshy hood.

'Please, Greg. Hurry, I can't bear it...'

He pressed his face into the fragrant bounty of her sex, pushing his index finger inside her and exulting at the tight wetness of her vagina, its gently twitching muscles which sought to swallow him up. Bliss. It was pure bliss to taste her sweetness, to have her honey trickling on to his tongue and down his throat. Ecstasy.

Black River's lips kissed the nape of his neck. Then his hands crept down over Greg's body, exploring, arousing. Greg felt the Indian's dick against his backside, a hard baton of flesh. It felt good, exciting, and he pushed back against Black River's belly, enjoying the sensation. He was full of joy, of love, of a new and unbounded lust for life.

For life – and for sex. For anything and everything that felt good. And this felt damn good. As he licked and lapped at Mila's sex he was laughing inside, laughing and exhilarated and more turned-on than he could ever remember.

THE GOLDEN CAGE

Black River's hands emerged from the swirling, shifting veil of white steam, and stroked down the curve of Greg's buttocks, easing them apart with a caress of pure gentleness.

Greg did not flinch or try to fight against this new embrace. Why should he? It was what he wanted.

It was like entering a new world. Discovering a new way of seeing things, a universe full of unsuspected, unexplored possibilities.

Black River had been right after all.

Greg and Mila stood at the north rim of the Grand Canyon, gazing across the bed of the Colorado River and towards their distant, unfathomable future. The late evening sunlight cast ever-changing patterns on the stark promontories and sandstone pinnacles along the canyon. It was almost immeasurably huge: eighteen miles across at its widest point, something so big that it dwarfed the two figures who stood alone at the viewing rail.

'Do you really think things could come right for us?' whispered Mila. It seemed a blasphemy to raise her voice in this sacred place.

'I don't know. I want to think that they could, but . . . I don't know. I daren't hope.'

Mila fingered the jade tiger in her jacket pocket. It felt warm, comfortable, enduring.

'You know what Black River said. We have to dare. Or would you rather just roll over and give in?'

What had happened back there on the reservation, in Black River's steam lodge, had changed something for ever. A cynic might say all that had happened was a drug-induced orgy, an hallucinogenic haze, but to Mila and Greg it was something more spiritual. Something that had altered their whole slant on the world and made them question whether or not they had to be victims.

'I want to make love to you, Mila Kirovska.'

'Here?'

'Here, at the very edge of the Grand Canyon. And I don't care who sees us.'

'That's fighting talk, crazy Englishman.'

Tenderly, Greg unfastened the top two buttons of Mila's shirt and slipped it down over her shoulder. He kissed the bare skin.

'Fighting wasn't exactly what I had in mind.'

Chapter 15

Mila sat in the Chevy, waiting for Greg to return from the foodstore. She looked out of the car window at the old Mormon town of St George, Utah. It seemed unremittingly, almost creepily wholesome.

Young men with dark suits and gleaming bridgework strolled down the broad main street. They looked disconcertingly identical, and so did their well-scrubbed girlfriends. Mila wondered why Greg had been so keen to make a detour and come here.

Five minutes later, he arrived back at the car with two huge brown paper sacks of groceries, which he slung into the back before sliding into the driver's seat. He leaned over and gave Mila a quick kiss.

'Plenty of food but I couldn't buy anything to drink except mineral water and fruit juice. They've got funny drinking laws in this part of the world.'

'That doesn't bother me – it's too hot for alcohol.'

'Ready then?' Greg enquired, sliding the key into the ignition.

'For what?'

'For a drive round town!'

Mila gazed about her, mystified, as the car moved off into the slow-moving traffic.

'But it's...'

'Yeah, I know. Gives you the creeps, doesn't it?'

'But if you think it's so horrible, why did you want to come here?'

'Out of curiosity.' Greg glanced at the town plan he'd bought for fifty cents in the Seven-Eleven. 'And maybe for a little revenge.' He needed to make a right, a left and then drive straight on down East St George Boulevard until he hit the outskirts of town.

'Revenge? What have you got against this place?'

'It's not really the place, it's what it represents. You see, ten years ago my company opened its first US office in St George. I don't even know if it's still here, but I've been fantasising about chucking a brick through the window.'

'You wouldn't!'

'You're probably right. But I might just go and spit on their brass plate. It'd make me feel a whole lot better.'

They drove on through the town. It was pretty enough – a jumble of old houses and new developments, huddled together at the foot of a broad, reddish-brown sandstone cliff. Some of the buildings were quite impressive, particularly the nineteenth-century Mormon Temple at 200E and 500S, but the overall impression it gave Mila was one of claustrophobia.

'Look – there's Brigham Young's old house.' Greg jabbed a finger at a crowd of tourists, their camcorders and floppy sun hats practically obscuring the façade of a much-restored adobe house. 'He used to spend the winter there. Nice and warm, you see – it's sheltered here.'

'Lucky him,' yawned Mila, thinking of the winters back in St Petersburg, the biting winds coming in off the sea and the great drifts of snow, so deep that they sometimes piled

THE GOLDEN CAGE

up waist-high outside the door of Alexander's apartment building. It all seemed very far away and – in spite of everything that had happened – she realised that she didn't regret what she'd done, none of it. At least, she wouldn't if only she and Greg could find a way of extricating themselves from trouble and making a fresh start.

'It's somewhere along here ... I remember. Can you see it anywhere? A grey building, four storeys, with smoky glass windows.'

'Is that it?' Mila pointed at an office block as they glided past.

'Not that one, it was much tattier than that.'

'How about that one?'

'Yeah, that's the one ... wait a minute though ...'

Mila opened her mouth to say something, but no words came out. Even after they had driven past and out towards the suburbs, what she had seen was still indelibly imprinted on her mind. The image of a huge, polished sign over the front entrance.

The sign which read: 'HOBART INDUSTRIES INC.'

'Hobart? Surely it can't be the same Hobart. There must be loads of Hobarts in the USA.'

'Yes. I'm sure you're right.'

Mila sounded totally unconvinced and Greg could hardly blame her. He knew little about this guy Orin Hobart – had hardly even heard of him until Mila had told him about her ordeal – but he knew enough now to understand why she should be so afraid of him.

'It's too much of a coincidence, Mila. Orin Hobart taking over a Gemini Electronics office. Besides, I'm sure I'd have got to hear about it. Wouldn't I ... ?'

235

'Yes. Of course you would. I'm just being stupid.'

'You're a lot of things, Mila, but stupid isn't one of them.'

They drove on in silence for a couple of miles, heading south-west through the suburbs and on to empty roads, more or less in the direction of Interstate 15. This was a strange land, thought Greg to himself; elemental, savagely beautiful and in many ways hostile too. Alone, friendless, without transport, you wouldn't survive long up in those 11,000-foot, sky-scraping peaks, looming above the crazy jigsaw puzzle of sandstone canyons and fiery red desert.

In a place like this, almost anything could – and probably would – happen. Including Mila's former 'master' taking over the old Utah office. Or was that stretching coincidence just a little too far? Greg took out his handkerchief and swabbed the sweat from his brow. It was scorchingly hot – somewhere up in the high nineties – but he felt cold; cold, itchy and paranoid, all at once. What was it his old boss used to say? Just because you're paranoid, it doesn't mean they're *not* out to get you . . .

'There's someone up ahead,' said Mila, jolting him out of his black thoughts. 'They look like they're in trouble.'

Greg screwed up his eyes to peer into the distance. A shimmer of heat-haze hovered above the lurid shape of an old mobile home, painted in swirling patterns of psychedelic pink and orange. Not so much painted as vandalised, thought Greg to himself. A thing like a TV aerial was sticking up out of its roof, and it was surrounded by a huddle of youths in tatty T-shirts, peering into the engine and apparently engaged in heated debate.

'Acid-heads,' he commented as the Chevy drove slowly closer to the stranded van.

'Acid-what?'

THE GOLDEN CAGE

'You know, hippies, drop-outs, New-Agers. Could be trouble. Better give 'em a wide berth, eh?'

'No, Greg, let's help them. They've broken down.'

'But they look weird. And what if—'

'What if what?'

'What if it's a trap – something designed to catch us?'

'If it's a trap, someone has gone to an awful lot of trouble. Don't you think there would be easier ways of catching us?'

'I just don't want to take any chances, OK?'

'Please, Greg.' She played her ace. 'You helped me, remember?'

Greg gave a sigh of surrender and steered the Chevy towards the side of the road, parking it behind the broken-down mobile home. He got out of the car and started walking towards the van.

'Need any help?'

Four faces turned towards him. It was worse than he'd thought. Two of them had scraggy goatee beards, one had a tattoo of the Eye of Horus on his arm, and the fourth had waist-length dreadlocks secured by a stupid-looking red spotted bandana.

'Hi, man. That's an English accent, right?'

'Right.'

'Cool! Hey guys, this dude's from England.'

'No kidding?'

An oil-smeared hand was thrust in Greg's face and before he knew what had hit him he was exchanging handshakes with the four most dubious-looking individuals he could remember meeting since his student days.

'This is Jeff, right, with the bandana? And that's Big Mac and the dude with the hat is Castro.'

'I'm Greg. And this is Mila.'

237

'Pleased to meet you, Mila. You sure are one beautiful lady, if you don't mind my saying so.'

Mila found herself giggling like a school kid. There was something so disarming about this bunch of misfits.

'Why, thank you.'

'Oh, and I'm Danny. D'you dig the beard?'

'It's ... er ... it's great, yeah.'

'You really think so? Only I wasn't sure.' Danny fingered the silky black tuft of beard. 'Jeff says it makes me look like the Sheriff of Nottingham.'

'Jeff's a dweeb,' pointed out Castro, wiping oily hands on the seat of his black denims.

'Say, you don't know anything about engines do you, Mister Englishman?' cut in Big Mac. 'Only Danny's been trying to fix this fucker for about an hour and if he doesn't do it pretty damn soon I reckon I'm gonna have to go against my strict Buddhist principles and kill him.'

'Bad karma,' nodded Danny.

'I'll take a look,' shrugged Greg. 'Can't promise anything though.'

He stuck his head under the bonnet and breathed in the familiar scent of the engine. My, but that smell took him back to his teenage days, when he and his brother had 'rescued' wrecked cars and put them back together again. He'd been an entrepreneur even then. Pity he hadn't stuck to the motor trade.

'Try the engine, would you? I need to hear it turning over.'

Castro jumped into the driver's seat and gave the key a turn. The engine misfired a few times, but nothing.

Greg fiddled about a bit.

'Now try it again.'

THE GOLDEN CAGE

Still nothing.

He scratched his head. In spite of his reluctance to get involved with these guys, he was starting to enjoy himself. It was years since he'd had the fun of tinkering with an engine – getting himself good and messy and not having to wear a suit.

He rolled up his sleeves.

'OK punk,' he announced to the engine with a smile of grimmest satisfaction. 'Make my day.'

The sliding side door of the mobile home was open and Mila perched herself on the edge. Danny and Big Mac were sitting on the ground, cross-legged in the dust. Mila couldn't help noticing that, despite the horrible sawn-off shorts, Danny had very nice legs, tanned and muscular. Very nice indeed...

'You and this Greg guy, you're an item, right?' Danny enquired.

'Right. Well, sort of,' replied Mila, not entirely sure what she ought to say. 'We're on holiday together, travelling across the States.'

'Lucky guy,' whistled Big Mac. 'Where you from, anyhow?'

'Russia. St Petersburg.'

'Well whaddya know!' Danny thumped the ground with delight. 'We've been asked to play the next White Nights rock festival in St Petersburg.'

'Only maybe,' Big Mac cut in. 'If we can get a new drummer and if they'll let Jeff in. Jeff's a bit of a pothead,' he explained. 'OK, we all are, only Jeff got caught so the Ruskies aren't crash-hot on giving him a visa.'

'You're musicians?'

Danny laughed.

'Kind of. That's not what my dad used to call us, though!'

He scrambled to his feet and mimed a guitar break. 'The Flying Insekts at your service, ma'am.'

'We travel all round the States in the van,' explained Big Mac. 'As long as people will pay us, we'll play. It's a way to get money to live, so's we can spend more time on what we really care about.'

'Which is?'

'Research into Fortean phenomena. You know, UFOs, bizarre killings, urban myths, the paranormal...'

'Anything so long as it's weird,' agreed Danny. 'Anything the Government doesn't want ordinary dudes like us to know about. Especially conspiracies...'

'What sort of conspiracies?'

Danny laughed.

'How long have you got? You name it, we got it here in the good old US of A. Commie conspiracies, fascist conspiracies, conspiracies to assassinate the President, conspiracies to cover up the truth about alien invasion, conspiracies networked on the Internet...'

'Do you know,' added Big Mac, 'there's even an international society of sicko perverts – you know, S/M and C/P freaks? These rich businessmen lure innocent babes by setting up "friendship agencies" all over the world.'

'There's one in St Petersburg,' added Danny.

'Once they get them over here, they take away everything: their money, their passports, their identity – and turn them into slaves.'

'Sick,' agreed Big Mac.

Mila felt her stomach turn over.

'How do you know this?' she asked, trying desperately not to show her alarm.

'Research.' Danny indicated the interior of the van.

THE GOLDEN CAGE

'Want to take a look? We have some hot technology in here.'

Danny climbed into the van and Mila got in beside him. The interior might have been quite roomy if it hadn't been stuffed with sleeping bags and billy cans – and a spaghetti-like jumble of wires.

'Computer, satellite link, tracking devices...' Danny reeled off the names of the various pieces of equipment. 'CB, police frequency radio, all kinds of things for watching and listening.'

'Jeff's the electronics whizz-kid,' explained Big Mac. 'He builds the stuff and we use it. Want a demonstration?'

He flicked a switch and, seconds later, a shrill electronic whistling sound filled the air. Mila clapped her hands to her ears.

'Switch it off! Switch it off! It's hurting.'

But Danny and Big Mac weren't listening. They were peering at a handset, at a little green dot flashing on a tiny screen. Castro rushed up to the van.

'What's going down?'

'There's some kind of bugging device around here, guys.'

'A bug? Jeez! Where?'

'I don't know yet.' Danny slid slowly out of the van, the bleeps getting faster and shriller as he moved across the dusty ground. Mila watched him from the van, her heart in her mouth as she watched him walking towards the Chevy.

'It's in the car, dudes. It has to be in the car.'

'No!' Mila gave a soft gasp of horror as Danny opened the driver's door and slid into the front seat of the Chevy, running his fingers along the underside of the dashboard.

'Got it!' He got out of the car and Mila saw he was holding up a little round silvery thing, no bigger than a button.

'Oh my God, oh my God.' Greg, up to his arms in engine-oil and grease, stood stock-still, his eyes fixed on the tiny silver disc.

'Well, I'll be...' announced Danny, throwing the bug into the air and catching it one-handed. 'You guys sure must have annoyed somebody real bad.

''Cause whoever they are, it looks like they bugged your car.'

The silver disc lay dismembered on Jeff's workbench.

'See? That's the tracking device, that thing there. It's Japanese, nice bit of precision electronics. These guys were made for long-range tracking assignments.'

'So whoever it is... they might still be a long way away?'

'Sure. Or next door. There's really no way of knowing.'

'You guys know who's got it in for you?' enquired Danny, swigging the last of a bottle of Sol. 'Or shouldn't we ask?'

'Let's just say it might be safer if you didn't know,' replied Greg grimly.

'So what do we do now?' demanded Mila, her eyes still fixed on the tiny, impersonal symbol of evil. And there were other questions in her head, unanswerable questions she dared not ask: like who had planted that bug and why.

'I think we should get away from here.'

'If you want, I can disable the bug, no problem,' said Jeff, a screwdriver stuck behind his ear. 'Or maybe it would be better if I just, say, confused it a little?'

'Confused it?'

Jeff smirked like a naughty schoolboy.

'If I just adjust this... and this... just a little, I can throw the signal out by... oh... anything up to a hundred miles in any direction. Whoever's after you will still think

THE GOLDEN CAGE

they know where you are, only of course you won't be there at all.'

'What d'you think?' asked Greg.

'Do it,' said Mila.

'OK. Done. There y'are. Stick that back under the dash and no one will ever know it was tampered with.'

'Thanks, Jeff.' Mila sank down on to a giant floor-cushion. She felt hot, flustered, and drained by the stress of the last half-hour.

'Can I interest you guys in a little recreation?' suggested Danny.

'Hadn't we better get going – in case . . . ?'

'Hey, stay cool. There's no hurry, not now I've fixed the bug. They don't have the first idea where you are. Lighten up, get down, hang loose.'

'Oh, I don't really think . . .' began Mila, but Danny waved aside her protests.

'Hey, just one second, little lady. You don't know what I'm proposing yet. Besides, we've gotta thank you guys for fixin' our van. He winked. 'Now, I'd say you and Mister Englishman were pretty adventurous, am I right?'

Mila didn't answer but her lips twitched a reluctant smile.

'Aw, c'mon. Ready to try anything, right?'

'Well – maybe. That depends what it is, *Mister American*.'

Danny rummaged through a pile of clothes, books and electrical spare parts, and uncovered a cupboard door.

'What we have in here,' he announced proudly, 'is gonna blow your minds.' He winked. 'And your erogenous zones.'

'You better believe it,' winked Castro. 'We're talking good times. *Real* good times.'

243

Reaching into the cupboard, Danny hauled out what looked like a couple of wetsuits.

'Jeff built these,' he said. 'We've never had a chance to try them out with a real woman before.'

'Mostly they tell us to rack off,' explained Jeff cheerfully. 'For some reason they seem to think we're perverts or something.'

'What *are* these?' Mystified, Mila gathered up one of the suits. It was more of a harness really, an elaborate arrangement of straps and buckles and pads, festooned with multicoloured wires. The other seemed much the same.

'Ever heard of virtual sex?' Jeff asked.

'You mean – like virtual reality?' Greg wiped his oily hands on a clean rag.

'Yeah, right on. Well I've been doing a few experiments and I've designed these VR sex-suits.'

'I don't understand,' protested Mila. 'What is this "virtual reality" you seem to know so much about?'

'It's a whole new way of experiencing things you wouldn't normally do. You can go anywhere, do anything – all you have to do is put on the suit and the helmet. You can even have sex, and it's completely safe in every way, no risks, no diseases, no emotional complications. It's computer-generated, see. The suit has electronic pads and probes to make things feel ... well, more realistic.'

Mila ran her fingers over the shiny rubber suit. It all sounded rather unlikely.

'A thing like this ... it can do all that?'

'Feels pretty damn good, you can take my word for it. That headset ... it has electrodes in it, they pick up exactly what you're thinking and turn it into reality! Wanna try?'

'I couldn't!'

THE GOLDEN CAGE

'"Course you could. Look.' Jeff got to his feet. 'Me and the guys ... we got things to do, OK. The van's not big enough for us all to sleep in, so we're going over there to pitch the tents. You feel like trying this stuff out, just put on the suit and turn on that control switch – this one on the panel, yeah?'

The four ambled off carrying the tents, leaving Greg and Mila inside the van.

'Do you think Jeff was right?' asked Mila. 'About the bug?'

'He ... seems to know what he's talking about.'

'So you don't think we need to get moving again tonight?'

Greg stared into the middle distance, momentarily distracted by black imaginings.

'Look, if they don't know where we are, we've got nothing to worry about. If they do ... well, running's not going to help, is it? Sooner or later, we'll have to face them.'

'Hobart?'

'Or the cops. Whichever.'

'How do you think the bug got into the car? And when?'

'I'm not sure. I thought we were being careful, but obviously we weren't. I guess it could have been at that weird party in Chicago – or maybe even those cops who stopped us back in Kansas.

'But whoever it was, we can't keep on running for ever, can we? So we might as well accept the Flying Insekts' hospitality for tonight at least. Maybe even explore a few possibilities ...'

Greg arched an eyebrow. His eyes fell on the VR suits.

'How about it?'

'We couldn't.'

Mila looked at Greg and they both burst out laughing.

'I don't need some electric suit to know I want to fuck you,' declared Greg, gathering her up into his arms and pushing down the neck of her shirt to kiss her bare shoulder.

'Mmm, that feels good. But...'

'But?'

'But this might feel good too.' She fingered the suit, wrapping it around her.

'You want to try?'

'I want to try.'

Greg picked up one of the suits.

'Is this the guy's, or the girl's? And how the hell do you put it on?'

'Well ... I guess first of all, you have to take off all your clothes,' Mila breathed sultrily.

'All of them?'

'Every one.' Mila began unbuttoning Greg's shirt.

'Know what? I think I'm going to like this game.'

Greg enjoyed the butterfly-soft caress of Mila's fingers as they eased his shirt down over his shoulders and he wriggled his arms out of it. The belt-buckle was a bit fiddly and he undid it for her, too hungry for her to waste time in an agony of frustration – however delicious that frustration might be.

Mila unbuttoned his 501s and they dropped silently to the floor of the van. Kicking off his shoes he stepped out of them. His cock pushed insistently against the inside of his shorts, the pale blue cotton damp and clinging from the first wetness of his desire. He did not take them off immediately, but began work on Mila, her body a quivering knot of delicious tension beneath his greedy fingers.

So soft, so firm, so deliciously warm. Could any other

THE GOLDEN CAGE

living creature feel as wonderful to the touch as Mila Kirovska? Greg knew she was incomparable, perfect, exhilarating. So how ludicrous it was to think that some electronic suit could go any way towards enhancing his pleasure. All his body wanted to do was get intimately reacquainted with hers, and it wanted to do it right now.

Mila's clothes seemed to offer themselves up to his hands, her buttons smoothly unfastening, her shirt and skirt sliding off as fast as his fingers could unfasten them. Her bra – a pretty, underwired confection of white lace embroidered with dusky-pink rosebuds – seemed to fall into his hands in a soft whisper as the catch yielded to his touch. And her matching lace panties kissed her thighs as they slipped willingly down from hips to toes.

Now naked, Mila responded by sinking to her knees and pressing her face against his crotch, still veiled by the blue cotton briefs. She pushed her lips against the tip of his dick, kissing the swollen flesh through the moist fabric, and he growled, stroking and teasing her hair with his fingers.

'Who needs virtual reality?' he whispered. 'When I have the real, living, breathing you?'

She teased down his pants with her teeth, easing them perhaps a quarter or half inch lower with each seductive nip of her teeth, then kissing and licking the new band of bare flesh which she had exposed. It all took an age: an unbearable, wonderful age which drove Greg to the point of distraction.

'Don't you know how much I want you?'

'I hope it's as much as I want you.'

'Hurry, Mila. I have to feel you . . .'

At last her teeth pulled his briefs down so far that his bursting, straining cock sprang out, free at last and aching for a taste of Mila's sweet, rose-red lips. She licked his shaft like a kitten lapping cream, and he trembled for the sheer ecstasy of it. He wanted to come, yet he wanted to delay his climax for as long as he possibly could. When she started licking his balls he wondered how much he could possibly bear.

'Put on the suit now, Greg.'

Mila's plea left him dumbstruck. All he wanted was to have her, here on the floor of the van and now she was asking him to put on that stupid VR suit.

'Oh, Mila, I'd much rather...'

'Go on, Greg. Just for me. I'll put my suit on too.'

'It probably doesn't even work. You know what these techno-dweebs are like.'

'Greg!'

'OK, OK.'

It was sheer agony to let her caresses leave his yearning cock, but if that was what Mila wanted, so be it. He took the suit which Mila handed him.

'This is mine? You're sure?'

'Look, darling. It must be yours. It has the sweetest little leather sheath for you to put your dick in.'

She was right. In most respects, the suits were identical, with electrical stimulation pads over all of the body's most sensitive areas and special gloves designed to simulate every possible aspect of a lover's caresses. But whereas the male suit had a sheath to stimulate the penis, the female one had a sort of inflatable rubber dildo, programmed to inflate and harden as arousal increased, finally entering the vagina like a lover's penis.

Mila helped him on with the suit. At first he just felt stupid, but as the tight rubber closed about his body, he began to understand why Jeff had been so enthusiastic about it. Even before it was switched on, it felt sensual – as

THE GOLDEN CAGE

though with every small movement many hands were caressing him, hands that knew every way to give him pleasure.

His dick slid easily into the tight leather sheath, quickly discovering the delights of its textured inner surface. With each tiny movement his dick slid across a tapestry of fine ridges which caressed him with a subtlety and skill which surprised him.

'Now you,' he said.

The sight of Mila slipping into her VR suit was far more erotic than he had anticipated, a little like having a lover who was half woman, half sensual android.

'Oh Greg, it feels...'

'Tell me.'

'It feels like you're sliding your tongue over and over my clitoris, and the tip of your dick is just touching the entrance to my vagina.' She closed her eyes in pleasure as her hips swayed, learning to enjoy the sensations produced by the tight, ridged pad strapped between her thighs. 'Oh Greg ... are you ready?'

'Ready. Put on your headset. Hurry.'

The helmets were heavy, a little like motorcycle headgear, but modified so that a broad, black perspex visor covered the face, blotting out the outside world. It was a peculiar sensation, disorientating yet exciting.

'Switch it on, Greg. Quickly, I can't bear to wait.'

He reached out blindly and found the two switches. Click. Click. The inside of his headset lit up.

'WELCOME TO SEXWORLD.'

'SELECT PARTNER PREFERENCE: MALE/FEMALE?'

He fumbled with the buttons on his belt.

'FEMALE'.

'READY TO PLAY.'

The voice was like a whisper inside his head, inviting him to play a new and thrilling game. When he spoke, his voice sounded hoarse and trembly.

'What can you see, Mila?'

'A man, Greg. He's naked. I can't see his face, he's wearing a mask but I so want him to be you...'

'I can see a woman, Mila. She's beautiful. She has long, dark hair. She's not you and yet she is...'

In response to the commands on the headset, Greg pressed buttons on the belt control panel.

'BREASTS: SMALLER/LARGER?'

'LARGER.'

'HAIR: LONGER/SHORTER?'

'LONGER.'

'SHAVEN OR UNSHAVEN?'

'SHAVEN.'

'Oh Mila. Oh my God ... she's you. She's right here beside me, I can *touch* her.'

'I'm touching you, Greg. Can you feel me? My hands are running down your belly, not quite touching your cock ... Touch me, Greg. I want you to make love to me.'

It was an incredible fantasy, unbelievable and yet so real. It was as if there were not two people there, but four: two Gregs, two Milas. Two partners, two equal sources of pleasure.

Greg had heard about VR systems before, of course he had, what with being in the electronics industry. But he'd never encountered anything quite so sophisticated as this. It was so subtle, so interactive that it seemed he only had to think of what he wanted and it happened. And, sure enough, his fantasy became reality as the fantasy-Mila wrapped her thighs about his waist and, moving slowly up

THE GOLDEN CAGE

and down, began to fuck him to the point of ecstasy and beyond.

One thing was for sure: Jeff was wasting his time chasing UFOs and playing bass in the Flying Insekts. The guy was a genius. If Greg ever got out of this mess and had the chance to put his life straight...

Mila knew the man was Greg, not by his masked face, but by the gentle skill of his caresses, the way his leather-gloved fingers toyed so beautifully with her backside as he took her on the floor of the van, on fours like a dog with a bitch.

The dildo felt huge inside her. Inflated to capacity, it was stone-hard as any man's penis, and as she moved her hips it thrust smoothly in and out of her sex. The electronic pads stimulated her nipples and thighs and clitoris so beautifully that it felt as though Greg was making love to her entire body.

Good. Good, it was so good. Almost good enough to chase away the fears.

'Give it to me, Greg,' she breathed, and they came together, in a shattering climax which left them utterly spent.

When Jeff came back from pitching the tents, he found Greg and Mila asleep in each other's arms, curled up on the floor of the van – still wearing their VR suits.

Dreaming of a new and better reality.

Chapter 16

It was darkest, bleakest night in the Nevada desert, but even from many miles away you could make out the knife-sharp laser beam from the Luxor pyramid, lancing upwards into the impenetrable black of the sky. The road was long, straight, monotonous, leading inexorably towards the distant horizon, glowing with the many-coloured lights of Las Vegas blazing in the darkness like some bonfire of the gods.

It wasn't difficult to see why people tended to pass straight through Nevada without stopping. To say that it was desolate was an understatement. Endless dry, sage-bush plains, army firing-ranges, knife-sharp mountain peaks and the occasional neon sign or drive-in burger bar made for a pretty depressing vista.

In any case, Greg and Mila weren't really in the mood for admiring scenery. They had scarcely spoken since they'd left Danny and the boys and crossed the Utah State border into Nevada. They both felt the same way: a sense of foreboding gnawing at them like a vulture stripping flesh from a carcass.

It was Mila who spoke first.

'Maybe we shouldn't have hung around with the boys for an extra night.'

'Maybe.' Greg gripped the steering wheel a little harder,

and tried to fight down the sensation of panic. He, too, was wondering why they'd let Jeff and Danny persuade them to linger in Utah.

'What if . . . the people who are following us know where we are?'

'Jeff said he fixed the bug.'

'What if he made a mistake? What if Hobart knows and he's coming to get us?'

'Then there's nothing we can do about it. In any case, all of this is probably down to me. I bet that bug was planted by the cops who stopped us in Arizona. They've probably been tailing me ever since I left Boston, and just want to see where I'm headed. There's no reason why they should be in any hurry to re-arrest me. I mean, it's not as if there's any danger of my escaping.'

'But why tail you like this?'

'Perhaps they think I'll lead them to one of my "accomplices". I'm supposed to be an international arms-dealer, remember.'

'How can they believe that?'

'The evidence is pretty damning. Some bastard must have had his work cut out to make sure that I played the fall-guy. I just wish I knew who it was.'

'Are you still going to the police when we get to San Francisco?' Mila looked across at Greg. He kept looking obstinately to the front.

'Yes.'

'Don't do it, Greg. We could get away, I'm sure we could. Make a life somehow. Maybe get across the border into Mexico. I don't have to go back to Russia . . .'

Greg took a deep breath.

'There's an attaché case full of money in the boot, right?'

'Right. It might be enough for us to...'

'Not us, Mila. You. Where I'm going I won't need it. It's all yours.'

'What the hell are you saying, crazy Englishman?'

'I am saying that the money is all yours. I can drop you and the money in Las Vegas and then we'll go our separate ways. It'll be safer for you that way. OK?'

'Is that what you want?'

Greg said nothing.

'Greg, answer me. Is that what you want?'

'I'm trying to do what's right, Mila. Why do you have to make it all so bloody impossible?'

'Because I bloody love you, that's why, crazy Englishman.'

Instead of kissing him on the lips, she bent over him, slowly unzipping his flies. Her tongue met the tip of his penis and he let out a long, low moan.

'You could at least play fair.'

'Oh Greg, didn't anybody ever tell you? Life isn't fair.' She kissed and licked his cock-tip, lapping up its salty juice. 'Now please, just shut up and drive.'

Of all the places Mila had seen on their odyssey across America, Las Vegas was perhaps the most predictable. The place was the international capital of tackiness.

And yet, mused Mila, it was much grander and prouder and more joyfully blatant than she had expected. It wasn't in the least bit embarrassed about being what it was: a people's palace of sleaze, tat and glitz. A glittering temple, dedicated to the worship of greed.

It was the middle of the night when they emerged from the hotel and on to The Strip. That was the first lesson Mila was to learn about this extraordinary place: in Las Vegas, people didn't sleep. In fact, night and day simply didn't exist.

The Strip was a tumult of seething humanity, a melting-pot for people from all over the world, united by a single burning ambition: to achieve The Big Win. A few would win. The overwhelming majority would lose. Some would lose everything they had on the roll of the dice or the spin of the roulette wheel.

'Care to see a show?' enquired Greg.

'What sort of show?'

He dived into his pocket and brought out two coloured strips of paper.

'I bribed the bellhop to get two tickets for Caesar's Palace tomorrow night. The Tony Scorpio late-night cabaret.'

'Tony Scorpio! Oh Greg, how did you know? I've been a big, big fan ever since I was a kid – even when the Soviets banned his records!'

'Well just fancy that, eh? You a fan of mega-capitalist Tony Scorpio, and all the time I thought you were a good Soviet girl.'

There was a casino right next to the hotel. To be precise, there was a casino actually inside the hotel – you couldn't go more than five yards in Vegas without coming across some novel way to part you from your cash. Think of a new money-making scheme and you could guarantee Vegas had thought of it first: all-day, all-night casinos, topless cabaret shows, huge great hotel and gambling complexes with themes like Ancient Greece, Hawaii or even Undersea World.

They strolled around The Strip, Mila dazzled by this place where a dozen different shades of neon transformed night into day; Greg enjoying the buzz of being somewhere

THE GOLDEN CAGE

so alive and so anonymous. In spite of his fears he felt himself relax a little. Their chances of being recognised here, of all places, were comfortingly low. Faceless Vegas was a great place to lose your unwanted identity as well as your cash.

'So – what do reckon to Las Vegas?' enquired Greg as they ate Moroccan delicacies from one of the all-night casino buffets.

'It's incredible,' declared Mila. 'Pinch me, I'm dreaming.'

She gazed around her. It was like being in somebody else's dream – her own imagination couldn't have conjured up any of this. This particular casino's theme was an Arabic one, and the restaurant took the form of a huge tent, made from acres of multi-coloured fabric swathed across the walls and ceiling.

Diners lounged around on big, soft cushions, stuffing their faces with cheap food or feeding succulent tidbits to their lovers. Away from the main gaming rooms, the atmosphere was rather quiet and intimate, with soft music playing in the background. It was tacky, yes, but it was something else too. Sensual.

Greg leaned over Mila and she accepted a forkful of spiced lamb, her tongue licking the sauce from her lips in a way which Greg found wonderfully provocative.

'You're trying to turn me on, aren't you?' he whispered.

'Do I need to try?' enquired Mila with apparent innocence.

'What do you think?' Greg moved closer and, when she thought no one was looking, Mila slipped her hand up his thigh until it met the firming bulge of his manhood.

'I think . . . that I wish all these people would go away and let me try some more.'

'What would you do to me?'

'These cushions are so lovely and soft,' teased Mila in a breathy whisper. 'Wouldn't you like to do it right here?'

'Right now.'

'In front of all these people?'

'Baby, I'm so hot for you I don't care.'

They kissed, Mila pushing a morsel of sticky honey-pastry into Greg's mouth with the tip of her tongue. The honey melted, sweet as sex juice, on his tongue.

'People are staring,' murmured Mila as he licked the last of the honey from her lips.

'They're just jealous, because they aren't kissing the hottest, sexiest, most gorgeous woman in the whole of Vegas. No, the world!'

'Flatterer.'

'Flattery will get me everywhere – won't it?'

'That depends on where you want to be.'

'Bed. With you.'

Mila took a sip of wine and shared it with Greg in a passionate kiss.

'Uh-huh.'

'If you prefer,' he unfastened the top button of Mila's shirt and traced a heart across the top of her breasts, 'We could make love right here.'

'How! People are watching.'

'No they're not. They're *eating*. Nothing comes between an American and his food. They won't notice a thing.' He kissed her again. 'Why don't you ... sit on my lap?'

Realisation of what Greg had in mind made Mila giggle.

'You're crazy!'

'That's me, the crazy Englishman.'

THE GOLDEN CAGE

To be perfectly frank, Greg was constantly surprising himself with his own audacity. He'd never used to be like this, taking insane chances, risking everything. Then again, in those days he'd had something to risk. Perhaps it was only when you had nothing left to lose that you realised how much there was to gain...

'Carefully, now,' he whispered. There was only a thin, filmy curtain of coloured muslin between them and the next pair of diners. If they'd wanted to, they could have listened in to every word, every passionate sigh. But the middle-aged couple were far too interested in their dinner to pay much attention to the young lovers sitting a few feet away from them. 'So very, very carefully.'

The music swooped and trilled in the background, liquid and sensual, masking the sounds of halting, shallow breathing. Above, half-hidden in the hanging folds and veils of muslin, a ceiling fan turned slowly, stirring the fabric so that it swayed and billowed gently in the man-made breeze.

Greg was right, thought Mila. No one was paying them any attention. No one except perhaps the guy in the white tuxedo with the embroidered silk cummerbund. He must have been in his late twenties or early thirties, tall and lean with rather hawkish features. She wondered who he was. The manager, maybe. Or just someone who liked to watch people. He was sitting at the bar, a glass in his hand, surveying the scene. Once or twice his eyes met Mila's and she wondered if he knew...

She slid as smoothly as she could on to Greg's lap. He was sitting cross-legged on the cushions, like some exotic eastern pasha, and she almost began to believe that they really were in the mysterious middle east, and that she was a harem slave.

For a few minutes all they did was embrace. Greg pushed aside the dark curtain of her hair and planted kiss after kiss upon the nape of her neck, the swell of her bare shoulder. She leant back against him, her head tilted back and her eyes mesmerised by the distant shadow of the ceiling fan.

'Would you like me inside you?' Greg's whisper sounded deafening, although no one else could possibly have heard it. To her shame, she found herself blushing, her cheeks burning. Surely the man in the white tuxedo knew ... he was looking right at them, his eyes burning into her, a half-smile playing about his lips.

'We shouldn't ... not really,' she murmured. Not that she was even convincing herself.

'We should. We really should.'

'Someone will see.'

'Let them. Can't you feel what you're doing to me?'

There was no mistaking the hard, demanding presence which was pressing itself against the back of her skirt, trying to burrow its way between her rounded buttocks. Greg was very, very hard for her, and the thought of his arousal intensified the pleasure of this crazy, wonderful wickedness.

'I can feel.'

'It's all for you, Mila, no one else. Never anyone else. Don't you want me too?'

'You know I do.'

'He wants you too, Mila. That man over there in the white tuxedo, can you see the way he's looking at you?'

So Greg had noticed too! She wasn't imagining it after all. Slowly turning her head, she glanced across at the man. This time he wasn't looking at her – or at least, he didn't seem to be.

THE GOLDEN CAGE

'No, Greg, you're wrong.'

'Am I? Oh Mila, he's crazy for you just like I am. He can't take his eyes off you. He's insanely jealous of the way I'm touching and kissing and caressing you.'

'Greg,' she pleaded, giggling with excitement. 'Greg, stop it, you're making me . . .'

Greg gave her earlobe a playful nip with his teeth.

'Horny?'

'Oh . . .'

'You're so horny and I want you my darling. Let me pull up your skirt.'

Luckily, Mila was wearing a long, flowing skirt of printed Indian cotton, which floated about her in a multicoloured cloud and hid the true obscenity of her passion. To any casual observer, she was just sitting on her lover's lap, enjoying his kisses as they embraced, his left hand resting on her hip.

But his right hand, unseen, was creeping underneath the billowing skirt and stroking it away from her buttocks and thighs.

'Raise yourself, just a tiny fraction . . . a little more . . . that's it, oh yes, my darling.'

She lifted herself and he eased the folds of material out from underneath her, ruching them up. She felt his hand on her thigh, stroking the smooth flesh, his fingers exciting her, tracing patterns on the bare, suntanned skin, still fragrant from the shower.

'You smell so good,' he murmured, licking and biting her neck as his fingers caressed her. 'Apple blossom and candyfloss and cinnamon. And pure, pure sex.'

Mila gave a tiny wriggle of protest as Greg slid his finger underneath the leg of her panties and started toying with the moist haven between her buttocks. But they both knew this was what they wanted, this secret pleasure which only they could share. She could feel the hot, sweet ooze trickling out of her, on to his fingers, and his gentle caresses mesmerised her with desire.

'Want me?'

'Want you.'

His fingertip toyed with the tight membrane of her anus and she could barely keep from squealing with excitement. It was so, so sensitive – almost to the point of discomfort – yet she wanted more, more, more. His fingernail scratched her lightly and instinctively, the puckered mouth dilated to welcome him, engulfing the tip of his fingers with a lingering kiss.

'Oh my darling. My darling Mila, you excite me so much.'

She could not reply, robbed of all reason and all coherent speech by the intrusive caress of Greg's beautiful, wicked fingertip. Her backside wriggled back a tiny fraction and she swallowed him up to the first knuckle. He moved his finger in a spiral motion, so that the nail teased and stretched the soft, yielding walls of her rectum, and she began to shake and pant.

'Softly, Mila. Softly. Remember, we're not alone.'

It was the sheerest, the most delicious torture to know that she must control herself at all costs. A cry, an incautious movement, any sign might give the game away. She pursed her lips, her teeth clenched, the tension making every nerve in her body jangle with effort.

'I'm going to slide into you now, Mila. Are you ready for me?'

'Don't make me wait any longer, Greg. Don't torture me!'

'Up just a little. Just a little more. Wait . . .'

THE GOLDEN CAGE

She felt his right hand slide underneath her, heard the faint swish of his zipper sliding down; then the warm hardness of his manhood was pushing and nudging into the wet welcome of her sex. His strong hands were both under her skirt now, placed on either side of her thighs, and he was pulling her smoothly down on to the spike of his penis, impaling her so completely and so beautifully that she wanted to sing for joy.

'Not too fast,' she gasped as they began to move together. 'Not too hard, someone will see.'

'No one will see. There, I've got you, you're quite safe. Let me set the rhythm.' Greg spoke in staccato whispers, his own excitement scarcely under control as he kissed and fucked her, sliding her smoothly up and down on his sex.

Despite the air-conditioning, Mila felt suffocatingly hot. Sweat was trickling down her back, making her blouse stick to her so that it clung to her breasts. They quivered as she moved up and down, her thigh muscles tensing and untensing at each new stroke.

Opening her eyes, she looked across the room. No one was paying the slightest attention to them. No one except a man in a white tuxedo. His eyes seemed hooded, half closed, as though he wasn't really looking at them at all, just contemplating some point in the middle-distance as he sipped his champagne cocktail.

'Greg ... Greg ... that man ...'

'Hush, baby. Let me do it to you. Let me show you how much pleasure I want to give you.'

'He's watching. He knows ...'

'And I know how much you excite me. Do you know, Mila? How much you arouse me?'

His fingers slipped round in front of her, still underneath

the veiling skirt, and began stroking lightly over the ripe swell of her pubis. This new stimulation was more than she could bear.

'Greg. Oh Greg, you're making me ... you're going to make me come.'

'Come, sweetheart. Come, baby. Come for me.'

No, no. She didn't want to, not with the creepy man staring at her like that. She was sure he was staring at her, afraid that it might be someone who knew who she was. Maybe even someone spying on her for Orin Hobart.

'Come for me. I'm going to come for you, darling. Can't you feel me getting harder? My balls feel so heavy ... they're aching and throbbing like they're going to explode ...'

'Coming ... I'm coming ... don't want to ... but I'm coming'

'Now, baby. Now!'

He exploded into her, a micro-second before her sex muscles clenched in the first, magnificent spasm of orgasm. This time she could not suppress the tiny, shuddering cry which escaped from her lips, nor prevent her body from shaking convulsively as spasm after spasm overtook her in a flood of ecstasy.

'Mila, you're the best. The only one. You're incredible,' gasped Greg.

When the pleasure had ebbed away and she was once again conscious of her surroundings, Mila found herself still held tightly in Greg's embrace, his hands on her thighs and his heart thudding like a bass drum.

Looking across the restaurant, she saw that the man in the white tuxedo was smiling at her. There could be no doubt about it this time – he really was looking straight into her eyes. Lifting his glass to his lips in a toast, he drank

THE GOLDEN CAGE

down the champagne. Then he set down the glass and simply walked away, out of their lives.

Las Vegas really was the craziest place.

Mila stood in the first of the gaming rooms at the Vegas Palace and wondered how so many strange people could all be in the same place at the same time.

The room was the height of whorehouse opulence: a huge, glittering salon in 1890s' decor, complete with flock wallpaper, plaster mouldings on the ornate ceiling and dozens and dozens of mirrors. The carpet was so thick it was like walking across a sandy beach.

The contrast between the room and its function could not have been more striking. It was completely filled by row upon row of gaming-machines, giant one-armed bandits sparkling with coloured lights and bleeping, buzzing and crunching as they devoured dollar after dollar. Very occasionally, a thunderous clatter and a blaze of electronic music would announce that some lucky person had won a cash prize – paid out in small denomination coins of course, to make a more impressive sound as the money clattered into the tray.

Right in the middle of the room were a row of much larger machines, blow-up versions of the other one-armed bandits, larger than life and flashing like the control panel of a 747.

'Jackpot machines,' commented Greg. 'They pay out a one million-dollar top prize.'

Mila's eyes widened.

'A *million*?'

'As I live and breathe. Of course, the odds are about ten billion to one, but that doesn't stop these poor deluded buggers parting with their cash.'

'Oh Greg, look – look at that woman. Over there.'

Mila nudged Greg in the ribs and he followed her gaze towards a young woman in a white pleated, halter-neck dress and white stilettos. The immaculately coiffured peroxide hair, false eyelashes and pillarbox-red lipstick completed the look in all its bizarre perfection.

Greg chuckled.

'So Marilyn's alive and well and living in Vegas. I wonder if we'll meet Elvis next. Did you ever see *Honeymoon in Vegas* . . . ?'

'Wonderful, aren't they?' breathed a voice at Mila's elbow. She spun round. A woman with chestnut hair piled up on top of her head, Cruella DeVille make-up and a tight velvet minidress, was stroking her fingers over the surface of one of the jackpot machines.

'I'm sorry?' Mila wondered for a second if the woman was actually speaking to her at all, but then she turned and smiled, a little pouting smile, soft and sensual.

'The machines. Beautiful.' She smoothed and stroked the hot metal, its low electrical hum like the purr of a sleeping tiger. 'And powerful. Don't you think so?'

'I've never really thought about it,' admitted Mila.

The woman took hold of Mila's hand, very gently, and placed it on the smooth chrome of the handle.

'Feel it. Feels good, huh? Throbbing with power, like a great big dick. Don't you just wish you could climb on and have that big chrome dick inside you?'

'Well, I . . .'

'Course you do, honey. Every woman craves a dick as big as this one – isn't that so, mister?' She eyed Greg, who shrugged, momentarily speechless. What could he say? This was the first time he'd ever met a woman who wanted to make love to a slot machine.

THE GOLDEN CAGE

Mila slid her hand away.

'It's nice meeting you...'

'Stay awhile. You don't understand now, but you will. The feeling when you pull that great big old handle and the power and the thrill...'

'...but we have to go now,' Greg cut in firmly.

'We have tickets for the Tony Scorpio show,' explained Mila.

The woman raised her eyes heavenwards in blank incomprehension.

'Lordy, child,' she sighed. 'Some people do have the strangest tastes...'

The man in the white tuxedo slipped into one of the phone booths in the foyer of the Vegas Palace Hotel, dialled the number and waited, tapping his fingers impatiently on the receiver.

Ring. Ring. Click.

'Hobart residence. Cora Whitemore speaking.'

'This is Steadman. I have to talk with Hobart. Now.'

'*Mister* Hobart is in bed. It is the middle of the night, Mr Steadman. Can it not wait until morning?'

'Stop pissing me about, Cora, and get Hobart.'

'I shall be reporting your rudeness to Mr Hobart,' snapped Cora coldly. 'I have no doubt that he will be most interested to hear about your discourtesy towards me.'

'Screw you,' muttered Steadman as Cora slammed the receiver on to the hall table and he listened to her bad-tempered footsteps climbing the stairs to the first floor of Hobart's summer 'cottage'. Not that he would screw her, he thought to himself. The bitch was so sour she looked like she sucked lemons for a living.

O'Brien rapped on the glass of the booth.

'You through yet?' she mouthed.

He nodded, grimacing 'Cora.'

'You want me to deal with her?'

He shook his head. Someone was coming to the phone. Picking up the receiver.

'Hobart here. This had better be good. I do not find incompetence appealing, and your handling of the electronic surveillance has certainly been incompetent.'

'Oh it's good all right. They missed the second bug.'

'You know where they are?'

'Vegas.'

'Indeed?'

'Yeah. And they're being none too discreet.'

'They? She's still with a man? Do you know who he is yet?'

Steadman flicked open his notebook, consulted the illiterate scribblings.

'As a matter of fact we do. Name of Delaney, Greg Delaney. English, apparently. And he's in some sort of trouble with the FBI, but I couldn't get any more than that...'

'Delaney! Holy shit.'

The hairs were standing up on the back of Hobart's neck. As if it wasn't bad enough for his slave to insult and defy him like this, she had to take up with Delaney, for God's sake. They had never even met, but Greg Delaney was a very dark shadow in Orin Hobart's soul.

How could it have happened? Hobart was sure he'd covered his tracks but no, here was that English slime Delaney, crawling back up from the carefully demolished ruins of his career to claw at him like a dead man's hand. He didn't understand how this could have gone so wrong. He'd been one hundred per cent sure that Delaney had never even heard of him, let alone connected him with . . .

A thought struck Hobart. How long had Delaney been controlling Mila? He must have been, there was no other explanation for it. How else would she have known what to steal from him?

'Right. Keep me posted.' Hobart crashed the receiver back on to the stand. His mind worked fast, calculating the likely consequences. And for that ripe, devious, oh-so-infuriating Russian slut they would be painful ones. He would make sure of it.

Chapter 17

Reno. 'The biggest little city in the world', that's what they called it. To Greg, it looked more like Blackpool Pleasure Beach with a snow-capped mountain where the Tower ought to be.

Still, if the town was sleaze personified, the setting was spectacular, the snowy Sierra Nevada looming over the town and the Truckee River winding right through the middle.

'No waiting, just drive in,' announced the neon sign over the doorway of the Starlight Wedding Chapel. Thirty-five dollars, all in, would get you the full works: taped music, plastic flowers and a quickie wedding, in a pink chintz parlour with heart-shaped seats. Stay an extra six weeks and you could get a divorce too.

Get married, get divorced, gamble away your life savings: that was just about all there was to do in Reno. Well, almost...

In search of somewhere a little quieter to stay after two days and nights in Las Vegas, Greg and Mila drove round Reno. They soon realised that 'quiet' was a purely relative term around this part of the world.

That was how they came to end up at the Happy Cowboy Honeymoon Hotel.

Mila bounced playfully on the gigantic, heart-shaped bed.

'It's soft. Greg, come and feel how soft.'

He turned back from the window and sat down on the bed beside her. This sure was one crazy place: pink satin everywhere, mirrored ceilings and wardrobe doors, a sunken bath in blush-pink marble and a little marble fountain with a gold-plated statuette of a naked woman, ice-cool sparkling wine fountaining out of a pitcher in her hands.

'Oh Greg, you're not still sulking about Tony Scorpio! I didn't even go backstage.'

Greg slipped his arm round her waist and kissed her.

'You did enjoy having him grope your bum though, didn't you?' He let his hand drop to her backside, feeling its firm curve through the thin silk of the bathrobe.

Mila giggled.

'He's a very attractive man.'

Greg pulled a face.

'He's an idiot.'

'You're just jealous.'

'Why should I be jealous?' Greg gave the end of Mila's nose a playful lick. 'He's old and balding and I'm blond and gorgeous ... and I've got you.' He kissed her again, more tenderly this time. 'I have got you, haven't I?'

'For as long as you want me.'

He embraced her, feeling her heart beating through the thin bathrobe. How could he even begin to tell her the tumultuous feelings that were crowding and fighting inside him?

'I still feel guilty about this,' he told her. 'About letting you stay with me. It's pure selfishness, you know – I should make you go away, for your own safety.'

'We've said all this before.'

THE GOLDEN CAGE

'And it was true then, too. What if Jeff didn't disable the bug? What if . . . ?'

She silenced him with kisses, her lips brushing gently over his closed eyelids, his cheeks, his chin.

'What if you made love to me?'

She sank back on to the shimmering magenta satin of the bedspread. It felt coolly sensuous against her bare legs and forearms, filling her with the urge to wind and slither and twist like a sexy serpent.

Looking up, she couldn't help catching sight of her reflection in the mirrors on the ceiling – not just one, but sixteen of them; big glass squares, each at slightly different angles so that lovers might look up and see themselves coupling in sixteen different ways. Idly her fingers toyed with the knotted sash of the bathrobe and succeeded in untying it. The sash fell away and the robe slid open, revealing a broad band of pink thigh and belly, and one matchless, ripe, pink-nippled breast.

'Watch me, darling. You don't need to do anything, not yet. Just watch.'

She wriggled out of the robe so that it lay like a scarlet stain across the magenta satin. Her skin seemed very fragile and pinkish-white against the strong reds and deep pinks. Greg watched entranced as she began caressing herself, beginning with shoulders and throat, belly and thighs, and working towards the sensitive centres of her desire.

'Do you like it when I touch myself?'

He growled his appreciation, his mouth meeting her fingers and kissing them as they stroked up the taut plain of her belly.

'I love it.'

'Where shall I touch myself? Tell me where.'

'Touch ... your nipples. I want to see how you stroke yourself when you want to give yourself pleasure.'

She was more than happy to oblige. The warm sensuality of this place was really getting to her, and she found the immense vista of mirror-screens an incredible turn-on. Her eyes gazing up at the mirrors, she moved her hands to cover her nipples.

At first, she merely covered her breasts, cupping them in her hands and making little circular movements which had the effect of rubbing her nipples lightly across her palms. It was horny and fun, but mostly for herself. Greg couldn't see what she was doing, couldn't see how erect her nipples were getting, and she could sense his yearning.

She slid her hands across until her fingers were just touching her nipples.

'Watch me, Greg. Watch me in the mirrors.'

He didn't want to take his eyes off Mila, but when he looked up at the mirrors he had the shock of his life. He'd known they were there, of course, but he hadn't been prepared for the huge surge of excitement he felt at the sight of Mila stroking her own breasts – reflected in sixteen different poses.

'Oh sweet Mila,' he murmured. 'You are so, so incredibly sexy. You make my cock ache for you.'

'Watch. I can do more.'

So much more, thought Greg as he watched her rolling and pinching her left nipple whilst her right hand skated lightly down over breasts and sternum and belly, towards the ever-beautiful garden of her pubic mound.

She was freshly shaven, and the golden ring in her pussy-lips sparkled, inviting the most intimate kisses and caresses. Greg was wild with need for her, but he knew

THE GOLDEN CAGE

that pleasure would be all the greater if it was a long, long time in coming.

Mila's fingers paused, just inches from the margin of her love lips.

'Where shall I touch myself next?'

'Touch your pussy for me. I'd love to see how wet you are.'

His mouth was dry, his pulse racing as he watched her part her shaven labia, spreading its soft pink petals with knowing fingers. A sweet drift of spicy fragrance wafted from her sex, making him dizzy with the intoxication of lust.

'Oh ... you smell so good.'

He breathed it in, the drift of sweet muskiness, and it seemed to fill his entire being, like an elixir of blissful forgetfulness.

'Mila ... I want to touch you and taste you and feel your wetness round my cock ...'

She gave a girlish laugh, drunk with the excitement of this place.

'Don't be so impatient. Don't you know, all the best things are worth waiting for?'

He knew she was right, but it drove him into a blind frenzy of lust, watching her fingers parting and spreading the soft pink lobes of her womanhood. The interior of her sex was a deeper, wetter pink, its delicate coral folds rippled and coruscated like the pearly lining of some exotic tropical shell. The light caught the flesh as her fingers slid across it, and it glistened like wet glass.

Mila felt the awesome power of desire, her own and Greg's, meeting and sparking its own electricity as her fingers explored the soft, moist folds of her intimacy.

'Look, Greg, I'm stroking my pussy. Can you see my clit?'

'It's beautiful. Like a little flower-stalk.'

'I can feel it getting bigger and harder. Watch...'

His eyes devoured the beauty of his lover's sex, her fingers gently smoothing around the concentric folds of her inner love-lips, spreading them wide so that he saw not only the head of her clitoris, peeping from underneath its pink hood, but the deep, succulent well of her vagina.

He leaned back and looked up at the ceiling mirrors. Sixteen different Milas smiled down at him, their slim thighs parted and their shaven pussy-lips gaping wide in the most intimate of kisses. He saw himself too – a tense and watchful figure, shaken and dominated by his own desire, his cock a savage spear of hunger.

'I have to have you,' he whispered hoarsely.

'Soon. Why don't you massage me first? There's a bottle of oil in the bathroom. You could warm it...'

The idea appealed to Greg, even through the red mist of lust which had crept over him. To smooth oiled hands over that beautiful body would be a great and sensual pleasure.

'In the bathroom, you say?'

She smiled, running the tip of her tongue over her juicy red lips.

'In the cabinet. Hurry back to me.' She pulled his face down to hers and he tasted cold, sweet wine on her breath.

Greg slid off the bed and went into the en-suite bathroom. His cock ached like a bruised limb, his balls heavy as sacks of stones. Oddly, the sensation was a profoundly pleasurable one, perhaps because he knew it was the prelude to a far greater pleasure. The incredible

THE GOLDEN CAGE

excitement of having Mila's warm, wet sex stroking and kissing his manhood, her strong and slender thighs tight about his hips.

Oil? Oil. He found it, not in the bathroom cabinet but on a little heated shelf above the bath. It was a pale golden colour, like clarified honey. Wrapping his fingers around the bottle, he felt its tropical warmth and smiled to himself. Clearly the management of the Happy Cowboy Honeymoon Hotel had thought of everything.

He took the bottle back into the bedroom, and was struck anew by his lover's amazing sexual potency. She lay across the discarded satin robe, her body a white rose among crimson petals, her fingers fluttering like a butterfly's wings in the heart of her sex.

'Hurry, Greg. I can't wait for you to do this to me.'

Mila's voice was a whispered groan, a heartfelt plea for more and yet more pleasure.

Greg unscrewed the bottle top and breathed in the fragrance of the oil. It had a light scent, flowery with just a hint of something darker and muskier – something very, very sexy. He wondered what they put in this stuff. He read the label: 'Oil For Lovers – a subtle blend of flower essences, ginger oil and secret oriental herbs and spices.'

He didn't know if he could believe the blurb on the label, but the oil certainly felt good as he poured a little into the palm of his hand – very good indeed. Maybe it was the ginger – he remembered reading somewhere that ginger oil was a great sexual stimulant. At first there was just the sensation of warmth, but then the other sensations surfaced, like overtones in a simple harmony. A tingling, softly burning sensation flowed through him and he gave a murmur of surprised pleasure.

'Good stuff,' he commented. 'I think we're both going to enjoy this.'

Mila's body writhed slowly and sinuously on the bed as he knelt over her and let a thin trickle of oil fall into the valley between her breasts. She shuddered and closed her eyes as his fingers began working it into her flesh, smoothing and skating across the firmness of her breasts and torso.

'Mmm . . . ah . . . Greg, that's so good!'

'Feels good for me too. Can you feel the way it sort of burns . . . the warmth . . . it's incredible.'

Incredible, too, the effect on Mila as he massaged the oil into her skin. Her breasts seemed to grow firmer and pinker, their nipples standing proud and hard as carved wood as the warm oil seeped through the pores.

He poured some more oil on to Mila's belly. It dripped and trickled into the well of her navel, forming a little honey-gold pool, then spilling out in golden, spidery threads which crept across and down her smooth skin.

With both hands now, in broad, sweeping, circular movements, he smeared and smoothed the oil into Mila's skin. He scarcely knew who was the more aroused – his lover or himself. The potent ingredients in the oil had seeped through the skin of his palms and entered his bloodstream heightening every sensation in his whole body.

'Stroke my pussy, Greg. Stroke my pussy with the oil.'

Mila lay on her back, her knees drawn up and her thighs spread wide. As she looked up, she could see the many reflections above her, reflections of a woman for whom nothing existed at this moment but the need for sensual pleasure.

She knew that the oil was powerful, had already felt the

THE GOLDEN CAGE

intense sensations it could produce. But when the first, warm trickle of oil made its way between her parted sex-lips, Mila gave a cry of astonishment, excitement, tinged with just the faintest hint of apprehension. How much more unbearably intense would the sensations become when Greg's fingers began smoothing and massaging the oil over the head of her poor, swollen, already-throbbing clitoris?

She was soon to find out. The piped muzak did nothing to drown her high-pitched squeal of pleasure as the oil began to do its work, raising Mila's level of arousal to the point at which she wondered just how much more she could bear.

'I need you. Need to have you inside me, need you now,' she murmured as Greg's fingers teased the inner folds of her sex.

'I could make you come with just my fingers,' whispered Greg. 'I could stroke you, ever so softly, until you come all over my hand.'

'No – want you inside me. I want to come you inside me. Come into me.'

Greg needed no further encouragement. He was half crazy with the need to join with her.

Mila was pulling him down on top of her, his manhood nuzzling into the softness between her pussy lips. But at the last moment, he drew back.

'Greg!' protested Mila.

'It's OK, sweetheart.' He bent over to kiss her and their bodies slid across each other, his sweat mingling with the sweet slick of oil on her breasts and belly. It felt so, so good. 'I want us to be able to watch ourselves having sex. Wouldn't that be great?'

'Yes. How . . . ?'

'I lie on my back, like this – OK? Now, you lie on your back but at right-angles to me. That's right. Put your legs across mine... now lift up that gorgeous backside... aah, oh yes, that feels so good...'

Holding apart her buttocks, Mila slid down on to the hard spike of Greg's erect penis. It slipped into her like a hot knife into butter and, as it slid between her outer sex-lips, it became smeared with some of the warm, spicy massage oil.

The effect was immediate – the powerful oil anointing not just Greg's penis but the wet and welcoming inside of Mila's sex. Their desire leapt forward in a crazy stampede of longing and it was all they could do not to let it take control of them.

'Slowly, darling... slowly as you can,' breathed Mila as she began lifting and lowering her backside, tilting her hips to set the slow, luxurious rhythm of their coupling. 'Watch, darling...'

Looking up, Greg's eyes met Mila's in a myriad reflections; the mirrors sending back sixteen different images of their glistening bodies, moving together in perfect synchronicity. It was incredible to look and watch yourself making love – to look into your reflection and meet your lover's eyes, sparkling with that same, shared ecstasy.

'Touch yourself,' he begged. 'It turns me on so much to see you touching your own pussy.'

Mila's thighs parted a little further and he shuddered with excitement as he watched the long, hard shaft of his prick disappearing between the lobes of Mila's sex. When he saw her begin to masturbate, her fingers rubbing and sliding again and again over the glistening folds, he knew that he had never felt quite so aroused in his entire life.

THE GOLDEN CAGE

He had known extremes of pleasure before, of course he had. But only with Mila Kirovska had he begun to explore pleasure to its outermost limits.

Later, in the hotel bar, Greg and Mila took time out to survey the scene. It was nothing if not surreal.

The Happy Cowboy Honeymoon Hotel certainly lived up to its name. The bar was decorated as a Wild West Saloon, complete with dancing girls in basques, frilly skirts and feathers. The patrons ranged from the odd uncomfortable-looking type in a business suit to lovey-dovey newlyweds in cowboy boots and stetsons, kissing and cuddling under a row of stuffed buffalo heads.

'I could fancy you in one of those outfits.' Greg nudged Mila's arm and pointed out a girl in a fringed suede skirt, so skimpy that the fringes barely stopped short of her panties. 'Mind you, I could fancy you in anything.'

'Typical,' pouted Mila. 'I always knew you English were chauvinist pigs.'

'Forgive me?'

'If you buy me another drink.'

As the bartender was refilling Mila's glass, a girl in a white mini-dress entered the bar, hesitating in the doorway for just a few moments as though searching for something or someone. Then she crossed the floor and went straight up to Greg and Mila.

'Hi,' she smiled.

'Er . . . hi.' All this up front American friendliness took some getting used to, thought Mila, who saw demons lurking behind every smile.

'My name's Cindy.' The fluffy blonde stuck out her hand and it seemed the polite thing to do to accept it. 'I was wondering if you guys could lend a hand . . .'

'Well, I don't know,' began Greg. 'We're busy right now...'

'Say, you're English, right?'

'Right.'

'Oh, Kenny and me, we just love your English accent.'

'That's nice.' Greg couldn't think of anything else to say. 'What sort of help did you need?'

'You see, me and Kenny, we're getting married in the hotel. Only our folks couldn't make it, and we need two witnesses. I was kinda wondering... it would be real fine if you'd agree to help us.'

Mila glanced round the crowded bar. Suspicion kicked in: it had become almost a reflex to suspect everyone, even if they did look completely fluffy and vulnerable.

'Why us?'

The girl giggled.

'I don't know. You just look kinda... nice. Will you do it? It'll only take ten minutes, and we're having a champagne reception in the El Dorado Suite...'

Mila and Greg looked at each other. Greg shrugged. It would be churlish to refuse. After all, there couldn't be any harm in helping out the girl. Could there?

Darsey O'Brien and Caleb Steadman waited edgily in the hotel chapel.

'Maybe we moved too soon.' Steadman checked the ammunition clip and shoved the handgun back in its holster.

'We agreed. This was the right time, the right place.'

'Sure, but what about Hobart? Shouldn't we have told him we were planning to move in?'

'Keep your cool and this will work out just fine.' O'Brien flashed her accomplice a cold, wicked smile.

THE GOLDEN CAGE

'And maybe we'll get to have a little fun with the girl before we give her back to Hobart. He won't give a damn if she's a little ... shop-soiled.'

Steadman put his hand up for silence.

'Now. I can hear them coming.'

They sat down on the lilac-cushioned chairs, backs towards the door. To a casual glance they looked just like two guests at a wedding party. Somewhere in the distance, schmaltzy organ music played on a continuous tape-loop.

'In here,' said Cindy, her pert bum wriggling inside the tight white mini-dress. Mila couldn't help wondering what kind of girl got married in a dress like that, but then again there was no accounting for Americans.

They followed Cindy into the chapel. There was no one in there except two guests, sitting facing the imitation stained-glass window with its hideous picture of two lovers standing hand-in-hand in a field of startled-looking sheep.

'Where's your fiancé...?' began Greg, but his voice tailed off as the two people got to their feet and turned round. One of them, the man, was carrying a gun and it was pointed right at his chest. 'Bloody hell. We've been tricked.'

'Yes,' said the woman with the most chilling smile Greg had ever seen. 'Hell. We know all about Hell and so will you before today is over.'

'I'm sure Mr Hobart will be pleased to get back what belongs to him,' added the man, his face expressionless but his voice sour as curdled cream. Mila froze. It was the man from the casino. The one who had been watching them make love.

'Run,' said Greg. 'Run, while you have the chance.'

But Mila was rooted to the spot, her whole body trembling, her mind paralysed. All she could think about was Hobart, Orin Hobart who had sworn she would never escape him. How could she have been stupid enough to believe that she could ever get away?

'Really, Mr Delaney, you have all the worst qualities of the English,' commented Steadman, walking quickly towards Greg and twisting his arm effortlessly behind his back. Greg felt the barrel of a gun press into the curve of his spine, cold and hard and uncompromising. 'Pointless altruism, honesty, sentimentality, a sense of fair play. Is it any wonder you lost your precious Empire?'

Mila gave a squeal of anger and pain as Darsey O'Brien took hold of her by the hair.

'Get off me. НА Помощб! Оставбте меня в цокое! Get *off* me!' she spat, suddenly recovering both her anger and her will for freedom.

'Yes, you'd like that, wouldn't you?' commented O'Brien, unconcernedly. 'But I'm afraid that's not possible. And if I were you, I'd learn to shut my mouth and be more obedient, little Russian bitch. Mr Hobart will not deal with you as gently as I do.'

'Walk,' said Steadman, pushing the gun into the small of Greg's back.

'Why should I do what you say?'

'Because if you don't, I shall shoot you.'

'I don't particularly care if you do.'

'But you'd care if we shot your pretty little bitch of a companion, wouldn't you, you stupid Englishman?' purred O'Brien. 'Been having fun with her, have you? Have you taught her some new tricks she can use to please her master?'

'Bastards,' hissed Greg.

'You're learning fast,' replied Steadman drily. 'Now move. Out through the hotel lobby.'

THE GOLDEN CAGE

'Where are you taking us?' demanded Mila.

'Full of questions, isn't she?' observed Steadman.

'I'm sure Mr Hobart will be able to cure her of that. Now, move – slowly, and don't you dare make one sound, understand?'

Silence.

'I said, do you understand?' O'Brien twisted Mila's hair, jerking her head back.

'Yes,' hissed Mila between clenched teeth.

Mila's mind was a turmoil of fear and anger and explosive resentment as Darsey O'Brien marched her out of the wedding chapel and into the hotel lobby. It was crowded but no one paid any attention to the small group making its slow progress across the lobby.

No one – except Tex Oakley.

Reno was the Big City as far as Tex Oakley was concerned. He'd lived almost all of his forty-three years on a cattle ranch in Wyoming, and if it hadn't been for his grandaddy's inheritance, he'd probably have lived the next thirty there as well, never moving, never seeing anything of the world.

Reno was his first big adventure. Next, if this worked out, maybe he'd go further afield – New York, maybe. Europe even. But for now, Reno had bright lights aplenty for a hick cowboy from the other side of nowhere.

Naïve he might be but Tex liked to think he knew how to behave around a lady. And that definitely did not include pulling her hair and sticking the barrel of a Colt & Wesson in her back. His hand was already on his own side-arm as he strode forward and stopped dead in front of Darsey O'Brien.

'Get out the way,' snapped O'Brien, her cool momentarily snapping. This was all they needed – some part-time gun slinger with a brain the size of a pea and a heart the size of Texas.

'Beggin' yer pardon, miss, but are these people troublin' you at all?' enquired Tex.

'Please...' gasped Mila. She felt the pistol jab into her back and a tear escaped from her eye, trickling down her cheek. 'Help us.'

'Shut up,' muttered O'Brien. 'I said, get out of my way,' she repeated.

Tex simply stood his ground and raised his voice. This time some of the other people in the lobby turned round and started taking notice. At six-foot eight, with a voice to match, Tex was the sort of guy who tended to get noticed.

'Let the lady go,' he said, very calmly. His eyes flicked across to Greg, struggling frantically now despite the gun at his back. 'And her friend.'

'We're Federal Agents,' snapped back O'Brien. 'And you're obstructing the arrest of two dangerous criminals.'

'Is that so?' Tex looked into Mila's eyes. If she was a dangerous criminal, he was Dr Crippen. 'Then you won't mind showing me your ID.'

Steadman panicked, drew his gun and pointed it at Oakley. His hand was trembling as his finger stroked the trigger. The barrel glinted in the sunlight, and Mila heard someone scream, gasps running round the lobby.

'He has a gun.'

'Call the cops.'

Steadman waved the gun in Tex's face.

'This is our ID, geddit?'

'Fancy your chances of blowing me away, do you?' enquired Tex, a slight tinge of amusement in his voice.

'Don't tempt me, home boy.'

A split second later, Steadman let out a cry of anger and

THE GOLDEN CAGE

pain as the bullet from Tex's .45 sent the gun spinning from his hand. The whiplash effect was so savage that he let go of Greg and clutched at his wrist.

'For God's sake, Steadman,' raged O'Brien, but she could sense the moment slipping away from her. She was fast, but not that fast. And that mad bastard of a cowboy kept on staring at her, the gun rock-steady in his hand.

'Now, let her go.'

Nevertheless, O'Brien might have held out for success, if Greg hadn't made a grab for the gun in her hand. It was a clumsy attempt, doomed to failure, but O'Brien loosened her grip on Mila just long enough for the Russian girl to wrench free. When she recovered her balance, O'Brien saw that Oakley had both her and Steadman covered.

'Bitch ... come here, you bitch ...' she screamed after Mila's retreating back. 'You know you can't get away from me.'

But it was too late. Already Mila and Greg were running for their lives, out down the front steps of the hotel, towards the car park, towards their best chance of staying alive.

The ghost town of Wild Horse was just off Interstate 80. The tourist industry hadn't bothered with it since it was patched up and used in a silent film, way back in the Twenties. Wild Horse was pretty much as it must have been when the gold prospectors left it to die, almost a century before. It had long since ceased to decay, its old bones fossilised by year after year of baking, dusty heat.

'They won't think of looking for us here. At least, it won't be the first place they look.'

Greg and Mila stood in the middle of what had once been the main street – the only street. It had everything a ghost town ought to have: a creaking sign, swinging from a rusty iron hook; the remains of a general store and livery stables; even balls of tumble weed, spinning and scudding across the dusty earth like the startled spirits of old settlers.

'It's spooky,' whispered Mila, the lengthening shadows adding to the mysterious aura of the place.

'Spooky, but well off the beaten track. We'll stay here tonight, think about what to do next.'

'What *are* we going to do, Greg?'

Greg took Mila into the shade of an old verandah, and they sat down on the bleached wood. It groaned a little under their weight, but was still surprisingly strong after so many years of total neglect.

'We're going to San Francisco,' he said firmly. 'At least, I am. And if you come with me I can get you to the Russian Consulate.'

'San Francisco . . . but what if they already know we're headed that way?'

'The thing is, I need to go to San Francisco, it's something I promised myself I must do. And if they come for us again, this time we'll be ready for them.'

'They're dangerous, Greg. They'll stop at nothing . . .'

'I know.'

'Maybe you should leave me. If you're not with me, maybe they'll leave you alone.'

'Leave you? You mean, like you were going to leave me?'

'Yeah. Yeah, I know.'

'Forget it, Mila. We're in this together.' They kissed and in spite of their fears the old excitement returned, their shared desires overwhelming their anxieties.

'At least we have the money,' he said.

'Only because you were stupid enough to leave it locked in the car!'

He laughed.

'Some people aren't as stupid as they seem, Mila. Even me .'

Chapter 18

San Francisco. The city by the bay. A tumbling, jumbling beauty of a city, with steep, narrow, picturesque streets climbing hills whose summits were lost in a haze of sea-mist.

Cable-cars jangled up impossible gradients towards breathtaking views of the bay, of misty blue waters and the Golden Gate Bridge; and, ghostly and sinister on the horizon, the looming rocky shape of Alcatraz Island.

The engine of the yellow Chevrolet groaned and whined as Greg eased it up the hill towards the twenty-four square blocks of downtown San Francisco that were the teeming heart of Chinatown. It wasn't a good day for driving through the city – the big parade was on, and every freak in town was out in full costume. Straights and gays, lesbians, bisexuals, leather freaks and rubber queens. San Francisco was putting two fingers up to middle America and Mom's apple pie.

'Where are we going?' asked Mila. 'You still haven't explained why it was so important to come to San Francisco.'

'I have to pay my last respects to the family of someone I knew,' said Greg slowly, steering the car away from a police control-point, set up to mark the course of the procession. 'He was once a colleague of mine.' He swallowed hard, a lump rising in his throat. 'Actually he was more of a friend.'

'Tell me about him.' Mila laid her hand on Greg's.

'His name was Anthony Ho. He was Chinese-American, but we met in England at a conference. I got him hired to manage the West Coast side of our business operations. He was young, keen, hungry to succeed. A great guy too.'

'What happened?'

'He died.' Greg found it hard to concentrate on his driving. 'About a month ago. They said it was suicide. I didn't believe it then and I don't believe it now. He was killed.'

'But why?'

'I don't know. Maybe he knew too much. But what I do know is that it was just after he died that things started to go wrong for me. Horribly wrong. I have this terrible feeling that Tony died because of me.'

'No, surely not . . . you can't blame yourself.'

'I can't be sure – can't be sure of anything any more. But at the very least I owe it to him to pay my respects, talk to his sister. Then, and only then, I'll feel able to walk into that police station and give myself up.'

Grant Avenue was a mass of souvenir shops, ornate golden gateways cheek by jowl with neon signs and painted wooden balconies. He swung the car into Stockton Street, where the senses were assaulted by the pungent aromas of spice stores, bakeries, fish stalls and exotic produce.

'Not far now. I . . . hold on, what the hell . . . !'

He hadn't really noticed the station wagon before. But now, as he saw it creeping up alongside, Greg remembered seeing it just behind them as they drove in from

THE GOLDEN CAGE

Sacramento. At that moment, the driver turned the wheel sharp left and deliberately rammed the side of the Chevy.

Oh my God ... The words pounded round in Greg's head again and again, as he turned to glare at the driver of the station wagon and saw the two familiar faces looking back at him. Smiling at him, colder than an Alaskan sunset.

'It's them! They must have followed us here from Reno,' screamed Mila.' Greg – get us out of here!'

'I'm trying, believe me I'm trying.'

Greg stamped on the gas pedal and the old Chevy lurched forward, engine protesting and wheels squealing. He was a good enough driver but it was an elderly car, and he could see from the way the station wagon was performing that it had been souped up. It was hopeless trying to outrun Hobart's gangsters.

'Is the money still on the back seat?' he gasped as he swung the Chevy round the corner, going straight through a red light and almost running over a fat woman with a poodle.

'Yes, why?'

'Lean over and grab it. Next chance we get, we're going to make a run for it.'

Things were moving quite slowly and calmly inside Greg's head, which was peculiar really, because Death Race 2000 was happening on the street. It was chaos – cars sounding their horns, vans swerving out of the way, a man on a motorbike shaking his fist ... and any minute now the police were bound to turn up to find out what all the commotion was about. Right now that sort of attention was exactly what Greg and Mila were trying to avoid.

The next street gave Greg what he was looking for – a moment's cover. The thoroughfare was lined with market stalls and filled with shoppers and a long, slow-moving line of traffic. Swinging the Chevy round the corner, Greg took a sharp left through a crowd of protesting shoppers and managed to conceal the Chevy in a narrow alleyway. They sat there in silence for several long minutes, silently praying that the station wagon had shot past them on the main road.

'Out – quickly. It won't take them long to realise what we've done. Give me the money, it's heavy. You concentrate on running.'

He took the attaché case and they dived out of the car and into the crowds. Greg knew they had no more than a few minutes' grace. The two investigators were clearly skilled operators. It wouldn't take them long to find the Chevy, work out where Greg and Mila had gone. Besides, for all he knew they had the whole city covered.

'Which way?' gasped Mila.

'That way – towards the parade.'

He didn't really know what he was doing or where he was going, only that the parade meant noise and colour and bustle. And wherever there were lots of people, there would be opportunities for two people to hide themselves.

They came through on to California Street, running slap-bang into a wall of colour and sound and tickertape. A slow procession of floats was making its way through the city. 'San Francisco Gay Pride' read a banner on one float. 'Dykes On Bikes' proclaimed a second, carried by two bikers in skintight black leather and silver bondage jewellery. 'Big Is Beautiful' chanted a group of ample ladies in scarlet and black Lycra, dancing as they followed the 'Chinese Women's Support Group' down the street.

THE GOLDEN CAGE

Greg felt Mila freeze, her hand suddenly gripping his.
'What is it?'
'There, Greg – over there, on the other side of the road. It's them. I don't think they've seen us yet, but . . .'

But it could only be a matter of time. Greg had to hand it to these two vultures, they sure were thorough. He had the feeling that no matter how far they might go, no matter how hard they might try to hide themselves, these two would never give up.

There were two options open to them now: stand their ground and allow themselves to be caught, or make a run for it. The first wasn't even worth considering. If they were going to go down, they would go down fighting.

Greg pulled Mila a little further back into the encircling crowd, fairly certain that the two investigators could not see them from the other side of the road. Where to now? Without the car they couldn't get far. If they tried to hire one it was a fair bet the office would lead their pursuers straight to them. There was only one thing for it: they had to stay in San Francisco and – somehow – disappear off the face of the earth.

A float was wobbling and rumbling its way towards them. Looked at objectively it was faintly ridiculous – a big industrial lorry decked out as a scene from a Roman orgy, all drapes and lopsided pillars, with an assortment of scantily-clad women eating grapes as they reclined on couches. The sign read 'House of Nymphs.' To Greg it was a godsend – a faint possibility of escape.

'See that float – the one with the Vestal Virgins on it?'
'Yes, why?'
'All those drapes at the back . . . I'm sure no one would notice if we climbed up and hid underneath.'

'But – how?'

'It's going pretty slowly. Just as it passes, I'll lift you up. Duck underneath the drapes.'

'What if someone sees?'

'They won't.'

'And if they do?'

He tried to hide the panic in his voice.

'Smile and eat a grape.'

'What about you?'

He kissed her, with a sort of firm finality.

'I'll be right behind. Now, get ready. And hold on tight...'

As the lorry drew level with them, Mila curled her fingers around the soft leather of her shoulder bag, patting the hard stone inside. Somehow she felt better, knowing it was still there. Funny how the little jade tiger had become something of a talisman. If she wasn't careful, she was going to end up as superstitious as her Aunt Anna Petruschkova. If she lived that long...

'Up – go on, up. Quickly.'

Mila felt Greg lifting her up and – watched by a few bemused members of the crowd, she managed to claw her way up on to the back of the lorry. The glamorous 'nymphs' were far too busy waving and blowing kisses to the crowd to notice the Russian girl slipping underneath the hangings at the back of their display.

Greg followed, losing his footing for one breathtaking moment that almost had Mila crying out with fear. *Once more, Greg*, she was mouthing at him. *Once more, you can do it.* It was all happening in slow-motion, though the whole episode couldn't have lasted more than a minute. His fingers scrabbled at the tailboard of the lorry, found a handhold, grasped it for dear life and hauled himself up.

THE GOLDEN CAGE

It was touch and go as to whether he'd make it – and if he didn't, he'd be a sitting target for Orin Hobart's hired thugs. What could be more noticeable than a man hanging from the tailboard of a lorry?

Just as he was heaving himself over the edge and towards safety, one of the women on the float turned in his direction. His heart stopped, his breath turning to solid ice in his chest.

That was it. He'd been rumbled. End of story. Give himself up, that's what he'd have to do. Sacrifice himself and hope Mila could get by on her own.

'Well I'll be ... if it isn't a gentleman caller!' The woman was very statuesque, terrifically handsome, fully six feet tall and with a voice like rough silk.

'Please ... please help me,' mouthed Greg. 'Somebody's trying to kill me. The police ...'

She regarded him for a split second, and in that moment Greg was certain she was going to tell him to get lost. Then, to his immense surprise, she put out her arm and pulled him the last few inches on to the float.

'Honey, I don't know what kind of trouble you're in but my kind don't have no special fondness for the cops, if you get my meaning. I ain't seen you, OK?'

Speechless with gratitude, Greg scrambled under the mass of drapery at the back of the float, and took Mila into his arms. He wasn't a moment too soon. As the parade turned the corner, he saw two figures – a woman with red-blonde hair and a tall, rangy man – running across the street to the exact spot where they'd been standing.

As the adrenaline rush started to ebb away, Greg felt cold and shivery. He drew Mila towards him, desperate for ways of reassuring her, of telling her that it was all over now and she'd be safe.

The trouble was, he could sense that it was just beginning.

'They were here. I know they were here.'

Caleb Steadman glared at the spot where, a few minutes before, he was convinced that he had seen Mila Kirovska and Greg Peterson.

'You were obviously wrong,' sneered O'Brien. 'As fucking usual.'

It wasn't exactly the right thing to say. Maybe she'd wanted to provoke him, it was kind of hard to tell with Darsey O'Brien. Aggression seemed to turn her on; she was always at her hottest when sex was dangerous or just plain crazy. Taking her to bed wasn't so much about making love as making war.

Steadman's cock stiffened as he turned and spat out his riposte.

'And I suppose you're always right, Little Miss Perfect? Like you were right about trying to jump them in Reno?'

'If you hadn't pulled a gun on that dumb cowpoke...'

'So it's all down to me now, is it?'

'Yeah. Wanna make something of it?'

They were squaring up to each other, eyeball to eyeball, faces flushed with resentment. Curious how it turned Steadman on to see his partner like this. He'd always thought of his sexual tastes as fairly conventional until he'd met up with her and embarked upon a month-long orgy of sexual excess.

O'Brien had corrupted him. He liked it.

He pushed her up against the wall and felt the hardness of her body.

THE GOLDEN CAGE

'Any time, bitch. Any time.'

Not even giving her time to spit in his face, he pulled away and started pushing through the crowds. A few seconds later she caught up with him.

'Where are you going?'

'Back to Delaney's car. I want to check it for anything useful. And they might come back, try and use it to get away.'

'They're dumb, but they're not *that* dumb. Not even that retard Delaney would think of going back to the Chevy.'

'We need to check it over. They may have left the jade tiger there.'

'Not if Hobart's right and they know how much it's worth to him. So, what then, wise guy?'

'Back to the station wagon, I guess. I'll think of something. They can't get far without transport and we have agents covering all the hire offices.'

He turned out of the main road into a narrow, dingy alleyway which led between tall, weatherboarded nineteenth-century houses; walking quickly, keeping one step ahead of her, head down and hands in pockets. He didn't want her to know how much her venom was turning him on.

'Admit it, Steadman. This time you goofed. Big time.'

'Nobody goofed. Except maybe you. You should never have taken this assignment on in the first place. Hobart's sick in the head, you know that?'

'He's a billionaire. I like billionaires.'

'He's obsessive – and obsession is dangerous. If you really wanna know, I don't particularly want to put my neck on the block for a fucking fruitcake like Orin Hobart.'

'Aw, c'mon Steadman. Stop making excuses and face up to the truth. You just don't have what it takes. Do you?'

This time she hit the target and he spun round to confront her, eyes blazing cold fire in his lean, tanned face.

'I've got what it takes to keep a bitch like you in line.'

'Yeah? Really?'

'One more word from you, O'Brien, and I'm gonna show you just how much.'

A slow smile crept over O'Brien's face, curving her deep-red lips into an expression of perverse pleasure.

'I gotta take a leak,' she announced.

Steadman hadn't expected this, and O'Brien knew it. That was the thing about him, he was so much more naïve than he thought he was, so little in control of his own sexuality. How could he possibly begin to imagine that he was in control of hers?

'Here?' This was a new game. Steadman wasn't yet sure whether he liked it, but hey, it had possibilities. 'In the street?'

He glanced around. The alleyway was deserted right now, and in shadow, but the parade was still in full swing at one end and the other led into a main tourist thoroughfare.

'Right here. You wanna watch?'

Steadman's lip curled. What a cool, cool piece of ass she was.

'It turns you on, doesn't it? Having people watch.'

She blew him a sarcastic kiss.

'Don't you mean it turns *you* on? You really do have to stop lying to yourself, Steadman.'

THE GOLDEN CAGE

She didn't even bother turning away from him; just started rolling up the hem of that tight, tight mini-skirt. It was a cotton skirt but there was lycra in the mix and it made it cling tighter than a young whore's ass to O'Brien's firm, juicy thighs. Steadman watched, entranced, as she inched it up to reveal more and more of those lightly tanned legs, until at last she reached the very top.

No underwear, of course, but then he hadn't really expected her to be wearing any. Darsey O'Brien wasn't in the habit of wearing panties – she said they 'made her pussy itch', or 'made her feel confined'. But Steadman knew the real reason was the thrill she got, walking through the streets bare-assed, knowing what all those men would think if only they knew too...

Her luxuriant, red-blonde curls formed a perfect triangle at the apex of her thighs. He couldn't take his eyes off them, cursing himself for his weakness. She could do anything she damn well liked with him. There was a devil inside her and it seemed to have been sent to earth expressly to torment him.

Pulling her skirt high on her hips, she squatted down. Steadman drank in the superb curve of her backside, the muscular tension of those beautifully parted thighs, the golden bush that marked the entrance to her secret garden.

She relieved herself right there in front of him, the ochre-yellow stream splashing gently on the cobbled roadway as it ran away into the gutter.

'That feels good,' sighed O'Brien. 'Mmm, you've no idea how good it feels. Like bringing yourself off and just letting go...'

'You're a shameless slut, Darsey O'Brien.'

'And you're a pervert who likes to watch girls piss.'

Oh, but it was turning him on. He didn't want it to – it was slightly humiliating after all – but there simply wasn't any way to resist the excitement that was coursing through him.

'I'm a man, Darsey. A man who thinks it's about time he taught you a lesson.'

She laughed as she stood up, smoothing down the skirt over her backside.

'Enjoyed that, did you?'

'Not as much as I'm going to enjoy doing this.'

Lust overtook him like a crimson tide, and at that moment Steadman couldn't have cared less if half of San Francisco had turned up to watch. His fingers fumbled with his fly, unzipped, groped inside and pulled out the wet-tipped shaft of his cock.

O'Brien tossed back her collar-length hair. It framed her face like a golden cloud, making her seem like some corrupted angel, the soul corroded from within but the external beauty flawless and radiant.

'Doing what, Steadman? Still think you can handle me, do you?'

Steadman's reply needed no words. Strength flooded through him and he slammed O'Brien back against the wall. He had the advantage of surprise and for a moment at least, she didn't even wriggle; just looked at him with round eyes that sparkled with astonished pleasure.

His heart thumped in his chest as he took hold of the front of her blouse, screwing the silk up in his fist and ripping, tearing it from her breasts – bare, golden breasts whose dusky brown nipples jiggled and trembled as he pushed her hard against the wooden exterior of the house.

Belatedly, she tried to push him away; but by now he held her fast. What's more, he had sensed the pleasure within her and knew that it would weaken her, betraying her resistance to him.

'I'm going to have you now,' he told her, quite matter-of-factly. 'And it's going to be the best damned fuck of your whole life. Okay?'

'Go screw yourself,' she spat, but the habitual vehemence was fast ebbing away. He could feel the pulse in Darsey's wrist, fast and thready, as the adrenaline rush hit her and surrendered her to him. He could smell her sweat, mingled with the unmistakeable muskiness of sexual desire.

'I'd rather screw you.'

She thought he was simply going to lift her up and wrap her thighs about his waist, forcing her down on to his prick. Already her sex was dripping juice at the merest thought of it – the smooth, velvet pleasure of their fucking. She would claw and bite him a little, show her displeasure while all the time she was getting off on the play-violence of it all.

Steadman was playing, too, only he was taking the game a little more seriously. Months of resentment and frustrated lust had built up inside him and now they were all spilling out. He had wanted to put her in her place for so, so long. Wanted, too, to show her that she was not as in control of her own pleasure as she thought. That there was one man, at least, who could take it from her by force.

O'Brien kicked out and bit his hand as he flipped her over like a pancake, pushing her breasts up against the wall. The wooden ridges pressed into her softness with unforgiving teeth, but the discomfort only served to heighten their mutual excitement.

'Get your filthy hands off me!' she spat. But her voice was scarcely louder than a whisper – and certainly not loud enough to summon assistance. Steadman smiled to himself. He'd been right. She wanted it as much as he did. If she could turn sex into a fight, so could he.

'I'll *get off* when I choose, not before.'

Her leg kicked backwards, almost but not quite catching him in the balls. Deftly he turned her resistance into a submission, using the opportunity to push up her skirt.

'You want me *that* bad, huh? Well, mustn't disappoint you, must we?'

O'Brien was seeing a whole new side to Caleb Steadman. All these months they'd been working together and she'd thought he was just a puppy-dog, the sort of man she could mould and toy with and turn into whatever she wanted him to be. Boring. Well, today she was being pleasantly surprised.

Her skirt was up round her waist again now, more like a belt of twisted fabric than a skirt. It did nothing to cover her – the globes of her bottom were bare and beautiful. He gave them a really good, resounding slap.

'Bastard!' squeaked O'Brien, but her face was squashed against the wall and the sound disappeared into the wood.

He did it again. It was fun. The way her backside quivered at the slap, turning first white then a pretty marbled pink, really turned him on.

'You have a fine ass, bitch. You should show it off.'

O'Brien squirmed, but it was useless. Besides, she was enjoying it – a lot more than she was prepared to admit to Caleb Steadman.

'It's high time someone taught you a lesson,' observed Steadman. *Slap, slap, slap*. It felt so good to feel his palm tingling and heating up as he administered the smacking of a lifetime to Darsey O'Brien. She probably hadn't been

```
*        LD KERRISDALE              **
LY FOR LESS TO U.S. - ASK FOR DETAILS


EMPLOYEE DISCOUNT                  2493
8 DISC CARLTON CARD               4.00 B
8 DISC B&D IRON                  39.98 B
        EMPLOYEE DISCOUNT         7.98-
   **** TAX      5.04  BAL       41.02
F      VISA                      41.02
        007209
        CHANGE                     .00
        (P)ST     2.52
        (G)ST     2.52
5/10/96 19:11 0010 11 0292 15877
     (B)OTH = G.S.T. + P.S.T.
LONDON DRUGS LTD. G.S.T. #R103378972
```

SATISFACTION GUARANTEED

Your satisfaction is guaranteed at London Drugs. If any merchandise purchased isn't to your complete satisfaction, return it to any London Drugs store within 15 days in the original packaged condition with proof of purchase for a complete refund, exchange or adjustment to your satisfaction.

Nobody does it better®

SATISFACTION GUARANTEED

Your satisfaction is guaranteed at London Drugs. If any merchandise purchased isn't to your complete satisfaction, return it to any London Drugs store within 15 days in the original packaged condition with proof of purchase for a complete refund, exchange or adjustment to your satisfaction.

handled like this since she was a little girl – and that was most likely half of the problem. Darsey O'Brien needed some discipline in her life.

Yes, it was fun watching the golden flesh turn to a marbled pink which in turn deepened to a warm crimson. So much fun that he knew he had to have her now, or explode with excitement.

He stopped spanking her, and she lay panting underneath him, muttering obscenities which could not quite mask the excitement throbbing through her overheated body. She stank of sex, every pore wafting the scent of musky, sweaty desire.

Steadman's hand pushed between O'Brien's buttocks. Her crack was dripping wet with the juices flooding out of her sex. He smeared a glossy, slippery trail from sex to anus, lubricating the twitching membrane of her most secret cavity.

Anticipating his next move, she again tried to kick him away; but he was ready for her and in any case, the feel of his fingers smoothing over and over her rose was soothing away her resistance.

It wasn't difficult for Steadman to pull apart O'Brien's buttocks and slide his manhood into the tiny, winking eye which nestled in the amber furrow between them. He felt O'Brien's whole body stiffen, and then suddenly she was pushing back against him – not resisting him, but taking him deeper into her, opening up the heart of her secret intimacy as his penis scythed into her.

As he enjoyed her, his cock throbbing with the brutal pleasure of this one, small victory, he cursed himself for his naïvety. She was meeting him halfway, taking his will and making it hers.

He should have known he could never defeat Darsey

O'Brien. The best he could hope for was to couple with her on her own, savage terms.

'Come in, my dears. You're very welcome.'

Greg and Mila walked through a side-door into the interior of an old wooden house, one of the painted nineteenth-century buildings which were scattered so prettily across the hills of San Francisco.

'Lori, Petronella – we have guests.'

Mila stood agape in the hallway of the house. It was draped with crimson velvet and veils of silver and gold gauzy fabric which gave the place an atmosphere of unreality.

'What . . . what is this place?'

The tall woman answered with a sweeping gesture, taking in the high, draped ceiling, the huge, curving staircase and statues of naked women peeping out from between the hangings.

'Welcome to the House of Nymphs. My name is Asta and I am the mother of the house.'

The mother? Mila wondered what Asta meant by that.

'Ah, here are two of my daughters now. They'll take good care of you, won't you dears?'

Two more women appeared at the top of the stairs, pausing on the landing then scurrying down to greet the new arrivals. They were tall, like Asta, but they didn't look much like her daughters. One was very thin and gaunt, with a mass of dark hair, the other a platinum blonde with generous breasts. There was something ever so slightly odd about them, but Greg couldn't quite put his finger on it.

'You look like you could use a hot bath and a good meal,' observed Asta.

THE GOLDEN CAGE

'That's very kind...' began Mila. 'You see, we've...'

Asta put up her hand.

'That's OK. You're in trouble with the cops and we've been there a time or two ourselves. You can tell me about it later if you feel like it. Now, go with Pet and Lori, and I'll see you afterwards in the Grand Salon.'

As Greg and Mila followed Petronella and Lori up the wide, curving staircase, Greg suddenly realised what it was that had seemed odd about these women.

They weren't women at all. Come to think of it, neither was 'mother' Asta.

All three of them were men.

Chapter 19

Hot sex, warm coffee and crumbly croissants, all on a misty balcony overlooking the waking city. It was the perfect way to start the day – so perfect, you might never guess that everything was so horribly wrong.

Cross-legged on the balcony, Mila curled up in the crook of Greg's arm and sipped her coffee.

'Who'd have thought it?'

'Asta, you mean?'

'Yeah. A man...'

The House of Nymphs had certainly turned out to be a place of unusual fascinations. 'The House of Freaks', Asta had laughingly called it, half-humorous, half-edged in bitterness. It was a house of transvestites and transsexuals, many 'in transition' between genders, living there until they had saved up enough money to take that final, irrevocable step. Most were men who wished to become women; a few were women who dreamed of being men. They lived here together, in this haven of acceptance, this temple of unquestioning sexuality where they could be exactly what they wanted to be.

And Mother Asta presided over it all, at once glittering and homely, imperious and warm. Greg found her hard to come to terms with – even though he knew 'she' was a man, he found himself admitting that she was attractive.

Aurelia Clifford

There was a knock at the bedroom door.

'Come in.'

The door opened and a tall figure swept in. Even at seven in the morning, Asta looked immaculate. Her make-up was just-so, her dark-red hair piled on top of her head, with long curled tendrils caressing her cheeks and the nape of her neck. She was wearing a wine-red sequinned dress, with shoestring straps and a low-cut neckline which revealed the swell of deceptively real-looking breasts. The gown skimmed an enviable figure, with a nipped-in waist which any woman would have been proud of. A side-split reached from mid-calf to thigh, exposing a length of tanned, smooth-shaven leg which Greg found instantly arousing.

'Did you sleep well?'

'Yes thank you.' Mila brushed crumbs from the baby-doll nightie one of Asta's 'girls' had given her to wear. 'It's so kind of you to let us stay here. You don't even know what we've done.'

Asta toyed with the black ostrich-feather boa which kissed her bare shoulders.

'Well, my dears, if your guilty conscience is pricking you so badly, why don't you tell me? They do say confession is good for the soul, though I must say I've never found that myself.'

Mila felt a twinge of reluctance. Things had been bad for so long that she found it hard to trust anyone.

'You say you're in trouble with the police?' continued Asta.

'Yes and no,' replied Greg. 'Well yes, I am. Bad trouble. I'm being framed for something I didn't do . . .'

'Inevitably,' commented Asta, with just a hint of irony.

'. . . and now I'm in very deep shit indeed. I'm going to

turn myself in, but first there's something I need to do in San Francisco.'

Asta turned her eyes on Mila.

'And what about you, my dear? Is that a Russian accent? Your English is so good it's hard to tell.'

'I'm Russian, yes.'

'So you're an illegal alien?' Asta crossed her legs and the dress fell open, baring a long, sleek slope of waxed thigh. 'Well, that's not the end of the world. Petronella's in the very same boat – she's Cuban, you know. Poor darling. It's only her little understanding with the Chief of Police that keeps her from being deported.'

'It wouldn't be so bad,' sighed Mila, 'but there's someone out there who's determined to destroy my life ... someone who thinks he owns me, and who'll do anything to get me back.'

'Which explains why we were running away from two thugs with guns yesterday,' explained Greg.

'I see.' Asta ran jewelled fingers through her forest of dark-red hair. 'Well, I don't like to endanger my daughters, and the House of Nymphs abhors violence of all kinds ...'

'It's OK, we'll leave,' said Greg, getting to his feet. 'This morning, if you like. You've been kind enough already.'

Asta gave an impatient snort.

'You Englishmen, you are *so* impetuous. Maybe that's why you make such hopeless lovers?' She laughed. 'Don't worry, you can stay as long as you want. I believe your story. And even if I didn't ... well, let's just say I have a fetish for Englishmen and pretty Russian girls.'

She looked them up and down.

'Ever done any acting?'

'No. Why?'

'The House of Nymphs is not a charity, Greg. We all

have to find ways to bring in money so we can support our dear sisters. Petronella does a little modelling, Cass and Rosita have exclusive clients who appreciate their unique personal services. And my dear Lori is something of a cult film-maker. Haven't you ever thought that you'd like to see yourself immortalised on film?'

Greg and Mila stared at Asta. Both were arriving, from different directions, at the same conclusion.

'You make ... films here? At the House of Nymphs?' asked Mila.

'Sex films, that's right, my dear. Erotic *oeuvres* to suit the most discerning of palates. We show them here sometimes, when I hold our soirées in the Grand Salon. The girls organise a fashion show, then we have a little sexual entertainment while the films play. I believe they are extremely well received – Lori is such an artist, a true perfectionist.'

'And ... what does this have to do with us?' enquired Greg, although he had already guessed. 'What is it you're asking us to do?'

'I want you to become film stars – beautiful, sexy, immortal stars of the silver screen. Won't that be wonderful?' Asta's face lit up as she spoke, as though she really was turned on by the thought of film-sex. 'And I want you to star with me.'

'I'm not quite sure I could,' replied Mila, very quietly. She was thinking of all the pictures Hobart had taken of her, pictures designed solely to degrade and destroy her.

Asta looked a little sad.

'Don't you think I'm attractive?'

'Yes, of course you are, but...'

Reaching up, Asta slipped down the shoulder straps of her dress, letting them fall down over her upper arms; then

THE GOLDEN CAGE

pushed down the sequinned top so that it hung down from the waist. Greg felt his manhood stir in appreciation of Asta's magnificent breasts – so firm, so round, so silky-smooth, with the most enormous nipples he had ever seen, pink and flat as saucers. *Real* breasts. Silicone dreams. He gaped like a goldfish.

'You see, darlings, I've always had a pet fantasy,' Asta continued. 'Maybe you'll think it's a little weird, but hell, we're all freaks here, and why shouldn't freaks have a little fun? I've always had a fetish for getting it on with two lovers at the same time – a man and a girl.'

Seeing Mila's raised eyebrows, Asta hitched up her skirt, revealing the bulge of a cock beneath red satin panties.

'Have no fear my darlings, I'm still *entire*. I can still give you pleasure. Both of you.'

Orin Hobart wrapped the bullwhip around his clenched fist. It felt good – supple, strong, vicious. Fragrant too, with the scents of dozens of different slaves, lovers who had existed solely to furnish him with the perverse pleasures he craved.

It had been far too long since his whip had tasted the sweet, succulent flesh of Mila Kirovska, and with every day that passed he grew more ravenously hungry for her, more furious at the incompetence of those he had employed to find her. And so he had come to San Francisco himself to make sure they didn't slip up again.

He hardly knew which loss disturbed him more – the jade tiger, with the explosive secrets it embodied, or the slave he purchased, broken to his discipline, and allowed to slip between his fingers.

A vicious flick of the whip sent its tip cracking down through the air, and on to the bare back of the Chinese girl he had bought from a man in a drinking-club near Sam Wo's. She was sweet and tender flesh – almost a virgin, only sixteen and completely unschooled to pain. Consequently she roared every time he struck her. At first that had amused him, but he was growing tired of her already. He needed a greater challenge.

He needed Mila.

He knew she was here in San Francisco, here with that idiot Englishman who had already caused him far too much trouble. Anger rising in him like black bile, he drew back his arm and brought the whip down a second time. The girl yelped and arched her back, the olive skin already criss-crossed with a patchwork of red welts.

'Be silent!'

'Please, sir! Don't hurt me any more, please!'

He sent the bullwhip curling and cracking through the air a third time.

'I will do anything . . . anything you tell me to.'

'Anything, Mae-Ling? You're absolutely sure about that?'

'Whatever you say. Anything at all. Just stop beating me. Please stop, I don't like it. I want to go home now.'

'If you do not cease your pathetic whining I shall do a good deal more things you don't like,' replied Hobart. He contemplated the girl as he chastised her: a pretty enough little thing, whiplash slender and lithe as a serpent. It was vaguely pleasurable to watch her writhe and twist, trying to free her wrists from the ropes binding them to the bed head. Her ankles were bound, too – with looser ropes attached to the foot of the bed, and forcing her to keep her thighs apart.

But he had not had her yet. He hadn't felt the urge to penetrate her. In general, he liked to whet his appetite by

THE GOLDEN CAGE

first breaking his victim's spirit. It was a pity this one's spirit was so lacking in substance. Even before he had laid a finger on her she had been offering to obey his every command. What kind of a turn-on was that for a man like Orin Hobart? It wasn't enough for a slave to *give* him her obedience – he needed the satisfaction of taking it from her.

The trouble with Mae-Ling was that she was more like a child than a woman – too easy, too irrationally fearful to put up any resistance. Not like sparky, sassy, insolent Mila. How he had punished her for her defiance! How his lust had boiled at the challenge of breaking her.

Much more of this girl's infantile behaviour and he would scarcely be able to raise enough interest to take her. This was not what he had intended at all – the girl had been purchased as an agreeable diversion while he watched and waited. Waited for Mila and Greg to betray themselves by some foolishness, some incautious move which would deliver them – and the jade tiger – into his hands.

He wanted that diversion and he wanted it now. He wanted Mila to be here, knowing instinctively what pleased him, what perversities and cruelties it took to make him iron-hard. Hobart decided on another approach.

'Your father says you are a dirty whore, Mae-Ling,' he commented coolly, stroking the tip of the bullwhip up and down the length of the girl's spine.

Her back rippled like an eel's at the touch of the whip, now so deceptively and treacherously gentle.

'My father lies,' sobbed the girl, her voice muffled by the sweat-soaked bedcover on which she lay.

'You dare to call your beloved father a liar?'

'I hate him. He tells untruths about me.'

'I don't believe you, Mae-Ling. He tells me you are the

dirtiest, filthiest little whore in Chinatown,' continued Hobart. This was promising. He was at last provoking some sort of reaction. Maybe he could stoke it up into rebellion.

'No! I am a good girl.'

'A good girl who fucks her sister's husband?'

'It is not true...'

'That's not what I've been told. You see, your father has told me everything about you. That's why I decided to pay such a good price for you. He told me that he found you with Chung-Hue in the cellar under the restaurant. You were sucking his cock, weren't you, Mae-Ling? Is that any way for a nice young lady to behave with her sister's husband?'

This time Mae-Ling did not speak. She was sobbing with anger, her limbs thrashing as she tried to free herself from the cords which bound her. Good, thought Hobart. Very good. Now she is really mad at me for humiliating her. She wants to kill me, she hates me so much. The pain she can bear, but not the shame.

'And when you had done, you drank it all down. Your father saw you. He says you had spunk all over your lips and you were licking the last drops from your brother-in-law's dick.'

'My father is a filthy liar,' sobbed Mae-Ling.

Perhaps, perhaps not, thought Hobart with an increasing degree of satisfaction. This was more like it. It didn't matter one way or the other whether Mae-Ling's darling papa had told the truth about her sexual exploits. What mattered was the girl's delicious anger. Now she was giving him something he could enjoy breaking.

'Chung-Hue must have liked having you licking him, because the next thing your father saw, you had made him hard again. You were kissing his balls, taking them into

THE GOLDEN CAGE

your mouth, stroking your fingers between his ass cheeks. Your father's right, you really are the filthiest little whore...'

'And you are an evil, lying bastard,' spat Mae-Ling.

'Say that again,' purred Hobart, the whip flexing in his hand.

'Bastard. Evil bastard...' She sobbed out her defiance, her wrists reddening as she wriggled to free herself and the ropes chafed her delicate skin.

Hobart gave her a flick of the whip – not a full stroke, he didn't want to dampen her resistance even before it had begun. A little bite, just incisive enough to make her buck and wriggle and squeal with angry resentment. Little by little, he was going to make her give him what he wanted.

'You let him do it again, didn't you?' He carried on talking, very calmly, certain that she was listening through the sobs and the curses. 'And not just once, either. Your father says Chung-Hue lay down on the ground and you sat on his dick, pumping those lovely firm thighs up and down on him. I bet those pretty little tits of yours jiggled like Jell-o...'

'Let me go! Let me go now. I won't listen...'

'You will listen, Mae-Ling. And I know you want to. I know it's making you hot for me, hearing me tell you all about what you were doing in that cellar.

'Do you want to hear some more?'

He didn't wait for her to reply. He knew she did. He could tell from the staccato rhythm of her breathing that he was getting through to her. Whether what he was telling her was real or a fantasy didn't matter any more. All that mattered was that they had both begun to believe it.

'Of course you do. A dirty little slut like you can't wait to hear about all the wicked things she's been up to when she thinks nobody's looking. Do you remember what you did after that, Mae-Ling? Sure you do. You sucked him till he was hard for you again . . . and then you let him fuck you in the ass.'

'No!' Mae-Ling's breath escaped in a gasp of horror.

'Not denying it, are you? Silly girl. You can't fool me. You see, I know what you like. *Everything* you like.'

He gave her one good, hard crack of the whip and this time she squealed – not so much in pain as in rage. He knew what she was feeling now and it stiffened his cock in a way he had not experienced since Mila had betrayed him.

Ah yes, Mae-Ling wanted so badly to kill him, to put her red-nailed fingers about his neck and claw him till the blood spurted in a scarlet arterial fountain. Such a pity she wouldn't be able to make her dream come true. He'd have to help her live out another of her fantasies, instead.

'Did he have a big penis?' He raked the whip down her spine and over the small, hard mounds of her buttocks. They clenched as he touched them, fearful and yet anticipating pleasure. 'Was he well-hung? Come on, Mae-Ling, I want to know.'

'It's lies, all lies. I won't tell you lies.'

Hobart contemplated the whip in his hand, its glossy-black serpent's body whispering of pleasures past and still to come. Seductive images chased themselves across his mind. With a smile of recognition, he turned the whip round so that its handle was pointing towards her – a long, thick length of wood, covered with woven leather.

'Really? Then perhaps I shall have to remind you. Was he as big as *this*?'

He pulled apart Mae-Ling's buttocks and pushed the

whip-handle into the deep crack between. The tiny, puckered rose of her anus twitched, dilated then tensed at the first touch.

'No, no, no!' she squealed, her whole body resisting what was about to happen and yet ... somehow wanting it.

'Why should you be afraid? You've done it before, haven't you? How often did you let him? You haven't told me yet, Mae-Ling. Was he as big as this?'

Her anus dilated and – lubricated by the abundant ooze from her sex – the handle drove into her. How she twisted and turned. How she resisted him. Yet with each movement she made to free herself, she only succeeded in pushing herself harder on to the whip handle, impaling herself upon it like a butterfly on a pin.

Hobart manipulated the whip with skill, possessing the girl with a subtlety that seemed to keep her forever on the edge between discomfort and pleasure. A warm, erotic sensation of power crept over him and he unzipped his penis from his pants. It felt hot and hard in his hand. It would feel even better when he slipped it into Mae-Ling's welcoming sex.

And best of all when it was spitting its venom over the upturned contrite face of Mila Kirovska.

When they reached the garden of the House of Nymphs, Greg and Mila found that Lori had already set up her cameras and was ready to begin shooting.

'Darlings,' she smiled, sashaying towards them across the lawn. 'You've no idea what a novelty this is ... a real pleasure ...'

Lori kissed them both on the cheek and Mila had to think hard to remember that 'she' wasn't a she at all. She was a he – or was she? There were so many people here who were 'in transition' between the sexes that it was hard to classify anyone.

There was Mother Asta, her magnificent silicon-enhanced breasts belying the hard bulge of cock and balls between sleek, shaven thighs. There were her 'girls', all pouting lips and big hair, tight corsets and skilful padding lending a helping hand to their nascent feminine charms. And of course there was Jo, the camera operator, to all outward appearances a crop-haired eighteen-year-old boy in sneakers and jeans – until you knew that Jo was short for Johanna.

In this fantasmagorical world where nothing was quite the way it seemed, it was Greg and Mila who felt like the freaks.

'Now, darlings, I'd just like to explain the scenario if I may.'

Mila decided it was easiest just to think of Lori as a woman. She even sounded like a woman, the voice soft and low and rather sensual.

'There isn't much of a story – well let's face it, it's not the story we're selling is it, darlings? It's set in the Garden of Eden, and I want you to play Adam and Eve.

'We'll start with you discovering each other for the first time. You can take your time, darlings, just let it come. And don't be shy. Do whatever feels good, right?'

'Er . . . right,' replied Greg somewhat sheepishly. He'd never really thought of himself as a potential porn star, and even if he had, now probably wasn't the moment he'd have chosen to launch his career.

'How about you, sweetie? Not nervous are you?' Lori patted Mila's dark hair into place, rearranging the flower garland so that the petals framed her face and trailed down over her bare shoulders.

'Just a little.'

THE GOLDEN CAGE

'Don't you worry, the nerves will just fly away, you wait and see. Now Asta... you're ready, Asta?'

Asta swept into the garden, her dark-red hair unpinned and falling over her strong, white shoulders. She wore the tightest dress Mila had ever seen – a skin-tight sheath of iridescent, metallic fabric which glittered red, green, violet, blue as she walked towards them. Its skirt ended in a long 'tail' which was attached to a silver bracelet about her right wrist.

'Darling, you look wonderful,' enthused Lori as they embraced. She turned back to Mila and Greg. 'Asta will be playing the Serpent, who enters your cosy little paradise and shows you the way to the true paths of pleasure.

'Now, if you'd just like to undress, we can begin.'

Mila rather reluctantly surrendered her cloak to one of Asta's girls, and found herself completely naked in Asta's flower-filled garden.

'Beautiful, darling. Simply beautiful. You know, I'm hoping to have a body just like yours one day. When I can get the last of the money together... OK now, if you could just lie down on that little marble bench over there, the one by the pool. Pretend you're asleep, yes? Greg, I want you to emerge from the bushes and kinda discover Mila just lying there. OK?'

'Y-yes. OK.'

Mila stretched out on the bench. It was rather chilly to her bare skin, and to her chagrin she could feel herself coming out in goose bumps. San Francisco wasn't the hottest of places, even in the middle of the summer, and today a fine sea-mist was hanging over the city. She hoped Greg would find a way to warm them both up...

The one thing that was really bothering her in all this was the thought of having sex with Asta. What would she do?

How would she respond to this strange, hermaphroditic creature with warm, soft breasts and a big, hard cock?

But there was no more time for thinking. Lori was speaking again.

'That's right, darling. Stretch yourself out on your side, so we can get a good view of those beautiful breasts. Petronella, tidy her hair would you? That's lovely . . .

'OK. Ready everyone? Positions and . . . action.'

Right on cue, Greg stepped forward from the shadows. He'd thought he would die of embarrassment, but when it came to it, all he could think of was Mila. Every time he saw her he fell wildly in lust with her all over again, and she looked like heaven, lying there on that marble bench with her dark hair covered in flowers and her breasts smooth as ivory. She looked like some wonderful statue, waiting to be brought to life with a kiss.

Somewhere at the back of his mind he was listening to Lori's directions, but he was moving to the rhythm of his own desire.

'That's right, Greg. Come forward, let us see that lovely big cock. Oh wonderful, it's getting hard. Why don't you touch it . . . stroke it a little? Jo, let's get a close-up of that . . .'

He walked towards Mila and, reaching out, ran his hand over the sleek curve of her shoulder, back and rump. She gave a little sigh of pleasure but did not open her eyes. The sensation of touching that smooth skin was miraculous to Greg – he really did feel as if he was discovering her for the very first time.

As his fingers brushed across Mila's cheek she opened her eyes and smiled up at him, reaching out her arms to him. He pulled her up into a sitting position and bent to kiss her.

THE GOLDEN CAGE

'That's it. Now darlings, I want you to explore each other's bodies. Mila, touch his dick. Isn't it beautiful?'

'Beautiful,' whispered Mila dreamily. 'I want to kiss it.'

'Good, good. Stand close to her, Greg, let her take you into her mouth. Jo – I want a close shot of him sliding between those pretty lips. That's good, so very good.'

Greg gave little murmurs of pleasure as Mila's tongue explored the mysteries of his sex, gently moving his hips back and forth so that his dick now disappeared from view, now emerged from between her pursed lips, glossy with her saliva. His hands toyed with her breasts, reaching down to stroke and squeeze them as his pleasure intensified.

'OK, now lay her down on her belly on the grass and start kissing her. Jo – make sure Camera Two can zoom in on Mila's lovely backside. Can you get a shot between her legs as she opens them up? That's it Mila, sweetie, raise your ass so Greg can pull apart your buns and kiss you there.'

He drank deeply from her secret well as he pressed his face between Mila's arse cheeks, licking and gently biting at the glossy-wet folds of her inner labia. His poor, neglected prick was dancing a fandango of frustration at the base of his belly, simply longing to scythe its way into that wet pleasure garden. But Lori's voice was calling out still more directions.

'Simply gorgeous, darlings. So horny. Now get her up on to her hands and knees . . . that's it, doggy-style. Jo, I want some really close-up penetration shots here, right? Now go to it Greg, do it to her *real* hard. Remember, she's the first woman you've ever made love to . . . to first woman in the world.'

He gave a groan of genuine release as his dick at last found its true home, in the soft warm heart of Mila's sex.

'Aah. Ah, darling, do it to me,' gasped Mila, pushing back against him, answering his thrusts.

'Out a little further this time, Greg – mmm, just right. Slow and sensual now, you're in the Garden of Eden. Everything is perfect and beautiful. Jo, close-up. Focus on that lovely wet hole and that beautiful hard shaft. Greg – when you feel yourself coming, I want you to pull out. We need to see the jism spurting . . . you got that?'

Greg was on automatic pilot now, his own desire taking over. Pull out? The very thought was anathema. All he wanted to do was thrust, and thrust and go on thrusting. But as his crisis approached he was surprised to find himself obeying Lori's directions almost automatically, withdrawing from Mila's wet haven and pressing her buttocks around his shaft, using her deep, velvety valley to make those last few, agonising strokes.

At last the semen spurted out of him, thick, white, cooling as it spattered in pearly droplets over Mila's back and backside. As the long and perfect climax of passion peaked and ebbed away he slipped his fingers underneath Mila's belly and stroked her to her climax, holding her there for many long moments.

They rolled on to the grass, Greg astride Mila, playful now. They kissed and petted, laughing in their innocent pleasure, their bodies streaked and moist with their own juices.

Until the Serpent walked into their world of unspoilt innocence.

'Darlings,' she hissed, her eyes twinkling with mischief as she tossed back her mane of dark-red hair. 'You have nothing but your ignorance to guide you. Let me enlighten you. Let me show you the paths to a more . . . sophisticated pleasure.'

THE GOLDEN CAGE

She unhooked the tail of her dress from its bracelet and it fluttered in iridescent waves about her feet. Slowly, slyly, she slid down the side zipper of her dress and it began to peel away from her flesh, like a snake discarding its old skin.

First the full, generous swell of her breasts, impossibly perfect. Then the narrow waist, the shaven belly ... and at last, as the dress fell to the ground, Mila and Greg saw the full magnificence of the cock, bulging beneath the red sequinned pants.

Asta walked across the grass in her panties and red high-heels. Greg and Mila gazed up at her like children, utterly mesmerised. With a smile, Asta slid down her panties, let them fall to the ground and stepped out of them.

'Now darlings,' she began, 'which of you would like to suck me first?'

Greg walked quickly through the streets of San Francisco, his hat pulled down and his collar pulled up. He wouldn't have risked going out at all, if it hadn't been important. But he had promised himself that he would see Anthony Ho's sister and he hadn't wanted to endanger Mila by taking her along too.

As it turned out, the best he'd been able to do was fix up a tentative meeting for the next day. Jessica Ho had been reluctant to see him at all – not perhaps all that surprising if she'd heard about Greg's big trouble with the police.

So that meant at least one more day in the House of Nymphs. Greg couldn't help a wry smile as he thought of this morning's artistic endeavours. If he'd been told, six months ago, that he and a Russian lover would be romping with a transsexual in a hardcore porn film, he'd probably have died laughing.

Turning the corner into Dubois Street, he knew at once that something was amiss. Petronella was sitting on the front steps of the House of Nymphs, her dress torn and her bruised face running with mascara-laden tears.

Oh my God, he thought to himself. *Mila. Something must have happened to Mila...*

He ran the last few yards.

'What's wrong, Petronella?'

She gazed at him blankly for a few seconds before her eyes registered any sign of recognition. He took her by the shoulders and shook her.

'What's happened? Tell me.'

'People ... a man and a woman. They had guns.' Her spare frame shuddered with hacking sobs. Greg felt the hairs standing up on the back of his neck.

'Guns. But what...?'

'They smashed everything, roughed us up, turned everything upside down. Kept going on and on, saying they'd shoot us if we didn't tell them where the tiger was. And Greg...'

Her eyes met his and he knew what she was going to say before she spoke the terrible words.

'They took Mila.'

Chapter 20

'You should not have come. There is great danger.'

Jessica Ho was visibly trembling as she lit a cigarette and threw the match into the ashtray. Greg caught hold of her wrist, imploring her to look at him.

'Anthony and I were friends, Jessica. Good friends. I had to come and pay my last respects...'

'You have done that.' She glanced nervously around the Chinese cafe. 'Now you must go.'

'I can't. Something terrible has happened.'

'I heard. You are in trouble with the police.'

'Worse than that, Jessica. Much worse. It's my lover, Mila – she's been kidnapped.'

Jessica's expression softened for an instant, then hardened again.

'I can't help you.'

'I think you can. Or at least, I hope you can. I have a hunch.'

He looked up and saw that Jessica's eyes were brimming with tears. Her obvious terror shocked him.

'Please, Jessica. Just tell me what I need to know and I'll go. I swear I'll never contact you ever again.'

She took a deep breath.

'What do you want to know?'

'About Anthony. About what happened to him.'

'He died.'

'He was killed, Jessica, you and I both know that. What I need to know is why.'

'I don't know.' Her voice was flat, masking the deep sorrow behind it. 'I honestly don't know for sure – but at a guess I'd say it was because he knew too much.'

'About the company?'

She nodded.

'Things started to go wrong about a year ago. First there were burglaries, then threats. I think someone knew Anthony was suspicious about some kind of fraud in the company. Then we heard that his franchise operation was being taken away from him for "financial irregularities".' She looked at him with her dark, accusing eyes. 'You were the Finance Director. You must have known it was all lies.'

Greg shook his head. He knew he'd been a blind fool, walking around with his eyes closed for God knows how long. Maybe that was why he'd been picked to be the fall guy in all this. Him and Anthony Ho.

'I didn't know anything about it until months later, when I got this really peculiar memo about "internal restructuring". The next thing I heard, Anthony was dead.'

'It was supposed to be an accident,' said Jessica bitterly. 'They said he fell from the balcony. But how could he have fallen? When the police came to the apartment, they found the balcony doors *locked from the inside*. And there was something else. Something they stole from him.'

'What?' Greg pricked up his ears.

'Something Anthony thought no one else knew about. A little ornament I gave him when we were kids. A jade tiger.'

THE GOLDEN CAGE

Greg's hand trembled as he opened the bag he had brought with him, took out the stone statuette and showed it briefly to Jessica.

'Like this one?'

All colour drained from Jessica's face.

'That's ... that's it! That's the one. Where did you get it?'

'Mila had it. She got it from ... look, I can't explain now. Maybe later, if things work out.' He slipped the tiger back into its bag conscious of the danger of prying eyes. 'What I need you to tell me is why was this tatty little tiger so important to Anthony? And why would it be important to someone like Orin Hobart IV?'

At the mention of Hobart's name, Jessica flinched.

'I'm so sorry,' she whispered. Her eyes were very bright, as though she was holding back tears.

'Sorry?'

'For what I've done. Or rather what I haven't done. I knew you were in deep trouble with the authorities, but I didn't come forward – how could I? I was pretty sure that if I tried to tell them you were innocent, what happened to Anthony would happen to me.

'You see, that tiger isn't all that it seems, Greg. It's hollow inside. If you split it open you'll find a computer memory card inside. On that card Anthony stored all the names and dates of the illegal transactions he'd traced through the company computer network. It was supposed to be his "insurance policy". But they killed him before he could ...'

A tear rolled down her cheek. Greg stared at her in stunned silence, then hesitantly reached out and touched her hand.

'I'm really sorry,' she repeated.

'I know.' Greg felt no anger, only pity. 'I'm sure I'd have done the same. What matters is, you've told me the truth now – and if I can get my act together it might just save Mila's life.'

He got up, holding the jade tiger very securely in its bag. It had been Anthony Ho's insurance policy and now it was his. Now he had to pray that it paid a better dividend for him than it had done for his old friend.

'Come to the Golden Gate Bridge tomorrow, midnight. Bring the jade tiger or the girl dies.' That's what the note had said. He'd be there. Whatever else happened, he wasn't going to let Mila down.

Orin Hobart gloated over his latest and greatest victory. Once again the girl was his. Soon the jade tiger would also be back in his possession, and this time – to make very sure – he would destroy both of them. Delaney too. To allow the affair to go to trial was just too much of a risk. The Englishman would just have to suffer an unfortunate accident, whilst resisting arrest.

'So, my dear slave,' he purred, sipping chilled Chardonnay from a rather exquisite crystal glass. 'Are you not pleased to see your Master again?'

Mila, chained by a dog-collar to a ring set in the wall, showed her defiance in the only way she could. She spat in his evil, smirking face.

Hobart snapped his fingers and Cora handed him a clean handkerchief to wipe away the spittle. She had been a loyal servant. Hobart was considering rewarding her with a slave of her own. She would make a wonderful slave-mistress.

'So, the bitch has learned bad manners,' commented Hobart. 'Disobedient *and* insolent.'

He smiled as he wiped the spittle from his face. The

THE GOLDEN CAGE

Chinese girl had long since been disposed of. He had no use for her now that he had Mila: his one true obsession. How his cock ached with the anticipation of all the sweet cruelties he would inflict upon her in the days to come.

Plans were already neatly laid out in his head. In the autumn, when he moved back to New York from his summer home in Massachusetts, he would take her with him. This time he would make very sure that there was no possibility of escape. The Manhattan apartment had been very discreetly modified to include a fully-equipped punishment room and that is where Mila would live during her training.

Once she had learned the virtue of discipline he would reassess her position in his life. If fully trained she might, perhaps, fulfil the role he had originally intended for her: that of high-class whore. With her natural skills she would be useful in seducing rivals and so advancing his business and political ambitions.

Naturally, if she refused all his attempts to domesticate her, he would have to get rid of her. It was the only logical thing to do. Strange how he felt a twinge of pain at the thought, bizarre how his heart leapt whenever he looked into those deep, dark eyes, so full of hatred and pain.

'You would think she would be grateful to you, sir,' remarked Cora sniffily. 'Bringing her to America, letting her live in your beautiful home, lavishing so much time and attention on teaching her the proper way to behave...'

She stroked her black-gloved hand across Mila's cheek, leaping back with a curse of pain as Mila bit her, sinking her teeth right through the thin leather and into the flesh.

'Little slut!' screeched Cora, striking her across the face.

'I'll teach you to behave, you little vixen.' Mila made no sound. She just turned her face toward Cora. And smiled.

Inside, Mila was scared. Really scared. Black despair lapped like a fathomless ocean at the edges of her mind, but she could not, must not let it flood in. She had to fight it. Greg would find a way to help her, she knew he would. Prayed that he would...

Hobart pushed Cora aside.

'You may leave us. I shall deal with her.'

His grey eyes surveyed his prey and his prize. His. No one else's. And certainly not Greg Delaney's.

But he would soon have his revenge on Delaney, tomorrow night when the poor dumb fool came to the Golden Gate Bridge, delivering himself right into Hobart's hands.

'Your education has been sadly neglected,' he observed. 'You have learned bad habits. That will never do, will it, my pretty little slave?'

He drank a toast to success and set the glass down on the table. Then picked up the bullwhip. And began.

The lights of San Francisco twinkled in the darkness, crowding the hills like millions of eyes, watching, waiting. Greg took the cable-car down to the terminus, then started walking, head down and hands in his pockets.

In the artificial light the orange towers of the Golden Gate Bridge looked unreal, much too big and too fantastical to be true. He stopped and looked around. Traffic never stopped completely, night or day, but at this time of night things had slowed down, the columns of cars gliding hypnotically across the 4,200-foot span. At Fort Point, the old brick-built fortress stood in darkness, the surf pounding away on the rocks below and the gravity-defying roadway soaring above, almost as if it wanted to dissociate itself from both land and sea.

Greg could feel his heart pounding in his chest. He wasn't cut out for this cloak-and-dagger stuff. Undoubtedly he was doing everything wrong. But he was doing the best he could – for Mila.

He started walking again, but his legs felt like lead and his mouth was horribly dry. Walking. Taking slow, rhythmic steps along the walkway on to the bridge. Moving painfully slowly towards the very centre, where they would be waiting for him.

Should he have brought a gun? Asta thought so, but what was the use of a gun if you didn't know how to use it properly? He'd only risk getting himself – and Mila – into even bigger trouble. Assuming there could be any bigger trouble than this.

It was quite a windy night, and he could feel the roadway moving under him, the quiver and rumble of the passing traffic vibrating the surface and the wind making it sway slightly. Somehow it brought home the fragility of everything. Glancing down, he saw that the sparkle of the sea was obscured in places by a drift of sea-mist, rolling in on the tide like a fluffy white blanket.

'Delaney.'

The voice drew his attention and he looked up, screwing up his eyes as he peered into the distance. There were shapes ahead of him – one standing on its own and two – no, three – in a huddle a few yards further on.

He kept on walking. Four of them. He hadn't expected four. He might have guessed they'd come mob-handed. A few more yards and he'd be there.

'Good evening, Mr Delaney. So glad you could join us.'

The glint of a gun made Greg's heart skip a beat but he

did not betray his fear. This must be Hobart. He had expected a mean, cruel-faced man, but he looked disappointingly ordinary for the devil incarnate.

'So I had a choice, did I?'

'That rather depends on how much you care about saving your pretty little friend.'

'I want to see her. Now.'

Hobart nodded.

'Bring her forward.'

He gestured with the barrel of the gun and his companions came forward out of the shadows. Greg recognised them instantly as the man and woman who had pursued them first in Reno, then through the streets of the city. But he wasn't looking at them. He was looking at Mila, her hands cuffed behind her back and a gag bound tightly across her mouth.

Mila struggled, but there wasn't much point in putting up more than a token resistance. Why, oh why, had Greg let Hobart lure him here? Didn't he realise he had no chance at all? Her eyes screamed 'Don't trust him, Greg, don't trust him,' but he seemed not to understand. Or if he did, he disregarded the danger.

'Let her go.'

Hobart laughed.

'Dear me, Mr Delaney, have you learned nothing at all from your experiences? I thought by now you would be a little less naïve. Why should I let her go before our bargain is concluded?'

'Why should I trust you to let her go once it is?'

'Very true. But I am the one with the gun, Mr Delaney.'

'And I am the one with the merchandise.'

'You have brought it with you as I instructed?'

Greg ignored the question.

THE GOLDEN CAGE

'I said, let her go.'

'Out of the question.'

'Then bring her nearer to me. Somewhere where those two bastards can't get their disgusting hands on her.'

Hobart turned to Steadman and O'Brien. 'Handcuff her to the handrail. That way she can't get away, and Mr Delaney's delicate sensibilities won't be offended.'

Greg fought down his anger. Losing his temper wasn't going to get him anywhere. He watched as Steadman brought Mila forward and fastened one end of her handcuffs to the rail. Now at least she had one hand free. It was a start. Ignoring Hobart, he stepped forward, kissed her, pulled the scarf from her mouth.

'Mila, darling, are you all right? What have they done to you?'

Her dark eyes pleaded with him.

'Greg – please go now. Don't trust him. He'll destroy you.'

'I can't go. I can't leave you. Are you all right?'

'Y-yes. But listen to me...'

'Much as I hate to interrupt this touching scene,' broke in Hobart, 'We have business to discuss.'

'Tell those two to get away from us. Right away.'

Hobart hesitated, then nodded. Steadman and O'Brien backed away.

'On the other side of the roadway.'

Hobart gave a cynical laugh.

'You make a lot of demands, Mr Delaney. For a man with a gun pointing at his head.'

'The other side of the roadway – or don't you want the jade tiger any more?'

Hobart's breath escaped in a gasp of irritation. Killing Delaney here and now was a possibility, but it was a very public possibility. Definitely something he'd prefer to avoid. And then there was the tiger...

'Steadman – O'Brien. Do as he says.'

The two investigators retreated with visible reluctance, dodging between cars and vans to the other side of the roadway. Greg had seen the gun holsters and didn't try to kid himself that he was any safer. But it was one small triumph.

'Very well, Delaney,' snapped Hobart. 'I have done everything you asked of me. Now give me back my property.'

Greg took a few steps forward. He didn't much care about the gun in Hobart's hand. He just had a burning desire to kick Orin Hobart's smug teeth down his throat.

'Do you know something, Hobart?'

'What?' They were only a few feet apart now. It made Hobart feel faintly uneasy. He jabbed the gun at Delaney. 'Keep your distance. Now, are you going to stop wasting my time and give me the tiger?'

Greg made great play of patting all his pockets, then shrugged.

'Sorry,' he smiled. 'I knew I'd forgotten something.'

Hobart's expression changed from smugness to blind fury.

'You did *what*!'

'Can't think how it slipped my mind. Only it occurred to me, you see, that once I've given you the tiger, you don't need me any more, do you? You can do away with me and Mila and tidy up the mess in your life, just like you tidied up Anthony Ho.'

'I strongly advise you to stop playing games and give me that tiger, Delaney.'

'I told you. It's my insurance policy, somewhere very

THE GOLDEN CAGE

safe. *Life* insurance for me and Mila. What are you going to do about it? Shoot me? Because if I don't turn up safe and sound in one hour's time, my friends will take that tiger straight to the police. Then it will be all out in the open, won't it? And I don't think the good people of Massachusetts will be too keen on electing a senator who's also an international arms-dealer.'

Hobart's lips twisted into a cruel smile.

'No, Mr Delaney. I'm not going to shoot you. But my colleagues here may feel obliged to shoot your dear friend Mila. Unless of course you tell me where to find what she has stolen from me...'

Hobart turned his head away for a split second – just long enough to look at Steadman and O'Brien – but Mila was waiting for her chance and she seized it joyfully. Kicking out with her spike-heeled shoe, she caught Hobart on the calf, making him stumble and curse.

Everything happened very quickly from that moment on. Greg was vaguely aware of one shot – maybe more – one ricocheting off the superstructure of the bridge and missing his face by inches. But there wasn't time to count or duck or run away. The next thing he knew, he was launching himself through the air at Orin Hobart, a red mist of anger clouding everything but the desire to put his hands round that man's throat and squeeze, and keep on squeezing until there was no life left.

To his surprise and immense pleasure, he caught Hobart off-balance. It was the perfect rugby-tackle – his full weight hitting Hobart in the solar plexus. Winded, he stepped back, faltered, falling against the handrail. Shots rang out around the two struggling figures, but in the darkness and the confusion of passing cars, Steadman and O'Brien couldn't be sure of hitting the right target.

'You're a loser,' Greg heard Hobart hiss. 'You can never defeat me.' And suddenly Hobart's strong fingers were round his throat and he could feel the strength in him beginning to fade. If it hadn't been for Mila, lashing out a second time, maybe he would have been done for.

Hobart's grip slackened momentarily and with a final, supreme effort of will, Greg shoved Hobart away from him – so hard that the American fell back against the parapet. He put out his right hand to save himself, but this time it met empty air.

And all at once he was falling off the bridge, tumbling down into the misty blackness, his scream cutting the cool summer air like a rusty blade. No one could remember when the scream ended, or the silence as the waters closed over his head.

Time stood still. No one moved. A car stopped. Someone shouted — a woman screamed. Darsey O'Brien raised her gun, aiming it at Mila Kirovska's head, but Steadman knocked it away.

'Are you crazy, O'Brien?'

'The bitch deserves it.'

'Sure, but do you want to go to jail that bad? Look, we don't owe Hobart – he owed us. There's nothing left for us here but trouble. Besides, he notified the cops about Delaney, remember? They should be here any minute now.' He turned and, seizing O'Brien's arm, dragged her away and into the gathering crowd.

Mila and Greg just stood staring at each other. Somewhere nearby the wail of police sirens cut the night air. There were running feet. Blue lights and guns, lots of guns. A hand took Greg by the shoulder, pulled his arms roughly behind his back. He felt the cold click of steel about his wrists.

THE GOLDEN CAGE

'OK, sir, if you come quietly it'll be better for all of us. Cut the woman free, Officer Blomberg, will you?'

'Mila . . . is Mila all right?'

'Sure, your friend's just fine. A little cold maybe, in that short dress.' The cop leered at Mila, shivering in a tiny black silk shift. 'Now, sir, if I'm not very much mistaken you're Mr Gregory Ryan Delaney. A lot of people have gone to a lot of trouble to find you. In fact, we've a couple of Federal Agents waiting to talk to you right now.' He muttered into his radio: 'Information received correct. Suspect apprehended.'

'As a matter of fact,' replied Greg, 'I've a few things I'd like to say to them. About a jade tiger.'

Epilogue

The police were very understanding, all things considered. They never did recover Orin Hobart's body, but the coast guard didn't seem particularly surprised. There were some peculiar currents at work in San Francisco Bay, apparently. It might wash up on a beach somewhere, maybe not.

In any case Mila and Greg didn't give much thought to Orin Hobart. They were too busy celebrating the fact that they were free. Free!

Once the police had recovered the jade tiger from the luggage locker at Transbay Greyhound Terminal, they handed the memory card over to the Federal authorities. It turned out that Anthony Ho's research had been more than thorough. They found lists of names, dates, transactions totalling hundreds of millions of pounds. And there wasn't the faintest shadow of doubt as to who'd been behind it all – one Orin Wycherley Hobart IV.

Hobart had been using corrupt officials in the Signet Corporation to front his arms deals for years now. Sensing that the FBI were on his tail, he had swiftly covered his tracks, planting information that would put Greg Delaney in jail for twenty years. The irony was that he'd never even met Delaney. You could call it bad luck, but on the contrary, Greg reckoned his luck had never been so good.

After all, he'd ended up with his freedom, an attaché case full of money . . . and Mila Kirovska.

As they boarded the plane at San Francisco International Airport, Mila clutched her new passport tightly, still half expecting that it would be taken from her, along with her precious new life.

'Is this really happening?' She slid into the window seat and looked out at all the bustle of the airport. The late summer sunshine was mellow, warm, reassuring.

Greg sat down next to her, and slipped his hand on to her thigh.

'Believe it. Tomorrow we'll be in England.'

To be honest, he could only just believe it himself. In return for Greg and Mila's full co-operation and 'invaluable assistance' in the Hobart investigation, the FBI had arranged new papers for Mila – even extending to an EC passport which would allow her residence in the UK for as long as she wanted.

It hadn't been easy, but they'd finally managed to track down Jeff, erstwhile bass player with the Flying Insekts. Between them they'd thrashed out a great plan to develop and market Jeff's VR program. With Mila's language skills, maybe they'd even break into eastern Europe.

'Tell me it's all going to work out for us.' Mila squeezed Greg's hand.

'I promise. A new life. This is a fresh start for both of us.' He kissed her hand, taking her fingers into his mouth. 'You'll be able to work on that sexy Scouse accent of yours.'

'Creep.'

'Sex queen.' They kissed so passionately that the man across the aisle asked to be moved to a different seat.

Ten minutes later they were airborne, San Francisco

receding until it disappeared beneath a blanket of sunlit cloud. The past didn't matter any more – all that mattered was the future.

Together.

A Message from the Publisher

Headline Liaison is a new concept in erotic fiction: a list of books designed for the reading pleasure of both men and women, to be read alone – or together with your lover. As such, we would be most interested to hear from our readers.

Did you read the book with your partner? Did it fire your imagination? Did it turn you on – or off? Did you like the story, the characters, the setting? What did you think of the cover presentation? In short, what's your opinion? If you care to offer it, please write to:

> The Editor
> Headline Liaison
> 338 Euston Road
> London NW1 3BH

Or maybe you think you could do better if you wrote an erotic novel yourself. We are always on the lookout for new authors. If you'd like to try your hand at writing a book for possible inclusion in the Liaison list, here are our basic guidelines: We are looking for novels of approximately 80,000 words in which the erotic content should aim to please both men and women and should not describe illegal sexual activity (pedophilia, for example). The novel should contain sympathetic and interesting characters, pace, atmosphere and an intriguing plotline.

If you'd like to have a go, please submit to the Editor a sample of at least 10,000 words, clearly typed on one side of the paper only, together with a short resumé of the storyline. Should you wish your material returned to you please include a stamped addressed envelope. If we like it sufficiently, we will offer you a contract for publication.

Also available from LIAISON, the intoxicating new erotic imprint for lovers everywhere

SLEEPLESS NIGHTS

Tom Crewe & Amber Wells

While trying to capture the evening light in a Cotswold field, photographer Emma Hadleigh is intrigued to discover she has an audience. And David Casserley is the kind of audience any smart young woman might be intrigued by – he's charming, he's attractive and he's sensational when it comes to making love in a cornfield. What's more, like her, he's single. But single doesn't necessarily mean unattached. And, as they are both about to discover, former lovers and present intrigues can cast a long shadow over future happiness...

0 7472 5055 3

THE JOURNAL

James Allen

Before she married Hugo, Gina used to let her hair down – especially in the bedroom. And though she loves her husband, sometimes Gina wishes he wasn't quite so straitlaced. Then she discovers that there is a way of breathing a little spice into their love life. Like telling him stories of what she used to get up to in her uninhibited past. The result is the Journal – the diary of sexual self-analysis that Hugo writes and which Gina reads. When she tells her best friend Samantha what it contains, the journey of sensual exploration really begins...

0 7472 5092 8

Adult Fiction for Lovers from Headline LIAISON

SLEEPLESS NIGHTS	Tom Crewe & Amber Wells	£4.99
THE JOURNAL	James Allen	£4.99
THE PARADISE GARDEN	Aurelia Clifford	£4.99
APHRODISIA	Rebecca Ambrose	£4.99
DANGEROUS DESIRES	J. J. Duke	£4.99
PRIVATE LESSONS	Cheryl Mildenhall	£4.99
LOVE LETTERS	James Allen	£4.99

All Headline Liaison books are available at your local bookshop or newsagent, or can be ordered direct from the publisher. Just tick the titles you want and fill in the form below. Prices and availability subject to change without notice.

Headline Book Publishing, Cash Sales Department, Bookpoint, 39 Milton Park, Abingdon, OXON, OX14 4TD, UK. If you have a credit card you may order by telephone – 01235 400400.

Please enclose a cheque or postal order made payable to Bookpoint Ltd to the value of the cover price and allow the following for postage and packing: UK & BFPO: £1.00 for the first book, 50p for the second book and 30p for each additional book ordered up to a maximum charge of £3.00.
OVERSEAS & EIRE: £2.00 for the first book, £1.00 for the second book and 50p for each additional book.

Name ....

Address ....

....

....

If you would prefer to pay by credit card, please complete:
Please debit my Visa/Access/Diner's Card/American Express (Delete as applicable) card no:

Signature .... Expiry Date ....